Sing Them Home

Pam's saga novels, *There's Always Tomorrow*, *Better Days Will Come*, *Pack Up Your Troubles*, *For Better For Worse*, *Blue Moon*, *Love Walked Right In*, *Always In My Heart* and *Sing Them Home*, are set in Worthing during the austerity years. Pam's inspiration comes from her love of people and their stories, and her passion for the town of Worthing. With the sea on one side and the Downs on the other, Worthing has a scattering of small villages within its urban sprawl, and in some cases tight-knit communities, making it an ideal setting for the modern saga.

Sing Them Home

PAM WEAVER

PAN BOOKS

First published 2018 by Pan Books
an imprint of Pan Macmillan
20 New Wharf Road, London N1 9RR
Associated companies throughout the world
www.panmacmillan.com

ISBN 978-1-5098-5717-3

Typeset by Palimpsest Book Production Ltd, Falkirk, Stirlingshire
Printed and bound by CPI Group (UK) Ltd, Croydon, CR0 4YY

*This book is dedicated to my cousin Jeanette
and her husband Steve Luxton, Thank you for fondly
remembered holidays, all your encouragement
and for being such wonderful fans.*

CHAPTER I

Pip Sinclair was just going outside with a bucket of warm water when she saw her neighbour from two doors down hurrying along the alleyway that ran behind their houses. She was about to call out to her, but something made her hold back.

Lillian Harris looked very smart in a new spotted pinafore frock with dark blue contrast at the neck and sleeves. Pip remembered seeing the material. The dress was made from two others, both of which Lillian had bought in a jumble sale, but you'd never know. How clever.

Her daughter, Flora, was also there, and was dressed up too. But when Pip saw Lillian glancing around furtively, she pressed herself against the shed door. She couldn't explain why, but she felt like she was witnessing something she shouldn't. Lillian hurried her little girl along and crossed the road for the bus stop. Pip frowned. Where were they off to, and why all the secrecy?

Pip reached the tin bath on the grass and tipped the

1

water inside. Hazel jumped up and down gleefully. At four years old, having a pretend swimming pool in the back garden was very exciting. Six-year-old Georgie was more philosophical, but he was already putting his toy boats in the water as Pip swirled it round to make sure the temperature was even.

It was a lovely warm day, and under normal circumstances, Pip would have taken her children down to the beach. It was only ten minutes' walk away, but ever since 1939 the shoreline had been covered in sea defences. Barbed wire, concrete blocks and pillboxes had replaced the donkey rides, deckchairs and ice-cream kiosks. Worthing was on the front line as far as an enemy invasion was concerned.

The children began to squabble.

'Now listen, you two,' said Pip firmly. 'If you're going to argue, I shall tip the water out and we'll all go inside.'

'But she's—' Georgie began. His mother raised a finger and gave him a stern look, so he turned back to his game murmuring, 'It's not fair.'

Pip got herself a cup of tea and sat in Peter's old deckchair to relax. Usually she had several other children to look after while their mothers were at work, but not today. It was nice to have her own children to herself for a change. Her thoughts drifted towards her husband. He was somewhere in the Far East. She wondered what he was doing. It would be a darned sight hotter out there than here, and he didn't much like the heat. Poor old Peter. He'd be the colour of a lobster by now. She leaned back and closed her eyes. Where on earth was Lillian off to?

3 p.m.

As soon as they jumped off the bus, they turned the corner and Lillian saw him. Her heart skipped a beat. He was leaning against a tree smoking a cigarette. His Canadian uniform was the same as worn by most of the world's armies: khaki jacket, cut short at the waist, with slip-on shoulder titles, pleated breast pockets and a field service cap worn rakishly over to one side. It was designed with practicality in mind, but it also made him look really handsome.

She squeezed her daughter's hand and walked boldly on.

'Are we nearly there, Mummy?' asked Flora, but her mother, distracted, could only answer with, 'Umm?'

It was a glorious day. It was hard to believe that the country had already been at war for three long years. Lillian felt a tinge of guilt. She must be mad. She really shouldn't be doing this, but life was hard. It was also very dull. She felt old before her time. It was ages since a man had even noticed her, let alone paid her a compliment. Then he'd come along. She worked hard all day 'doing her bit', so why shouldn't she get out and enjoy herself? She was still only nineteen, for goodness' sake.

All at once he turned slightly and saw them. 'Hey, you came,' he said with a lazy smile.

She hesitated, chewing her bottom lip anxiously.

Flora looked up at her. 'Is that man my daddy, Mummy?'

Lillian let slip a nervous laugh. How could she explain this to a three-year-old? Flora hardly knew her father. He'd been called up just days before she was born, and he'd only seen her a few times when he came home on leave before he was sent overseas. 'No,' she said, 'this isn't your daddy.' And looking the Canadian straight in the eye, she added, 'Uncle Woody is a friend.'

Woody crouched down to the child's level. 'You must be Flora,' he said, holding out his hand. 'With all those lovely golden curls, you can only be a princess. I'm very pleased to meet you.'

The child grinned and then glanced up at her mother for approval. Lillian nodded and the little girl shook Woody's hand. As he rose to his feet, Woody stuck out his elbow and Lillian threaded her arm through his. Then they turned towards the Ilex Way (her suggestion) and began their stroll.

They had agreed to meet in Goring because Lillian was concerned that people might recognize her in Worthing and she was anxious not to be the subject of idle gossip; after all, she was a married woman, and he was a stranger, a long way from his home. They might not be able to recall where they'd seen her (who remembers a railway porter, anyway?), but she didn't want anything getting back to her mother. Dorcas had strong views on the sanctity of marriage. And besides, it had taken Lillian a long time to find war work that suited her. She liked her platform duties at Worthing and didn't want to risk being given the sack.

Lillian had lived with her mother all her life. She'd never even left home when she and Gordon got married. They couldn't afford the rent on a place of their own, and now that his army pay had been reduced, it was well-nigh impossible. It made her angry to think that just because he was a POW and wasn't actively fighting, she was expected to exist on next to nothing, especially when she had a child to support, but that was the way it was. Luckily, living with Mum meant that she had a babysitter when she had to work different shifts.

'This is a beautiful place,' said Woody, breaking into her thoughts, and he was right. The avenue was nearly a mile long and ran due east from St Mary's Church, Goring-by-Sea, to the village of Ferring. It was wide and yet, at the same time, shady. Apparently, the Ilex, or Holm, oaks had come from somewhere in the Mediterranean and were planted in the previous century by the then owner of the Goring Hall estate. The public had been kept at bay by a pair of ornamental gates at either end of the walk until 1940, when they had been removed as part of the war effort. The avenue had now become popular with strolling couples. He stopped walking and looked down at her. 'Almost as beautiful as you.'

Lillian felt her face flush. 'Don't be daft,' she said,

doing her best to make light of it, but he'd already made her heart beat faster.

He leaned over her and cupped her face in his hands. As much as she wanted to be kissed, something made her step back. 'Careful,' she said with a nervous laugh. 'I'm a married woman, remember?'

He apologized immediately and she wished she hadn't reminded him. They resumed their walk.

'Tell me about him,' he said. 'Your husband.'

Lillian was slightly surprised that he'd asked. She shrugged. 'There's not a lot to say. He got called up just as the war started. He was part of the British Expeditionary Force and was captured at Dunkirk.'

How strange. She felt slightly dispassionate about him now. He may be her husband, but after three years of separation, she might as well have been talking about a complete stranger.

'I get the odd postcard,' she went on, 'but Gordon was never one for letter-writing.'

'You must have been very young when you married,' he remarked.

'Sixteen,' she said, adding with a resigned snort, 'and in the family way. I had my daughter a week after my birthday.'

He made no reply. Why did she tell him that? She'd said too much. It was embarrassing. She looked away, remembering. It had been a difficult time. She shouldn't have let Gordon have his way in the first place, but he'd sweet-talked her into believing that she'd be safe. They'd done it every time they'd met after that. He couldn't get enough of her, until she'd found out she was pregnant. After that, he was horrible. He kept shouting at her and saying she'd ruined his whole life – as if it were all her fault! And then they had to face their families. There followed weeks of rows and blame, until the day she and Gordon stood side by side in church and said, 'I do.' She shook the memory away, and spotting her daughter heading for a patch of stinging nettles, called her back.

'What about you?' she said as they carried on walking. 'Tell me about your life in Canada.'

'I'm the oldest of six,' he said, catching her hand in his and lacing their fingers. 'My mom stays at home, and my dad works in a bottling factory. He was over here in the Great War. Well, not here, but in Europe.'

'And that was supposed to be the war to end all wars,' she said drily.

Flora was trying to pick some poppies, but so far she only had the heads.

'Pick them at the other end of the stalk, darling,' Lillian called. They went over to help her, but the child was already bored. She ran off to chase a butterfly.

Beyond the trees, they could see a golden cornfield, and at the far end, a few people were busy gathering in the harvest.

'Imagine being lord of the manor with this as your driveway,' Woody said. He reached out and took her hand again. 'Allow me, m'lady.' And he pulled her sharply towards him.

Until she was this close, she hadn't realized how

startling his eyes were. Blue, but more than that, they were a lovely, ethereal violet blue, the colour of cornflowers. His kiss, when it came, was as light as a feather, tender and caressing. He was so gentle. Gordon's kisses had always been impatient, a means to an end, and they had to be quick, even after they were married. There was forever something to be scared of: being caught with his trousers down or being overheard by her mother. She closed her eyes and let this feeling of being with Woody absorb her. She could feel her senses rising, and with them the desire. They only stopped kissing when Flora tugged at her skirts.

They looked down to see her holding something green and wriggly in her hand. 'Look, Mummy. Mummy, look. A pillercat.'

A woman walked by with a little dog, a poodle on a red lead. She glared disapprovingly at Lillian. Lillian recognized her as the woman who had just started working in the ticket office at the station.

'Good afternoon,' Lillian said politely. The woman didn't reply, so Lillian poked her tongue out at her receding form. Woody laughed.

All too soon they'd completed the walk and were on the way back. They had spent such a wonderful afternoon together that she promised that next time she had an afternoon off, she would get her mother to babysit and would come alone. 'I'll tell her I've got to go to work or something,' Lillian promised, 'and then we can be together.' It was only because her mother had gone over to Lancing to visit her sister, Aunt Lou, that Lillian had been able to come. Dorcas had wanted Lillian to come with her, but Lillian had said she preferred to spend a little time on her own with Flora. She hadn't mentioned that she was meeting Woody, of course.

They agreed to meet at the dance a week on Saturday but she made him say his goodbyes by the entrance to the Ilex Way, and then she and her daughter caught the bus. She waved discreetly to him from the window and settled down for the short journey back to Worthing. Having waited for a girl cyclist to pass, the bus pulled out into the road and he was gone. Lillian smiled to herself. What a lovely afternoon she'd had. For the first time in a very long time, it felt good to be alive. How exciting to have someone special in her life again. She wasn't a bad girl. She hadn't done anything really wrong. She touched her mouth. It still tingled a little. She looked out of the window as she felt her cheeks begin to colour. With Flora sleepy and curled up on her lap, Lillian spent the rest of the journey reliving the memory of his wonderful kisses.

7 p.m.

'A cup of tea before you go?'

Stella, who was putting her shoes by the back door, glanced up at her mother-in-law's face. Judith Bell's expression said it all. She didn't want her to go, not just yet.

Judith, a small, birdlike woman in her early fifties,

was in her WVS uniform. When war came, she was already one of the key organizers of the Worthing branch. Her first job had been coordinating the evacuees from London, and everyone agreed that she'd done a magnificent job. Since that time, Judith had proved herself able to put her hand to almost anything, from manning the WVS canteen van for the Canadians erecting the town's sea defences to setting up first-aid courses for beginners. Stella couldn't help admiring her mother-in-law. It was a mystery how she managed to do everything. Of course, like many women of her ilk, she had a daily woman to do the housework, but she still managed to fulfil her duties and maintain her high standards.

As for Stella, she was an attractive girl with fair hair and a ready smile. She was quite happy to stay a little longer. She still hadn't told her in-laws the reason she'd turned up out of the blue. 'That would be nice, but I'll have to make it quick. I've been out all day on my bike and I really do want to get back home.'

'But there's no school tomorrow, is there?' Judith said, as she reached for the kettle in her neat and spotless kitchen.

'No,' Stella conceded, 'but I have to play the piano for Mrs Hurrup-Gregory's ballet class. They're getting ready to put on a bit of a show for the Canadians.'

'Ooh, is it going to be open to the public?' said Judith. She had put a tray cloth on the tea trolley and was now arranging the Royal Albert bone-china cups. 'I do so love the ballet. I haven't seen one for ages.'

'I'm afraid not,' said Stella, 'but I might be able to get you in if you'd be willing to help backstage.'

'When is it?'

'Two weeks' time.'

Judith pulled a face. 'Oh rats. I shall be on a course in London.'

Stella's father-in-law, Desmond, came through the back door and put half a bucket of fruit on the floor.

Judith shrieked. 'Desmond,' she cried. 'Shoes!'

Desmond returned to the doormat and dutifully kicked them off. His wife turned her back on him as she finished getting the trolley ready, so Desmond and Stella exchanged a sympathetic smile. He looked forward to Stella's visits. Their only son, Edmund, Stella's husband of five years, was serving somewhere in North Africa and they all shared an anxiety about him that was never fully expressed.

When Stella arrived, the three of them had spent a few minutes strolling around the garden while Desmond picked some strawberries and vegetables for her to take home. For a few precious minutes, they'd been able to forget that the country was at war and that their nearest and dearest was far away from them, risking his life to bring peace. But she'd have to tell them her news soon. She couldn't leave it much longer.

Judith put the teapot onto its stand. 'I'll take this through,' she said.

As the sound of the rattling trolley faded, Desmond produced a canvas bag and began putting new potatoes inside.

'Not too many,' Stella cautioned. 'There's only me, remember?'

Desmond nodded. 'There's a few tomatoes, some runner beans and some carrots,' he said. 'Do you like gooseberries?'

'Ooh, yes, please,' said Stella, and a couple of handfuls went into the bag as well.

Desmond straightened up. 'Now, my dear, if there's anything you need . . .' he said, patting her arm.

Stella nodded. 'I know where to come. Thanks.'

Desmond was a man of few words. He was very fond of his daughter-in-law, and he'd once told her that as soon as he'd met her, he'd known why his son had fallen for her. The pat on the arm was only a small gesture, but she knew it was heartfelt.

The conversation when she'd first arrived had begun with Johnny (he hated his first name, so Stella called him by his second name), but they'd quickly run out of things to say. Then Judith had hurried indoors to find a letter he had sent her. It was weeks and weeks old, but she and Desmond had only just received it. Being in a war zone, Johnny wasn't allowed to say anything that might be useful to the enemy, so information in his letters, when they had them, was sparse. Desmond had handed it to Stella and watched her read it.

Stella had a letter too, which she carried in her handbag, but she only showed them part of it. 'The rest is . . . well, you know . . .' she'd said, keeping the pages back. She blushed modestly and no more was said.

From what they'd read in the papers, they'd all guessed that he was still in the North African desert with the Eighth Army. He had been part of the relief of the besieged city of Tobruk at the end of 1941, but in February, Rommel's Panzers had regrouped and the Eighth Army had been pushed back. By May, according to the BBC, fighting had broken out again, and in the middle of June, the whole country had been devastated to hear that Tobruk was in German hands once more. The *Daily Telegraph* had reported that Rommel had taken twenty-five thousand prisoners, and since that time, they had heard nothing much from Johnny. Judith wept at night, and Desmond did his best to comfort and console her. Stella had tried to cope with her worries on her own, but in the end, she had biked up to Broadwater and told her own mother. Phyllis had helped her through the difficult first few days, but then all they could do was wait.

Stella suddenly felt embarrassed that she hadn't told them about the telegram in her handbag as soon as she'd arrived. She'd been looking for the right moment, but so far she hadn't breathed a word.

'You look worried, my dear,' said Desmond.

Stella sighed but couldn't bring herself to meet his eye. 'I've got something to show you both,' she said. Desmond stared at her blankly. 'Shall we go into the sitting room?'

He nodded, and it was obvious from the expression on his face that his heart was already sinking. Desmond was a man who kept his dark thoughts at bay by staying busy in the garden. Stella's in-laws employed a full-time gardener, but the grounds of their home, the Knowle, in Chesswood Avenue, Worthing, were large and there was plenty to keep them both occupied. Most of the flowers were gone now. Every square inch was devoted to the production of food, and even the area round the rhododendron bushes had been fenced off and given over to two allotments.

Judith spent most of her time doing her WVS work, and she was also on various committees. Stella, who had trained as a teacher, had returned to work and was now at Christchurch School on Portland Road. She had begun her career in St George's School at the High Street end of Lyndhurst Road, but when she had married Johnny, in 1937, she had stopped work. The marriage bar meant that the day they became Mr and Mrs Bell, Stella was no longer allowed to be a teacher. It was a bittersweet blow, but shortly afterwards, St George's was earmarked for closure. It felt like the end of a chapter, and before long, the pupils were dispersed to other schools. As things turned out, when a bomb was dropped onto a shop and two houses directly opposite the school in October 1940, everyone agreed that it had been a good job that the school was closed. Had Jerry hit his target (the gasworks next door) during term-time, the consequences didn't bear thinking about.

By 1941, the town had a shortage of teachers and Stella, who had no children of her own, was invited back. Glad to be busy again, she had been in the infants class for a whole year. Now, in August, the children were having their summer break.

'Tea's getting cold,' Judith called.

Stella and Desmond padded into the sitting room in their stockinged feet.

'Stella has something important to tell us, my dear,' Desmond said as he threw himself into his armchair. He looked weary, Stella thought. The war was clearly taking its toll. Judith looked up anxiously.

'I've had a telegram,' said Stella.

Desmond leaned forward in his chair and stared at the floor.

Judith pulled a handkerchief from under her watch strap and pressed it to her lips. 'Oh, Desmond . . .'

'No, no,' Stella said quickly. 'He's not dead, but he has been taken prisoner.'

Her in-laws' relief was palpable. Stella handed the yellow paper to her father-in-law, who read it aloud.

'*Based on information received, records of the War Office have been amended to show Lieutenant Edmund John Bell is a prisoner of war of the Italian Government. Further information to follow.*'

'Well, that's good, isn't it?' said Judith. 'I mean, he's not dead, and Italy is a nice place.'

Desmond smiled. 'Yes, my dear. I'm sure it's better than being a German prisoner of war.'

'Can we write to him?' Judith asked. 'I mean, where exactly is he?'

'Apparently, we send everything to the usual BFPO address,' said Stella, 'and they will forward it on.'

Judith stood to her feet, and walking over to Stella, gave her an awkward hug. 'Thank you for coming over to tell us straight away,' she said. 'If ever you feel you need someone to talk to, you know where we are.'

Swallowing the lump in her throat, Stella managed to choke out a 'Thank you.'

They drank their tea, and shortly afterwards, they said their goodbyes. Stella gave them a wave and set off, her bicycle basket weighed down with goodies. She was tired now. During the afternoon, she had taken herself off for a ride over to the villages of Ferring and East Preston, and now she was finding it hard to keep her weary legs going. She had planned to relax with a good book for the evening, but when she got back home and discovered the telegram, she had pushed all tiredness aside. She knew at once that she couldn't leave Johnny's parents in ignorance.

Despite the lateness of the hour, the sun was still warm. High above the town, she could hear the drone of aircraft, but the terrible night raids of previous years were long gone. Back in 1940, the skies had been black as wave after wave of German bombers headed for London. The RAF boys stationed all around at Ford, Tangmere and Westhampnett had done their best, but for a while, it was hell on earth. The pattern of the war had changed and now they were experiencing daylight raids. Of course, the cities suffered the most, but not even Worthing was without its tragedies.

As Stella turned into Cranworth Road, the familiar wail of the air-raid siren began. What should she do?

There were no shelters nearby, the closest being Beach House Gardens, on the seafront, or Stoke Abbott Road, north of the town. Perhaps she should turn back to Chesswood Road. She had slowed for a moment to gather her thoughts when the low moan of an aircraft engine filled the air. It sounded very near to the ground, and Stella was aware of people opening their front doors to look out. The engine cut out for a second or two and then restarted. Looking towards the town, she saw a German plane coming from the direction of Madeira Avenue, travelling diagonally from the area of the pier. Smoke was pouring from the rear end. It was clear that it had been hit and was damaged in some way. It clipped a couple of chimneypots but kept going. Stella, frozen to the spot, stared in horror as it headed towards her.

'Get in!' a voice behind her bellowed. 'For God's sake, get inside!'

Dropping the bike, Stella ran up the short path to the front door. A woman, a complete stranger, grabbed her arm and pulled her roughly towards her house. At the same time, she heard a whining screech and the sound of falling masonry as the plane's wing hit the wall of the Home Guard HQ on the corner of Lyndhurst Road and Farncombe Road, about a hundred and fifty yards away. The wreckage ricocheted across the street and ploughed into a house on the opposite corner. As Stella fell inside the woman's house, she caught sight of a burning ring of fire spinning along the road. It was followed by an almighty explosion and a rush of hot air propelled both herself and the woman towards the stairs, taking their breath away. The sky above the crash was suddenly filled with dense white smoke. The woman staggered against the hall-stand as the front door was snatched away from her hand and banged against the wall. Stella was flung against the banister with such force she lost her footing and tumbled onto the mat. The whole house shook, and all around the street, they could hear the sound of breaking glass. Inside the house, though, although the windows rattled, the glass didn't break, probably because the front door was still wide open.

There was a moment of stunned silence, which was suddenly broken by the terrified screams of two little children.

CHAPTER 2

White as a sheet, Stella's rescuer pulled herself upright and wobbled to the bottom of the stairs as the two terrified children raced down and flung themselves into her arms. 'It's all right,' she said in a cool, calm voice that belied the shock she'd just experienced. 'Mummy's here. Shh, shh. You're quite safe.'

Stella, still trembling, felt the tears in her own eyes as she pulled herself to her feet. Feeling a bit dizzy, she leaned against the balustrade and tried to calm herself. She gradually became aware that her head hurt where she'd hit the banister, and her left ear was stinging.

Her rescuer was about her own age, slim with slightly reddish-brown hair. She had a pretty face and hazel eyes. Her children – Stella presumed they were hers – a boy aged about five or six and a little girl, slightly younger, with soft curls, were both in their nightwear, he in pyjamas and she in a short, white nightie.

Once the children were comforted, the woman looked up. 'Are you all right?'

'I can't thank you enough,' Stella said, conscious

that her voice was wobbly. 'Pulling me in like that, I feel sure that you saved my life.'

The woman shrugged her shoulders. 'That's what the card is for.' And it was only then that Stella noticed the blue card in the window next to the front door. First started as an indication of a 'safe house' for children caught out in an air raid, the council and local voluntary services had encouraged people to maintain the use of the card for the sake of any passer-by caught outside during a bombing raid with no protection. Everyone suffered from the constant, lingering, unspoken fear of a massive attack and wholesale slaughter on the streets. As it was, the people of Worthing were all too often caught out by German pilots machine-gunning at random as they made for home after a bombing raid further up the country.

'You're very pale,' the woman said, 'and look – you're bleeding.'

Stella put her hand to her ear and her fingers came away bloodied. She swayed slightly.

'Mummy has to help this lady,' said the woman, standing up. 'She's been hurt.'

The little girl clung to her mother's skirts as she took Stella into the kitchen of the house and sat her at the table. The back door was wide open. The children stared wide-eyed as their mother reached for a tin on top of a cupboard and brought it down. Inside, there were bandages, cotton wool and other paraphernalia used to tend to minor cuts and bruises. The woman poured some Dettol into a pudding basin and topped it up with warm water from the kettle. She then set about dabbing Stella's ear.

'It's not too bad, but I think your earring must have caused some damage,' she said. 'The hole is certainly a lot bigger. Shall I take it out for you?'

Stella nodded. 'Thank you.'

'My name is Philippa,' the woman went on as she handed Stella her earring, which she'd rinsed in the Dettol. 'Philippa Sinclair, but everybody calls me Pip, and this is Georgie – he's six – and Hazel. Say, "How do you do?" children.'

The children dutifully did as they were told.

'I'm very pleased to meet you, Georgie and Hazel,' said Stella, at last beginning to feel more like herself. 'And how old are you, Hazel?'

'Six,' said Hazel.

'Four,' her brother corrected.

Stella smiled.

The front door was still open and sounds drifted in from outside. People were calling anxiously to each other, asking if they were all right or if they needed help. Somewhere very close, a fire was raging.

'I think I should go out there to lend a hand,' said Stella as Pip cleared away the mess, but as they rose to their feet, the two women were distracted by someone in obvious distress calling a name. It was coming from the rear of the houses, not the street. Stella and Pip went to the back door and looked out. A woman was running along the alleyway behind the house hysterically calling for someone called Flora.

'That's Auntie Lillian,' said Pip, more to her children than Stella. 'Georgie, you stay here and look after your sister. I won't be a minute.'

The two women hurried to the back gate, and Pip called out, 'Lillian, what's happened?'

Lillian was completely distraught. Turning her tear-stained face in their direction, she wailed, 'I can't find Flora. Have you seen her? My little girl is missing.'

'Where did you last see her?' said Stella, straining her neck to look over the fences. She didn't have a clue what the child looked like, but somehow that didn't register for the moment.

'She was in the garden,' said Lillian hopelessly. 'When the explosion happened, all the glass in the windows of the house next door blew out, and when I went outside to look for her, she wasn't there!'

Lillian was clearly a lot younger than either Pip or herself. She was an attractive girl with curly fair hair swept back from her elfin face with a kirby grip.

The air was thick with the smell of aviation fuel and burning. Here and there, the trees were festooned with ribbons of flame. They could still hear people shouting out as they ran from their houses with buckets of water or blankets to beat out the flames, and somewhere on Lyndhurst Road, the bell of a fire engine rang out.

'How old is she?' Stella asked.

'Three.'

Stella did some quick thinking. A three-year-old wouldn't venture very far from home, no matter how scared they were. Could she have doubled back indoors without her mother seeing? 'When she heard that big crash, she must have panicked,' Stella said. 'Are you absolutely sure she didn't dodge back inside the house?'

'I've already looked,' wailed Lillian. 'I've . . . Well, no . . . Oh, I don't know . . .' She threw her arms up in despair. 'Oh, where is she? Flora . . . Flora.'

'Why don't we go back into your place and double-check that she's not there?' Stella said gently.

The three of them retraced Lillian's steps, Georgie and Hazel joining them as they passed by their gate. Stella stayed with the child's mother, doing her best to reassure her that they would find the little girl, but a quick search of Lillian's home and garden by Pip and her children yielded nothing.

Georgie tugged at his mother's sleeve. 'She's in the pirate den.'

'Surely she wouldn't have gone out this way,' said Stella, walking to the end of the back alley and towards the carnage on Lyndhurst Road. Everyone followed her, and when they got there, they had to agree. It was obvious that the plane had broken apart on impact. The road was covered with burning debris, hot and dangerous. The ring of fire Stella had seen out of the corner of her eye as Pip pulled her indoors turned out to be a landing wheel that had detached itself from the plane and rolled half a mile down the road before coming to a stop. Judging by the number of people helping in the carnage, there had been some serious injuries, and perhaps even loss of life.

Fierce flames surrounded the house on the corner. Two fire engines were in attendance, together with several men in uniform. Candia, which stood behind the wall struck by the aircraft wing, was the headquarters of the Home Guard, and the Canadian soldiers were billeted in the area. They had turned out in force to lend a hand. Neighbours were running around with buckets and bowls of water trying to douse the flames, but it was a bit like throwing a thimbleful of water at a volcano. A man on the edge of the pavement was yelling at a group of boys scavenging for plane debris in the wreckage to get back. At the rear of the house the plane had crashed into, the men had spotted two women at an upstairs window. It didn't take much thought to realize that their escape was cut off by the flames. Pip pulled her children away, anxious that they shouldn't see something horrible. When the women opened the window to shout for help, the Canadians told them to jump. Their skirts fanned out as they fell, but happily, the men broke their fall and the women were able to walk away practically unscathed.

Pip, Lillian and Stella still hadn't found Flora, though.

'Mummy,' Georgie insisted. 'Mummy, I told you where she is.'

'Oh, Georgie, don't be silly.' His mother sounded a little exasperated. 'You were in bed. How can you possibly know where Flora is?'

24

Georgie gave his mother a self-satisfied grin. 'She's hiding in the pirate den.'

'Georgie, dear,' said Pip, 'this isn't a game.'

'But, Mummy, she is. I know she is.'

'That's enough!' said Pip crossly.

But the urgency of his voice stirred something in Stella. In her experience, children like Georgie had a wonderful imagination and what might seem unbelievable to an adult could have a grain of truth. It was certainly worth exploring. 'Excuse me, Pip, but may I?' she began. 'I don't wish to contradict you, but perhaps Georgie could show us this pirate den?'

'There is no den,' said Pip. 'He's making it up.'

'I'm not, Mummy. Really I'm not.'

The three women looked at each other. Stella got down on her haunches and smiled at him. 'Can you take us there, Georgie?'

Georgie made to set off, but his mother said, 'He's got no shoes on.'

His wellingtons were by the back door, so he made do with them. Georgie hurried down the back alley away from Lyndhurst Road. Pip swung her barefooted daughter onto her hip and they quickly reached the end of the alley. Georgie turned left, hugging the wall.

Stella could tell by the look on Pip's face that she was still unconvinced. 'He's not allowed to come this far,' she said. 'This is a waste of time. There's nothing down there.'

'How do you know about this place, Georgie?' Stella asked.

'The big boys showed me,' said Georgie.

'I've told you not to hang around with the big boys,' Pip said crossly. 'They get up to all sorts of mischief. There's no telling what they might get you and Hazel to do.'

Georgie eyed his sister. 'It's all right, Mummy. Girls aren't allowed.'

If the female sex were not allowed in the den, it appeared to be lost on him that all the adults present were female.

They found themselves in a derelict garden. The house was all boarded up and looked rather forbidding.

'Nobody has lived here for years,' Pip remarked. 'There's talk of pulling it down.'

And what better place for boys to have a secret den? Stella thought to herself. Round the back, they found a half-collapsed garden shed covered in brambles, but it was obvious that someone had been using it. A footpath worn down by constant use led directly to the door, which hung open at an angle. Above the lintel, someone had made a reasonable attempt at drawing a skull and crossbones on the wood. Above that, in chalk, were the words 'Kep out epeseally girls.'

Lillian ran on ahead, and as she bent to go inside, they heard her strangled cry of anguish.

CHAPTER 3

The house on the corner of Homefield Road and Lyndhurst Road still had the plane embedded in it. The
house was called Reydon and belonged to a Dr Marjory Davies, a GP, and a popular one at that, which
was most likely why so many people had turned out
to help. Their relief was palpable when word got
round that the doctor was on leave and staying somewhere in the Bournemouth area on holiday, but by
then the body count had already reached seven. Five
German airmen and two other men were dead by the
time the fire crew found a survivor in the rubble. He
was alive, but only just.

'Take it easy, old chap,' said the fireman. 'We'll soon
have you tucked up in bed.'

The fire chief had seen some terrible injuries in his
time, but he'd swallowed hard when the fellow was
pulled to safety. He looked like a huge stick of charcoal,
black from head to toe, his clothing still smouldering.
He was trembling uncontrollably, but the first-aider,

called over to help, knew he probably wasn't in that much pain. With several thicknesses of skin so severely damaged, the nerve endings would have perished as well. As soon as they saw the remains of his uniform, they knew he was one of the soldiers from the First Canadian Army, which was under the command of General McNaughton. One of the locals mentioned that he had been billeted in the doctor's house.

The first-aider could tell at once that the victim hadn't a hope of survival, though that didn't stop him barking out his orders. 'Put him on this stretcher. Gently. Gently does it. Now get this man to hospital immediately!'

9 p.m.

When Lillian found Flora, she was appalled by her injuries. When the plane came down, Flora had been in the garden looking for Mr Floppy, her cuddly rabbit. They had been late for tea after their excursion to Goring, and consequently, Flora had been late to bed as well. Lillian had thought she would sleep straight away, but how could she? Mr Floppy was missing. They searched the house, and then Flora remembered leaving the rabbit outside.

'I left him by the shed, Mummy,' she'd said.

It was still light, so Lillian was happy to let Flora look for herself. She'd waited by the back door until she had been distracted by a knock on the front door by what turned out to be two Jehovah's Witnesses. As luck would have it, having both doors open at the same time saved the windows from being blown out, but when the plane came down, all three women were knocked off their feet. The Jehovah's Witnesses didn't stay long. As they ran down the street, Lillian staggered to her feet and went to look for her daughter, a search that had eventually ended in the dilapidated shed of the derelict house.

Flora had been burned. It was clear that aviation fuel or perhaps some debris from one of the bombs had fallen on her head. Lillian guessed that was why she had run in the opposite direction. Her hair must have been on fire, and in the child's mind she had to get away from it, but of course running had only made matters worse. The lovely golden curls on the right side of her head had gone, and her ear was blackened. When her mother came into the shed, Flora was in shock, trembling, very pale and limp, but she still clung to her rabbit.

Pip, who was as white as a sheet herself, took her children home, while Stella helped the distraught Lillian to get her child to the hospital.

When they arrived, the entrance to Worthing Hospital was like a war zone. People milled around, some in a daze, some with visible injuries, ranging from cuts caused by broken glass to severe burns. It was obvious that the medical staff on duty were overwhelmed.

Because she was a child, Flora had priority. A doctor

saw her and gave her a sedative. After examining the child's head, he decided she should stay in hospital and told the nurse to clean up her injuries. There were no beds on the children's ward, so there was no option but to take Flora into the female ward. The nurse put the child to bed and pulled the screens round.

'Perhaps you could wait outside,' she said kindly, 'while I put a bandage on.'

Lillian didn't want to go, but as Flora was quiet, Stella was able to persuade her to wait in the corridor. They hadn't been there long before the ward sister, a dragon of a woman, ordered them to leave.

'But she's the child's mother,' Stella protested.

'Visiting time is over,' said the sister, tight-lipped. 'She can come back tomorrow at three.'

'I'm not going until I can kiss my daughter good-night,' Lillian said defiantly and through gritted teeth.

The two women squared up to each other until the sister grudgingly backed down and said, 'Very well. Two minutes,' and turning to Stella, she barked, 'You stay here.'

Lillian returned to her daughter's bedside. Her face had been washed, and she had a large white bandage on her head. She looked so little in the adult-sized bed, so young, so vulnerable. Lillian was torn. How could she leave her baby like this? What would happen if Flora woke up in the night? She'd be scared. She'd want her mummy. She tucked Mr Floppy beside her and pulled the covers up to Flora's chin; then she leaned over and kissed her cheek. One of her tears dropped onto her daughter's face. Lillian wiped it away very gently with her finger.

'Night-night, darling. See you in the morning.'

Flora didn't stir. Her eyes were closed and her breathing steady.

The nurse came back to take the screens away. 'It's not as bad as it looked,' she said, glancing behind her with a smile. 'Don't worry. A good night's sleep and she'll be as right as ninepence.'

'Thank you,' said Lillian, her eyes bright with unshed tears and her voice cracking.

'Nurse Stokes!' The sister's sharp tone sent the young nurse scurrying.

Lillian made her way back to the corridor.

'Let me take you home,' said Stella gently as she reappeared. Behind them, they could hear the sister's caustic remarks as she told off Nurse Stokes.

'Will you listen to that,' Lillian breathed. 'What a bloody battleaxe.'

Stella hesitated for a second before saying, 'I know it's a cliché, but your daughter is in the best place, and there's nothing more you can do.'

'You're right,' said Lillian, nodding miserably. 'And at least she's got Mr Floppy.'

9.15 p.m.

Everyone was focused on getting the survivor out of the wreckage and to hospital as quickly as possible.

31

Part of the house had collapsed, and there was the constant danger of falling masonry. The fire had died down somewhat, but nonetheless the rescue was hazardous. Men ignored the heat under their working boots as they struggled to manoeuvre the stretcher from the top of the building to the street below. No one was aware that Billy Stanford and Gideon Powell, two of the 'big boys' Georgie had been forbidden to play with, had defied the man who had shouted at them to 'clear off' and had come back. For them, the race was on to find something worth pinching: a trophy, some spoils of war they could boast about. One of the lads from Clifton Road had a piece of shrapnel, and the choir-boys from St Botolph's Church had a piece of the Heinkel that had come down on High Salvington in 1940, but that was regarded as a bit of a cheat. Apparently, one of the boys' dads was a first-aider who worked in a garage on the Findon Road. He'd been called out to help and had picked up the trophy to give to his son. The boys from Lyndhurst Road School had a piece of a German parachute, which they'd found in 1941, but so far Billy and his mates didn't have anything worth bragging about. This wreck was right on their doorstep and far too good an opportunity to miss. What they needed was something that couldn't be beaten. The trouble was, the fire was destroying everything worth taking. Gideon was trying to grab what looked like a logbook when another man yelled at them to 'Get away from there.' When he threatened to cuff them, they legged it, but they went round the back and came towards the house another way.

The pilot must have tried to eject because he was hanging from a tree by his parachute straps. He was quite dead, and unfortunately too high up to get to without being seen. The boys scoured the ground.

'I thought you were told to clear off,' came a voice behind them. It was one of the Home Guard from the place opposite. 'Now, get on home before I tan your hides.'

Reluctantly, Billy and Gideon dragged themselves away.

'Did you get anything?' asked Gideon.

Billy shook his head. Gideon opened his hand to reveal a piece from a belt buckle.

Billy took in his breath. 'Cripes.'

Gideon grinned. 'I reckon it belonged to the pilot.'

Billy slapped his friend on the back. 'Just wait until the gang see this one.'

9.30 p.m.

The four volunteers ran down the debris-strewn road with the stretcher. As soon as they arrived at the hospital, the soldier was rushed into a single room, with a consultant and a bevy of nurses following.

The consultant didn't disturb his patient very much. Turning to the sister, he shook his head. 'Make him as

33

comfortable as you can,' and they all heard the hopelessness in his voice.

One of the nurses and the sister gowned themselves up; then the nurse prepared a trolley. When she was ready, the sister began laying gauze strips soaked in an alkaline solution over his burns. He opened his eyes and she was startled to see what a beautiful piercing blue they were. The contrast of his clear eyes staring out from his blacked face wrenched at her heart, but pulling herself together, she quickly became the professional again and smiled. 'Hello, soldier,' she said quietly. 'That was a bit of a bugger, wasn't it, but you're in hospital now.' His lips parted slightly, but there was no sound.

About ten minutes later, the consultant returned to see how they were getting on. The sister stepped to one side as he leaned over his patient. 'Any reaction?'

'He opened his eyes a few minutes ago, sir,' she said.

The blue eyes came back.

'Hello, old chap,' the consultant said kindly.

For a moment or two, the body on the table shivered, but he made no sound as they saw him pass away. The change was hardly discernible – just a flicker and then the cornflower-blue eyes became empty, though they still stared at the ceiling. The consultant turned briskly on his heel and left the room.

The sister laid the strip she had been about to apply to his shoulder back onto the sterile tray and sighed. 'Sixty per cent burns,' she murmured. 'He hadn't a hope.'

'They say the plane was carrying some of those new phosphorous bombs,' said the nurse.

The sister took a deep breath. 'I'll leave you to clear up, Nurse,' she said stiffly. She left the room, keeping her back to the girl lest she see the tears standing in her eyes. No wonder the man's injuries had been so terrible. When in contact with air, phosphorous burned and stuck to any surface it hit. He must have been covered in it. It was a miracle he'd survived for so long, but there had been little that anyone could do. He was very young – nineteen or twenty – but there would be no recognition of his contribution to the war, not when he'd ended up losing his life in a miserable accident in which an enemy plane hit the place where he was staying. What a waste of a life. What a terrible, bloody waste.

On the women's ward, Flora was sleeping peacefully when the ward sister came towards her bed. She was gowned and masked, and carried a pair of forceps. She glanced around furtively; then, satisfied that no one was looking, she picked up Mr Floppy by the ear and pulled the toy away from the bed with the forceps.

'Dirty, filthy thing,' she murmured. Some of the stuffing from the toy's arm dropped onto the floor. 'Ugh.'

Holding it out in front of her, she marched down the ward to the sluice room, and as soon as the door closed behind her, she dropped it into the bin.

CHAPTER 4

In order to miss the chaos on Lyndhurst Road, Stella and Lillian had come out of the hospital through the back entrance. By the time they reached Cranworth Road, the police and ARP were going house to house telling all residents that they would have to leave. It was bad enough to have debris, broken glass and fire damage everywhere, but now they were being told there was an added hazard: unexploded bombs and live ammunition in the wreckage. The authorities deemed it too dangerous to ignore, so word got round that every-body had to find alternative accommodation for the night.

Lillian's mother was back from Lancing and opened the front door. 'Thank God you're all right,' she said. 'I was beginning to wonder where you were.' She looked pale but was clearly relieved to see her daugh-ter. 'Where's Flora?'

Lillian told her what had happened and did a quick introduction. Dorcas was alarmed, but the sound of raised voices outside jolted them back to the here and now.

'Better hurry up and get yourself a change of clothes,' Dorcas said quickly. 'We've only been given fifteen minutes to get ready.'

'Where will you go?' Stella asked.

'They've opened the Foresters' Hall in Newland Road,' said Dorcas.

'They can't possibly fit everybody in that poky little place,' Stella blurted out before she'd had time to think. 'And you certainly won't get much sleep.' The two women were relieved when she added, 'You're welcome to come to mine if you like.'

'Are you sure?' said Lillian. 'Where do you live?'

'Salisbury Road.' She saw Lillian and her mother exchange glances. 'I know it's a bit of a hike,' she went on, 'but at least I can offer your mum a proper bed.'

'Well, there is one thing,' Dorcas said cautiously. 'If that bomb went off, we'd be well out of the way.'

Lillian looked anxious. 'But what will happen to Flora? The hospital is very close.'

'Don't worry,' said Stella. 'Let's try and look on the bright side. Those bomb boys are amazing. They'll soon get it sorted. Nothing is going to happen.'

As they walked back into the street, the officials were still banging on doors to get people moving. Stella hurried to Pip's house to collect her bicycle, but just as she got there, Pip came out pushing an old pram, her two children, still in their nightclothes, tucked up inside. As soon as she saw Lillian and Dorcas, Pip's first words were, 'How's Flora?'

Lillian told her the bare bones of the story as they

were being jostled along the street by the ARP, and Pip heaved a sigh of relief. Strangely enough, although Stella's bike had been righted, the fruit and vegetables in the basket hadn't been touched. She walked along beside them, pushing it. The children seemed slightly bewildered by all that was going on, so Stella tried to make a game of it, and a few fresh strawberries magically appearing in the pram helped the situation as the untidy procession continued until it reached the end of Chesswood Road. It was here that Stella extended her invitation to Pip and her family, and it was gladly accepted.

While everybody else squeezed themselves into the Foresters' Hall, Stella's new-found friends continued to the end of Newland Road and headed back towards town.

'You all right, love?' Dorcas suddenly said.

Lillian was dabbing her eyes with the end of her sleeve. 'Oh, Mum, I can't stop thinking about Flora.'

'She'll be fine,' said her mother. 'You worry too much.'

'But what if she wakes up in the night?'

'She's got that nice nurse with her,' Stella reminded her, adding as an afterthought, 'and she's got her rabbit.'

Lillian nodded glumly.

'I don't understand,' Pip whispered to Stella as they walked along. 'Why is she so worried? I thought you said it turned out that Flora wasn't too badly injured.'

'She's probably worried about the sister on the

ward,' Stella said confidentially. 'She was a bit of a dragon.'

Lillian spun round. 'A bit of a dragon!' she exclaimed. 'The woman was an absolute nightmare.' Dorcas gave her daughter a nudge. Georgie and Hazel were wide-eyed and listening.

'Well, never mind,' said Dorcas, mainly for the benefit of the little ones. 'With a bit of luck, Flora will be home tomorrow.'

They walked on, each lost in her own thoughts, until Lillian said to her mother, 'I never asked you – how was Aunt Lou?'

'Her bunions are playing up.'

Slightly ahead of them, Stella suppressed a smile. First bombs and now bunions. If nothing else, life's problems were very varied.

It was beginning to get dark. They could still hear aircraft droning overhead, but they were miles up and most likely heading for London. There were no street lights, of course, so at the beginning of the war, all town-centre kerbstones had been painted with white stripes. Three years on, they were worn and scuffed, and the white bands painted round the base of trees that lined the streets hadn't fared much better, so to avoid slipping off the pavement, they were walking in the middle of the road. They were quite safe. There were no cars about.

They turned into Salisbury Road.

'Here we are,' Stella said at last.

The house was fairly substantial compared to Lillian and Pip's two-up, two-down terraced houses, and there was a garage on the side. 'You live here on your own?' Pip asked.

'At the moment, yes,' said Stella. 'But I'm not alone. I live on the ground floor. The billeting officer has just allocated me a couple of girls from the Land Army. They have the rooms upstairs.'

'I thought they only worked on farms,' said Lillian.

'They've been seconded to help at a nursery in East Worthing,' said Stella. 'They're crop-picking.'

Stella opened the front door, and they left the pram in the substantial hallway before she invited them in.

'This is lovely,' Pip remarked. 'How long have you lived here?'

'Since 1937,' said Stella. 'I came the day we got married. Please, make yourselves at home.'

They put the children in the spare bedroom upstairs, and under protest, Dorcas was given Stella's bed, which was in what would have once been the dining room. As soon as everyone else was settled, the three women turned the sitting room into their sleeping quarters.

'I see you've got a piano,' said Lillian. 'Lucky thing.'

'It's my mother's old one,' said Stella. 'She's a music teacher.'

Lillian ran her fingers along the keys but didn't press them enough to make a sound. 'I've always fancied playing the piano.'

'Who is the man in the picture?' Pip asked. They

were pushing back chairs to make room on the floor and forming mattresses out of cushions and blankets. Pip was pointing to a picture in a silver frame. In it, a good-looking man in army uniform smiled into the room.

'That's my Johnny,' Stella said wistfully. She gazed at it lovingly, and her heart gave a guilty lurch. What with everything else going on around her, she hadn't given him a thought for ages. How could she forget him so easily? 'My husband.'

'Is he overseas?' Lillian probed.

'He's been in Tobruk.'

'Blimey,' Pip murmured. The news bulletins had been full of Rommel and the taking of Tobruk. The Libyan port had suffered an overwhelming onslaught, with heavy tanks crashing through the perimeter fences. It was a bitter blow, and thousands of Allied soldiers had been taken prisoner. 'He's not . . . Is he?'

Stella nodded. 'He's still alive. As a matter of fact,' she sighed, 'I just heard today that he's been captured.'

'Oh, Stella, I'm so sorry.'

'Where exactly is Tobruk?' asked Lillian.

'The Middle East,' Stella said, 'but my husband is apparently a prisoner of the Italian Government.' She paused. 'My mother-in-law seems to think that being a prisoner of the Italians is better than being with the Germans.'

'Looks like we're both in the same boat,' said Lillian drily.

'What do you mean?' asked Stella.

41

'I mean you're not the only one,' said Lillian with a sigh. 'My old man is a German POW.'

'Oh, Lillian,' said Stella sympathetically. 'I wish I hadn't said that now. I'm sorry. I just didn't think. Is he in Germany? Are they treating him well?'

Lillian shrugged. 'I suppose so. He doesn't write much.'

'How long has he been a prisoner?'

'Ever since Dunkirk.'

'Dunkirk!' Stella blurted out.

Lillian laughed sardonically. 'You know, everyone talks about the miracle of Dunkirk, but they forget about the thirty or forty thousand men, including my husband, who were captured.' She tossed her head. 'Still, one good thing – unless he can escape and get back home, I guess Gordon's war is over.'

They fell silent until Pip, who up until now had kept quiet, said, 'She's right about us being in the same boat. My husband was captured earlier this year after the fall of Singapore. He's a POW of the Japs.'

'You never said,' Lillian said accusingly. 'How could you keep it to yourself all this time?'

Pip shrugged. 'I was trying to keep it from Georgie and Hazel,' she said. 'I don't want anyone saying anything in front of them.'

'You could have trusted me,' said Lillian.

Pip looked embarrassed. 'I'm sorry.'

Throwing a couple of redundant cushions onto the upright chair at the table, Stella tried to lighten the mood. 'Anyone fancy a cup of tea before we bed down?'

The suggestion was greeted warmly, so Stella went into the kitchen. While she was gone, first Pip then Lillian had a wash in the tiny bathroom. Afterwards, having got ready for bed, they settled down.

Stella handed each of them a welcome cup of tea. 'I've taken the liberty of lacing it with something,' she said. 'It's been a long day.'

No one objected.

'Will you go to the hospital first thing in the morning, Lillian?' Pip asked.

'That old dragon of a sister said visiting hours didn't start until three,' said Lillian. 'I'm working tomorrow anyway, so I'm sure Mum will go.'

'Would you mind if I went to see her as well?' asked Stella.

'Of course not,' cried Lillian. 'The more the merrier.'

The tea was wonderful, and the nip of brandy warmed their throats on the way down. Stella sat on the edge of the cushion-less sofa because the exposed springs dug into her legs, Pip sat cross-legged on the cushions that were lined up on the floor, and Lillian leaned back on some blankets with a sigh.

Pip reached out and squeezed her arm. 'She'll be fine.'

Lillian nodded. 'I know. I just wish that awful woman wasn't there.'

'She'll be off duty and tucked up in her own bed by now,' said Pip.

'You're right,' said Lillian, cheering up.

'Actually, she made me quite cross as well,' said Stella. 'There was no need to behave like that.'

They fell silent for a second or two. Stella sipped her tea and looked at her new friends. They were both attractive women but very different. Pip wore her chestnut-brown hair long, but swept up at the sides and curled under. It looked a little wild right now, but after the day they'd just had, that was only to be expected. She had a peachy complexion. Despite being a mother twice over, she was slim, and Stella admired her long, delicate fingers, though her nails were short and chipped. Lillian looked much younger: probably only about twenty or twenty-one. Her blonde hair was curly, and at first Stella thought she'd had a perm, but now that she was really close up, it looked natural. No, she must be younger than that. She still had a few childhood freckles over the bridge of her nose.

When they'd finished their tea, and while Stella took the cups into the kitchen to rinse them under the tap, the girls bedded down. Pip had her face to the wall, and Lillian had pulled her blanket over her head. When she was ready, Stella turned out the lights and the room became pitch-black. Not even a chink of light showed: the blackout curtains saw to that. She lay down on the sofa and tried to get comfortable. Even though she'd put a couple of coats over the springs, they still dug in. She couldn't sleep anyway. All she could think about was poor Johnny. She hoped her mother-in-law was right and that the Italians treated their prisoners of war well.

It didn't take long for the tears to fall. Although silent, they soaked the pillow under her head and trickled off the end of her nose. She heard one of the others trying to blow her nose quietly. Then someone cleared her throat.

'We're all awake,' Lillian said into the darkness. 'Does anyone want to talk?' Her voice was thick, as if she had a heavy cold.

'I wouldn't mind,' said Pip. It would be good to talk about Peter, and it would stop her thinking about little Flora and her burns. Lillian wasn't to know, but the sight of her daughter in that state had brought back some uncomfortable memories.

'Shall I put the light on?' Stella asked.

'No!' cried Lillian. 'Please don't.'

There was a silence; then Pip said, 'She's right. It might be easier to talk in the dark.'

'So?' said Stella. 'So who wants to go first?'

'We've been told so little,' Pip complained. 'I had a telegram telling me Peter was a prisoner of the Japanese Government, but I have no idea where he is.'

'Gordon sent me a postcard saying he was being well treated,' said Lillian, 'but that's about it.'

'And I've heard nothing,' said Stella. 'Not from Johnny, anyway.'

'Gordon didn't actually write on the card,' said Lillian. 'There were tick boxes next to the sentences. He ticked two, one saying he was a POW and another

45

saying he was being well treated. You just have to hope it's true.'

Pip gave her nose a hearty blow. 'I wish Pete could write to me.'

'I don't know how you bear it,' said Stella. 'To be honest, I'm scared.'

Pip sighed. 'So am I. They say the Japs are ruthless.'

The other girls didn't say anything, but they were all remembering the stories that had filtered back to Blighty after the fall of Hong Kong. The newspaper headlines screamed, 'Horror at Japanese Atrocities,' and Mr Anthony Eden, the British foreign secretary, told an appalled House of Commons that not only were the Japanese refusing to let the British bury their dead but that fifty British officers and men in the over-run HQ had been found bound head and foot and bayonetted to death. The Japanese Army not only had a reputation for being callous and despicable but had also refused to sign the Geneva Convention with regard to their treatment of prisoners of war.

'I guess we all feel the same,' Pip went on, 'but it's best not to dwell on it. We have to keep going. They have to have something to come home to.'

'What do you think, Lillian?' Stella said eventually. 'Your husband has been a prisoner the longest.'

Lillian was aware that the other two were crying. She wasn't. Glad of the darkness, she swallowed hard. 'She's right,' she said. 'You have to keep going.'

'You're so brave,' said Pip.

'No,' Lillian protested. 'Not really.'

46

'Yes, you are,' said Stella. 'I'm not sure that I could be as calm as you.'

'Like you said, my husband has been gone a long time,' said Lillian. 'I thought I would die when I got the news, but you cope. It gets easier as time goes on.'

Stella blew her nose again. 'Oh, Lillian, you're amazing.'

'Please,' Lillian protested, 'don't put me on a pedestal.'

'Why not?' asked Pip. 'You're an absolute inspiration.'

Lillian could feel the tears coming to her own eyes now. Her friends were grieving, wounded because the men they loved weren't coming home until the war was over. Thank God it was so dark in the room. She was glad they couldn't see her face. It was burning with embarrassment and shame. How could she tell them the truth? How could she explain that she really didn't care if Gordon never came back? Oh, she didn't wish him harm, and she hoped with all her heart that nothing bad would ever happen to him. She honestly hoped he would survive the war. She just didn't want him back home, especially now that she'd met someone as wonderful as Woody.

CHAPTER 5

PETER SINCLAIR, JAPANESE POW

If I was able to write to you, my darling, this is what I'd say.

It looks as if we're in for a pretty rough ride until all this is over. I'm so thirsty, my tongue is really swollen, and it feels like the sun has burned the skin on my shoulders right through to the bone. Bloody painful. Mind you, I'm sore all over. After a couple of beatings and then being tied to a post for a day and a night, I can hardly walk. Thank God a couple of the lads were detailed to help me into the hut. I couldn't have done it on my own, but at least with their help, I had some dignity.

When we were captured, the Kenpeitai were sent in. They wanted to know what equipment we had – how many ships, how many planes, how many men, all that sort of thing. I began by trying not to say anything – just my name, rank and number – but in the end, just to make them stop, I had to say something. So I made up some numbers. Equipment: basic. Planes: forty, the rest all shot up. Men: no more than twenty thousand. None of it true, of course.

The Japs took everybody by surprise. We'd all been led to believe they were nothing more than a bunch of Boy Scouts when it came to fighting. Everybody was convinced they'd invade by sea. How wrong can you be? They came swarming in like bloody locusts through the jungle and mangrove swamps. We hadn't a hope. They're pretty ruthless too. Some of the lads have been telling us that the Japs have killed everybody in the hospital. They've doused the Australians with petrol and set them alight, and they've even killed civilians for no better reason than they wanted to. In our briefings before the fighting started, we were told that according to the Geneva Convention 1929, prisoners should be treated humanely at all times. They should be protected from reprisals, acts of violence, insults and public humiliation. Well, I can tell you that's a bloody laugh out here.

Of course, if I could write, I'd say none of that. I'd tell you I'm fine. I'd say I am missing you. I'd tell you I can't wait to come home and that it won't be long.

I'm on a cot now, and someone is cooling me down with a bit of rag soaked in water. Dear God, how am I going to survive? If I could write, I'd tell you how much I love you. I'd say whenever I close my eyes, I can see my darling wife and my kids. We're all on the beach and I'm building a sandcastle for Georgie. Yes, that's what I'd tell you. I can't believe how fast my boy is growing up. Will he even know who I am when I see him next? Oh God, I've got to get through this. I want to come home again. I want to hold you in my arms once more, my darling Pip. I want to kiss my little girl goodnight and tuck her into bed.

The adrenaline is pumping through my veins again. I can feel a cup on my lips. The water isn't clean, but by Jove it tastes wonderful.

CHAPTER 6

Pip was up first. Years of keeping an ear out for the children had conditioned her so the moment she heard a padded footfall on its way to the kitchen, she was wide awake. However, it took a second or two more to remember where she was. She lifted her head. The other two were still sleeping soundly, but it was morning. She could tell that by the faint haze round the edges of the door.

She got up carefully and crept silently out of the room. There were low voices and the smell of toast coming from the kitchen. Pip pushed the door open and the two land girls looked up sharply.

'Oh, hello,' said one.

Pip put her finger to her lips and closed the door quietly. 'Any tea in that pot?' she said, sitting at the table with them.

One girl reached for another cup and saucer. 'I'm Vera,' she said, 'and this is Brenda.'

'I'm Pip Sinclair,' said Pip, stifling a yawn.

'Are you working with us?' asked Brenda.

Pip explained briefly what had happened and why

she was in Stella's kitchen so early in the morning. 'I'm sorry if we disturbed you when we came in.'

'Didn't hear a thing,' said Vera, 'but we did wonder about the pram in the hallway when we came downstairs this morning.'

'That plane coming down must have been the awful bang we heard last night,' said Brenda, glancing at her companion. 'We thought a sea mine had gone off.'

'Stella told us you were crop-picking,' said Pip, sipping her tea.

'Cucumbers,' said Vera. 'Eight ruddy greenhouses stuffed full of them. There must be millions of the damned things.'

Brenda giggled.

'What on earth will you do with them all?' gasped Pip.

'We're packing them for Covent Garden,' said Vera. 'The owner's son died and he had a breakdown. The government couldn't let good food go to waste, though I doubt he'll be allowed to grow them again next year.'

'I should hope not,' Brenda chuckled. 'Not much muscle-building power in a cucumber.'

Vera glanced up at the clock. 'Come on, Bren,' she said, getting to her feet. 'It's ten past six.' She gathered her flask and some sandwiches. 'Nice to have met you.'

When they had gone, Pip had a quick wash and made another pot of tea. A minute or two later, Lillian put her head round the door. 'Blimey, look at the time. I'm on duty at seven.'

Stella woke to the sound of children's voices. Her back ached, and she had a dent at the top of her leg where the springs had dug in. She was alone in the room. By the time she had emerged tousle-haired in the hallway, Pip had already dressed her children and was putting them back into the old pram.

'Sorry to rush off,' she said, 'but the kids want their breakfast.'

'You can have your breakfast here,' said Stella.

'That's very kind of you,' said Pip, 'but I run a small nursery in my front room and one of the children comes in just before eight. If I don't get a move on, I'll be late.'

'Where are the others?' Stella asked.

'The land girls went to East Worthing to pick cucumbers, Dorcas went home, and Lillian went to the station.'

'Off out for the day?'

'No,' said Pip. 'She works there. She's a porter.'

'Of course,' said Stella. 'I had a sneaky feeling I'd seen her somewhere before.'

'I've cleared up a bit in the kitchen,' said Pip, opening the front door. The early morning sunshine flooded in. 'Thanks for everything. You were an absolute brick.'

Stella waved her hand to kindly dismiss the compliment and the door closed. For a second or two, she stood in the hall and tried to collect her thoughts. It was very quiet, and for the first time since Johnny went, she felt utterly alone.

When her mother had told her to grab her things the night before, Lillian had taken her uniform. She was on an early shift this morning. When women were conscripted into war work in 1941, Lillian had been among the first to volunteer. The government required women between the ages of eighteen and sixty but started off with single or widowed women in the twenty-to-thirty age group. These women were assigned to munitions factories, heavy industry and ship-building, sometimes miles away from home. Other women joined the three services, the Women's Auxiliary Air Force, Women's Royal Naval Service and the Auxiliary Territorial Service.

It didn't take long before the shortage of manpower led to the inclusion of married women and older women in the scheme. Women with small children, like Lillian, weren't exempt either. Those who didn't have a relative or friend who could look after their children were expected to make use of the nurseries the government had set up. Luckily, Dorcas was only too delighted to look after her little granddaughter, and so long as they made sure their shift patterns didn't clash, everything worked out very well. On the rare occasions when both were working, Pip looked after Flora for a while, and she didn't charge too much.

Dorcas Cooper was part of a hush-hush thing called Radar, based on High Salvington. She wasn't allowed to talk about it (the Official Secrets Act and all that), but she spent her time up there counting aircraft. When Lillian registered, there was a chronic local shortage on the railway. No fewer than five local station staff had been called up to be part of the British Expeditionary Force, so Lillian was told to report to Worthing, where she began work as a railway porter. She had a uniform consisting of a jacket with the metal initials 'SR', for 'Southern Railway', on the lapel and a peaked cap, and for the first time in her life, she wore trousers.

It was hard going at first. She had to load heavy mailbags onto the station trolleys and wheel them to the train. There was usually someone inside the train to help, but there were occasions when she had to propel them through the doors of the waiting train by herself. She also had passenger luggage to stow on the train, and it was the porter's job to make sure all the train doors were slammed shut before the guard could blow his whistle and wave his green flag. Only then could the train move off.

Another one of the porter's jobs was to keep the platforms clean, so in between trains, Lillian swept the concourse and emptied the bins. It was an endless task because the soot got everywhere, but Lillian took a pride in her work. Not only were the platforms spotless but she even went to the trouble of wiping the enamel advertisements as well. The plaques extolling the virtues of Rinso washing powder, Cut Golden Bar tobacco and Camp coffee had never gleamed so brightly.

The trains were always busy. The Railway Executive Committee's poster campaign 'Is your journey really necessary?' fell on many a deaf ear. If the trains weren't packed with troops being moved all over the country, they reunited families or sent people to new places of work many miles from home. Despite the noise, the dirt and the hard work, Lillian loved being part of a giant moving machine. In fact, she often sang as she worked.

'You've got a nice little voice there, Mrs Harris,' Mr Rawlings, the stationmaster, said on one occasion. 'You ought to be on the stage.'

Although she worked as hard as ever, Lillian didn't feel like singing today. In spite of her resolve not to, she was still worrying about Flora. It was already afternoon and she had been separated from her daughter for almost twenty-four hours. Was she in pain? Lillian was willing to bet that all her lovely curls had gone on one side of her head, and even though it was bandaged, it was probably sore. The burns on her shoulder and body were covered in cream. They weren't so serious. The burn on her head was much worse. Would Flora keep the bandage on? After all, she was only three. Lillian glanced up at the station clock. Twenty past three. Dorcas would be with her now.

The news that a plane had crashed in Lyndhurst Road was the talk of the day and rumours flew.

'I heard that the Germans were machine-gunning people as it came down,' said Iris Keegan, the woman who ran the station cafe.

The doors to the canteen were wide open on account of the heat, so Lillian, who was checking the level of sand in the fire buckets, couldn't help over-hearing.

'They say a couple of Canadian soldiers were killed,' said a passenger.

Lillian frowned and made a mental note to ask Woody when she met him at the dance on Saturday week if he had known any of the poor chaps.

'One of them Germans was hanging in a tree by his parachute,' someone else said.

'And two girls who were working for the doctor,' said Betty Shrimpton, who worked in the ticket office and was on her break, 'jumped from the upstairs window.'

Iris poured her customer another cup of tea. 'My neighbour told me that one of them Canadian soldiers put his hand up her knickers,' the customer said.

'Wouldn't surprise me,' said Iris. 'Always strike me as a bit gung-ho, that lot.'

Lillian suddenly saw red. 'That's not true,' she said, coming into the cafe. 'Those boys saved her life.'

Looking around at her audience, Iris laughed sardonically. 'I bet he did.'

'They jolly well did!' Lillian said crossly. 'Those girls would have burned to death if it wasn't for those men.'

'And what makes you the expert?' Betty asked.

'Because I live in the next street,' Lillian retorted. 'I

was there. I saw what happened, and you've no right to cast such aspersions.'

Iris threw some empty plates into the sink with a clatter. 'I don't know, I'm sure. I was only repeating what I heard,' she said haughtily.

'Well, you should make sure of your facts first,' Lillian retorted.

'Mrs Harris.' The stationmaster's sharp tone right behind her made Lillian jump. 'When you've finished with that, come to my office.'

Lillian stared after him as he strode back down the platform.

'Sounds like you're in for a rollicking,' joked another passenger, coming out of the cafe.

Lillian tossed her head and cleared up her things. She wasn't going to back down, but the passenger might be right. She shouldn't have sounded off like that in front of them. Mr Rawlings certainly sounded very serious. Maybe she'd done something else that was wrong. Her mind raced over all the tasks she'd completed this morning, but she couldn't think of anything out of the ordinary. In fact, she merited a gold star! It was only as she topped up the sand in the last fire bucket that it occurred to her that it might have something to do with Flora. Her heart went cold. But how would Mr Rawlings know that her daughter was in hospital? Apart from her set-to with Iris, she hadn't even mentioned what had happened the previous day. She didn't want to talk about it. It would only encourage endless questions, which was why she hadn't bothered to correct Iris about the machine-gunning. Nobody had got shot. She caught her breath. Had the hospital rung the station? Were they trying to contact her? If they were, then something must be badly wrong. She virtually threw her cleaning box into the store cupboard; then locking the door with a trembling hand, she ran to the station-master's office.

Back in the cafe, Iris wiped down the counter with her dishcloth. 'Stuck-up little madam,' she said as she watched Lillian hurrying down the platform. 'She had no right to talk to me like that. I hope he gives her the ruddy sack.'

CHAPTER 7

Stella made her way towards the women's ward of the hospital. Having spent her day starting and restarting snatches of music for Mrs Hurrup-Gregory's little dancers in the ballet class, she was feeling rather tired. They had met in a hall along the Richmond Road, five different classes of girls ranging from three to fifteen years old. Mrs Hurrup-Gregory had a reputation for being a firm but fair woman and had a list of achievements and awards as long as her arm. Stella had been both impressed and full of admiration for her skill in getting twenty or more unruly children to behave so beautifully. Unfortunately, by the end of the morning, Stella had a backache from sitting in a constant draught, though that didn't stop her wanting to visit Flora as she had promised.

When she reached the ward, the bed occupied by Flora the night before had another patient in it.

'She's gone to the kiddies' ward,' said a pale-faced staff nurse when Stella asked. 'Straight down the corridor and to the right.'

Stella headed off, but just as she was passing the

sluice room, the door burst open and Nurse Stokes came out. Looking around furtively, she pushed something into Stella's hand and whispered out of the corner of her mouth, 'I saw what Sister did. I found it in the bin.'

Leaving Stella slightly confused, she hurried away. Stella looked down. She had a paper bag in her hand. She was about to call out or open the sluice-room door when the thwump of the swing doors leading to the ward told her she was no longer alone in the corridor. She turned to see the ward sister coming towards her. Stella froze to the spot, but not before she had swung the bag behind her back.

'Yes?' said the sister accusingly. 'Can I help you?'

'Oh . . . er,' Stella fumbled. 'I came to see Flora Harris, but I was told she'd been moved.'

'The children's ward is straight down the corridor and you'll find it on the right,' said the sister, repeating what Stella had already been told. 'We moved her there because she wouldn't stop crying and it disturbed the other patients.'

Stella didn't move.

'Is there anything else?'

'Er . . . no. No. Thank you, Sister.'

Stella turned on her heel, doing her best to keep the paper bag out of sight.

The children's ward was a fairly recent addition to Worthing Hospital. It had been opened in 1939 by the Princess Royal, Princess Mary, the only daughter of King George V and Queen Mary, but the event had been largely overshadowed by the outbreak of war. The Princess Royal was well respected and liked, and since that time had been commended for dedicating so much time to her war work in addition to her role as the controller commandant of the ATS.

The sound of little voices led Stella to the door, but when she peered through the glass, she could see Flora already had visitors. Dorcas and Pip sat either side of the child's bed. Planning to leave them to it, Stella took a step back, but Dorcas had spotted her and stood up. A second later, the door opened.

'How nice of you to come,' said Dorcas.

'I knew Lillian was working,' Stella explained, 'and that you intended to come, but I thought just in case . . .'

'You go on in,' said Dorcas. 'I'll wait outside for a bit.'

'No, no,' said Stella. 'How is she?'

'She's all right, although she's been a bit upset because they've lost her toy,' said Dorcas. 'They think they'll take the bandage off tomorrow and then she can go home.'

'Home tomorrow? That's good, then.' Stella turned to go. 'Well, I'll leave you to it. Give Lillian my regards, and I hope Flora makes a good recovery.'

'Thanks for coming,' Dorcas called after her, but Stella gave her a dismissive wave.

Outside in the hospital grounds, Stella opened the paper bag. Inside, she found a toy rabbit, all sooty and badly in need of a wash. One arm was virtually severed, and some of the stuffing had fallen out, but she recognized it at once. It was Mr Floppy. She knew he was being sorely missed by Flora, but Stella could hardly return him in his current state. He was covered in old tea leaves from the ward kitchen and he smelled awful.

What with everything that had happened, Stella had a sudden urge to visit her mother, so rather than bike straight home, she rode north of the town. Phyllis Bailey lived on Grove Road in Broadwater, where she was a music teacher. Before the war, her mother had rattled around her large house on her own, but now it was full of Canadian officers. Mrs Bailey kept two downstairs rooms and the kitchen for herself, while they had taken over the rest of the house. Although she welcomed the company, it had been a struggle for her to hear male voices again. There hadn't been a man in Knightsbridge House since Stella's father had died, in 1923, but now, at any given time, there were at least six of them, twelve or more when they invited others round.

Having so many people billeted there did, however, have its advantages. It seemed like the Canadians ditched far more food in their bases than Phyllis and Stella were given as a weekly ration. The men knew that people like Phyllis were proud, so nothing was said, but every now and then, a pound of butter or a bag of sugar would appear in her larder. The men ate at their base camp, so Phyllis understood that anything she found had been deliberately left as a gift. They were tactful – it was never too much so as to be embarrassing, but it was always welcome. Phyllis shared her bounty with her daughter and a few close friends, but she was careful. The authorities took a dim view of anything that smacked of black market-eering and the penalties were high.

Mrs Bailey was listening to the radio when her daughter walked in. 'Stella, darling, what a lovely sur-prise!'

They made tea in the kitchen and Stella carried the tray back into her mother's sitting room and sat down.

'Are you all right, dear?' said Phyllis. 'You look a little pale.'

Her mother listened with a horrified expression on her face as Stella related the events of the night before.

'Thank God you're all right,' she said. 'Have you eaten?'

Stella shook her head.

'Then you're to sit there while I get something. The boys brought me a tin of salmon last week. I can't remember the last time I ate real salmon. I was going to save it for a special occasion, but I think tonight we both need spoiling, don't you?'

The stationmaster was sitting behind his desk. Lillian had entered the room at the behest of his gruff 'Come,' but he didn't look up. She had butterflies in her stom-ach, and her anxiety had made her breathless, but she knew better than to interrupt what he was doing. She stood to attention while he finished writing a memo.

The room was one of ordered chaos. Neat piles of

papers on the desk left only an area the size of a sheet of foolscap paper to work on. Mr Rawlings had a black Bakelite telephone at his left hand and a framed picture of his grandchildren at his right. She knew he missed seeing them now that he had been brought out of retirement to take the place of another man who had received his call-up papers. A row of pencils, pens and an inkwell separated him from the front of the desk. On the wall behind where he sat, several bulldog clips nailed to the wall held different sheets of paper, lists of various descriptions: staff rotas, details of railway shipments, memos from head office and a calendar. Even the filing cabinet squeezed in next to his chair groaned under the weight of files on the top.

Lillian shifted her feet awkwardly as she waited, but Mr Rawlings wasn't a man to be hurried.

Eventually, he looked up, as if aware of her presence for the first time.

'Ah, Mrs Harris,' he said, leaning back in his chair. 'I'm glad of this opportunity to raise a few points with you.'

From his relaxed manner, she decided this was nothing to do with Flora, but Lillian's mind still went into overdrive. She'd obviously done something he didn't approve of.

'There's a matter we need to discuss.'

He wasn't going to sack her, was he?

'Please, sit down.'

There was a small chair by the wall. Lillian pulled it in front of the desk and lowered herself onto it. Mr

Rawlings pressed his fingertips together. 'I have been very impressed with your hard work and commitment,' he began. 'You have applied yourself well to your work, and you have certainly raised the standard.' He smiled. 'People are always complimenting me on the cleanliness and outward appearance of the station,' he continued.

Lillian began to relax. Coming from him, this was high praise indeed.

'You do your tasks with cheerfulness and dedication.'

The unease Lillian had felt when she'd walked into his office began to creep back. He was overloading her with compliments now. There was a 'but' coming. She could feel it in her bones.

'However . . .'

Lillian held her breath.

'. . . life never stands still,' he continued, 'and in these difficult days, we all have to embrace change.'

Lillian stared at him with a blank expression.

Mr Rawlings cleared his throat. 'Not to put too fine a point on it,' he went on, 'I have been allocated another worker.'

Lillian's heart sank. So it *was* the sack. What was she going to do now? Since Gordon had been incarcerated by the Germans, his army pay had decreased. The government deemed that since he was no longer a fighting man, they didn't need to pay him a full wage, and subsequently, Lillian, along with all other wives of prisoners of war, was expected to manage on much less. It seemed grossly unfair. She was not only without a breadwinner but she had a child to support too. This job had been a godsend: close to home, with varied shift patterns, which meant that some days she could spend a lot of time with Flora, and a reasonable wage as well. Of course, she didn't get as much as a man, even though she was doing exactly the same job, but at least she got more than a shop girl.

'Mr Knight, the new man,' Mr Rawlings went on, 'has lost the sight in one eye. War injury. He's also subject to bad headaches, so he can't do what he used to. I had to think carefully about what he could manage.'

'But you think he can manage to do my job very well,' said Lillian bitterly.

'Precisely,' said Mr Rawlings, clearly delighted by Lillian's understanding attitude.

'And I get the sack,' said Lillian dully.

'Oh no, no, Mrs Harris,' cried Mr Rawlings. 'Far from it.'

Puzzled, Lillian frowned.

'The post that was offered to Mr Knight,' Mr Rawlings continued, 'was driving the railway goods van, and having seen his predicament, I can't possibly ask him to do that.'

'I don't understand,' said Lillian.

'It would be something completely different,' said Mr Rawlings, 'but I'm sure you could rise to the challenge.'

Lillian moved to the edge of her seat. 'You're asking me to drive the van?'

'Yes, that's right,' said Mr Rawlings. 'As you know,

there are two deliveries a day. Whatever is in the van goes out first thing in the morning. Then you should be back at lunchtime ready to collect the afternoon deliveries. Well, I don't need to tell you, do I? You know the routine.'

Lillian was speechless.

'As soon as the afternoon parcels are gone, you can go home,' said Mr Rawlings. 'So what do you think?'

'I think it sounds like a fantastic job,' Lillian blurted out. 'When do I start?'

Mr Rawlings consulted his roster. 'The present driver has a few weeks to go,' he said. 'He's been called up. Mr Knight starts tomorrow, so I thought you might like to show him the ropes for the rest of this week and next, and start the following Monday with the current driver.'

'That sounds perfect,' said Lillian. She flashed him a smile. She was already imagining herself at the wheel, flying around the Sussex countryside.

'Marvellous,' said Mr Rawlings. 'I'll get all the paperwork done and we'll be under way.' He stood up and offered her his hand, which she shook warmly. 'Well done, Mrs Harris. I knew I could rely on you.'

Lillian's head was whirling with plans as she returned the chair to the wall.

'Oh,' said Mr Rawlings, 'I forgot to mention. There will be a little more money. Fifteen shillings, to be exact.'

A pay rise as well, thought Lillian. Even better. 'Thank you, Mr Rawlings.'

'It may take a while to get used to the van,' he said, turning back to the paperwork on his desk. 'She's a bit temperamental, but I'm sure you'll soon get the hang of it.'

'Absolutely,' said Lillian breathlessly.

She had her hand on the doorknob when he added, 'I take it that you can drive, Mrs Harris?'

Lillian turned with an indignant expression, and putting her hand on her hip, she tossed her head. 'Oh really, Mr Rawlings. I can't believe you asked me that,' she said with a scornful chuckle. 'Can I drive . . . ?'

CHAPTER 8

'Don't be so utterly ridiculous!' Dorcas snapped. 'It can't be done.'

'It has to be, Mum,' said Lillian doggedly. 'I want that job.'

They were crossing Homefield Road on their way back from the hospital. The mess on the corner had largely been cleared away from the pavements, thanks to the Canadian troops billeted in the area. Traffic was flowing again, and barriers had been erected. A jagged hole and a pile of rubble were all that remained of Reydon itself. The papers had said nine people in all had died: four Canadians and five German crew members. Of the sightseers who came, most stood by the remains of the wall on the other side of Lyndhurst Road, which had been stacked neatly in the grounds of Candia, and shook their heads in disbelief. In the normal course of events, there was no love lost for the Germans, but everybody agreed it had been a terrible tragedy.

'But you've only got twelve days,' said Dorcas

crossly. 'How on earth do you expect to learn to drive in less than a fortnight?'

'It can't be that difficult,' Lillian retorted. Her face was set.

Mrs Cooper threw her hands into the air. 'There's no reasoning with you when you're in a mood like this, my girl.'

They had met at Flora's bedside. As soon as her shift was over, Lillian had dashed to the hospital to spend the last half an hour of visiting time with her daughter. As she had expected, her mother was there, and Lillian was pleased to hear that Pip had spent some time with Flora as well. It was a pleasant surprise to discover that Stella had popped by too.

'Philippa didn't stay long,' said Dorcas. 'She seemed a bit upset about Flora's face, but she said to give you her regards.'

'She comes across as a really nice woman,' Lillian remarked.

What little visiting time she had left went all too quickly, and it broke Lillian's heart to leave her daughter sobbing in the nurse's arms.

'Be a good girl and the nice doctors and nurses tell me that after you've had the bandage changed tomorrow, you can come home,' she said encouragingly. But Flora wailed as her mother and grandmother walked out of the ward.

Too upset to talk, Lillian and Dorcas had walked from the hospital in silence, until Lillian broached the subject of having driving lessons. It was then that she told her mother about the van driver's job and they began their argument.

'You should have told Mr Rawlings you couldn't drive,' Dorcas said petulantly.

'And then I would have got the sack,' said Lillian.

'He might have asked someone to teach you to drive,' said Dorcas. 'From what you've said, he thinks very highly of you.'

'Which is why he's offering me that job,' Lillian insisted.

They had reached the house. Dorcas opened the front door and went straight into the kitchen. She began by winding down the pulley and taking the clothes down ready to iron.

'We could do with the money, Mum,' said Lillian, following her mother into the kitchen, 'and he promised me an extra five bob a week.' Should she tell her mother it was fifteen shillings? Lillian didn't want to. She had plans for the other ten bob.

'And what about the driving test?' said Dorcas, determined not to be defeated just yet. The pulley swung erratically as she snatched down the clothes. 'That'll cost you seven and six, and how are you going to fit it in?'

'I don't have to take one,' said Lillian, ducking away from the wooden rungs. 'They suspended all that for the duration in 1939, remember?'

'But surely you'll have to prove that you're capable of driving?' Dorcas insisted.

'I guess Mr Rawlings will ask the van driver,' said Lillian.

Dorcas sighed as she tugged on the rope to make the pulley go back to the ceiling. She knew it was pointless trying to make her daughter see sense. Lillian had always been headstrong and impetuous, which was why she'd had to get married at sixteen, but this madcap idea was just plain stupid. 'How are you going to pay for the lessons?'

'Who said anything about paying?' said Lillian. 'There's more than one man in this town who would give me a free lesson or two.'

Her mother looked shocked.

Lillian chuckled. 'Don't worry, Mum. I won't get myself into any trouble again, I promise.'

Two doors away, Pip was glad of her new-found friendship. She liked Stella a lot. She had known Lillian for some time but only as the mother of one of the small children she occasionally looked after. Most working mothers in the country were supported by the nurseries set up by the government for women doing war work, but because there were no munitions factories or heavy industry in the area, there was a singular lack of them in Worthing. Those women with preschool children who did go out to work had to rely on relatives or friends, which was why Pip had set up a small nursery in her own home.

She soon gained a good reputation for her nursery. She only had a few children at a time – five, including her own – but she had a lot more names on the books. She provided indoor and outdoor playtimes, and taught them songs and counting. She read stories and played games. The children who came to her were very happy.

Before the war, Peter, her husband, owned a builders' merchant's in Lyndhurst Road. When he was called up, with no one to run the business, Peter had shut it down, but he'd kept the premises. Pip had divided the shop in two. One half was being used as a general hardware store, run by the Powell family, and the other was rented out to Mr Stanford, a cobbler. The rents for the two shops brought in a steady income, which augmented Peter's army pay, so she was better off than most. The nursery idea benefited everyone. Pip had plenty to keep her mind occupied, and it stopped her dwelling on the past. Her children had lots of playmates. The government inspectors were happy too. They liked the fact that she was contributing to the war effort by enabling several mothers in the area to work and provide for their own families. Pip didn't charge a huge amount to look after their children, but she had a good business ethic, which meant she more than covered her costs.

Pip hadn't always been so shrewd. Soon after Peter left, she'd fallen victim to a bit of a scam. Terry Wilcox had put her in touch with a farmer who wanted to sell some land, so Pip had bought twenty acres. At five pounds an acre, it seemed like a good deal, but after she'd parted with her money, she'd discovered that the land was waterlogged. It was a costly mistake, and one she certainly wouldn't be making again.

She missed Peter. Their marriage wasn't a passionate affair. It could be more accurately described as comfortable. At eighteen, she'd met him at a village-hall dance, where he was playing in the band, and they had married a year later, in 1935. She'd told everyone she had no family of her own. It was better that way. Peter was a hardworking man who put his family first. Before the war came, Pip always had birthday presents, happy Christmases and holidays. He spoiled her when the children came along, and unlike a lot of his generation, he was a hands-on father. Up until February this year, she had received letters from him quite regularly. They were long and chatty. Despite the war, life in Singapore had carried on as normal. His talent as a reasonable musician had opened the doors to some amazing opportunities outside of his official duties, like playing in places like Raffles Hotel and the Singapore Club. The fall of Singapore changed all that.

As seemed to be so often the case, the British were woefully unprepared for war in the East, even though the intelligence had warned them of the ever-growing menace from Japan. The considered opinion of most of the powers-that-be was that because the Japanese were small of stature, they were weak and ineffective. Officers were convinced that if an assault ever came, it would begin from the sea. No one expected the Japanese to come overland through Malaya. In just a few days, the RAF had lost all its fighter planes, the battleship HMS *Prince of Wales* and the battlecruiser HMS *Repulse*, which had been sunk solely by enemy air power. The casualties were mounting. Resistance against the Japanese invasion by the locals and the British forces on the islands was fierce, but the Allies were running out of food and water. Surrender was inevitable. Peter had been captured by the Japanese and was now a POW somewhere in the Far East.

Having tidied her children's toys away, Pip sat down with pen and paper. A methodical woman, she wrote to him two or three times a week. She had no idea if he was getting her letters, but she forced herself to believe that he was alive and well, and still reading them.

Dear Peter,
We've had a bit of excitement here. A plane came down ~~in Lyndhurst Road~~ . . .

She crossed that bit out. Perhaps it was better not to say exactly where the plane came down for fear, at best, of falling foul of the censors or, even worse, giving the enemy some useful information.

. . . nearby. The children and I are fine, although I have had a bit of a problem making Georgie stay in the garden. He's so inquisitive and wants to see what's going on down the road. I've caught him wandering around the alleyway twice. No damage at all when the plane came down, and we made friends with a teacher who was passing by at the time.

Pip paused and chewed the end of her fountain pen. Should she mention Flora's injury? No, she decided. Better to keep it light.

Just lately, the weather has been lovely, with blue skies and a light breeze off the sea. The children are as brown as berries. They send their love. Hazel keeps drawing her daddy pictures. They're too precious to send as they might get lost in the post, so I'm keeping them in a box for you.

Well, that's all for now. Keep smiling.
All my love,
Pip xx

She put the letter in an envelope and addressed it to his regiment. Even though he was halfway round the world, if it didn't get blown up or sunk on the way, with a bit of luck he'd be reading it by the end of the month. She smiled to herself. Oh, the wonders of modern communication.

Lillian had a driving lesson lined up for the next day. Cyril Johnstone, who was working on the station as a painter and decorator, was eager to help her out and would be waiting for her in his car as soon as she'd finished her shift, in Station Approach. She'd sworn him to secrecy, but sadly the lesson itself wasn't to go well.

He began by staring at the front of her blouse as she climbed into the driver's seat.

'Right,' she said, making sure it was buttoned all the way to the top. 'So how do I start it?'

His hand rested on the back of her seat as he leaned forward. 'Turn the key in the ignition, darlin'.' His breath on the side of her face was sour. 'Press your left foot down onto the clutch. No, not that one. That's the brake. Now press all the way.'

His tone was very suggestive. Lillian frowned. 'I'm serious about this, Cyril,' she said curtly.

'Course you are, darlin',' he said, removing his hand from the back of the seat.

She turned the key and the van sprang into life. Pressing her foot on the clutch, she felt his hand cover hers on the gearstick. She didn't like it one bit, but between them, they eased the car into first gear.

'Now you press the accelerator,' he said. The car moved forward. 'Good girl.'

His hand was still over hers on the gearstick and he pushed it into second gear.

'Do you mind not sitting so close to me?' she said as she spotted Iris coming out of the station.

Cyril gave her a brown-toothed smile and moved away, but not enough to please her.

She'd made it twice round the loop of Station Approach before she'd had enough of his body odour so close to her to want to finish the lesson. He'd eventually taken his hand from the top of hers on the gearstick, but then he'd kept patting her leg as he complimented her.

When she finally got back home, Lillian was all hot

and bothered. There was no time to dwell on that, though: Flora was home. She lay on the sofa under a lightweight blanket. She was pale but clearly delighted to be back. The bandage was gone. From the left side, Flora looked the same as always, but the lovely golden hair on the right side of her head was missing. The exposed skin looked enflamed and sore. It was also stained with iodine. The burn reached her chin, and although her ear was intact, it was very red, and Lillian could see signs of broken blisters. The sight of it tore at her heart, but she stifled her pain as she put her arms out.

'Darling, you're home!' she cried as she ran to the sofa and enveloped the child in her arms.

'I was allowed to take her home during visiting time,' said Dorcas, standing over the two of them with a contented smile. 'We've read some stories together, and Flora has been dressing Dolly, haven't you, sweetheart?'

Flora hugged her mother and smiled shyly.

The subject of driving lessons wasn't mentioned. Neither woman wanted to be the cause of any tension now that Flora was back.

'Did they say anything about her hair?' Lillian whispered when Flora was looking at her picture book again.

'They seem to think some of it will grow back, but it may not be like it was,' said Dorcas.

Lillian gulped. 'Oh, Mum.'

'Now, now,' Dorcas said firmly. 'She'll be fine. When it's healed, we can put a little bonnet on her for a bit.'

Just before teatime, there was a knock at the door. It was Stella.

'Come in, come in,' cried Lillian happily. 'Look who's home.'

Stella was delighted to see Flora and to meet her properly for the first time. Seeing her daughter's puzzled expression, Lillian said, 'Auntie Stella helped Mummy to find you when you were poorly. She took you to the hospital.'

'I'm glad to see you are a bit better,' said Stella. 'I've brought someone to see you.' She handed Flora a parcel wrapped in faded pink tissue and tied with some red ribbon. With her mother's help, Flora managed to take the paper off without tearing it, and Dorcas folded it neatly. No one said anything, but it was an unwritten rule that the same paper would be used over and over again. Wrapping paper was a luxury, and the pink tissue would be put in a drawer for another time and another present.

Under the final layer, they found the familiar toy rabbit, cleaned up and with a bandage covering the neat stitching on his arm. He also sported a bright yellow bow round his neck.

'It's Mr Floppy!' Flora cried happily as she hugged him close.

Lillian had a confused look on her face. 'They told me it was lost,' she began. 'How . . . ? I mean, where . . . ?'

'The sister had put him in the bin,' Stella said confidentially. 'That nice nurse fished it out when she wasn't looking and gave it to me in a brown paper bag. It was filthy, of course, what with the soot and all the muck in the bin, but it was nothing a good wash wouldn't cure. His arm had lost some of its stuffing, so I added some cotton wool and bandaged it.'

'You are very kind,' said Lillian, 'and you've made a little girl very happy. Thank you.'

'My pleasure,' said Stella.

'Stay for tea,' said Dorcas.

'Oh no, I couldn't possibly,' said Stella. 'I have to get back. The land girls . . .'

'Surely you've got time for a cup of tea,' Dorcas insisted.

They turned to look at Flora. She was sleepy, struggling to keep her eyes open. Now that she had Mr Floppy, she had relaxed. Lillian pulled the blanket up to her chin and they all crept out into the kitchen.

'So you will stay?' asked Dorcas.

Stella hesitated for a moment or two, then said, 'Why not?'

Dorcas busied herself with cups and saucers, while Stella sat at the table, and Lillian stood in front of the mirror over the fireplace and tried to tidy her unruly hair.

'Busy day at work?' Stella asked to make conversation.

'Frustrating,' said Lillian.

She was interrupted by a tap on the back door. It was Pip.

'Just popped in to see how the patient is.'

'You must have smelled the tea,' said Dorcas. 'Sit yourself down, dear. Where are the children?'

'Mrs Doughty from across the road has invited

them to play with her two,' said Pip. She turned to Lillian. 'So what's happening with Flora?'

They went over the same ground again with the addition of the return of Mr Floppy, and by the time they were halfway through their second cup of tea, Lillian had launched into her hopes for the new job and her driving lessons.

'I thought Cyril would be a good choice for instructor,' she said ruefully, 'but he was more interested in getting his hand on my leg, the lecherous old basket.'

'But he's old enough to be your father,' Dorcas scowled.

'Well, that didn't stop him!' cried Lillian.

The other women laughed.

'I've a good mind to tell his wife,' said her mother.

'I'm telling you,' Lillian went on, 'I spent more time worrying about his hand than watching the road. If I'd had a skirt on, I dread to think what might have happened. I couldn't get out of that blessed car quick enough.'

'Oh dear,' Stella commiserated as she dabbed at a tear of laughter in her eyes.

'One thing is for sure,' said Lillian. 'I'll have to find somebody else to teach me. I can't possibly go out with him again.'

The four of them sipped their tea.

'I don't suppose you've got a car lurking in that garage of yours, have you, Stella?'

Stella looked over the rim of her cup and smiled. 'As a matter of fact, I have.'

CHAPTER 9

'Somebody's been in here.'

Billy Stanford and Gideon Powell were inspecting their den. The old shed to the side of the derelict house at the end of the street had been their hideout for several months now. They guarded its whereabouts with their lives. Only members of the DD Gang (the Desperate Dan Gang) were allowed in, and they could only enter by using the secret password. The boys had taken the name from their favourite character in the *Dandy* comic. Desperate Dan was, of course, the world's strongest man. He could lift a live cow with one hand, and the pillow on his bed was filled with building rubble. Dan's beard was so tough he had to use a blowtorch to shave, and because he was a goody, it was the ambition of every boy in the gang to grow up to be just like him. The gang consisted of eight. Each boy had taken an oath, swearing that if he divulged any of their secrets, his tongue would be cut out. Nobody had the stomach to carry out such a threat, but Gideon had read all about such things in his book of *Arabian Nights* stories. There was even a picture of Abdul

Abulbul Amir, a fierce Turkish warrior who couldn't be beaten, so cutting out a boy's tongue would be nothing to him.

They kept their collection in the den. Anything from old pram wheels to a service lapel badge, obviously dropped by a serving soldier, a pair of goggles to bits of shrapnel. Now that they could add some finds from the plane crash to the trophy box, it was imperative that nobody pinch it.

'What do you mean, somebody's been in here?' Gideon asked.

Billy pointed. Their notice forbidding girls to enter had been tampered with, and the door swung from only one hinge. 'That door is big enough for an adult to get inside now.'

'Then we'll have to move everything and hide it somewhere else,' said Gideon.

'Put everything in that tin box,' said Billy.

They stuffed it in the box, all except the goggles and their spent bullets.

'I daren't take them home,' said Billy. 'My mum would skin me alive.'

'Don't look at me,' said Gideon. 'I've got three sisters. I could never hide anything from them.'

Billy looked thoughtful. 'Let's give them to Georgie Sinclair,' he said.

'Are you sure you can trust him?' Gideon asked. 'He's only a kid.'

'If we tell him Abdul Abulbul Amir will get him, he won't say anything.'

'Abdul will cut out his tongue,' said Gideon, acting it out. 'And string him up from a tree.'

'Just like he did that German pilot,' said Billy, giving a delicious shiver.

It was Sunday. The three female friends gathered with their children at Stella's place to take a look at Johnny's car. They hadn't dressed up for the occasion. In fact, Pip was in dungarees, and Lillian wore some very old slacks. They had decided to make a day of it by pooling their rations for a meal and letting the children play in new surroundings. Pip had brought some of her nursery toys, and Flora was having her first outing since the accident. Her face and neck was still red, but the burns were not that deep. Funnily enough, neither Georgie nor Hazel made any mention of the change in the way Flora looked. They treated her exactly the same as they always had done. In fact, it didn't take long before the children were settled and happy, especially when Stella had produced some old clothes they could use for dressing up.

'Have either of you heard from your hubbies?' Stella looked at the two women over the rim of her cup of tea, but they shook their heads. 'I've had a letter from Johnny,' she went on.

'Since he's been a prisoner?' said Pip. 'Well, that has to be good, doesn't it? At least you know he's alive.'

'Does he say where he is?' Lillian asked.

'A place called Benghazi,' said Stella. 'He says he's being well treated.'

'They all say that,' said Lillian. Pip gave her a kick under the table. 'Well, they have to,' she said indignantly. 'You've got to read between the lines.'

'He does say that his rations are not up to much,' said Stella. 'Hang on, I'll go and get it.'

When she'd left the room, Pip said, 'Be careful what you say. Don't go upsetting her.'

'I won't,' Lillian frowned, 'but you have to be realistic. It won't be easy for him stuck in a place like that. It'll be bloody hot, for a start.'

Stella was back. Her letter, when she took it out of its envelope, was only one page. '*My dearest*,' she read aloud. '*As you will know, I am a POW of the Italians. We are being well treated in a place called Benghazi. I don't have much stuff, but a chap from the South African Tank Corps gave me a blanket. It gets very cold here at night. We have rations, which include a pint of water a day for everything. I think of you and long for the day when we can be together again. I hope this finds you well. I'll say cheerio for now, Freckle-Face, and God bless. All my love, Johnny.*'

There was a silence in the room when she'd finished; then Pip said, 'That's a lovely letter, Stella.'

'Freckle-Face?' said Lillian.

'A pet name for me,' said Stella, her cheeks colouring slightly. She put the letter back into its envelope, and turning her back to her friends, she reached up and put it on the top of the dresser. Her shoulders trembled and they knew she was fighting a tear or two.

Lillian was the first to move. Standing up, she said, 'I'd better check on how Flora's doing.'

Pip followed, but not before she had given Stella's shoulder a gentle squeeze as she walked by.

'A pint of water for everything?' Lillian hissed in Pip's ear when Stella was out of earshot. 'Bloody hell, that's hard.'

'Don't say anything to her,' said Pip. 'It's best that she doesn't understand.'

'For God's sake, she's not stupid,' Lillian retorted.

A little later, Stella emerged from the house with a bunch of keys. The lock on the garage door hadn't been used since Johnny shut it up at the beginning of the war. As soon as petrol rationing began, they had decided they would keep their car but not use it. They would enjoy their excursions to the countryside once the hostilities were over. The door creaked, resisting her gentle pull, until she gave it a good yank and the daylight flooded in. The car had been jacked up off the ground.

'I don't know a thing about cars,' Stella had admitted the day they had decided on this venture, 'but Johnny said jacking it up would protect the wheels.'

The garage smelled musty and unused, which of course it was, but it was neat and tidy. Johnny was clearly a man who liked order and everything in its place. Their first job was to get the car off the jacks. Lillian had a vague idea of what to do, having seen some of the activity in the goods yard at the station, so it didn't take long to get the car onto its wheels again. Stella produced a foot pump, and Lillian was given the task of getting air back into the tyres.

They knew there would be no petrol in the tank, so over the past few days all three of them had tasked themselves with asking friends and relatives for as many petrol coupons as they could spare. They'd managed to get four between them. They weren't sure how much petrol four coupons would buy, but Pip set off for the local garage with the empty petrol can. Stella lifted the bonnet, but she had no idea where to begin, so she satisfied herself with cleaning the car's interior. When Pip came back, the car was looking good, but she quickly realized that she was the only one who knew how to do the really important things. She cleaned the spark plugs and filled the radiator with water.

'How come you know so much about cars?' Stella asked admiringly.

Pip shrugged. 'I just picked it up along the way, I suppose.'

Everything else was cleaned and polished, and by lunchtime, they honestly believed that once the petrol was in the tank, the car would be roadworthy.

'Oh no!' cried Lillian as they began to fill the petrol tank. 'The garage must have made a mistake. It's pink!'

'So?' said Stella with a shrug. 'What does that mean?'

'It means if we're caught with this petrol in the tank, we'll be in trouble,' said Pip. 'This stuff is only for designated drivers. You know, the doctor or some essential war worker.'

'Well, that's put the kibosh on everything,' said Lillian. 'What are we going to do? If we get stopped and they find out, we could end up in prison.'

'All is not lost,' said Pip. 'Have you still got your gas mask?'

'Yes,' said Stella. 'It's inside somewhere.'

'Then get it,' said Pip.

No one bothered much with their gas mask now. At the beginning of the war, people were vigilant and carried it everywhere, but with the threat of gas attacks proving unfounded, anyone spotted carrying a gas-mask box would more likely have their sandwiches inside than the mask itself. After a few minutes, Stella re-emerged from the house with her gas mask in its box. Pip placed it over a bucket and began to pour petrol through the visor.

'What on earth are you doing?' cried Lillian.

'This takes out the colour,' said Pip, and sure enough, pink petrol went in but the petrol in the bucket had its normal transparent bluish tinge.

'How did you know about that?' said Lillian, her voice full of awe.

'Don't ask,' said Pip, and the other two laughed nervously.

They ate their lunch in the garden with the children, who, flushed from the sunshine, sat on a blanket and ate fish paste, shredded cheese and beetroot sandwiches, followed by a few more of the strawberries grown in the garden belonging to Stella's in-laws.

When they'd finished, it was obvious that Flora was tired, so they laid her on the sofa in Stella's sitting room. While Georgie played trains and Hazel drew her daddy a picture, Pip was happy to sit with them all, and if she was honest, she was glad of the rest.

Now was the moment for Lillian to set off with Stella for her first driving lesson.

They decided to drive to Goring-by-Sea, but first Stella had to get the car out of the garage and onto the road. She was a bit nervous because she hadn't driven for three years. Luckily, it started after the third attempt, but as Stella revved the engine, the car belched a pall of black smoke from the exhaust. It felt like touch and go, but joy of joys she managed to inch it forward with no further mishap. Lillian had made two 'L' plates out of cardboard and string, which she hung on the front grille and from the handle on the back of the boot.

When the car was on the road, Stella got out of the driver's seat and climbed into the passenger side. By this time, Lillian was a bag of nerves. Would she manage this? Stella made it look easy enough, but to hold all that power in your hands was rather daunting.

'Good luck,' Pip called from the front door.

Lillian gave her a wave; then taking a deep breath, she climbed into the driver's seat. Yes, she told herself sternly, she jolly well could do this. She had to. She wanted that job. She needed it. It was part of the plan.

Stella turned out to be a patient teacher. First, she explained the terminology, something Cyril had failed to do. 'This is the gearstick; this is the accelerator, the

89

brake pedal, the clutch and the handbrake. This pull knob is called the choke. You may need it in cold weather, but you don't need it right now.'

There was so much to remember: press your left foot on the clutch, right down as far as it will go; first gear, second gear, up and over into third gear and finally fourth. Lillian was horrified to realize that she not only had to remember all that, but with her left hand on the steering wheel, she had to do hand signals with her right arm out of the window as well!

'Arm straight out for going right,' Stella explained. 'Arm held upright at a right angle from the elbow for turning left, and a slow up-and-down movement to signal that you are stopping.'

The car bunny-hopped along Salisbury Road into Richmond Road, but before long Lillian could manage a reasonably smooth gear change. The change from second to third gear was the most tricky. The car made a loud grating noise almost every time. It was exhausting and stressful, but by the time they had reached the village of Ferring, about four miles from the centre of Worthing, Lillian was beginning to enjoy herself. Then Stella threw a spanner in the works by deciding that it was time to practise some three-point turns and reversing the car. The sense of panic came back.

'I think you've got the seat too close to the steering wheel,' Stella remarked as Lillian struggled to look over her shoulder to see where she was going. 'There's a lever under the seat. If you pull on it and push with your feet, the seat will go back.'

Lillian did her best, but the seat hadn't been moved for three years and the runner was unyielding. All at once, the seat shot back so far that only her fingertips were on the steering wheel. 'Oh . . . Oh!' cried Lillian. Her feet were nowhere near the pedals. The driver of the car behind tooted angrily as they trickled to a halt. He overtook them, shouting expletives as he went by. The two girls looked at each other and burst out laughing.

Once they'd got the seat into a comfortable position, Lillian wiped her brow with the heel of her hand. 'It's going to take me ages to get the hang of this.'

'Nonsense,' said Stella. 'You're a natural.'

Pip was in the loft. It was two days after Lillian's driving lesson and she was alone in the house. By way of saying thank you for looking after Flora, Lillian had taken Georgie and Hazel to her place to play.

Pip didn't normally go up in the loft, but she was looking for something special. The news that the King's younger brother, the Duke of Kent, had been killed in an air crash had profoundly affected her. It wasn't as if she knew the man, and she'd never even seen him in the flesh, but it was obviously a bitter blow to His Majesty to lose his brother, and all at once she'd wanted to look at an old photograph.

Pip had precious little from her past life before she'd met Peter. Young as she was, she had come to Worthing for a fresh start and to put all the sadness behind her. Up in the loft, she was searching for the old vanity case. It should have been easy enough to find because in among all the dark and shadow, it was white, but thus far she'd had no luck. There really was so much junk up here. When Peter came home, she'd ask him to clear it out.

She moved a small pair of steps and a tennis racquet fell down. She picked it up and tutted. With no brace, it was warped and several strings were broken.

That's for the victory bonfire, when we have one, she thought ruefully.

Apart from a few baby things, most of the stuff in the loft was Peter's. It brought a tear to her eye when she came across his old school cap and a rowing oar signed by all the boys in Chalkhill. All the houses in his school had been named after Sussex butterflies: Holly Blue, Chalkhill Blue, Common Blue and Adonis Blue. His school report book was on the top of his old trunk. The last time he was home, Peter must have come up here himself. She opened it and scanned a few pages at the back.

English: Peter has worked well and I hope he will be successful in the final English examinations. J.H.E.

Physical education: Satisfactory progress. S.L.F.

Peter was a class-one entrant to this school and I expect him to get a really good mark for his final certificate. The marks in the 'mock finals' afford few grounds for complacency. J. D. Neil (headmaster)

Her husband was a man who tried, but he wasn't a much better businessman than he had been a student. She'd understood that as soon as she'd married him. His builders' merchant business had only ticked over, and he hadn't been willing to listen to her suggestions. She was convinced that was the main reason why he'd closed everything down before he left. Of course, he'd given her a more palatable explanation. 'Darling, with two small children to care for and a house to run, I don't want you to have to worry about the business as well,' he said between kisses. 'We'll keep the premises, but we'll wait until I get back before deciding what to do with it, all right?'

And she'd agreed. However, since he'd been gone, with a better business plan and some forward thinking, she had turned a disused building into a profitable concern.

'Oh, Peter,' she said aloud, 'I do miss you.'

She lifted the lid of the trunk and slipped the school report book inside, and that's when she saw what she was looking for. It was right at the back of the attic, resting on a rafter. With a bit of an effort, Pip managed to clamber over a few things and reach it. Inside were some old clothes and a couple of books, but that wasn't what she was looking for. On the inside of the case, there was a ruched pocket containing a handkerchief and a map of the South of England. Next to the pocket was a slit in the fabric. It was well hidden, but Pip knew it was there. She slid her fingers inside. For a couple of seconds, she couldn't feel it and her heart constricted. When she drew it out, she sat down on the floor and turned it over.

It was a photograph of two people. She hadn't looked at it for seven years. Seven long years and it was just as she remembered it. The day it was taken had been sunny, the weather warm. She recalled the colours and how they had stood under the lilac tree, although being a black-and-white photograph, that would have been lost to anyone who wasn't there.

Pip ran her fingers across the dear face, and with an audible gulp, she began to weep softly.

CHAPTER 10

Lillian had a problem. She had arranged to meet Woody at the assembly rooms on Saturday night, but she knew her mother wouldn't approve. She could just imagine the furore if she told Dorcas the truth, which was why she had to dream up a really good excuse as to why she needed to go out in the evening. She decided to ask someone else to babysit. She finished work in the afternoon, and then had a driving lesson planned with Stella before she met Woody. The problem was, who was going to look after Flora?

'I wonder if you could do me a favour?' she asked Pip.

'If I can,' said Pip.

'I have to meet someone,' Lillian went on, 'Well, it's Stella, actually. We arranged for me to practise driving in the dark. With winter coming on, I shall have to know how to do it because it gets dark by four o'clock.'

'Sounds like a sensible idea,' said Pip. She was on her hands and knees putting the finishing touches to her stair carpet. She'd noticed the thread was a bit worn in places but had no money for a replacement; she did, however, have half a stair length on the landing, so she had decided to move the whole thing. It had been a long job. Once the stair rods were off and the carpet was lifted, it was obvious that it was full of dust. A good beating on the washing line created enough dust to challenge a sandstorm, but at last she was satisfied that it was clean. Then the stairs had to be washed, and the stair rods were given a polish before she was happy to put everything back in place. It only remained to spray it in situ with a good insecticide to prevent moth damage, which was what she was doing right now.

Lillian explained that her shift didn't finish until late evening and Dorcas had to be up on High Salvington at four to begin her own shift, so she had no one to look after Flora while she took her lesson.

'The thing is,' Lillian went on, 'I was wondering—'

'No problem,' said Pip, getting to her feet. She smiled to herself. It looked good, and the carpet had a whole new lease of life.

'I may be late home,' Lillian cautioned.

'She can sleep on the sofa until you get back,' said Pip, packing everything up to put in the broom cupboard. 'I'll pop round to get her from your mum in the afternoon while you're at work.'

Lillian smiled. 'Thanks, Pip. You're a pal.'

With that problem solved, Lillian had one other. She couldn't go to the assembly rooms in her railway uniform, so where could she change into her dancing clothes? It was clear that she couldn't go home first and then leave all dressed up: if Pip saw her done up to the nines, it would be only too obvious that she wasn't working late and then going for a driving lesson.

The idea didn't come to her until Saturday afternoon as she finished her lesson with Stella. As luck would have it, Stella was busting for the loo. Having carefully parked the car in the garage, Lillian turned to her with a smile. 'You run on in. I'll lock the garage door for you.'

Stella jumped out and went indoors. Lillian locked the car and pulled the garage door shut, but she didn't actually turn the key in the lock until she had changed into her dancing things. Pulling her raincoat around her to hide her dance clothes she dropped the garage key through the letterbox.

The plan worked like clockwork, and by twenty past eight (the dance began at eight o'clock), she was in the crowd outside the assembly rooms.

Woody was nowhere to be seen. In fact, there were hardly any service personnel around, and certainly no Canadians.

'Haven't you heard?' a girl replied when Lillian remarked on it. 'They all went over to Dieppe on some sort of operation.'

Now that the girl had mentioned it, Lillian did remember hearing on the news that a combined operation of British, American, Fighting French and Canadian troops had spent nine hours on French soil as part of a commando raid. They had set out at night and destroyed a gun battery and an ammunition dump. The attack was deemed a great success, but it was not without its casualties. Many men had been killed or injured, and fifteen hundred Allied troops had been taken prisoner.

'Those that got back safely,' another girl chipped in, 'are confined to barracks.'

Lillian hesitated. She had been looking forward to the dance, but because Woody wasn't around, it had suddenly lost its appeal. Just before she reached the ticket booth, she turned on her heel.

'Hey,' the girl called after her, 'where are you going?'

'Home,' said Lillian.

'Bet you haven't seen anything like this,' said Billy.

It was Sunday afternoon and the boys had invited Georgie into the den. He knew he couldn't stay long. Mummy would be cross with him if she knew he was here, but an invitation from the DD Gang was too hard to resist.

The boys had lined up their trophies on a piece of board. Georgie looked over them admiringly. Large chunks of shrapnel, a piece of material from a uniform, half an army-issue belt buckle, though it was unclear whose uniform it might be – English, Canadian or German – a battered mug and more shrapnel.

'I've got something too,' said Georgie.

'We're not interested in kids' stuff,' said a boy at the back. 'This is big stuff. Grown-up stuff.'

'What yer got, then?' asked Derek Fox. 'Go on, let's have a dekko.'

Georgie put his hand in his pocket and drew it out.

'Cor,' Gideon gasped. 'Where did you find that?'

'Blimey, that's the biggest bullet I've ever seen,' cried the boy at the back. He came up to the plank and made to take it, but Georgie got there first. 'It's mine,' he said, standing his ground. He snatched the bullet off the plank and rubbed it on his trouser leg. 'Nobody touches it but me,' he said, putting it back.

The boys were lavish in their praise.

'It's very big.'

'It's bigger than any of the others.'

'That's 'cos it's a machine-gun bullet,' said Georgie.

'How do you know that?' asked Billy.

'Because I heard a man say, "Bloody 'ell, Alf. This place is littered with machine-gun bullets," and that's when I picked it up,' Georgie said innocently.

'Whatever it is,' said Billy, his eyes wide with admiration, 'compared to the others, it's a Goliath.'

'You'd better not let your mum hear you swearing Georgie,' Norman Peabody cautioned.

Billy nudged him in the ribs. 'Anyway, we've got to find a new hiding place.'

'So we want you to keep some of our stuff,' said Gideon.

Georgie frowned. 'But Mummy doesn't like me keeping things like this.'

Although he was glad to be included, Georgie was a little afraid of the big boys. He turned Goliath and a couple of pieces of shrapnel over in his hands. It was all very well hiding stuff, but if he got caught, he was sure his mother would tan his bottom. 'I can't,' he began.

'Then I guess we'll have to tell Abdul,' said Gideon with a sigh.

'Who is Abdul?' said Georgie.

'Abdul Abulbul Amir,' said Gideon, narrowing his eyes. 'He comes from a place called Turkey, and he's a warrior.' He waved his arms as if he had a sword and was cutting his enemy to ribbons.

'He can't be beaten,' said the boy at the back. 'Not even Hitler can beat him.'

'And he'll cut your tongue out just like that,' someone else called as he clicked his fingers.

Georgie shivered.

'If you won't do it,' said Billy, 'we won't be able to let you be part of our gang.'

Georgie hesitated. He wanted to be part of the gang more than anything in the whole wide world.

'And of course,' Gideon added as his pièce de résistance, 'we wouldn't be able to stop Abdul if he wanted to cut your tongue out.'

Georgie paled. 'All right,' he said quietly. 'I'll do it, but when you want them back, don't tell my mummy.'

They loaded him up, stuffing his pockets and giving him an old canvas bag as well. As they watched him go, the boy at the back said, 'Are you really going to make him a member?'

'Nah,' said Billy. 'He's far too young.'

* * *

100

On the following Friday, it was Stella's birthday. The school holidays were long gone, and although she had enjoyed the three-week break from lessons, Stella was glad to be back at school. She had been back a week already, but there remained something rather special about walking into the classroom after having been away for a while. Perhaps it was the smell of the ink, or the chalk for the blackboard, or maybe it was the faint aroma of lavender polish on her desk. Everything seemed new and fresh. Of course, she hadn't been idle during the holidays. On her first day back, her arms had been full of new wall charts and plans for what she hoped would be exciting lessons for her pupils.

Out of the forty-seven names on her books, twenty-eight filed into the classroom and sat at their desks. When she'd called the register on Monday, she'd discovered that Rachel Becket had mumps, Annie MacGreggor was in hospital recovering from having her tonsils removed, Ivy Cookson had to stay at home to help look after her three smaller siblings because her mother had just given birth to her fifth child, and the Porter boys were helping to bring in the harvest on the farm. There had also been a note in her desk drawer informing her that Mrs James, the teacher who had arrived with twelve child evacuees, had taken her pupils back to London during the holidays. Two of her absent students, however, remained unaccounted for: twins Samuel and Susan Dennison weren't in class and hadn't been all week.

'Does anyone know where Sam and Susan are?'

she'd asked her class each day, but her query had been met with blank stares and a few shrugs.

On Friday, during the afternoon, she asked her pupils to write or draw something they had done on their holidays. She felt it would be a good topic to draw out conversation and a useful exercise to encourage memory and communication. Everyone knuckled down, some with their tongues between their teeth as they concentrated, others leaning right over the page as they wrote and a few spending a little time gazing upwards for inspiration. As she sat at her desk in front of them, Stella wondered what she would have written had she been their age.

She might have drawn a picture of the terrible events of three weeks ago: the plane crash and poor Flora's injuries were still fresh in her mind. Thankfully, the child looked a lot better now. Although her hair still looked a mess, the burns were healing nicely. If she hadn't drawn a picture of the crash, perhaps she would have written about her new-found friendship with Pip. She was a quiet, unassuming girl who had probably never strayed from the straight and narrow. Kind and honest as the day was long, she always seemed to be looking after others, particularly her children, to whom she was devoted. On her own, one might say she was perhaps a little too predictable and possibly dull, but maybe that was being unkind. One thing was for sure: she was the type of girl who would be a loyal friend for life.

Or perhaps she would write something about Lillian,

someone who lived life at ninety miles an hour. How could Stella ever forget giving her those driving lessons, or all the laughs they'd had along the way? Right now, Lillian was at the end of her first week in the railway goods van. Would it be her first and last, or the first of many? Stella admired Lillian's determination and single-mindedness, but she couldn't help feeling a little anxious for her.

At the beginning of her quest for that job, she had been a hopeless danger on the road. A couple of times when they were doing three-point turns, they had ended up with the back wheels of the car dangerously close to the steep sides of a ditch. On another memorable occasion, Lillian had been trying to turn right onto a main road. Halfway across, when both lanes were blocked, she'd stalled the engine. A lorry driver had honked his horn noisily and mouthed obscenities. In order to keep Lillian's level of panic to a minimum, Stella had deliberately glared at him through the windscreen as she waited for Lillian to move off. Under pressure from the impatient lorry driver, the gears crunched and groaned. The engine revved a couple of times, only to die when the car bunny-hopped and stopped. Lillian swore and cursed, but after a few gut-wrenching minutes, it all went quiet. The lorry driver whose horn-blowing had only added to Lillian's fluster threw himself over the wheel and began to laugh. Stella turned her head, only to find the driver's door wide open and Lillian standing on the other side of the road waiting for her to complete the manoeuvre.

As the days sped by, through sheer guts and determination Lillian had managed to master her driving technique, and although Stella wouldn't have said she was brilliant (far from it), she honestly believed that with perseverance she would soon be a competent driver.

Stella glanced up at the school clock. At this moment, Lillian would be heading back in the railway goods van with the old driver. With no driving tests available for the duration, it would be up to him to say if Lillian was fit to spend her hard-earned seven shillings and sixpence to buy a licence. Stella mentally crossed everything that she'd come through with flying colours.

Because it was her birthday, Stella had invited her two new friends and their children to her small party. She would use the opportunity to celebrate or commiserate with Lillian. Even if she failed, Stella knew she wouldn't stay down for long. She had a feeling that nothing would stop Lillian from getting what she wanted.

Looking around the classroom once more, Stella wondered about Samuel and Susan again. There had been no word from them all week, which was unusual. Their mother was a conscientious woman, keen for her children to do well at school. It wasn't like her not to send a note of some sort. Stella decided that if the twins weren't back on Monday, she would go round to their house and see what was wrong. It wasn't her job, of course, but if the Dennisons were in trouble, she preferred to offer a hand before she reported the children to the authorities as absentees.

Her mind drifted back to her husband and her heart lurched. Poor Johnny. What was he doing? Were the Italians treating him well? Please God that they were. The news bulletins had said little about North Africa since the fall of Tobruk. There were more pressing flare-ups in other places. A battle had been raging in the Arctic between a Russian convoy and German planes and U-boats. The losses on both sides were horrendous, and of course this was all being played out against the backdrop of another Allied attempt to defeat Rommel in the North African desert.

Stella looked up and saw a few upturned faces. It was three-thirty. School finished at four. 'Five more minutes,' she said, 'then put your hand up if you want to read your work out first.'

Pip arrived before the others. Her children were squashed together in the pram, with some goodies underneath. 'Happy birthday,' she said as Stella opened the door.

Stella had cleared the table in the sitting room and pushed it against the wall. Every chair she had was arranged round the room, and the cover on the piano was pulled back.

'Ooh,' said Pip, putting a plate of fresh blackberries on the table next to the grated carrot and white cabbage sandwiches, 'does that mean we'll be having a sing-song?'

'Why not?' Stella smiled.

Pip put another dish on the table.

'Is that cream?!' cried Stella.

Pip allowed herself a small grin of pleasure. It wasn't real, of course, but she knew from experience that it was a pretty good imitation. She'd actually made it herself by putting four ounces of margarine and four ounces of milk through her cream-maker.

The doorbell rang again and a few more friends and their children turned up, which meant Georgie and Hazel had someone to play with. The adults packed them off into the garden. There were no toys, but with an archway of roses and some sparse rhododendrons at the end of the garden, it wasn't long before the boys had initiated a game of Robin Hood, and the girls were happy to tag along until they were 'killed'.

In no time at all, the sitting room began to fill up, and so did the table. Thanks to her lodgers, Stella's mother came with a real birthday cake just like the ones they remembered from before the war. She'd even managed to find some old cake candles, though sadly only four of them. The rest of the spread included Spam sandwiches, cheese swirls, carrot sticks, potato drop scones and gypsy creams . . . There was no limit to people's ingenuity. The land girls Brenda and Vera arrived home and ran upstairs to quickly change into their smart dresses. By the time Dorcas and Flora were on the doorstep, Pip had started serving teas and the room was buzzing with conversation.

Lillian was late, but they had expected her to be. Stella opened the door to her wondering what sort of mood she would be in. Her face was so serious Stella's heart sank. As Lillian walked into the room, every eye turned in her direction. There was a pregnant pause, and then Dorcas came towards her daughter. 'Never mind, love,' she said quietly. 'Another time, eh?'

Lillian's face broke into a wide smile. 'I got the job, Mum,' she cried. 'I got it!'

Everyone crowded round congratulating her and giving her a kiss on the cheek or a pat on the back.

'Happy birthday, Stella,' she said happily as she pushed a small box into Stella's hand. 'And thanks for everything.'

'Oh, you shouldn't have,' Stella said shyly. Inside the box, she found a small necklace with an imitation drop pearl on the chain. 'Oh, it's lovely,' she cried.

'It's only Woolworths,' Lillian confessed.

'It's lovely,' Stella said more firmly. She looked around with a smile. She was a quarter of a century old and she'd had some wonderful presents: talc, a box of three handkerchiefs, some chocolate, a head-scarf from her mother and much more. She almost felt like a kid again. Only one person was missing . . .

'Come on,' said Lillian. 'Let's get this party under way.'

The children were given a plate full of food and some raspberry tea, which was simply a spoonful of jam in a cup of warm water, but the kids loved it. The adults talked, ate and drank tea until Dorcas produced two bottles of parsnip wine and then the glasses came out.

'Be careful of that stuff,' Lillian cautioned. 'It's got a kick like a mule.' But nobody was listening. Once they'd all charged their glasses, they toasted the birthday girl. Eventually, Stella sat down at the piano and all the old songs came out.

Mellowed by the parsnip wine, Lillian and Pip stood either side of the piano as Stella began to play 'Don't Sit Under the Apple Tree'. They blended their voices and it wasn't until they'd reached the final notes that they became aware that the rest of the room was hushed and they were the only ones singing. Turning from the assembled crowd, Lillian, Stella and Pip looked at each other in blank surprise.

'Blimey,' said Brenda, 'that made the hairs on the back of my neck stand up.'

'You sounded amazing,' Dorcas said. 'Just like the Andrews Sisters.'

Stella laughed. 'Don't be daft,' she said.

'No, darling, she's right,' said Phyllis. 'You should listen to what she's saying. When you sing together, you girls have got real talent.'

CHAPTER 11

Dear Lillian,

I hope this finds you well as it leafs me. Since last munf I have been working 12 hours a day mending roads. We are glad to be doing somefing. Its been a long 2 years. We get good Red X fod parsels. The Canadan ones are best. I has to share our ones between two but we has half a pound of sugar, and chocolates, and condensed milk. The Canadans send us butter, coffee, biscuits and fifty fags.

I often think of you and Flora. I miss you. I hope you are behaveing yoursef. That's all for now.

Your ever loveing Gordon

It wasn't much of a letter, and only the fourth she had received from him in the two years he'd been a POW. It was dated May 1942, and the stamp on the front of the envelope said, *Stalaag XXB Poland*. Lillian reread the words without emotion. She was glad for his sake that he was still alive and that he'd remembered their daughter, but she could have done without him telling her he was thinking of her. She knew now more than ever that she had made a stupid mistake when she'd got pregnant.

She loved Flora to pieces, but she should never have married Gordon. She had imagined that he was love's young dream, but what did she know of life when she was only sixteen? Fifteen when she got pregnant. Back then, it didn't matter that Gordon was always messing about at school and getting into trouble, but his letter revealed just how uneducated he was, and she resented him for it. Since the country had gone to war, she'd worked at the railway station; she'd met such interesting people on the platform; she'd learned to drive and got her new job. She was a different person altogether now. What on earth had they got in common except Flora? She'd met Stella and made better friends with Pip. She'd also met Woody, and he'd made her realize that there was so much more to life than leaving school, finding a boyfriend and getting married. Given the chance, she'd love to travel, to see a bit of the country, even a bit of the world, but instead she was doomed to be stuck with Gordon for the rest of her life. Well, not if she could help it.

It was great fun driving the van. She had a tight schedule, but she loved the challenge of finding the address and getting her round done as quickly as she could. Ron Knight, the man who had taken over her station duties, seemed a pleasant enough fellow. In fact, Iris Keegan in the station cafe couldn't speak more highly of him, and Betty Shrimpton had a permanent smile on her face when he was around.

'They should have given Mr Knight that van-driving job,' Lillian heard her telling Betty from the ticket office.

'Quite right, dear,' said Betty. 'But it's nice having him around the station.'

'It's all very well putting these young flibbertigibbets in trousers,' Iris went on, 'but they haven't got the strength. When I was her age, I was at home doing what I should be doing: looking after my child.'

'I wouldn't know about that,' said Betty. 'I've never married. Someone had to stay at home to look after Mother.'

'Exactly,' said Iris. 'Family comes first.'

That's right, Lillian thought acidly to herself. Put the knife in, why don't you? You never did like me much, did you, Iris? She was tempted to give the silly old duffer a piece of her mind, but she couldn't be bothered. Iris was from an altogether different generation, and Lillian had no intention of giving up her hard-won independence for domesticity. Besides . . . there was a war on!

Being in the cab on her own gave Lillian an excellent opportunity to practise her singing. She'd always loved singing, but it had been a bit of a revelation when the rest of the partygoers had been so encouraging. When everyone else had gone home, the three girls had talked about what had happened. 'If we work really hard,' Stella had said, 'we might be good enough to perform in public.' Perform in public . . . how exciting. Lillian had spent a lot of time thinking about it. Pip had liked the idea too, so they'd all agreed to meet together a couple of times a week to practise. Lillian could well imagine that Stella would be a hard taskmaster, but if they really were good enough, she might even get to perform to the Canadian troops. She smiled to herself as she tried to imagine Woody's face when she went out on stage.

To her great surprise, Lillian had to deliver a package to the Canadian camp, which was near the village of Goring-by-Sea. The camp was mostly tented, but there were a few Nissen huts. She was stopped by the guard at the entrance, but once she had clearance, she headed straight for the HQ to make her delivery.

As she waited to go inside, the sentry on the door couldn't resist flirting.

'Hey, honey, this has made my day,' he said with a laugh, 'seeing a gal like you driving the van.'

Lillian gave him a teasing grin. 'I bet you say that to all the drivers.'

'Hell, no,' he quipped. 'You're a lot better-looking than the other guy.'

The door opened. Lillian was invited inside; the package was delivered and the docket signed.

On the way out, the guard said, 'Maybe I'll see you at the dance on Saturday night?'

'Maybe, maybe not,' said Lillian. She climbed into the van and turned it round. As she drew level with him again, she wound down the window. 'By the way, do you know a soldier called Woody?'

'There's an awful lot of men here, honey,' he said, shaking his head slowly. 'I can't say I do. Is it important?'

Lillian shrugged. 'Not really, I suppose, but I was

meant to meet him the weekend you all went to Dieppe.'

'Do you know his proper name?'

Lillian didn't hesitate. 'Lemuel Dicken Woods.'

The guard shifted his feet awkwardly. 'Hang on a minute, ma'am,' he said, suddenly becoming more formal. 'I'll get the adjutant.'

Lillian was about to say, 'Don't worry,' but he'd already gone into the office. A couple of minutes later, he came back outside with another man.

'You were asking about Woody?' the other man said.

Lillian nodded.

'Then I'm sorry to have to tell you Woody was killed.'

Lillian felt the colour drain from her face. 'Killed?' she said faintly. 'What, in France?'

'No, ma'am,' said the adjutant. 'He died shortly before we went to France. You may have heard about it. A plane crashed into a house in the town. Woody was one of the guys billeted there.'

Lillian felt slightly sick. 'You mean the house near the hospital?'

'That's right,' said the adjutant. 'Do you know it?'

Tears smarted in her eyes, and Lillian swallowed hard.

'Are you OK?' the guard asked. 'You look kinda pale.'

'I'm fine,' said Lillian, putting her foot on the clutch. 'Did you know him well?'

Lillian shook her head, anxious to go. 'But I am sorry to hear that he's dead.'

She drove from the camp with dignity, but pulled up somewhere along the Goring Road on her way to her next delivery. She looked across the fields. Her hands were trembling. Woody was dead? It hardly seemed possible that while she was frantically searching for her daughter, he was dying not two hundred yards away. How could he have been so near to her house and she'd not known? Angrily she wiped a tear from the tip of her chin and fished out her handkerchief to blow her nose. Hell and damnation. She'd really liked Woody. How many other lovely people had to die before this bloody war was over?

Stella looked up and down the street, but the house wasn't there. She looked down at the piece of paper in her hand and frowned. She had copied Samuel and Susan Dennison's address straight out of the register, so there was no mistake . . . Or was there? The numbers on the houses on this side of the road ended at sixteen. Those on the other side of the street were all odd, but they included number nineteen, so where was number eighteen?

The children hadn't been at school for well over a week. Normally she would have reported their absence to the school office, who would in turn notify the Education Department at the town hall. If there was no valid reason for the children's failure to attend school, Mrs Dennison would be in trouble. The only reason

Stella hadn't reported her was that it was so unusual. Mrs Dennison was committed to making sure her children had a good education. Stella was aware that she was one of the few mothers who sat with her children at home helping them to read and do their sums. She was also aware that things weren't easy for her. The children's father was abroad fighting for king and country, so apart from the small allowance taken from his army pay, she was the sole breadwinner. Mrs Dennison had several part-time cleaning jobs, which Stella was willing to bet only paid her a pittance, but her children were a credit to her. Polite and well mannered, they were always clean and tidy, though their clothes weren't new. Stella felt there had to be a cast-iron reason why they were absent from their desks. Was their mother sick? Had the family moved? Anything was possible. People moved around the country to try and find a safer place to live.

She crossed the road and tried the houses there, but with a change of road, they began with number one on the left and number two on the right-hand side.

A chimney sweep pushing a bicycle with his brushes in the large box on the front came by.

'Excuse me,' Stella began. He turned his sooty face in her direction. 'I'm looking for number eighteen.'

He smiled knowingly and revealed tobacco-stained teeth. 'You needs to go through the twitten,' he said. 'Numbers eighteen and twenty are round the back.'

Stella followed his pointing finger, making her way past the high walls of a garden and the side of a house.

When she turned the corner, she could see another two houses tucked away out of sight. Remembering the history of Worthing, she recalled how in Victorian times, the haves, anxious not to mix with the lower classes and deal with their squalid living conditions, screened themselves from the have-nots by putting up high walls. It was more a question of out of sight, out of mind. She sighed. Things hadn't changed much. The houses were in poor condition even now.

Stella walked up the path of number eighteen. It was barely five or six strides to the front door, and judging by the width of the house, it probably only had one room downstairs and two small rooms upstairs. She knocked loudly on the front door and Samuel opened it.

'Hello, Samuel. Is your mother in?'

At first, the boy gasped in surprise, but with a wide smile he stepped aside to let her in. The door opened into an untidy sitting room. She had hardly got through the door when Mrs Dennison came from the direction of the kitchen wiping her hands on her apron. From her expression, Stella could see at once that she was embarrassed to have the children's teacher calling at her home.

'I beg your pardon, Mrs Dennison,' Stella said. 'Perhaps I should have waited outside . . .'

Mrs Dennison made an instant recovery. 'No, no,' she cried. 'Do come in, miss. Make yourself at home.' She began plumping up the cushions and removing old newspapers from the sofa. 'You'll have some tea? I've just made a pot.'

'I won't stay long,' Stella began. Mrs Dennison sniffed loudly and held her head high, and Stella, guessing that she had offended her, added quickly, 'But I never say no to a nice cup of tea.' Mrs Dennison smiled and her body language told Stella she'd made the right decision.

It was only as she sat down that Stella noticed that Samuel's feet were bare. When their mother came through from the kitchen with the tea, Susan followed her. Susan's feet were bare too.

'I've been wondering why the children aren't at school,' said Stella as Mrs Dennison put her best bone-china cup and saucer into her hand.

'I'm sorry, miss,' said Mrs Dennison, 'but their father came home from the war and he wanted us to all be together.'

Stella nodded. 'Quite understandable, but—'

'Just for a bit,' Mrs Dennison interrupted.

From the room above them, Stella heard the creaking of a bed.

'So,' said Stella, sitting back on the sofa in a relaxed way, 'Mr Dennison is home. How much leave has he got?'

'He won't be going back, miss.' Mrs Dennison turned her head away from Stella's gaze and cleared her throat. 'The truth is, he's not feeling so good these days. Since he got out of the army, he feels let down.'

'I'm sorry to hear that,' said Stella.

117

And Samuel blurted out, 'Jerry blew his hand off.'

'Sam!' his mother scolded.

Stella stared in disbelief and an awkward silence descended. 'I'm so sorry, Mrs Dennison.' It was a lame and pathetic response, but the revelation had caught her completely by surprise.

Mrs Dennison took a deep breath. 'That's why the kids have to stay home, see, on account of their dad.'

They heard a loud thud above them, as if someone had dropped a shoe or something, and a man's voice called, 'Nancy.'

Stella chewed her bottom lip uncomfortably. 'The thing is, Mrs Dennison, they have to go to school, not because I say so but because it's the law.'

Mrs Dennison gave her a helpless look.

'If they don't attend,' Stella went on, 'I am duty-bound to report the matter.' She looked up, alarmed to see tears standing in the woman's eyes.

'Please excuse my asking,' Stella began again, 'but I couldn't help noticing that your children don't appear to have any shoes. I have no wish to embarrass you, but . . .'

'They like running around without them,' Mrs Dennison said stiffly.

'Nance,' the voice called again.

'I'll send them along just as soon as I can get straight,' said Mrs Dennison, standing up.

Stella rose to her feet. It didn't take much to work out what was going on. Johnny's army pay had dropped when he became a POW. If Mr Dennison was no longer capable of fighting, he'd probably been sent home with nothing or very little. It was perfectly possible that he couldn't get a job. What could he do with only one hand? If only Mrs Dennison would let her help. Stella was sure she could find a pair of second-hand shoes from somewhere. She looked from Samuel's feet to Susan's and opened her mouth to say something, but Mrs Dennison got there first.

'Now, if you don't mind, miss, I have to go upstairs and help my husband. He can't do up his bootlaces with only one hand.'

Stella didn't know what to say. What should she do? What *could* she do? She didn't want to embarrass Mrs Dennison any more than she already had. The woman still had her pride, but if something wasn't done, her children would be condemned to a life of ignorance and poverty, or, worse still, put into care. It worried Stella that the children were barefoot. Was that the real reason they weren't at school?

'Nancy!' The shout from upstairs sounded more urgent and Mrs Dennison turned to go.

'Before you go, Mrs Dennison,' Stella said, fishing into her bag and trying to sound businesslike. 'I've brought them some homework. Until Samuel and Susan return, I'm sure that you'll agree they mustn't let standards slip. I would hate for them to fall behind. They are my most talented pupils.'

Mrs Dennison's expression softened at the compliment. Taking the schoolbooks from Stella, she nodded politely and added, 'Thank you, miss, and thank you for coming.'

Pip knew she was staring at Flora, but she couldn't help it. The little girl sat at her kitchen table alongside Georgie, Hazel and Sarah Hollick, a little girl Pip sometimes looked after. The children were painting. There had been a high turnover of canvases. Three vertical strokes in green paint and a blob of red at the top of the page and Flora was finished.

'What's that?' Pip asked.

'A princess.'

'What's the red bit?'

Flora turned with an indignant look and a frown. 'Her crown.'

'Of course,' said Pip with a smile. She put the finished work onto the dresser to dry before handing Flora another sheet of paper. In these days of paper shortages, she had been fortunate to find a whole roll of wallpaper lining-paper at the jumble sale. Damaged at the edges and rather discoloured, it was useless for papering walls but ideal for the children's paintings.

Flora concentrated on her next creation, which looked remarkably like the first. Sarah finished her painting, and as Pip put it up to dry, she took a minute to wipe a blob of yellow paint from the end of Sarah's nose. Hazel was still engrossed in her picture, a work so thick with paint it had become a murky grey and the brush was in danger of making a hole in the paper. Georgie was painting the plane crash again. Ever since that fateful night, although he refused to talk about it, what he had seen had surfaced in his artwork and his play. The event had become a little more fanciful each time, but the outcome was more or less the same: a house, a plane, lots of fire and people running away.

'What's your picture about, Georgie?'

Georgie shrugged. 'Can I do another one?'

Pip handed out fresh paper and everyone began again. She stared at Flora once more. Her hair was beginning to grow back, but she couldn't help noticing there was a little area behind the child's ear where the curls were missing. The skin was as shiny as a billiard ball and Pip wondered if the hair follicles had been permanently damaged.

Elsewhere, the burns on Flora's skin were healing nicely. She still had a couple of crusty scabs on her neck, but pink new skin had grown underneath. Lillian told her that the rest of the child's body was responding well to the creams the hospital had given her. Pip took her word for it. She had no reason to undress Flora while she was in her care.

She could only guess how frightening the incident had been to a three-year-old alone in her garden with fire falling from the sky. Pip closed her eyes as a distant memory of Marion's terrible screaming came back into her mind. For many a year she had refused to think about it, but ever since that day, it returned unbidden: that awful moment when she'd seen Marion flying down the stairs engulfed in flames. Pip shook herself back to the present, and as she did so, her fingers accidentally

121

touched Flora's neck. Dropping her paintbrush, the child scrambled from the chair and began batting her shoulder vigorously. 'It hurts, burning.'

Pip was horrified, and dropping to her knees in front of her, she held the child's arms. 'It was me,' she said. 'I touched you. It's all right. Nothing happened.' Pip felt her little body judder.

'Hot,' Flora said desperately. Big tears rolled down her cheeks.

Pip let go, and Flora began to brush her shoulder more vigorously. One touch, one stupid dip of her hand and she'd brought it all back to her. She could have kicked herself. 'It's all right,' she soothed as she held the child close. 'We're all indoors and you're perfectly safe.' Flora relaxed. 'I'm sorry, darling. I'm so sorry, Marion.'

The other children had stopped painting and watched them in mild surprise. Over Flora's shoulder, Pip's eyes met Georgie's. 'Mummy gave her a bit of a fright, that's all,' she said reassuringly. 'It's all right now.'

The girls returned to their work, but Georgie was still looking at his mother. 'Mummy,' he said. 'Her name is Flora, not Marion.'

CHAPTER 12

Stella kept up her visits to Johnny's parents even though they had no news to share. Since the telegram had come, way back in August, they had all endured weeks of silence. It didn't help when in November, the local paper, the *Worthing Herald*, published a long list of Worthing men who had been made POWs in the North African Campaign but Johnny's name wasn't there.

'Why haven't we heard from him?' Judith wondered.

'It could be a clerical error,' Desmond suggested, 'or maybe he's not counted in the numbers because he's escaped.'

'Escaped!' Judith exclaimed, grasping at her throat. 'Oh, Desmond, don't say such things.'

'I'm sorry, my dear,' he apologized. 'Thoughtless of me.'

Stella had been equally alarmed by the suggestion, but on reflection, it probably wasn't so far from the truth. Wherever he was incarcerated, she felt sure Johnny would feel honour-bound to try and get home.

Stella had been invited to dinner. The meal had been prepared by the maid. All Judith had to do was turn on the oven, and as soon as Stella had walked through the door, the wonderful aroma of rabbit stew with dumplings filled her nostrils.

'How's your mother?' Judith asked as she dished up.

'Very well,' said Stella. 'She's been helping me by listening to us singing.'

Desmond smiled. 'How's it going?' He and Judith had been keen to hear all about Lillian, Pip and Stella's singing group. 'Are you any good?'

'I think so,' said Stella. 'We've been meeting for a while, and the other girls are very enthusiastic.'

Judith dabbed her mouth with her napkin and looked up. 'What sort of things do you sing?'

'Mostly popular songs,' said Stella. '"Rhumboogie", "The Anniversary Waltz", "Kiss the Boys Goodbye", "Don't Sit Under the Apple Tree", that sort of thing.'

Desmond nodded approvingly. 'I like that one. A little wine, my dear?'

'Is it your own brew?' Stella asked.

'Elderberry,' said Desmond. 'It's quite light.'

'We wanted to sound like the Andrews Sisters,' said Stella, holding out her glass while he poured. 'But it was too hard trying to recreate the sound because they always sing with big bands.'

Judith smiled. 'What are you going to call yourselves?'

'Not sure yet,' said Stella. 'The Southcoasters, the Highdown Trio . . . Skylark was a favourite until we discovered somebody else had already thought of that.'

'So shall we see you at the assembly hall or the Connaught Theatre?' Desmond asked with a teasing grin.

'I doubt it,' said Stella. 'We want to be with ordinary people.'

'What does that mean?' said Judith.

'We'll go into works canteens, the hospital, factories, places like that,' said Stella.

The three of them had talked it over. She and Pip weren't seeking fame and fortune for themselves, though it was obvious that Lillian wasn't averse to such things, but they all agreed that the people of Worthing needed a little light relief. The town had been hugely disappointed when long-distance coach trips had been suspended because of the petrol shortage. Not only did it mean a serious drop in the number of day-trippers but it also meant that the locals were unable to travel themselves. Added to that, to save coal, train services had been cut by ten per cent. The year 1943 promised to be rather bleak, what with soaring food prices and an epidemic of shoplifting so bad that specially trained private detectives had been called in from other areas to patrol the shops.

'People need a morale boost,' Stella went on. 'Life can be so depressing at times. It's all "Do this" and "You can't do that." The whole country is sick of rules and regulations. We think everybody should have a little time to simply *enjoy* themselves.'

'Hear, hear,' said Desmond.

'A noble cause,' said Judith.

'This stew is delicious,' said Stella, deliberately changing the subject.

'Have some more, dear.'

Stella shook her head. 'No, no, that's enough for now.' She put her knife and fork together, and picked up her wine glass.

'You look miles away, dear,' Judith said to her husband. 'Is something wrong?'

'To tell you the truth,' Desmond began, 'I find myself in a bit of a quandary.'

'Tell us,' said Stella. 'Maybe we can help.'

Desmond took a deep breath. 'Well, my dear, as you know, since I retired, I've become a magistrate. A man was brought to the courts the other day charged with stealing by finding.'

Stella frowned. 'Whatever's that?'

'The story goes that he picked up a pretty bracelet in the street, put it into his pocket and went home.'

'And that was enough to bring him to court?' said Stella.

'He should have taken it straight to the police station,' said Judith.

'Perhaps he should,' said Desmond, 'but it was late at night. According to his solicitor, he'd just come out of a public house, it was raining hard, and he wanted to get home for his supper.'

'Honesty comes before a full stomach,' said Judith

in a strident tone. 'What sort of fellow was he? I'll wager that he had a criminal record.'

'I suppose it depends on what he did with the bracelet,' said Stella. 'Was it valuable?'

'He put it in a drawer and forgot it,' said Desmond, 'and yes, it was very valuable, worth more than two hundred pounds.'

'Did he plan to sell it?' said Judith.

'His solicitor said that he had no idea of its value,' Desmond went on.

Stella frowned. 'So how did the police find out about it?'

'The gentleman in question saw a notice in the paper,' Desmond continued, 'so he took the bracelet to the address, which turned out to be a jeweller's shop. The jeweller was out, so he left it and his details with the assistant. It was she who reported him to the police.'

'I still can't see what he did wrong,' said Stella. 'He returned the bracelet to its rightful owner, so where's the problem?'

'I hope you dismissed the case,' said Judith indignantly.

Desmond sighed. 'Actually, my dear, it wasn't my case. Old Bob Redding was presiding, and I'm sad to say that he convicted the poor fellow, even though he had a perfectly good character.'

'But that's awful!' cried Stella. 'That means anyone who finds something in the street would be better off keeping it than returning it to the rightful owner in case they get prosecuted for stealing!'

'I quite agree with you,' said Desmond.

'I hope they didn't send the poor man to prison,' said Judith.

Her husband shook his head. 'At least he was spared that,' he said. 'But he was fined five pounds.' He paused. 'I have to say I really felt for him. The chap only had one hand – apparently lost the other in the war. He'll have a dickens of a job to get work with only one hand and a criminal record.'

Stella took in her breath. 'Say that again. He lost his what?'

Desmond raised his eyebrows. 'He'd been invalided out of the army. He was shot in the hand and they had to amputate.'

Stella put down her glass. Her blood had run cold. She knew her father-in-law wouldn't tell her the name of the man, but it sounded awfully like Mr Dennison. In fact, it was too much like him to be a coincidence.

'Is everything all right?' Judith was saying.

'I think I might know the man in question,' said Stella. Her parents-in-law looked up at her in surprise. Stella put her finger to her lips. 'His children go to my school, or to be precise, they used to go but haven't for a while.'

'A problem family, then,' said Judith.

'I went round to their house,' said Stella. 'I think they can't come to school because they have no shoes.'

'But surely that's easily remedied?' Judith said.

'If the magistrate fined him five pounds, that was

probably all the discharge money he had left,' Stella protested. 'They don't give them much, you know.'

'I hope the father doesn't spend all his time drinking in pubs,' said Judith, beginning to stack the empty plates. She looked up at her husband. 'You did say he'd been to the pub, didn't you, dear?'

Desmond nodded.

'I didn't actually see the man,' Stella admitted, 'but his wife is a really good mother, and the children are very bright.' She was beginning to feel very angry. How could the magistrate be so unfeeling? Clearly the stupid man had no real idea of how hard life could be for some people less well off than himself. She couldn't imagine how awful it would be to be without shoes. Besides, the court's sentence was grossly unfair. If that person was Mr Dennison, no wonder he was depressed. What sort of a world was it when picking up a piece of lost property and taking it home was tantamount to stealing?

'Tell me where they live,' Judith was saying, 'and I'll make sure the children have shoes. This is exactly the sort of thing the WVS was created for.'

'I'm not sure I can,' said Stella. 'If this really is the same man, his wife is a very proud woman. I wanted to help them, but she wouldn't let me. You know, they truly don't strike me as dishonest people.'

Judith rose to her feet, the empty plates in her hands. 'A little gooseberry fool, Stella, dear?'

She nodded numbly. When Judith had disappeared

with the empty plates, Stella glanced at her father-in-law.

'Have you talked to the British Legion?' he asked. She frowned, puzzled. 'They help ex-servicemen and their families.'

They heard the sound of the trolley returning from the kitchen.

'Before you go home,' Desmond said, 'I'll give you the name of a contact. Some of these ex-army chaps have a way of doing things without it seeming like charity.'

Later that evening, when he helped her into her coat, Desmond pushed a piece of paper into her hand. 'Don't worry about telling Thornton about your family with no shoes. The Legion know how to handle this sort of problem, and if that chap is looking for a job, they can probably help with that too.'

'What can he do with only one hand?' said Stella.

Her father-in-law kissed her cheek. 'If there's a job to be had, they'll find it. The British Legion have contacts everywhere.'

Every week, sometimes twice a week, when the girls met to practise their repertoire, the vexed question of what they should wear would come up. Their taste in fashion was roughly the same, but it was hard trying to decide on a colour that would suit them all. Should they wear an evening dress, day dresses or a suit? The Andrews Sisters wore American Army uniform a lot of the time, so much so that it had become their trademark, but

Stella, Pip and Lillian weren't in the forces. Working on the railway, Lillian had a recognizable uniform, and Pip wore a uniform of sorts when she was doing her obligatory fire-watching duties, but neither uniform was very attractive. Then there was the problem of the style of costume for the stage. Lillian was slim, and Pip had a pear-shaped body, whereas Stella was curvy.

One evening after practice, Pip turned up with a slither of material in midnight blue. 'What do you think of this?'

'That's gorgeous!' Stella exclaimed.

'This chap has a bolt he can give me at a good price,' she said, 'but I have to be quick about it.'

'How many coupons will it take?' Lillian asked anxiously. 'Flora has grown so quickly I've just had to get her some new things. I don't have many left.'

Pip gave her an old-fashioned look and thumbed her nose. 'This fell off the back of a lorry.'

Lillian went to the mirror on the wall and held the fabric up to her face. 'I love it.'

'If we all had the same colour,' Pip went on, 'we could each make it up in the style that suits us best. You can sew, can't you, Lillian?'

Lillian nodded. 'You bet. I'd look best in a pencil-line dress.'

'I'd go for a sweetheart neckline,' said Pip. 'I'd have it fitted at the waist and with a slightly flared skirt. That would hide my hips.'

'Maybe we could all wear a string of pearls or something,' Lillian suggested.

'No,' said Stella, and she said it with such force it stopped the other two in their tracks.

'You don't like pearls?' said Lillian.

'I don't think we should have the material,' said Stella.

Lillian and Pip looked at each other in mild surprise. 'But it's the best suggestion we've had so far,' said Lillian. 'We all agree the colour is perfect. Why don't you like it all of a sudden?'

'I love the colour, and the idea is great,' said Stella.

'So what's the problem?' Pip demanded.

'It fell off the back of a lorry,' said Stella. 'We all know what that means. It's probably stolen, and it's definitely black market.'

'Oh, come on,' said Pip. 'Everybody does it now and then.'

'But I don't,' said Stella.

'Who will find out?' asked Lillian. 'If anyone asks, we could say it came from the market.'

'No,' Stella said again. 'Look, I turned a blind eye to the petrol, but I refuse to be involved in the black market any more.'

'What do you mean, the petrol?' said Lillian, widening her eyes innocently.

'Lillian, I'm not stupid,' said Stella. 'We all know that petrol was knocked off from somewhere. You'd never get that much petrol for so few coupons, and it was pink, for goodness' sake. Call me old-fashioned, but up until then I'd never bought anything on the black market, and I don't want to start now.'

'But you won't get caught,' said Lillian, shaking her head. 'I promise.'

'How do you know that?' asked Stella. 'No, I can't do it and that's that. I'm a school teacher, for heaven's sake. What sort of example would I be setting for the children?'

The other two looked glum.

'Anyway,' Stella went on, 'you two have far more to lose than I have.'

Pip turned her back and stared out of the window. Lillian lifted her head defiantly. 'It's perfectly safe if you do it in small doses,' she said vehemently. 'Nobody cares about the likes of you and me. I've been getting stuff off the black market for years and I've never been caught.'

'Supposing,' Stella said stubbornly, 'just supposing you did get found out. Who would look after Flora if you went to jail?'

'Now you're being ridiculous,' Lillian shouted. 'I'm telling you that won't happen!'

They were having their first row.

'I hope you're right,' said Stella crossly, 'but you can count me out.'

'Do you really think anyone is going to be bothered about a bolt of dress fabric?' Lillian insisted.

Pip turned back with tears in her eyes. 'She's right, you know.'

'See?' said Lillian. 'Pip agrees with me.'

'No,' said Pip, 'Stella is right. I never gave much thought what might happen to my kids if I got caught before. It's all very well for you, Lillian. You've got your mum to look after Flora. I don't have anybody to look after Georgie and Hazel. No, Stella is right. It's stupid and it's risky.'

Lillian turned away in a huff. She was loath to give up on a midnight-blue frock. It was years since she'd had anything decent or new. 'It's no more risky than getting an extra bit of meat from under the counter at the butcher's,' she added sulkily.

'But we'll be on stage, remember?' said Stella. 'Every woman in the place will know exactly what we've done.'

Lillian sat down heavily. 'But it's such a wonderful colour,' she said miserably.

Pip laid a hand on her shoulder. 'I know, and I'm sorry. I've been a perfect idiot. I never should have suggested it.'

'So now we're back to square one,' said Lillian. 'What are we going to wear?'

After a moment's thought, Pip said, 'You don't need clothing coupons for curtain material.'

'Oh great,' said Lillian. 'Blackout or heavy brocade. I'm sure we'll look fantastic in that.'

'Actually, she may have a point,' said Stella. 'Some curtain material is quite lightweight.'

'But it's always in such awfully dull colours,' said Lillian.

They all sighed.

'I guess it's back to the jumble sales, then,' said Pip bleakly.

CHAPTER 13

The big boys had found a way into the derelict house. They had always been thwarted by the barricaded doors and the boarded-up windows. The shed had been a great den until Flora ran into it the night the German plane came down and the adults found her.

At first, the boys were angry and blamed Georgie, but when Flora's injuries became clearer, they decided she had done the right thing.

'We are protectors of the realm,' Billy reminded them. 'It's our job to rescue people from the Hun. Even,' he added with a grimace, 'girls.'

But now that everybody knew about the shed, it wasn't much good as a secret hideout (which was why they had asked Georgie to hide their stuff), though they still enjoyed running around outside the house as they played Robin Hood or Hopalong Cassidy. What they wanted was somewhere where the grown-ups couldn't see them.

Today, Billy and the other boys had been playing in the grounds. He had been kicking. He had nothing to kick, so he was just kicking, but when he jumped onto a sloping bit covered in ivy that was jutting out from the wall, the wood under his foot splintered. It was a scary moment because he almost fell through. On closer examination, the boys discovered that underneath was a coal cellar. In a moment of daring, they broke in and jumped down. The cellar was dark and covered in mouse droppings. It smelled musty and damp, so they didn't want to stay there, but the really exciting bit was when they found a door that led to the rest of the house. The gang had a fantastic afternoon playing cowboys and Indians as they dashed along the corridors and ran upstairs, hid in empty cupboards and yelled down the echoey, brown-stained loo pan.

'We can keep all our treasure here,' said Gideon eventually. 'No one will ever find it.'

'We've got to get it back from Georgie Porgie first,' said Billy. 'Any idea where he put it?'

The rest of the gang shrugged.

'I think when he gives it back,' said Gideon, 'that we should make him an honorary member.'

'But he's only a little kid,' Billy protested.

'I'd vote him in,' said Norman.

'And so will I,' said Gideon.

'He's too young,' Billy insisted.

But Gideon wasn't about to give up so easily. 'We could make him our mascot until he's old enough to take the gang oath.'

And so it was agreed.

* * *

By the end of November, as the Christmas decorations began to appear in the shops, their singing had come on by leaps and bounds. They had agreed to adopt a close harmony as they sang, and for the past few months, they'd been adding stage moves to their routine. Phyllis, Stella's mother, had helped them from the word go. She was strict, but Pip and Lillian didn't seem to mind. She taught them how to do exercises to strengthen their vocal cords, and they learned how to look after their voices. While she was up in the loft looking for Christmas decorations, Stella had found an old wardrobe mirror. She laid it across the sofa so that they could perform in front of it and watch their every move.

Phyllis also gave them some golden rules. Drinking alcohol was bad for a singer, and one should never perform after a big meal. She encouraged them to do their exercises every day whether they were singing or not, and before long the girls found they had a greater range and singing was less of a strain.

'Deep breaths,' she cajoled. 'Bring it up through the diaphragm . . . No, no, you're singing through your nose . . . Let the note swell . . . Slowly, slowly and bring to a close.'

On Saturday night, they found out that the Andrews Sisters were on at the pictures in a film called *Buck Privates* with Abbott and Costello at the Plaza Cinema. With babysitters arranged for the children, the three girls set off together to see it. Afterwards, having seen the film twice, they discussed every move and tried to emulate the professionals. They discovered that by standing together, they could move slowly across 'the stage' if they swung their right leg outward and only made a small step. Once they'd got the footwork right, they paid attention to their hand movements. All this had to be done, of course, while keeping in sync with the tune and looking happy.

'I've just thought of something,' Pip suddenly said at their rehearsal. 'Supposing there's no one to play the piano.'

'Oh crumbs,' Lillian gasped. 'I don't really want to sing unaccompanied. What shall we do?'

'Perhaps your mum would help us out?' Pip suggested.

Stella shook her head. 'I think I'd prefer to play it myself,' she said.

'But we can't have you stuck down in the orchestra pit!' cried Lillian.

'We'll get them to put the piano on stage,' said Stella, 'and we'll sing round it.'

'Then you'd better practise a few moves standing round the piano,' said Phyllis. 'It's important that you look professional whatever you do.'

They spent some time practising new moves, which, although carefully choreographed, made them look casual and at home.

'Smile, girls,' Phyllis cajoled every time they looked too serious. 'Smile.'

It didn't take long before they had a repertoire of

five songs: 'I'll Be With You in Apple Blossom Time', 'Don't Sit Under the Apple Tree', 'I'll Be Seeing You', 'Fools Rush In' and 'I'm Sending a Letter to Santa Claus'.

'I've got us an invitation,' Stella told them one evening. 'My mother has asked us if we can sing in the canteen up at Broadwater. Apparently, an officer who is billeted with her is organizing the entertainment and has been let down at the last minute. I said we could go . . .'

Lillian took in her breath, and Pip gulped. 'But we haven't even got a name for ourselves yet,' she cried.

'And we still have nothing to wear,' Lillian wailed.

Stella looked uncomfortable and chewed nervously on her bottom lip.

'What?' said Pip with a frown.

'Mum told them we were Sussex sisters,' Stella said cautiously, 'and the organizers thought that was our stage name.'

'Sussex Sisters?' said Lillian.

'I like it,' said Pip.

'I think I do too,' said Lillian, nodding slowly. 'The Sussex Sisters it is, then.'

'But there's still the problem of a costume,' Pip reminded her.

'Siren suits!' cried Stella.

Lillian and Pip stared at her in disbelief.

'Siren suits?' said Lillian. 'Oh, please . . .'

'No, listen,' said Stella. 'The Andrews Sisters wear uniforms because they've been signed up. We're all civilians. Why not let the ordinary women feel they have a real part to play in this war? I've never seen anyone make a fuss of them.'

Lillian looked sceptical.

'You know she's right,' said Pip. 'We can make the factory worker and every hardworking woman feel special. They deserve that much, don't they?'

'Yes, but in a siren suit?' said Lillian. 'They're all baggy and covered in pockets. Hardly flattering.'

'If we turn up in a siren suit,' Pip went on excitedly, 'we'd be saying, "We know exactly what you're going through because we're one of you."'

'I suppose we can glam them up a little,' Stella suggested.

Lillian wasn't convinced. 'How?'

'I'd be quite happy to take them all in a bit, to give them some more shape,' said Pip. 'We could wear a colourful turban, and a bit of lippy would work wonders.'

'Would we have time?' asked Lillian. 'The show is next week.'

'I'll make time,' said Pip firmly, 'and there's no time like the present. Where's your suit, Stella, and have you got any dressmaking pins?'

'My suit is at home,' said Lillian dully. She was disappointed, and she showed it.

'That's fine,' said Pip. 'I'll make a start on Stella's, and you can pop round after work tomorrow evening.'

A slow smile played over Stella's mouth as she

fished around in her needlework box. 'You know what? The idea is really growing on me.'

'It would certainly put the Sussex Sisters in a class of their own,' said Pip, taking the pincushion from her and setting it on the table.

Stella was pulling on her suit. Pip brandished the scissors. 'Now, let's give this baggy old thing a bit of glamour.'

Oh, wonderful, wonderful: three letters from Johnny! It was Tuesday and Stella snatched them from the mat as she walked in through the front door. She felt light-headed and breathless with excitement. She was tempted to rip them open there and then, but she forced herself to reach for the letter-opener instead. She hurried into the sitting room and threw herself into a chair.

She put them in order; then she slid the opener along the first one and feasted her eyes on the familiar and much-loved writing.

My darling Freckle-Face,

I have so much to tell you. Life changed dramatically for me the day I was caught out in the sandstorm. It came rolling in like a huge black cloud 20ft high. The wind itself must have been at least 35mph. The lads and I were in the Katie ambulance, which only has canvas closures, not doors, so we had to cover our faces with a damp cloth and protect our eyes with goggles, or, in my case, sunglasses. It's very hard to breathe, and the sand gets into your nose, eyes, mouth and lungs. When it was all over, we were sitting ducks and so we were captured by the Germans. We were kept together in some sort of stockade until they handed us over to the Eyeties. It was then that we heard that Tobruk had fallen.

There were about 500 of us, not all British. After a couple of days, we were herded on board ship, South Africans, Indians and Aussies. It was hell on earth. Nobody was allowed on deck, and with only 10 buckets between us, you can imagine the stink. Some of the men already had dysentery, so it was no picnic, I can tell you.

I had no equipment, so as a first-aider, you can imagine how helpless I felt. Despite my best efforts, we lost a few men.

We spent two days down there before we reached port. After several hours waiting, we were lined up on the dock. I must have looked a pretty sight. I hadn't washed for over a month. I was lousy, ravenously hungry, and my uniform hung in tatters. It was only the thought of you, my darling girl, that gave me the will to go on. Before they marched us to camp, they took us into the town and put us in cages. The locals chucked rotten cabbages and tomatoes at us. Surprisingly, some of the tomatoes were only soft and tasted all right, so we were all grateful for the moisture.

After a day and a night, we were moved to a POW camp, where I had a shower. The weather was kind enough to be able to wash our clothes, and we walked around in our underpants while we dried them on the roof.

Things are a bit better now. There's talk of being moved to another camp, but so far we've made the best of it here. A chap from the South African Artillery, a PE instructor, has licked us back into shape, and the Red

Cross parcels add a bit of variety to the monotonous food.

It helps to think of you all back in Worthing. Your letters make such a difference. I had two the other day. I imagine you'll be eating Dad's strawberries before long. When I'm in bed, I hold your letters close to my heart and remember our times together. I try to imagine kissing the mole on your thigh and caressing you. I want to make love to you madly. It's hard to bear because it enflames me, but I miss you so much; Freckle-Face. Please don't forget me. That's all for now.

Your ever-loving Johnny

Poor Johnny. How awful. Stella became aware that her arm was hurting. In her rush to read his letters, she had pulled her left arm out of her coat sleeve but sat in the chair before releasing her right arm. As a consequence, she'd sat awkwardly and the sleeve was cutting off the circulation. She raised herself and pulled off her coat, dumping it untidily on the floor. Wiping her eyes and giving her nose a good blow, she opened the second letter. It was much shorter than the first.

Hello, Freckle-Face,

Please don't worry if you don't hear from me for a while. I have a plan.

All my love,

Johnny

She frowned. What did that mean, *Please don't worry if you don't hear from me*? She took in her breath noisily. He was going to escape, wasn't he?!

143

They shot people who tried to escape, didn't they? Her heart was in her mouth as she slid the letter-opener under the seal of the third letter.

My darling Freckle-Face,

I have just received no less than six letters from you! Oh, my sweet Stella, it was so good to read about Worthing and the things you've been up to. Thank God that plane came down where it did. I can't bear the thought of you being so close to it. Tell Pip I think she's the most wonderful girl in the world (apart from you, of course) for pulling you inside. I'm so glad you haven't forgotten me.

Thanks for the news of Mother and Dad. I also received a letter from her, but she says so little apart from her WVS work.

I have been moved to another prison camp, this time in Germany. I got away for a few days by pinching a motorbike, but I got caught out at a checkpoint because I didn't have any papers. It was good while it lasted.

Oh, Stella, how I wish you were here and I could take you in my arms. I miss having sex, and I miss you. Mr Cuddles can't wait to come into your garden again.

Stella giggled at his naughtiness and turned the page. What would the censor have made of that sentence? Would he have understood the intimate language? She felt her face flushing as she read on.

I don't have to worry about having nothing to do any more. They send us out in working parties every day. I set out at 5 a.m. for a local coal mine three miles away.

144

We get some black bread and sausage at 10 a.m., some
vegetable soup at noon and supper when we get back
to camp after a five-o'clock finish. As you can imagine,
it's pretty deadly.

Since I've been here, we haven't had any Red Cross
parcels at all. It looks like I shall be spending
Christmas here, so if I get the chance, I'll raise a glass
of water to you, Mother and Dad. Think of poor, lonely
Mr Cuddles, won't you?

All my love,
Johnny

She cried for a while after she'd finished reading
them. Everything sounded so bleak apart from his
brief moment of freedom. Having made a couple of
hankies soaking wet with her tears, Stella pulled herself together. Walking to the writing bureau, she pulled
out her fountain pen and some paper to begin a carefully worded and cheerful reply. Now that she knew
where he was, tomorrow she would put together a few
Christmas things and some necessities into a parcel.
He probably wouldn't get it until the new year, but she
was determined to brighten his day sometime soon.

145

CHAPTER 14

Their first ever singing engagement was on the following Saturday December 5th. Stella didn't mention it to the teachers at work. The preparations for the Christmas nativity play were well under way and she didn't want to distract them from that. That was what she told herself, anyway. If the truth be told, she wanted to see how the engagement fared first. Singing round her sitting-room piano was one thing, but singing in front of a crowd of strangers in a canteen was another entirely.

Pip had asked one of her neighbours to babysit for the evening, but she didn't say why. It was beginning to dawn on her that after carefully keeping out of the public eye for nearly eight years, being a member of the Sussex Sisters had suddenly made her very vulnerable. The sensible thing would be to abandon the idea, but she enjoyed singing, and besides, how could she disappoint the others? She kept telling herself she was miles and miles away from her old home and that the probability of anyone finding out where she was was remote, to say the least. Yet in this time of flux, when everyone in the country was on the move for one reason or another, it wasn't as improbable as it might have once been.

Lillian asked a friend to look after Flora. Dorcas would have been there, but she was on duty tonight. Lillian had been tempted to tell Mr Rawlings about it, but in the end, she had satisfied her desire for notoriety by telling Ron Knight. To her great surprise and delight, he'd expressed the desire to be there.

'But it's an army camp,' she'd protested. 'I'm not sure you'll be allowed in.'

Mr Knight had thumbed his nose. 'Ways and means,' he'd said mysteriously. 'Ways and means.'

There was just enough petrol left in Stella's car to get them to Broadwater and back. The performance was billed for seven-thirty, so Stella set out to pick the others up an hour earlier. It was a bit of a mad rush for Pip to make sure that the children were tucked up in bed before the babysitter came. She usually spent time reading them a story and saying prayers for Daddy, but tonight, all that had to go by the board when she heard Stella tooting the horn outside in the road at six thirty-four.

Nobody spoke as they travelled: they were far too nervous for conversation. Lillian was not only concerned about the performance but was also wondering how she would feel being in a room full of Canadian soldiers all dressed like Woody. They found the camp with no problem, and Phyllis was waiting with the guard on the gate. Once their ID cards had been checked and he'd opened the case in the boot to check the contents, Phyllis climbed in the back seat and guided them to the canteen, which was in a Nissen hut at the far end of the camp. The authorities had given them a small room behind the stage in which to change. It was more like a store cupboard, and Pip was glad they had opted for the siren suits. Getting changed into evening dresses or fancy gowns in such a confined space, surrounded by mops and buckets, would have been problematic. Something would have been ruined, for sure.

Pip had made a good job of the suits. Gone were the pockets over the breast that gave everybody a big, blousy look. Pip had swapped the plain collar on her suit for some pretty material and matched it with the pocket on the waist, thus drawing attention away from her hips. Lillian's outfit had tapered sleeves and some sparkling beads down the front as far as the waistband. She had added her own belt, which complemented the changes beautifully. Stella's siren suit had flared trouser bottoms rather than the usual gathered leg, and all of them had been taken in enough to make the girls look slim and attractive.

Once they had put on their colourful turbans, they made their way to the makeshift stage. The canteen was very noisy. Stella peeped through the side curtain.

'There's nobody at the piano,' she said, 'so it looks like I'm playing.'

'What's it like out there?' Pip whispered nervously.

Stella peeped again. 'It's packed, but they're all drinking at tables and playing cards.'

'Ready, girls?' someone asked.

They turned to see an officer with a clipboard standing behind them.

Lillian nodded.

'When I've introduced you,' he went on, 'get out there straight away. They don't like to be kept waiting.'

Pip squeezed Lillian's hand.

'And,' he added as an afterthought, 'don't take it personally if they boo.'

'What on earth do you mean?' said Lillian crossly.

'They're hard to please,' said the officer. 'We had a troupe from ENSA last week and most of them were booed off stage.'

'Isn't anybody else coming tonight?' said Stella, looking around. 'Where are the rest of the performers?'

'I couldn't persuade them to come back again,' said the officer. 'So just for tonight, honey, you're it.'

There was a stunned silence as the girls looked at each other with sinking hearts. 'Talk about a baptism of fire,' Pip muttered.

'Right, then,' said the officer. 'I'll get out there and introduce you.'

They watched him burst through the side curtain and struggle to make himself heard over the din.

'Five songs,' said Lillian. 'That's never enough to fill a whole evening. What are we going to do?'

'We haven't practised anything else,' said Stella. 'We'll do the lot and then go. It's their loss if they don't have anything else.'

'I think I'm going to be sick,' said Pip.

'Oh no, you're not,' said Lillian. 'Whatever happens, we're all in this together. If the act dies tonight, so be it, but at least we'll have given it our best shot.'

'Break a leg,' said Phyllis. They turned to Stella's mother with startled expressions. 'That's what they say when they go on stage,' she protested. 'It's a form of reverse good luck.'

On stage, the officer was facing them with his left arm extended as he bellowed, 'And here they are, the Sussex Sisters!'

'I hope this b-well works,' Stella muttered darkly as they ran through the curtain.

A few members of the audience looked up as they reached the piano, but most carried on with what they were doing. All around the room, the conversations continued unabated. In a corner near the back, some men were playing a noisy game of cards. Others stood at the bar shouting orders to the harassed barman, who was obviously rushed off his feet.

Stella sat down at the piano and played a short introduction before they began their first song, 'Don't Sit Under the Apple Tree'. They belted the song as loudly as they could, but it was only heard by the men in the front row. They obviously wanted to listen because the girls heard them telling their comrades to 'shut up', but it had no effect.

The girls finished the song to a paltry round of half-hearted applause.

When Pip glanced at Stella, she could see she was

almost in tears as they began their rendition of 'I'll Be With You in Apple Blossom Time'. The racket in the room hadn't dimmed in the slightest, and Stella only played a few bars before she stopped. It was hopeless. There was no reaction from anyone in the audience; in fact, no one seemed to notice they were on stage doing absolutely nothing.

'I think it's time to go,' Stella said quietly.

'But we can't give up in the middle of the act,' Pip whispered urgently.

'Why not?' said Stella. 'Look at them.'

'What's wrong, sugar?' a man called from the front seats. 'Why don't you come and sit on my lap and I'll give you somethin' to sing about.'

Stella and Pip blushed to their roots as he and his mates roared with laughter.

Something flashed in Lillian's eyes. Marching to the front of the stage, she put two fingers in her mouth. The room was suddenly filled with the loudest whistle Pip had ever heard. Everybody stopped what they were doing and turned round. Stella and Pip stared open-mouthed as Lillian, her legs akimbo and her hands on her hips, jutted her neck and glared into the crowd. When she spoke, she didn't shout. She didn't need to. A deathly hush had fallen across the whole room.

'I used to be impressed by the Canadian soldier,' she began in a measured voice tinged with anger. 'I thought him a fair-minded, honest chap who would give a girl a chance. That's why I considered it an honour to come here to sing to you tonight. We heard what you did to ENSA, and to be frank, we won't mind if you see fit to boo us off the stage, but at least have the decency to listen first!'

No one made a sound, until someone near the bar called out, 'All right, lassie. Off you go,' and with a leap of excitement, Lillian recognized Mr Knight. Their eyes locked and he raised his glass of beer in her direction. She could have jumped over the chairs to kiss his cheek.

Returning to the piano, Lillian said, 'Go on, Stell. Let's do it.'

Stella played the first two bars of 'I'm Sending a Letter to Santa Claus' and they began to sing. It was an emotional song about a little boy whose father was fighting overseas. The child was sending his letter to ask Santa Claus 'to bring my daddy safely home to me . . .' They began nervously, but as the room remained quiet, they gained in confidence. At least the men were listening now.

The song ended and the girls bowed. A few seconds later, the whole place erupted into loud applause. When they looked out onto the sea of faces, it was obvious that the words of the song had struck a chord. Several men were surreptitiously wiping away a tear.

As the applause died down, Stella sat back down at the piano. 'From the beginning?' she whispered. The others nodded eagerly, and so for the second time that evening, she struck up the introduction to 'Don't Sit Under the Apple Tree'.

* * *

Back at Stella's place later that night, the three of them flopped into chairs.

'I can't believe we did that,' said Lillian.

'You were amazing,' said Pip.

'Anybody fancy a bit of toast and jam?' Stella's offer was greeted with enthusiasm and she left the room.

'How's your little Flora doing now?' asked Pip.

Lillian was cuddling a cushion. 'Fine,' she said. 'It seems she was very lucky. Everything has healed well, and the doc reckons that in years to come, she'll hardly even have a scar.'

'That's good,' said Pip, pushing some sheets of music away so that she could spread herself out a little more. 'I notice her hair is growing back.'

'Mostly,' said Lillian. 'There's one patch that looks a bit thin, but with careful brushing, we can hide it fairly well.'

Pip shivered and nodded and shook away the memory of another person with burns, a person who still bore terrible scars to this day, scars that were all her fault.

'Are you all right?' Lillian said anxiously. 'For a moment there, you went awfully white.'

'I'm fine,' said Pip. 'A bit tired, that's all.'

'It's been a long day,' Lillian agreed. The smell of warm toast drifted through from the kitchen.

Pip stood up. 'I think I'll go and give Stella a hand,' she said. 'I'm more peckish than I thought.'

'Do you ever hear from your Peter?' Lillian asked. 'You never mention him.'

Pip shook her head. 'Not a dickie bird since he was captured,' she said sadly. 'I did have a letter from his regiment. They said they were doing all they could, but apparently the Japs don't recognize the Geneva Convention. The men don't even get Red Cross parcels.'

'How awful!' cried Lillian.

'What's awful?' said Stella, coming into the room with a tray of tea and toast.

'Pip says her Peter doesn't get Red Cross parcels,' said Lillian. 'Gordon gets British and Canadian parcels.'

The other two looked impressed, and they all sat down again.

'He says the Canadian ones are best,' Lillian went on. 'He has to share the British ones between two sometimes, but they get half a pound of sugar, sweets and chocolates, and tins of condensed milk. The Canadians send butter, coffee, packets of biscuits and fifty cigarettes. I'd volunteer to be a prisoner of war if I could eat all that. It's better than two ounces of butter a week, isn't it?'

Stella laughed, but Pip only smiled.

'Sorry,' said Lillian, immediately embarrassed by her crassness. 'That was a stupid thing to say. It must be such a terrible worry for you, and you've got no one to really talk to.'

Pip waved her hand dismissively.

'What about your family, Pip?' said Stella, passing the plates and toast round. 'I've never heard you talk about them. Do they live far away?'

'I have no family,' said Pip.

'What, none at all?' cried Lillian.

Pip took a bite from her toast and shook her head.

'God, that's terrible,' said Lillian.

'I've no wish to pry,' said Stella uncertainly, 'and you don't have to tell me if you don't want to, but what happened to them? Did they all die?'

'I went to live in a children's home,' said Pip, looking away.

Her voice was flat, and it was obvious she didn't want to elaborate. Lillian leaned over and squeezed her hand. Stella waited a second or two, then changed the subject to more mundane things.

CHAPTER 15

By the second Saturday in December, the festive season was well under way. Christmas carol singers gathered in Montague Street, and all the old favourites – 'Hark! the Herald Angels Sing', 'We Three Kings' and 'Silent Night' – drew the crowds. While Georgie, Hazel and Flora were becoming more excited by the day, the preparations for the festive season were giving Stella, Pip and Lillian a bit of a headache. The same tired old Christmas decorations came down from their lofts, but finding suitable presents that they could afford and having enough coupons to buy them was proving to be very hard. The few toys to be had in the shops were extremely expensive. Of course, you could get things at an inflated price and without coupons on the black market, toys that had 'fallen off the back of a lorry', but as they had been reminded, if you got caught, you could end up with a hefty fine or, even worse, a prison sentence. After their argument about the bolt of midnight-blue material, none of the girls had the stomach for risk-taking.

Pip had been preparing for Christmas for some

time. With no other relatives around and her husband a POW, she had to be mother and father, grandparent and aunt all rolled into one. With rent from her shops, money wasn't quite so much of an issue. It was availability that was proving difficult. Some months ago, she'd found a pretty-looking dolly in the Red Cross shop. Since then, she'd spent her evenings knitting the doll a complete wardrobe from odd scraps of wool. Georgie had asked Father Christmas for a train set, sadly an impossible request. There wasn't anything like that to be had in the whole of Worthing. Every available toy was war-related: a tank, a Spitfire or a battleship. Georgie wasn't in the least interested in them, so Pip was delighted when she found a battered sled in the junk shop on the corner of North Street and Lyndhurst Road. While he was at school or playing with friends at their houses, she was beavering away repairing a broken slat and painting it bright green. What a good job Pete was such a hoarder. The paint came from a tin she'd found in the shed, left over from when he'd painted the gateposts in 1939. Once it was ready, all she had to do was pray for snow!

Pip had to move a few things around to make room for the sled in the shed. At the back, she found a tin that rattled. She hadn't noticed it before, and when she opened it, to her horror, she found several spent bullets. Where on earth had they come from? She'd tackled Georgie about it that evening.

'They're not mine,' he'd protested. 'I'm looking after them for somebody.'

'Who?'

Georgie lowered his head and stayed silent.

'If those big boys have made you do it . . .' she began.

'Nobody made me do it, Mummy.'

'Well, you can tell them from me, I'm giving them to the police.'

'No, Mummy,' Georgie cried. 'You can't. They won't let me in their den if you do.'

'Georgie, I've told you before – stay away from them,' said Pip.

'But, Mummy—'

'But nothing,' Pip said firmly. 'I've said all I'm going to on the matter and there's an end to it.'

With an angry pout, Georgie turned on his heel and ran upstairs to his room.

'And from now on,' his mother called after him, 'keep out of Daddy's shed.'

In the run-up to the big day, Stella invited Pip to spend Christmas in Phyllis's house with her. At first, Pip refused, saying that she and the children might 'spoil' the family occasion. She was also afraid that Stella might be thinking that being on her own was a problem to her. She didn't want anyone feeling sorry for her. Luckily, Stella allayed her fears on both counts.

'If you come, we can pool our resources,' she said. 'We can share the meal. That way, we might be able to enjoy more than we could if we stayed on our own.'

Her suggestion made Pip change her mind, and straight away she was looking forward to it. She envied Stella and Lillian their close-knit families. It must be wonderful to have a mother on hand to step into the breach when needed.

When she'd been allowed to go back to work, Stella had initiated the school kitchen garden. It had proved to be very successful on several fronts. Not only did the school have plenty of vegetables all year round, but the children enjoyed their nature lessons outdoors, weeding, hoeing and, later on, harvesting the fruit and vegetables. Everyone in the school enjoyed wholesome food, and it was surprising how keen the children were to eat up their carrots and greens when they'd grown them themselves. Stella had adopted a crop rotary system for planting. This meant that the area used for peas, beans and onions the first year had Brussels sprouts, broccoli and swede the second year. In the third year, which would be 1943, she planned to have carrots, early potatoes and main-crop potatoes in that same plot. By dividing the whole garden up into three separate areas, she minimized the risk of clubroot and other diseases, and because she'd been the one to spearhead the project, the school cook made sure that she had some of the preserves the children had produced in their cookery lessons. As a result, Stella would be bringing a jar of pickled onions, a jar of pickled beetroot and two Kilner jars of stewed fruit to the Christmas meal.

It made sense to join together, and it promised to be

an enjoyable time. Pip belonged to a pig club, which meant that in exchange for her kitchen waste, which was used to feed the animals, she had a share of the meat when the pig was slaughtered. As the pig was expected to reach the required one hundred pounds in weight by Christmas, she would be able to bring a nice piece of pork to the table.

'My mother will love having the children,' said Stella. As she said the words, Stella felt her chest tighten. How she wished she and Johnny had a child of their own. She sighed, and catching the change in Pip's expression, she added quickly, 'I hope you don't mind if she spoils them rotten.'

'Oh, I think I can cope with that,' Pip said with a grin.

'My mother can't wait to have grandchildren of her own. Not much chance of that with this damn war on,' Stella added with a hollow laugh.

Thanks to her new job, Lillian would be a little better off this Christmas. Flora was to have a toy china tea set and a brown teddy bear with a loud growl when his tummy was pressed. Lillian knew she'd love it. Dorcas was busy too. Although they'd both agreed not to bother with presents for each other, she'd been saving her sugar ration to make home-made sweets. Lillian had to decline Stella's invitation for Christmas Day because she was expected to be with her aunt and the rest of the family in Lancing for the day. 'But if the offer still stands for Boxing Day . . .' she added with a cheeky grin.

The run-up to Christmas brought more invitations for the Sussex Sisters. They were mostly local and for lunchtime performances in works canteens, army camps and hospitals. They were selective over the ones they accepted. They couldn't go far. There wasn't time. Lillian and Stella only had their lunch hour.

Stella's headmistress had been very helpful, but she didn't want to take advantage of her. If the school day was changed slightly, Stella was able to go for her lunch a little earlier. Providing she was willing to set up her class with a project that could be unsupervised, she had just enough time to do a twenty-minute performance and get back for the rest of the working day. The other teachers agreed to pop in to check on the children, and everything went smoothly.

'I can't see this happening after the war,' Stella remarked to her mother, 'but people are more than happy to go the extra mile to boost the nation's morale.'

Lillian found much the same kind of cooperation at the station.

'The Sussex Sisters, lovely girls,' Mr Knight told anyone who had the time to listen. 'Do you realize one of them works on this station?' In fact, Mr Knight had been so lavish in his praise for the Sussex Sisters that Mr Rawlings was happy to release Lillian every now and then for an extra-long lunch hour.

'So long as your deliveries are done, Mrs Harris,' he

told her, 'the railways are keen to support you as you do your bit for our gallant troops in hospital.'

Iris and Betty were not quite so generous.

'And who's going to make sure she's done all her work?' said Iris, leaning over the counter in a confidential way as her friend Betty popped in for her afternoon break.

'I'm sure she won't take advantage,' said a customer. 'She seems like a hardworking girl to me.'

'Oh, she's that all right,' said Betty, her voice full of innuendo.

The door opened and a cold blast of air came in with Mr Knight. Iris looked up. Three-thirty. He'd come for his afternoon cup of tea. 'Nothing would surprise me,' she sniffed. 'That girl's got the morals of an alley cat.'

'I didn't mean it like that,' the customer protested.

'It seems it's one rule for her,' said Betty, looking down her nose, 'and something quite different for the rest of us.'

'If you're talking about Mrs Harris,' said Mr Knight when he overheard them grumbling, 'it does a man good to have a pretty girl sing to him when he's in hospital.' He smiled, remembering his own experience not so long ago when Anne Shelton came to the hospital where he was being patched up. 'You haven't heard them. They're terrific. I reckon they could beat Vera Lynn any day.'

Betty looked slightly embarrassed. 'We didn't mean to criticize, I'm sure,' she said, but Iris harrumphed and passed his tea, spilling some in the saucer on the way.

She remained tight-lipped until he'd left the room. 'That's as maybe,' she said acidly when he was out of earshot, 'but the girl is employed to work for the railway, not go gallivanting about the county and cavorting about on the stage.'

For Pip, rearranging her day wasn't too problematic. She didn't have to give the children she cared for lunch, anyway, as they'd all gone home, so by extending her lunch hour from noon until two o'clock, she had plenty of time. She didn't even have to find someone to collect Georgie. On the few occasions when Dorcas wasn't around to look after them, Flora and Hazel came along as well. They were as good as gold, and the nurses or the canteen staff, depending on where they were, enjoyed making a fuss of them.

The war ground on with no tangible sign of ending, and before long the girls fell into a well-worn pattern. People were war-weary and tired, but they spurred each other on with the promise that it would 'all be over by this time next year'. They didn't want reminding that every week was the same as the last: queuing, counting coupons, making do and going without. It was a miserable existence, but because everyone was in the same boat, they just kept going.

All the time, the Sussex Sisters were becoming better known and in greater demand. Their repertoire had increased to ten songs, and there was even talk of a record being made. Publicity became an issue. Stella was keen to make them better known and didn't mind very much how they went about it. Lillian was dead keen, but Pip seemed reluctant to be in the limelight. It was only when a reporter turned up to do an article in the *Sussex County Magazine* that she agreed to having a photograph taken. The other two were so excited. On the day it came out, in April 1943, Stella bought a copy for all the teachers in her school, and the headmistress pinned the article on the school noticeboard. Stella took a magazine to her parents-in-law. The result was predictable. Desmond and Judith were as delighted as her own mother, and Judith said she would buy an extra copy to send to her son.

Lillian put the magazine in the station waiting room, but it wasn't long before it mysteriously disappeared. Mr Rawlings pinned the article on the noticeboard next to the ticket office in the station forecourt, and throughout the day, passengers paused to read it. It put a smile on every face.

Pip sat alone in her kitchen to read her copy of the magazine. She studied the inside page very carefully. The offices of *Sussex County Magazine* were in Eastbourne, with branches in Worthing and London. London – her blood ran cold. She had been led to believe it was purely a magazine for Sussex. She never would have agreed to be in it if she had known they had offices in London. The address was Fleet Street no less. That meant it was more important than a locally produced magazine, didn't it? What was the range of distribution? Was it likely to go further afield than Sussex?

The contents of the magazine helped to make her feel a little less agitated. There was an article on Sussex sprites and goblins, another two called 'Nature Notes' and 'The Bells of Sussex', and one about village yew trees. The picture on the front cover was of a country church – hardly the sort of thing to be of interest to anyone outside of the county or without a real connection to Sussex itself. The article was half-way through the magazine. It was well written and enthusiastic, and the picture had come out well. But what if someone from her past read it? She chewed the side of her mouth anxiously. It had been years since she'd seen any of them. They probably wouldn't recognize her even if they saw the magazine. She smiled to herself. The *Sussex County Magazine*? She was fretting about nothing. Nobody she knew was going to read that.

'Oh, I forgot to tell you,' Stella began excitedly when next they met. 'I had a letter from Basil Dean.' She got up and went to the writing bureau in the corner of the room.

'Basil Dean?' said Lillian. 'I know that name, but where from?'

'He's the head of ENSA,' said Stella, removing a letter from the drop-down drawer. She took it from the envelope and handed it to Pip. 'He's invited us to audition.'

'An audition!' Lillian echoed.

'Apparently, our reputation has gone before us,' said Stella.

'What difference would it make if we were part of ENSA?' Pip asked.

'We'd get a lot more money, for a start,' said Lillian. 'I've heard that some of the performers get as much as ten pounds a week.'

Pip's eyes grew wide.

'I'm not sure we're good enough to ask for money,' said Stella, 'and it might mean that we'd be sent further afield, maybe even abroad.'

Pip took in her breath.

'But we all have commitments,' said Lillian. 'How could you carry on teaching if we had to go miles and miles to our engagements?'

Pip shuddered at the thought of being moved all over the country. There was no telling where she might end up. 'More importantly,' she said, seizing the moment, 'who would look after the children?'

Stella's smile died. 'Yes, of course,' she said. 'How stupid of me. You're both absolutely right. I was only thinking that we'd reach a bigger audience or get on the radio with the BBC, but you're right. The children come first.'

'Shame,' said Lillian, shaking her head and passing the letter to Pip to read. 'Fame and fortune might beckon, but I'm stuck with working on the railway.'

Pip was relieved. Just supposing they'd been sent to her old home town. Just supposing . . . She closed her eyes. Thank God they weren't going. What a lucky escape.

CHAPTER 16

Georgie wasn't stupid. He knew the big boys wouldn't be very pleased with him now that Mummy had found the bullets. He knew they'd been hard won. One boy, Leslie Hoare, had risked life and limb to collect three of them after a lone Jerry had machine-gunned the road near the station. Everybody said Leslie's uncle Eric was a hero. He'd been on his bike on his way to work when the Jerry plane came over. His uncle had spotted the pilot turning the plane and knew what was coming. As the plane screamed towards him, Uncle Eric had dropped his bike in the road and leapt over a low wall. The gunner sprayed the street and Uncle Eric's bike with bullets, then flew on towards the sea. Uncle Eric checked to make sure he didn't have a puncture, then without a backward glance, got back on his bike and rode off. Leslie had rushed outside and picked up three spent bullets before his mum yelled at him to get back in. Now thanks to Georgie's mum, the bullets were gone.

Leslie was furious when Georgie told them what had happened.

'You idiot,' he cried. 'Well, he can't be our mascot now!'

'She didn't find them all,' Georgie protested. 'I hid everything in different places.' The other boys stared at him in amazement as Georgie tipped out an old teapot with a chipped spout and a couple of spent bullets and an army great-coat button rolled across the table. 'I've still got the best bits of shrapnel,' he told them, 'but I couldn't bring them without Mummy finding out.'

The next minute, everyone was slapping him on the back and ruffling his hair and calling him a good egg. It made Georgie feel very happy, and he was even more so when they decided that he could be their mascot after all.

Lillian's sense of humour had become a trademark of their appearances on stage. Of the three women, she was the most at ease with performing in public. She was cheeky and flirtatious, and egged on by the audience, she gave as good as she got. When men heckled, she had a cheeky answer.

'Give us a kiss, darlin'.'

'Join the queue,' Lillian quipped.

Lillian was the one who came home with flowers and stockings, but although she enjoyed the banter with men, she never allowed anyone to overstep the mark. That's not to say she wasn't tempted, and why not? Some of them were very good-looking, but so far she had never put herself in a position to follow through.

'I had a postcard from Hitler yesterday,' she joked. 'He's on holiday in the Bavarian mountains. He said he'd like to do something that would make me really happy.' She posed in a coquettish way, with an innocent expression that made everybody laugh. 'So I wrote back straight away and told him to take a running jump.'

It brought the house down.

Lillian's favourite engagement was the Lancing carriage works. In the early 1930s, the carriage works had become one of three plants majoring in carriage construction owned by the railway. Just a year or two before, that number was pared down to two, the other being at Eastleigh. With the advent of war, requirements changed. There was a dramatic rise in the need for goods wagons, so the majority of their work became repairing bomb-damaged trucks. Passenger carriages were converted into mobile ambulances or military hospitals complete with operating theatres, which would be made available in the event of an invasion. In that eventuality, fighting men had to be protected at all costs.

One of the workers, Nigel, was a gifted pianist, so Stella was able to join Pip and Lillian on stage for their other routine. It made a welcome change from singing round the piano while Stella played.

Lillian couldn't help noticing just how good-looking Nigel was. Not only that but he was the perfect gentleman. Over a cup of tea after the show, and before he had to get back to work, he told her he'd been refused in the call-up because of a weak chest. Years of infections as a child had taken their toll on his body.

'You should think about a stage career for yourself,' she'd told him.

'I might be tempted if I was playing for a singer like you,' he'd chuckled.

Lillian gave him a playful shove. 'Behave yourself,' she'd grinned. 'I'm a married woman.'

By far and away her greatest problem on stage was the lecherous compère in one particular canteen. All the women complained about his wandering hands, and he wasted no time in latching on to Lillian. He was sly. As they stood together on stage taking a bow, she felt his hand on her waist. In no time at all, he was touching her bottom, and then, as they all bowed again, he ran his thumb between her buttocks. She elbowed him sharply, but it was difficult to get away from him with Pip pressed next to her on the other side. Lillian was helpless to do much about it.

As the audience drifted back to their places on the assembly line, she hissed, 'Keep your filthy hands off me.'

He played the innocent and apologized in front of the others, but as they walked out of the dressing room (a broom cupboard again), he grinned and leaned towards her and, out of earshot of the others, whispered, 'It's only a bit of fun, darling, and you know you like it.'

Lillian was furious.

'I can't bear that man,' she told Stella later. 'He's such a bloody creep.'

Stella seemed a bit surprised at the venom in her voice, until Lillian told her what he'd done.

'You should complain to the management.'

'And then what?' cried Lillian, exasperated. 'He'd sit there like butter wouldn't melt and they'd tell me I imagined it.'

Stella and Pip had to agree that would be about the sum of it. He wasn't called Sly Stan by all the women in the factory for nothing.

All alone in her cab doing her rounds, Lillian thought dark thoughts and plotted revenge. She had to find a way of making him look a fool that wouldn't rebound on herself. It took a while to work out a plan, but at last she was satisfied. The next time they took their bows on stage, Lillian stood beside Pip and Stella, but Sly Stan pushed his way between them, and sure enough his hand gravitated to her bottom once again. This time, Lillian pushed him forward. Her movement was so sharp he almost toppled over the front of the stage. There was a small moment of silence, but the women in the audience knew exactly what was going on and began to cheer and clap. Lillian wasn't finished yet, though. There was more to come. In a clear, ringing tone, she began a limerick.

'I said to a man in this place, "At times, you're an utter disgrace."'

The clapping and catcalling grew louder. Lillian turned to face Sly Stan, and wagging her finger, she continued fearlessly, '"Take your hands off my rump or I'll give you a thump and wallop you right in the face."'

As one, all the women in the factory rose to their feet. Sly Stan kept up his pretence of innocence by giving an exaggerated shrug of his shoulders and looking slightly surprised.

With her hand on her hip, Lillian began again. '"Is this why they call you Sly Stan? 'Cos you touch up the girls when you can? Touch me once more and I'll give you what for."' And here she made a breaking action with her hands. '"When I'm done, you won't be a real man!"'

The limerick wasn't all that good, but the hall erupted.

After several curtain calls, they reached the dressing room and closed the door before dissolving into fits of laughter.

A moment later, Stan put his head round the door.

'Don't you believe in knocking?' said Stella haughtily.

'I just wanted you to know,' he snarled, 'that we shan't be wanting you bitches again.'

The door slammed behind him.

Lillian turned to the others. 'Oh, I'm sorry.'

'Don't be,' said Stella with a laugh. 'You were amazing.'

'But I've lost us the chance to come back.'

'There'll be other performances,' said Pip, struggling out of her siren suit. 'I think you did everybody a favour. The man is an absolute creep.'

'That rhyme . . .' Stella began.

'It wasn't perfect,' Lillian admitted, 'but I was so angry with him I had to do something.'

'And it was brilliant,' said Pip.

A hundred miles away, Maud Abbott sat at her workroom table and stared into space, her hand resting on the wedding photograph. She had come across it while she was looking for a number-10 crochet hook. It was a bit of a mystery how it came to be in her needlework cupboard. She didn't even remember keeping it. She glanced down. How young she had been, how innocent. Her dress was a pale lilac, though in the black-and-white picture, it was only a grainy grey colour. It was made of silk and it draped round the gentle curves of her body as if she were a Greek goddess. If she closed her eyes, she could imagine the heady scent of the lily of the valley and violets in the corsage on her right shoulder. The day had been perfect. As the centre of attention, she had enjoyed every minute. What a pity the marriage hadn't lived up to expectation. Her mouth set into a hard line as the memory of her wedding night with all that heavy breathing and perspiration came to mind. She'd been both horrified and revolted. She'd hated every minute and dreaded each repeat performance. She shuddered as she recalled her husband pawing at her clothes, the coarse hairs of his leg rubbing against hers and the nauseating aim of it all. When she got to heaven, she would have a serious word with God about it.

She stood up suddenly, scraping the chair back noisily on the parquet floor. The photograph had to go, the same way as he had gone. All that was a lifetime ago, and a horrible memory she refused to trigger again. She tore the picture in half again and again and again. Heading for the kitchen range, she was still struggling to get the thought of 'it' out of her mind. She'd pretended that her monthlies lasted for two weeks; she'd pleaded a headache or tiredness. She never once willingly gave herself to him. To give him his due, he'd never actually forced her, but he'd never stopped wanting it. As soon as she'd got pregnant, she'd had the perfect excuse. He didn't like it, but he'd respected it, although the moment the twins were born, he'd wanted to start the whole miserable business again.

She lifted the lid of the range and an orange flame leapt greedily towards her hand. She dropped the pieces inside and slammed down the lid.

Behind her, she heard the garden gate click. Her daughter would be here at any moment. Reaching for the kettle, Maud put it on the hob.

'Have you seen this?' As she walked into the kitchen, Marion threw the *Sussex County Magazine* across the table.

Her mother picked it up. 'Where did you get this?'

'I was working in the reference library this morning,' said Marion. 'I had to put the library stamp on the inside page and I noticed the picture.'

The magazine was folded back to reveal an article

about the Sussex Sisters. Her mother frowned. 'Why should I be interested in this?'

'Look at the picture,' said Marion.

Her mother squinted at the page. With an exasperated tut, her daughter went to look for her glasses, then lowered herself expectantly into a chair as her mother began to read. She didn't have to wait long for a reaction.

'It's her!'

'That's what I thought,' said Marion, curling her lip. 'Just look at her. All dolled up like a dog's dinner, cocky cow.'

'Typical,' her mother scoffed. 'Well, I wouldn't give you tuppence to listen to her.'

'You know what this means, don't you?'

Her mother gave her a blank stare.

'It means we can find out where she lives, Mum. The timing couldn't be better. We're almost twenty-five.'

The girls were slowly but surely gaining a reputation. News of Lillian's stance against Sly Stan travelled fast, but it didn't impress everyone. Iris seemed as prickly as ever. After a particularly trying day, Lillian stopped by the cafe for a cup of tea about fifteen minutes before closing time. There were only three customers, all of them sitting at separate tables.

'Got any tea in that pot, Iris?' Lillian called cheerfully. 'My throat is as dry as a biscuit.'

A passenger was just on his way out of the cafe to

catch his train as she walked in. Lillian stepped aside to let him pass.

'You're one of the Sussex Sisters, aren't you?'

'Yes, that's right,' said Lillian with a smile.

'You girls came into the factory where my daughter works,' said the man, pumping her hand. 'They're worked to death and it was really getting her down, but after your performance that lunchtime, it bucked them up no end. Thank you – you're doing a grand job.'

'My pleasure,' said Lillian, deeply touched.

'You must put in hours of practice to be that good,' the man went on.

Lillian nodded and glanced up at the big clock. 'Got a practice tonight.'

The man only let go of her hand as his train rumbled into the station. Lillian gave him a mock salute as he hurried away.

'Nice to be appreciated,' said Lillian as she approached the counter.

Iris lifted the heavy stainless-steel teapot from the counter and placed it behind her on the draining board. 'This tea is stewed,' she said sniffily, 'and I don't have time to make a fresh pot. We close at five.'

Lillian smiled. 'Don't worry – that'll do so long as it's wet and warm.' She took a cup and saucer from the stack next to the hot-water urn and put it at the front of the counter.

'All the tea in this cafe has to be paid for,' said Iris, picking up a tea towel to dry up a couple of plates.

177

'I'm sure Southern Railway can't afford to dish out free cups to all and sundry.'

Lillian relaxed her stance. 'Come on, Iris,' she said good-naturedly. 'I really need reviving. It's been one hell of a day.'

Ignoring her, Iris carried on drying up.

Lillian fished around in her pocket and pulled out two pennies. Slapping them noisily onto the counter, she said pointedly, 'A cup of tea, please, love.'

Something flashed in Iris's eyes. 'Don't you call me "love",' she said indignantly. 'How dare you speak to me like that, you cheeky mare? You should have more respect.'

Now it was Lillian's turn to see red. 'My mother always taught me that respect,' she spat, 'was something you earned.'

Iris turned her back and tipped the teapot upside down in the sink. Lillian watched helplessly as the scalding-hot tea, and lots of it, disappeared down the plughole. 'What's the matter with you?' she demanded. 'You've had it in for me ever since I got here.'

'Don't be so ridiculous!' Iris retorted. 'I've got better things to do.'

'No, no,' said Lillian. 'It's true and you know it. Let's have this out once and for all.'

Behind her, Lillian could hear the few remaining customers leaving the room.

'Now look what you've done,' said Iris. 'You're driving everybody away.'

Lillian turned towards the empty room. Another

train was pulling up at the platform. When she turned back, Iris gave Lillian a triumphant glare.

'Like you said,' said Lillian, willing herself to stay calm, 'you're closing at five. Nobody else is coming in, so kindly explain exactly what I've done to offend you.'

Iris carried on with her work.

'You're jealous,' said Lillian. She could feel her own cheeks beginning to heat up, but she wasn't about to let this go, not yet. 'You didn't like it that despite all of your criticism, I got a promotion. Or maybe it's because of the singing group?'

The door opened and Betty Shrimpton came in with her hat and coat on. 'Ready?' she asked her friend, but Iris was preoccupied.

'Jealous?' Iris retorted with a hollow laugh. 'Why would I be jealous of a jumped-up little tart like you? Don't make me laugh.'

Lillian put her hand on her hip. 'Who are you calling a tart?!' she cried.

'Don't think I don't know what you've been up to, my girl,' Iris shouted back. 'You should be ashamed of yourself.'

'I don't know what you mean!' cried Lillian. 'Who's been talking about me?'

'It's all over Worthing,' said Iris. 'Making up filthy rhymes about people . . . It shouldn't be allowed. You do know you lost that poor man his job?'

For a second or two, Lillian was taken aback. What poor man? What job? And then it dawned on her. Iris must have heard about Sly Stan. 'Well, I'm sorry if he's lost his job,' she conceded, 'but that sleazebag had no right to paw me about. And he was doing it to half the girls in the factory, from what I heard.'

Iris tilted her head defiantly. 'Stan happens to live in my road,' she said.

'He can live with the King and Queen for all I care,' Lillian retorted. 'That doesn't give him the right to put his hand between my buttocks and feel me.'

'Ooh, you're disgusting,' said Betty, curling her lip.

'I'm disgusting?' Lillian cried indignantly. 'He was the one doing it.'

'You've got a bloody cheek,' said Iris, 'getting on your high horse like that. We all know the way you flaunt yourself about.'

'I have never flaunted myself at anyone,' said Lillian, 'and I'll thank you to mind your own business and stop casting aspersions.'

'All this from a person who *had* to get married?' Iris retorted. 'And from what I hear, you were hardly out of a gymslip.'

'What's that got to do with it?' Lillian demanded.

A mild-mannered voice behind them said, 'Now, now, ladies.'

Lillian turned to see that Mr Rawlings, the stationmaster, had come into the room. Outside, the platform was filling up with troops. Something must be on the move somewhere. They were already three or four deep on the platform and still coming.

'I'm sorry, Mr Rawlings,' said Iris, looking down her

180

nose, 'but I really must insist that this . . . this person be banned from the cafe. As you can see, her belligerent attitude has driven all the customers outside, and I really can't cope with her nastiness any more.'

'Me belligerent!' cried Lillian. 'All I did was ask for a cup of tea.'

'Ladies,' Mr Rawlings said, holding up his hands, 'that is enough. Settle your differences outside of working hours. I will not tolerate what amounts to a staff brawl while you're in uniform.'

'I paid for the tea,' said Lillian, pointing to her money on the counter, 'but she preferred to tip it down the sink rather than pour me a cup.'

'It was closing time,' Iris insisted.

There was a cry as some soldier outside spotted Lillian and knocked on the glass.

Mr Rawlings lifted his hand. 'Mrs Harris, please. Go home.'

'Oh, don't worry,' said Lillian haughtily. 'I won't be coming back in here even if you paid me.' She made to leave, but then turned back. Pointing a finger at Iris, she added, 'And I won't have you spreading vicious rumours and lies about my good reputation.'

'You lost that, my girl,' Iris added acidly, 'when you were seen kissing a Canadian soldier in the Ilex Way.'

At the same time, the door opened and a couple of Canadian soldiers pushed their way into the room.

Lillian felt her face flush. She had been seen? All those months ago, someone had seen her with Woody and Iris hadn't mentioned it until now? But who? She caught sight of Betty looking very uncomfortable and then she remembered. Betty had only just started in the ticket office, but she had been in the Ilex Way walking her dog when she and Woody had been together that day. Hot with embarrassment, Lillian turned on her heel. It took everything she had to hold her head high as she walked towards the door.

'Hello, sweetheart,' said the soldier, thinking she was coming over to him. 'You're one of the Sussex Sisters, aren't you?' He leaned towards her and planted a kiss on her cheek. 'You were lovely,' he said. 'Lovely.'

Lillian's step faltered as Iris called after her, 'Kissing in broad daylight, Lillian Harris? And you a married woman with your poor husband a prisoner of war. Shame on you. Shame, I say.'

CHAPTER 17

Stella had popped by Samuel and Susan's place after work, not because there was a problem, far from it, but to have a chat with Mrs Dennison. Since their first meeting all those months ago, things had radically changed for the Dennisons. The children were back at school, and Mr Dennison was in work, employed at the town hall by the finance department of Worthing Borough Council. He was also being trained as the council representative in the case of emergencies. He was to coordinate the council's response and take charge of resources and manpower in the event of a disaster or, worse still, an invasion. It was, according to his wife, a real feather in his cap and the kind of thing he'd always wanted to do. Not only that but Mrs Dennison was expecting another child. The twins were doing really well at school and it was for that reason that Stella had come to the house.

'Come in, come in, miss.'

'I can't stay,' Stella began, but Mrs Dennison's warm greeting was too hard to resist.

Ten minutes later, she was ensconced in the untidy

sitting room with a cup of tea and a small piece of home-made cake in front of her.

'I'm glad you've come,' said Mrs Dennison. 'It gives me an opportunity to thank you.'

'Whatever for?' cried Stella. 'I haven't done anything.'

'Oh, I think you have,' she said. 'We had a visit from you, and then only a little while later, the Legion come along and my hubby gets a job. A well-paid job at that.'

'Actually, it wasn't me—'

Stella was cut short when Mrs Dennison raised her hand. 'He hasn't made the connection, miss, but I have. They also gave us money to tide us over. A godsend it was, and I want to thank you. If there's ever anything I can do for you . . .'

'Please, Mrs Dennison,' said Stella, her cheeks growing pink, 'let's say no more about it.'

'As you wish,' she said with a smile.

'Mrs Dennison,' Stella began again, anxious to sound businesslike and professional. 'As you know, Samuel and Susan are bright and intelligent children, and I am sure they will have no trouble at all in passing the eleven-plus when it comes. However . . .'

Mrs Dennison leaned forward eagerly as Stella spoke.

'I think Samuel should try for a scholarship.'

His mother caught her breath.

'It will be hard work, but if we start as we mean to go on, there's no reason why he shouldn't take the examination for Christ's Hospital.'

184

Mrs Dennison stared at her with a blank expression.

'Christ's Hospital is a very old school,' Stella went on, 'with a reputation second to none.' She handed Mrs Dennison a picture of some of its pupils in uniform. The garb was somewhat old-fashioned, with a blue frock coat and breeches ending at the knee. The rest of the leg was covered with a bright yellow stocking that matched the lining of the coat.

'It looks very expensive,' Mrs Dennison remarked as she handed back the picture.

'If Samuel gets the scholarship,' Stella went on, 'the fees will be waived and the uniform will be free.' She could see that Mrs Dennison was impressed.

'Where is it?'

'Horsham,' said Stella. 'He'd have to be a boarder, of course.'

There was a long silence as Mrs Dennison thought about it. 'But what about Susan?' she eventually asked. 'We've always tried to treat them the same.'

Now it was Stella's turn to be impressed. Usually people had little ambition for their girls, only expecting them to get some menial job when they left school because it was assumed that they would get married before long. Clearly Mrs Dennison was an enlightened woman.

'There is a branch of Christ's Hospital School for girls, but it's about seventy miles away,' said Stella. 'It's in Hertford. That's north of London, near Welwyn Garden City.'

'And they offer scholarships too?' said Mrs Dennison.

Stella chewed her bottom lip. 'I'll be perfectly honest, Mrs Dennison. I don't know, but I can find out.'

Mrs Dennison looked thoughtful. 'It does seem a bit unfair if Susan is every bit as bright as Samuel not to give her a chance, doesn't it?'

'Indeed it does,' said Stella with a smile. She sipped her tea and ate a little of the cake. It was delicious and as light as a feather.

By the time Stella made her way home for the usual Sussex Sisters singing practice, it was already after five o'clock. She felt rather pleased with herself but also a little chastised. Mrs Dennison was right. Why shouldn't all girls get their chance at higher education? It was time to move out of the dark ages and set young girls free. After all, women had proved themselves to be perfectly capable of doing men's work while they were fighting, and some were doing highly skilled work at that. Once the war was over, what would happen? Surely women wouldn't be expected to return to house and home and a life of drudgery and boredom? No, she decided, that shouldn't be allowed to happen, and from now on she would do all in her power to broaden her pupils' horizons.

She'd got the idea of a Christ's Hospital scholarship from Judith.

'I've made a few enquiries,' her mother-in-law said the last time Stella had visited, 'and provided he gets good marks, there's no reason why he couldn't go there.'

Mrs Dennison had promised to talk it over with her husband before making any decisions, but Stella was confident that she wouldn't let him stand in the twins' way of what was a golden opportunity. The next couple of years would be hard work, but it would be worth it all if both her children passed that exam.

As she reached Richmond Road, a taxi came up Christchurch Road and turned left. When she saw the passenger, Stella did a double-take. The woman looked awfully like Pip, but what was Pip doing in a taxi? Stella waved her arm and called out, but as the passenger turned in her direction, something wasn't quite right. Although she was the same sort of age as Pip and had the same colour hair, it was much shorter, cut and permed into tight curls. Not only that but now that she'd turned her head, Stella could see that the whole of the right side of her face was deeply scarred.

Pip and Lillian were waiting on the doorstep when Stella arrived gushing her apologies. She would have mentioned the girl in the taxi, but it was obvious that Lillian was very upset. She'd been crying and Stella's first thought was that something had happened to Gordon. By the time they'd reached the sitting room, Lillian had told them all about her run-in with Iris.

'She seems determined to ruin my reputation,' Lillian wept. Stella and Pip had never seen her so upset. Lillian was always the one who laughed and joked her way through tricky situations. With her devil-may-care attitude to life, they weren't used to seeing her anything other than defiant when someone tried to put her down.

'I'm beginning to hate the woman,' she said, blowing her nose. 'I don't understand why she's doing all this.'

'Like you said,' Pip said as she put her arm around Lillian's shoulders, 'she's probably jealous.'

'It's this war,' said Stella. 'It's dragging on forever, and it brings out the worst in some people. We're all on edge the whole time. It's beginning to feel as if we'll never get back to normal.'

The others nodded their heads in sad agreement. All at once Stella rose to her feet. 'A day off,' she declared. 'That's what we need.'

Pip and Lillian sat open-mouthed.

'We'll take the children,' Stella went on excitedly, 'and jump on a bus going somewhere.'

'Where?' said Lillian faintly.

'I don't know,' cried Stella. 'Anywhere. What do you say?'

Lillian was already drying her eyes. 'I think it sounds like a marvellous idea.'

'I guess we could do with a bit of a break,' Pip conceded.

'That settles it, then,' said Stella. 'Leave it to me and we'll all go on a jolly.'

It took a while to decide where to go. It wasn't so easy when the beaches were covered in barbed wire and anti-tank defences. There were airfields around the area (Shoreham, Ford, Tangmere and Westhampnett), which blighted the countryside, and of course funfairs and outdoor entertainment that might draw crowds were seriously curtailed. Luckily, Stella had kept in touch with Brenda and Vera, the land girls her mother had billeted in her house when she, Pip and Lillian had first met. Vera was back home in Stoke-on-Trent, but Brenda was working on a farm just outside Pulborough. According to her, the bus went right by the gate, so they'd be most welcome to come for the day. The only demand she made on them, and it was hardly a demand, was that the Sussex Sisters would entertain some ladies from the local WI before they went back home.

When the big day came, the children were excited, even though they'd had to get up very early to make the most of their time. They all enjoyed the bus ride, and Brenda met them at the farm gate just after ten.

'I've got a surprise for you,' she said, once the greetings were over and they were heading towards the farmhouse. She extended her left hand and waited for them to admire the diamond-shaped ruby ring on her third finger.

'You dark horse,' cried Stella. 'I had no idea you were engaged. Who is he?'

'He's in a reserved occupation working on the farm,' said Brenda, beaming from ear to ear. 'Oh, Stella, he's so wonderful. He's kind and considerate, and he's so handsome.'

'You must be in love,' Lillian quipped.

Flora had spotted some chickens near the farm gate and was desperately trying to catch one. Georgie was more interested in the huge shire horses working in the field, while Hazel clung to her mother's skirts, overwhelmed by the strangeness of everything.

The farmer's wife, Mrs Elkins, was very welcoming, and after a cup of tea and a bun, they were given a ride round the farm on a low-loader behind the tractor. Pip leaned back and gazed heavenward. How wonderful to be out in the fresh air and countryside.

'You seem to have plenty of help,' Stella remarked as she watched the men hoeing a field of turnips.

'They're prisoners of war,' said Brenda. 'The Italians don't do much – they prefer to cook using herbs from the hedgerows – but the Germans are more hardworking.'

Sure enough, the Germans kept their heads down, while the Italians waved and called out to them, kissing the ends of their fingers with an exaggerated gesture at the same time.

After the tractor ride, they went round the farm buildings to look at the animals. The children were having the time of their lives.

The girls hadn't come empty-handed. Lillian had brought some of her mother's sugar ration. Since Dorcas had given it up for Christmas, she'd never gone back to using it. Lillian also brought some soap and a couple of flannels. Stella had brought some custard powder, and Pip had brought some tacks and rubber for mending shoes. Even the children had brought something: a painting or a drawing. Everything was gratefully received, and Mrs Elkins pinned the drawings all around the kitchen before they sat down to a delicious pigeon pie and vegetables. The POWs ate their lunch in the field, but the other farm workers joined the family round the table. Here, the girls met Sidney, Brenda's future intended.

'It's no wonder she's fallen for him,' Lillian whispered out of the corner of her mouth. 'He may not be the sharpest knife in the drawer, but he's certainly the best-looking.'

'Now, my dears,' said Mrs Elkins as soon as the clearing-up was done, 'Brenda is going to take you into Pulborough. You can leave the kiddies here. I'll look after them.'

'Oh no, Mrs Elkins,' cried Pip. 'We couldn't. It'll be far too much.'

'Nonsense,' said Mrs Elkins. 'My sister is bringing her boys up in a minute. They'll all have a wonderful time running about in the orchard. You go along and enjoy yourselves.'

She waved them off, calling, 'Don't forget you said you'd sing to my ladies.'

Pulborough was only a two-mile walk, and the weather was warm.

'I've got another surprise for you a bit later,' said Brenda.

The village itself was long and spread out. Close to the River Arun, it boasted some lovely Georgian buildings.

191

There was a pretty church, and a stone bridge over the river that dated back to Saxon times. The girls enjoyed their wander, and when they came to a rather posh-looking hotel, Brenda made to go in.

'What are you doing?' Stella asked.

'This is your surprise,' said Brenda. 'I've booked us afternoon tea.'

As soon as they walked into the hotel, Stella wondered if Brenda had made a mistake. It was very grand. They were faced with eight tables, each with its own crisp white linen tablecloth and silver cutlery, and chairs with rather faded pink powder-puff seats. Well-dressed matriarchs and their snooty friends occupied almost every table. At the far end of the room, beside a huge potted palm tree, a man in a dinner jacket tinkled the ivories of a white grand piano.

A waitress padded towards them with a tired-looking pink-and-gold menu tucked under her arm. With a slight bow, she ushered them to a window seat overlooking the formal gardens and they all sat down.

Brenda ordered cucumber sandwiches, a pot of tea for four and cakes.

The sandwiches, when they came, were as thin as tissue paper. The tea was in a pink rosebud china teapot, and the cakes looked out of this world. Brenda poured the tea, while Stella handed round the sandwiches. Lillian adjusted the plate of cakes so that her personal favourite was closest to hand. As they ate, they all made polite but hushed conversation. Pip was suddenly reminded of those teas at her grandmother's place when she had to sit bolt upright at the table and be on her best behaviour. As if on cue, the pianist began to play 'The Breeze and I'.

'Oooh,' whispered Stella. 'That's my favourite. Johnny and I love this song.'

Brenda lowered her eyes with a faint smile.

'Did you ask him to play it for me?' said Stella. Her eyes glistened.

'I don't believe this!' Lillian suddenly exclaimed.

'What?'

'There's a nail in my sandwich.'

'What?'

'A piece of fingernail.'

'Where?'

'There!'

'Good heavens above! She's right,' Brenda frowned. 'Well, I'm not paying all this money for you to have a dirty nail in your sandwich. Waitress!'

'Actually, it's not dirty,' Lillian protested.

'That's not the point . . .' Brenda hissed. 'Waitress!'

When she arrived at the table, Brenda wordlessly pointed to the offending article. Horrified by their discovery, the waitress beckoned the manager.

The manager arrived looking down his nose, as if he'd encountered a rather bad smell, until he saw the nail.

'Madam,' he gasped in an urgent whisper, 'I apologize. Most profusely.' And sweeping the plate away from her, he carried it all the way back to the kitchen. As he passed by the tables, he was accompanied by a little buzz of excitement, which grew louder as the other customers began to realize something a little out of the ordinary was happening. The girls could hear urgent whispers.

'A complaint? Did you say a complaint?'

'But they say no one ever complains here.'

'Something wrong with the sandwiches.'

'The sandwiches? Do you think mine are all right? Waitress . . .'

'Waitress!'

They heard the sound of raised voices coming from the general direction of the kitchen and everyone looked anxiously from one to the other. The pianist struck up a noisy rendition of 'This Will Make You Laugh'.

Two minutes later, the poker-faced manager swept out of the kitchen and made his way to their table. He was followed by a very red-faced man in a chef's hat and apron. He had the look of a man whose days were numbered.

'Madame, I must apologize,' gushed the chef in a heavy French accent, 'I yam mortified. *Je suis mortifié!* I cannot imagine 'ow this 'appen.' He glanced at the sour-faced manager and swallowed hard. 'I serve this 'otel for twelve years,' he went on, almost in tears, 'and this never 'appen before.'

He looked so desperate that the girls began to feel sorry for him. Was he really hinting that his job was on the line? Surely things wouldn't go that far?

'Please,' said Brenda, calming down. 'It's just that this was supposed to be a special occasion and—'

194

The manager glanced around the room at the sea of faces watching them. 'We shall of course reimburse you the cost of this tea,' he interrupted.

Brenda was still finishing the sentence she'd started. '. . . although I am a little disappointed—'

The manager put up his hand to stop her. 'I cannot allow that, madam. The hotel will pay for all your teas and give the lady who found the . . . er' – he leaned forward and muttered behind the menu – 'object . . . a voucher for another occasion.'

Lillian had become aware that the whole place was silent. The pianist had stopped playing, and all the other customers, though not looking their way, were obviously straining their ears to hear what she would say. Even Pip, Stella and Brenda waited with bated breath.

'Er . . .'

The manager leaned towards the table. 'No one ever complains here,' he said urgently.

'Then we shall say no more,' Lillian stuttered. 'Thank you for your generous offer.'

There was a collective sigh of relief. The manager bowed stiffly and followed the repentant chef back into the kitchen. As the swing door closed behind them, a heated argument ensued.

The pianist began playing and the rest of the customers resumed their conversations, although every now and then, a head would turn in their direction with a nod and a smile of approval.

Lillian dared not look at the others or she knew she'd

start laughing, but when the chef, his face flushed with embarrassment and his hat at a crazy angle, burst back out into the room, she struggled to keep the laughter in.

He descended onto their table with another plate of sandwiches perched on the tips of his outspread fingers and placed it in front of her with an exaggerated flourish. Then, thrusting his nose high into the air, he swept past the startled waitress, back into the kitchen. The whole charade was done in absolute silence, but as soon they were left to themselves, the buzz of conversation in the dining room rose to a noisy crescendo.

Behind their napkins, Brenda and the girls struggled to contain their giggles.

When at last the meal was finished and they stumbled through the door, the manager handed Lillian her voucher. They only just made it into the formal gardens before they all collapsed into uninhibited laughter.

'Are you going back to use the voucher?' Pip asked, as she wiped the tears from her eyes.

'I wouldn't dare,' Lillian giggled. 'It was a lovely place, and thank you for taking us there, but I'd never manage to keep a straight face.'

That set them all off again.

As they walked back to the farm, Lillian shivered. 'Ooh,' she said, reaching for her cardigan, 'it's getting a bit chilly.'

'I haven't laughed so much in ages,' said Stella. 'This afternoon has done us all the world of good.'

Lillian pushed her hand through the armhole of her cardigan and reeled back in pain. 'Ouch!'

'What is it?'

'My finger really hurts,' Lillian began. She glanced at her hand. 'Oh no!'

'What?'

'That broken nail . . .' she gasped, 'it was mine!'

CHAPTER 18

When the children at the farm had got together, they'd played shyly at first, but before long they were climbing trees. After a while, Mrs Elkins came out to tell them they could climb the big beech tree but not the apple trees or they might damage the fruit. Then she took Flora and Hazel indoors to play with the cat's kittens, and that's when the boys really got to know each other. Georgie had brought his cars in a bag, so when they'd had enough of climbing, they made a track along a fallen log. Brian and Christopher were evacuee children from Deptford in London, but they were going back home at the end of the week.

'Me mum finks it's much safer now,' said Brian. 'She says if Jerry bombs the place, we'll all go togevver.'

Georgie's eyes grew wide. 'Have you been in the bombing?'

Christopher shook his head. 'Nah.'

Georgie told them about the Heinkel 111 crashing into the house on the corner and the boys listened with rapt admiration as he told them about the German airmen, the Canadians and the fire. Apart from the odd bomb jettisoned over the fields as the Germans went home, Brian and Christopher had enjoyed relative peace and quiet in the countryside, although of course they thought it was boring. Georgie told them about his shrapnel collection and Goliath.

'We've got a tail fin,' said Christopher. 'Uncle Cecil reckons it's from a insenerary bomb.'

'What's that?' Georgie asked.

'It makes a big fire,' said Brian, waving his arms to show just how big. 'It set the trees alight in the wood.'

'Cor,' said Georgie, impressed.

'You can 'ave it if you like,' said Brian. 'We won't be allowed to take it home wiv us.'

'Anyway, they got them all over the shop in London,' his brother scoffed.

My darling Freckle-Face,

Thank you for your parcel, which arrived last week. It was wonderful to get a few things to remind me of home. Whenever I am alone, I hold the inside wrapping against my face. I want to smell your perfume and imagine you in my arms. Oh, my darling, it has been so long. Thank you for the photograph. I look at it all the time. After so long, I'm ashamed to say it was hard to remember exactly what you looked like.

When you see me, you'll find me much changed. I have lost about two stone in weight, and I keep getting boils up my nose. Bloody painful, I can tell you. I guess it's because of the poor diet. We've eaten all sorts to supplement our rations: squirrel, rabbit, all kinds of birds and even a frog or two – well, only the legs. My friend Reg got a few of us together and we went up to

the Red Cross depot and one of the lads managed to
collect a couple of parcels. We only get German rations
now and then, and it's mostly coarse black bread and
margarine. We make cakes for ourselves from crushing
Red Cross biscuits with the margarine. They wouldn't
do for the Peek Freans factory, but they taste a darned
sight better than the other muck. We sometimes get hot
drinks from the villagers who come out to meet us on
the way to the mine. God bless them, I say.

Mr Cuddles and I can't wait to get you between the
sheets again. I reckon when I come home, you'd better
take a week off to make up for lost time.

All my love,
Johnny xx

In the summer of 1943, the girls were back at the
Lancing carriage works for a lunchtime concert. As
soon as she walked through the factory gate, Lillian
found herself looking forward to seeing Nigel again.
The minute she saw him and he smiled, her heart
pounded wildly.

So far, the Sussex Sisters hadn't been caught up in
an air raid while performing, but that day, they were
unlucky. The sirens wailed almost as soon as they got
to the canteen, and Nigel made it his business to make
sure they knew exactly where to go. The railways had
devised a system whereby the workers had to go to the
air-raid shelters outside the works itself. Each shelter
was staffed by an ARP warden and an ambulance man.
As they entered the shelter, each man put his name on
a ticket. Lillian, Pip and Stella had to do the same. The

names were put into a round metal container, and as soon as everybody was inside, about a hundred of them, the warden threw the container outside the shelter and shut the door. The idea was that if the carriage works took a direct hit, any rescuers would know who had been in the shelter.

Not willing to miss the opportunity to cheer everybody up, Stella suggested they sing unaccompanied and an impromptu concert began, with the sound of dropping bombs all around them. When they emerged, some coaches had been destroyed and the panel shed had been damaged, but everyone escaped unscathed, and admiration for the Sussex Sisters had rocketed.

It was difficult for Georgie to get back to the gang members. Not only had his mother forbidden him from spending time with the big boys, but he also ran the risk of Hazel telling tales if he tried sneaking off. He couldn't wait to tell them the story of the tail fin and how the whole of the woods were burned down. 'If you thought the fire at Reydon was big,' he'd say, 'you should have seen how bad it was at Pulborough.'

The summer was almost gone and the nights were drawing in. Following their rendition for the ladies of the WI at Pulborough, the Sussex Sisters had been asked to sing for the annual general meeting of the WI in Worthing Assembly Hall. It was to be by far their largest audience. Members had gathered from all over the county for their first joint meeting since 1939.

The girls were still using their trademark siren suits, but by now they had made them look even more glamorous. Lillian had rhinestones on her collar. She had carefully picked them off an old evening dress she'd bought at a jumble sale. Pip had a sparkly belt round her waist, and Stella wore a small polka-dot scarf knotted cowboy-style round her neck. They had long since used up all their own lipstick and nail varnish, but such were the perks of fame that they had been given quite a few half-used lipsticks as presents. Their songs included several new ones, such as 'You'll Never Know' and 'Sunday, Monday or Always', but their audiences still enjoyed the old ones.

Their performance was to be the climax of the day, so most of the afternoon was taken up with reports and presentations in recognition of the selfless service the ladies of the WI had put into the war effort.

The Sussex Sisters had been asked to do two sessions. The first was to come at the end of the committee business. The rest of their performance would be performed after the members had had their tea. Remembering Phyllis's advice, the girls declined to eat before they sang, so they waited in their dressing room.

'Did you see that lady in the third row?' Lillian asked Pip.

'What lady?'

'She looked just like you,' said Lillian. 'In fact, if you hadn't been standing right next to me, I might have thought she was you.'

Pip's face paled. 'I didn't see her.'

'A woman with short, curly hair?' said Stella. 'I can't say I noticed her on the third row, but I have seen her before.'

'When?' Pip asked softly.

Stella shrugged. 'I don't know. It was months ago. I can't remember where. Oh, hang on, wait a minute, she was in a taxi. Why? Do you know her?'

Pip didn't answer, but her friends could see that she was troubled.

There was a sharp knock on the door and someone called, 'Two minutes.'

They all took once last look in the mirror and stood up to go.

'Where did you say she was sitting?' Pip asked as they made their way to the stage.

'Third row, fourth seat,' said Lillian.

By the time they reached the wings, they were already being introduced. 'And now we proudly present . . .'

'You can't miss her,' Lillian whispered close to Pip's ear. 'Her face is scarred.'

Pip froze.

The woman on stage flung her arm out towards them and cried, 'The Sussex Sisters.' The audience clapped wildly. Pip was rooted to the spot.

'What's wrong?' Stella whispered.

'I can't do it,' said Pip. 'I can't go on.'

'But you must,' said Lillian. 'They're waiting.'

The announcer tried again. 'Our very own Sussex Sisters.'

Stella gave Pip a gentle shove and all three were on stage. While Stella arranged her music at the piano, Pip scanned the audience. Her throat was as tight as a drum. How on earth was she going to sing? She felt clammy and sick. This couldn't be happening. This was the one thing she had always dreaded. Her eyes found the third row. In seat one was a portly woman with dark upper-lip hair, dressed in a tweed suit. In seat two was someone who appeared to be a younger version of the woman in a tweed suit. Her daughter, perhaps? In seat three sat an attractive woman with a big smile, who was clapping enthusiastically. Seat four was empty. Pip almost fainted with relief. Thank God . . . Oh thank God. Then Stella struck up a chord and they all burst into the Sussex Sisters' version of 'Zing! Went the Strings of My Heart'.

Their performance was one of their best. The ladies of the WI were lavish in their praise, and more than that, the Sussex Sisters received invitations to sing to individual groups in hospitals and church halls where the movement had an interest.

There was another buzz of excitement when a member of the public came running into the hall shouting, 'Mussolini has resigned! I just heard it on the radio.'

Suddenly, everybody was smiling. The first real crack in the alliance between Italy and the Nazi regime had come earlier that month, when Allied troops liberated Sicily. Rumour had it that the Italian dictator had met with Adolf Hitler somewhere in northern Italy to discuss what to do next, but it was believed that the meeting had been acrimonious and ended badly. Sicily had been the bastion of Hitler's European fortress, but now that the Eighth Army and the American Seventh had landed, all that was gone.

'It's going to be over soon,' cried Stella as she hugged Lillian and Pip in turn.

Elsewhere in the hall, some of the younger ladies were doing the conga.

Pip tried to be happy for everyone, but it was doubly difficult for her. After more than a year, she still had no idea if Peter was dead or alive. Despite repeated requests at government level, the regiment had no news to pass on to waiting relatives.

When they got back into their dressing room, there was a large bouquet of flowers in front of the mirror. Lillian gasped, 'Oh, how lovely!' They were home-grown, from somebody's garden, but all the same they were very impressive. Lillian pulled the card from between the foliage. 'Oh!' she said, surprised that the bouquet wasn't hers. 'It's for you.' She handed the card to Pip.

'Me?' Pip asked enquiringly.

'It's got your name on the front,' said Lillian with a grin. 'Have you got a secret admirer you haven't told us about?'

With Stella at her elbow, Pip took the card from the envelope. There were two words on the card and a kiss. Pip let it fall from her fingers as a gentle voice behind her said, 'Hello, Philippa.'

At first, Pip was totally transfixed. She didn't turn round. She didn't need to. She could see the woman's reflection in the mirror. 'No, no,' she whimpered. 'It can't be.'

Lillian and Stella were alarmed to see that she was shaking uncontrollably. Instinctively, they folded themselves between Pip and her unwanted visitor in a protective way. Lillian picked up the card from the floor and showed it to Stella.

'*Love, Marion x,*' they read.

Stella recognized the woman at once. She was Pip's lookalike, the woman she'd seen in the taxi a few months back. Up until Lillian mentioned seeing the same woman, she'd forgotten all about her.

Pip sank into a chair with a small moan.

'It's all right,' said the woman, coming further into the room. Stella and Lillian stood closer together, effectively barring her way.

'Look here—' Stella began, but they were interrupted by the organizer bustling through the door.

'My dears, you were fantastic,' she gushed as she handed Stella a small brown envelope. She didn't seem to notice the woman; in fact, she seemed totally unaware that anything was amiss. 'Everyone adored you,' the organizer hurried on. 'I'm sure we shall meet again. Oh dear, that sounded like a cue for a song, didn't it?' She chuckled at her own joke before continuing. 'So many people have been asking me for your contact details that

I am positive you'll be getting a lot more invitations from the WI.' She paused and Stella felt sure that this was the moment when she would remark on the tense atmosphere in the room or become aware of Pip's distress.

The other visitor remained where she was, though she had turned her head away.

'Well, my dears,' the organizer said again, 'I'd better be running along. Do take care, won't you? And,' she added in a jolly voice, 'see you soon.'

The moment she'd gone, Stella looked at the other woman. 'I think you'd better go too.'

'Oh, please don't send me away, not just yet,' she cried. 'I've been searching for Philippa for years.' She turned towards Pip. 'Philippa? It's all right, you know. There was no need to run off like that.'

Pip had begun to cry.

'Please let me go to her,' said the woman, trying to push past Stella and Lillian.

'You're upsetting her,' said Stella.

'Who are you?' Lillian demanded. 'What's this all about?'

'My name is Marion,' said the woman, 'and Philippa is my sister.' She paused and covered her scarred face with her hand. 'We're twins.'

CHAPTER 19

Lillian looked up anxiously. 'Is she all right?'

Stella had just taken some tea into her sitting room for Pip and her sister. Lillian was waiting in the kitchen. At Stella's suggestion, they had all made their way back to her house to give Pip and Marion a private place where they could talk.

'She still looks pale, but she's stopped crying,' said Stella. 'I asked her if she wanted me to stay, but she said no.' She sat at the table and poured herself a cup of tea.

'Blimey, that was a turn-up for the books, wasn't it?' said Lillian. 'I never even knew she had a sister, let alone that she was a twin. She's always led me to believe she was on her own apart from Peter and the children.'

'Me too,' said Stella. She rose from the table and went to her sideboard. Taking a small bottle of Vat 69 out of the cupboard, she poured a splash into each of their cups. 'Do you think I should offer some of this to Pip and Marion?'

Lillian shook her head. 'I reckon they'll both need a

clear head,' she cautioned. 'They've got a lot of talking to do.'

Stella sat down again. 'Although Marion is quite a bit shorter, they do look very alike, don't they? Apart from that terrible scar.'

'How do you think it happened?'

Stella shrugged. 'It looks like a burn.'

'From what she was saying on the way home, Pip seems to think it was her fault,' said Lillian.

They sipped their tea in silence and wondered.

'It makes me realize how lucky we were with Flora,' Lillian went on. 'She could have ended up looking like that.'

'But she doesn't have any scars to show for it now, does she?'

'Only that little bit behind her ear where the hair doesn't grow,' said Lillian.

'I didn't realize it was still there,' said Stella. 'Since you've had her hair cut, she looks lovely.'

'I wanted to keep it long,' Lillian said with a sigh. 'I used to put it into little plaits when she was younger, but after the accident, people kept noticing that bald patch. Having it in plaits made it show up more.' She ran her fingers through her own hair. 'I always fancied having plaits when I was a kid, but my hair was too frizzy.'

'Flora is a lovely little girl,' said Stella, leaning over and patting Lillian's hand affectionately, 'and she's the spitting image of her mother.'

Lillian gave her a wobbly smile, and they sipped more tea.

'Have you heard anything from Gordon lately?'

'He writes now and then,' said Lillian in a non-committal voice. She sighed, then noticing Stella's concerned expression, added, 'We don't have a lot to say to each other. The more I think about it, the more I feel that I made a terrible mistake when I married him. We've got nothing in common, except Flora, of course.'

'Oh dear,' said Stella.

'You do know that we had to get married, don't you?' said Lillian. She was being more frank than she'd ever been before. 'His parents, my parents – my dad was still alive back then – they talked it over and that was that. He and I had little say in the matter. When I woke up on my sixteenth birthday, it was my wedding day.'

'It happens to a lot of people,' Stella said sagely, 'but they go on to make a happy marriage. There's still time.'

Lillian shook her head. 'We've been apart too long. I've changed. He's changed. We don't want the same things any more.' She took a deep breath. 'What about you and Johnny? Are things still OK with you two?'

'As a matter of fact, I had a letter today,' Stella grinned. 'He's missing me like mad.' She felt her cheeks colour as his reference to Mr Cuddles came to mind, and when she made eye contact with Lillian, they both giggled.

'Funny thing,' said Lillian. 'I don't miss that at all.'

'Miss what?' said Stella, feigning innocence.

'You know perfectly well,' said Lillian. 'The sex.'

'You will,' said Stella, 'when you really love someone.'

When Stella left the sitting room, both Pip and Marion stared at the closing door. The atmosphere was heavy with embarrassment and pent-up emotions. Things needed to be said, but Pip didn't know where to start.

'Marion, I'm sorry,' she said brokenly.

'And I am too,' said Marion.

'Why should you be sorry?' said Pip, slightly surprised at her contrite manner. 'You were the one who got burned.'

'I said some terrible things. I never meant to drive you away.'

Pip was puzzled. It seemed as if she had always been at war with her twin. Whenever she thought of Marion, it was to remember something grossly unfair that ended up with her getting into trouble. Marion had wound her up like a clock spring. Her sister always got her own way because she would keep on and on until Pip snapped. She felt hot with shame as she recalled pulling her sister's hair or pushing her into the water butt when it was November and freezing outside. Another time when they'd had a hands-on tussle, Marion had ended up with a split lip. Their mother would never listen when Pip tried to explain what had happened. She wasn't interested in anything Marion had done or what had started it. All she saw was a bully, taking it out on her defenceless sister. As time went on, things only became more compounded. Pip had few friends, while 'poor' Marion was everybody's darling.

Things had been so different when Daddy was around. She and Daddy did everything together, while Marion stayed close to their mother. Their parents didn't get on either. The girls would lie in bed listening to their rows. Terrible rows that went on for days at a time, and then suddenly, Daddy wasn't there any more and they moved. Her mother told her that he had died, but even at five, she'd been a bit mystified as to why there had been no funeral. When Mrs Bingham next door had died, she'd had one, and everybody in the street went to it, even though Mummy said she was an interfering old battleaxe and nobody liked her. When Pip had questioned her mother about Daddy's funeral, all she'd got was a slap on her legs.

Marion put up her hand. 'What you did that day, I don't want to talk about it any more.'

Pip avoided eye contact and sucked in her top lip. Her mind was in turmoil. Part of her was thinking, But I want to talk about it. Don't you remember? When I went to the hospital to visit you, you said you never wanted to see me again as long as you lived. You told me to go to hell. You said you hated me. You said I'd ruined your life. At the time, it was understandable, of course, but it hurt so much.

She fished up her sleeve for her handkerchief and

pinched the end of her nose with it. It was sodden and useless. Her sister opened her handbag and offered her a clean one. Pip took it gratefully, wiped her eyes and blew her nose.

'I've never been able to get that moment out of my mind,' she said miserably. 'It still gives me nightmares – you flying down the stairs all in flames.'

Marion said nothing.

Her sister wore her hair short. She still looked attractive if you looked at the left side of her face, but on the right side, her skin looked like crumpled tissue paper. Pip could see that the scar went down her neck. Presumably, it was still as far as her wrist and her waist. She glanced involuntarily down at her leg. That was marked too, although the scars were more faded.

Closing her eyes, she leaned forward and put her hand to her forehead. 'I did try to stop you, you know,' she said unevenly.

Marion glared at her tight-lipped. 'No, you tried to stop me getting help,' she said coldly.

Pip looked up sharply. 'Marion, that's not true! I was trying to pull you to the floor so that I could roll you in the hearth rug.'

Marion looked sceptical.

'Why don't you believe me?' Pip cried. 'Why must you always believe the worst of me?'

'Me, me, me,' said Marion, and despite herself, Pip found she was slipping back into her childhood role with Marion winding her up until she exploded.

'Are you sure you didn't engineer the whole thing

because you wanted to go to the party with Richard?' Marion's tone was more familiar now – challenging and aggressive.

Pip swallowed hard. 'Richard?'

'Yes, Richard,' said Marion. 'Admit it – you always wanted him.'

Pip frowned. No. She'd never wanted Richard. He'd always seemed a bit wet. And why did Marion have to be so confrontational? True, her sister was the one who got the dates, while she (Pip) was forced to stay at home because she'd lost her temper yet again. Marion was always going off to something nice. The gymkhana, punting on the river, a concert in London – you name it and Marion was there. Nobody ever asked her out, not unless you counted Neville Paris, and he was the most awful drip.

Marion tossed her head. 'Richard stuck by me and he was wonderful.'

Pip glanced at her sister's left hand. 'You're married. You married Richard?'

'Good Lord, no,' Marion laughed. 'It wasn't quite the fairy-tale ending, but I've had my moments.'

For the first time since she'd met her sister, Pip smiled. 'I'm so glad that—'

'That these horrible scars didn't stop someone from loving me?' Marion challenged.

'No, no, I didn't mean it like that,' Pip protested wildly, 'and please believe that I never stopped loving you.'

'I know,' said Marion with a hollow laugh, 'and I'm teasing.'

Pip frowned. Why was her sister so awkward, so confusing? 'Where do you live?'

'With Mother,' said Marion.

That wasn't exactly what Pip meant, but she found herself looking away as the memory of her mother's angry face came to mind. She'd always known her mother liked Marion more than her, but that day in the kitchen, she'd been shocked by the venom in her voice.

They'd just come back from the hospital, where they'd left Marion seriously ill. Everyone else, Richard and Mrs Bliss, their next-door neighbour, who had come in to sit with Granny, had gone home. Granny was asleep and they were alone. Mum had sat at the kitchen table and wept for a long time. Pip had tried to comfort her, but she'd jerked her arm away.

'You needn't think you're going to get round me like that,' she'd snarled. 'Why did you move the fireguard anyway?'

'I didn't,' Pip had protested.

'Marion told me,' her mother snapped, 'and I must say it's typical of you. You're a wicked, jealous little madam. I can't believe you're your sister's twin. If I didn't know better, I would say that the day you were born, the nurses swapped you for somebody else.'

Pip had stared at her open-mouthed. 'Why are you saying all this, Mum? It was an accident. I wasn't . . .'

But her mother wasn't listening. She never listened.

Pip glanced over at her sister and sipped her tea. It was getting cold. She wanted to tell Marion all this, but wouldn't that be raking over old coals? Was it better to leave it unsaid? The pain was still there, but what was her pain compared to what her sister had gone through? Marion's scars were visible. Pip's were hidden deep inside.

'How is Granny?' she said, coming back to the here and now.

'Oh, of course you wouldn't know,' said Marion in a superior tone. 'Granny died. It was not long after you'd left.'

It was a shock. Pip took in her breath.

'It was all very peaceful,' said Marion.

'And Mum?'

'She's fine,' said Marion. 'Older but still the same.'

Still the same . . . Pip still couldn't shake off the memory of her mother's bitter denunciations. 'You always were horrible to poor Marion, even as a child,' she'd ranted. 'Well, this time you've gone too far, Philippa. Much too far!'

'Mum, I know you're upset,' Pip had begun again. 'You don't mean it.'

'In fact,' her mother said, getting to her feet, 'in the morning, you can pack your bags and leave.'

'Leave!' Pip had cried. 'But why? I didn't do anything, Mum. I wasn't even in the room!'

Her mother had swept out of the room, pausing only to add, 'You're exactly the same as your father, and do you know what, Philippa? I don't care if I never see you again.'

'Are you married?' said Marion now, interrupting her thoughts. 'I can see a ring on your finger, but in these uncertain times . . .'

'Yes,' said Pip. 'I'm married, and we have two children. Georgie is seven, and Hazel is five. My husband was caught up in the fall of Singapore. He's a Japanese POW.'

A strange look flickered across Marion's face. 'I'm sorry,' she sympathized. 'You must be having a pretty hard time of it.'

'I haven't heard from him since he was captured,' said Pip with a sigh. 'It's been over a year now and I still don't know if he's dead or alive.'

The two sisters fixed their eyes on each other. All at once Marion smiled and said, 'Poor you.' Pip felt a bit uncomfortable. Marion's tone wasn't exactly sincere, but then she added, 'Can I give you a hug?'

They stood up together and spread out their arms.

'Will I hurt you?' Pip asked anxiously.

'No, so long as you don't squeeze me too hard,' said Marion, and as they enfolded each other in their arms, Pip's silent tears fell while Marion's body stiffened.

CHAPTER 20

As the days went by, Judith had secured invitations for the Sussex Sisters to revisit the camps in the Broadwater area. The Allied troops loved them and were hoarse from cheering by the time the show was over. Aside from singing for the soldiers, it was good meeting up again with people who had been so supportive at their debut in village halls, hospital wards and WI meetings. Their number-one fan, Mr Knight, turned up for every performance and clapped enthusiastically. The girls made new friendships. Everyone had their own particular story to tell: a husband wounded, a brother killed, a relative made homeless by the bombing, children evacuated yet again and desperate to come home, or, on a happier note, children happily settled and thriving up North somewhere.

Lillian and Stella were dying to tell everybody about Pip's twin sister, but she had sworn them to secrecy. They weren't sure why but it was obvious that Pip had some reservations about Marion.

As for Marion herself, she told them she was working for the government exposing people involved in the black market. For that reason, she explained, most people held her at arm's length. When Pip found out, she was relieved that she hadn't got involved in any more under-the-counter purchases since the incident surrounding the bolt of midnight-blue material.

The odd thing was, Marion didn't invite Pip to stay with her, nor did she seem bothered about meeting Pip's children. Every time Pip asked about their mother, Marion was evasive about her too.

'I'm beginning to wonder why she's turned up at all,' Pip told Stella. 'She's very cagey about everything.'

'Has she been to your home yet?'

'No,' said Pip. 'She told me to meet her in Lyons tearooms.'

Stella gave her a quizzical look. 'Perhaps you should speak to her in a more direct manner?'

Pip looked away and shook her head. 'I can't. She's so prickly everything ends up in a row.'

'You're afraid of her, aren't you?' said Stella.

'Not exactly,' said Pip. 'I just don't want to go back to the way things were. She blames me for what happened. Oh, she doesn't actually come out with it, but it's always there, hanging over my head like a dark cloud. All those little hints and insinuations she drops, I can't bear it.'

'Oh, Pip,' said Stella. 'I'm so sorry. Look, if you ever want to talk—'

'I can't,' Pip interrupted.

Lillian had discovered that Nigel was dominating her thoughts. He was the first thing to come into her mind the moment she woke up, and all through the day, little things reminded her of him. Some chap at the station flicked his cigarette away just as the train pulled in. Nigel did that. A man in the waiting room was chewing the inside of his cheek as he concentrated on the crossword puzzle. Nigel did that too. She tried to imagine being with him and Flora as a family, and in her daydreams they ran up Highdown Hill or splashed in the sea at Goring in a world free from tyranny and war.

Whenever these thoughts intruded, she would pull herself up short. She'd tell herself she was wicked to think such things. She was a married woman with responsibilities. Nigel had never once led her on or even suggested any impropriety, but that didn't stop this perpetual yearning to see him again.

Marion had put in her appearance just a few months before the twins' twenty-fifth birthday. For Stella, that was the perfect excuse for a party, and it didn't take her long to get everything going. She was disappointed to discover that they couldn't do it on Pip's actual birthday, Friday November 27th, because Marion had arranged some family occasion and had made it plain that the girls weren't invited. It was an awkward moment. Lillian and Stella could see that their friend was embarrassed, and although it was perfectly understandable for Marion to want Pip to herself, the whole business made Stella feel uneasy. In the end, they arranged that Pip would leave Georgie and Hazel with Stella for the weekend. They would go to school as normal on Friday but come home with Stella afterwards.

Marion would collect Pip from her place that morning and take her to their mother's house. They would return to Worthing the following day, the Saturday. It seemed a little odd not to want to stay with their mother a bit longer, but in an effort to make the occasion special, Stella planned her party for the Saturday evening.

When Marion turned up in a car she drove herself, there was only Dorcas to wave them off. 'She looked more like she was going to a wake than a birthday celebration,' Dorcas told Lillian later that evening. 'There's something not quite right there if you ask me.'

Lillian brought Flora round on Friday evening so that she and Stella could start getting the room ready for the following day. There would be enough to do on Saturday, and to keep the children amused in the morning, Stella had promised to take them to see Father Christmas in his grotto in Bentalls, which was opening that day.

After tea, the children played in Stella's bedroom. They loved the dressing-up box, and before long they could hear the girls clip-clopping around in high-heel shoes on the parquet floor of the hallway, while Georgie was some sort of dragon or monster jumping out of cupboards or leaping from behind a chair to scare them away.

'Mum said Pip didn't look too happy when she set off,' said Lillian. 'How did she seem to you when she brought the children's things round?'

The two of them were in the sitting room blowing up balloons.

'Worried,' said Stella. She paused before adding, 'It's all a bit odd, don't you think?'

'I feel the same way,' said Lillian. 'I'm not sure about that Marion either. I mean, ever since they sat in your sitting room – that's what, about three months ago? – Since that first meeting backstage, she's only been to see Pip a couple of times, always in a tearoom, and the last time, she chose the very day we told her Georgie and Hazel wouldn't be there.' She laid a red balloon in her lap to tie the neck. 'I can't make her out.'

Stella, who was folding paper napkins, lowered herself onto a chair. 'I know she's gone through an awful lot, what with that terrible burn and everything, but to be honest, I don't like her much.'

'What a relief to hear you say that,' said Lillian. 'I don't like her much either. She's so different from Pip. Pip is fun to be around, she's loving and caring, but her sister seems . . . I can't put my finger on it, but when she's around, it's like poor Pip is walking on eggshells.'

'I know she hates the snide remarks,' said Stella.

'Snide remarks?'

'That first day, just as she was going, I don't know if you heard, but she said something like, "Every time you look in the mirror, you must see me as I once was."'

Lillian looked shocked. 'That's a bit unkind.'

'She was laughing about it, but you're right – it wasn't very nice.'

'I remember Pip told me once that it was her fault she got burned,' Lillian continued.

'As I recall, you said the same sort of thing when Flora got burned,' said Stella, 'but we all know it wasn't true. Knowing Pip, I'm sure whatever happened, it was an accident. She'd never do something like that deliberately.'

'Absolutely not,' said Lillian.

They sat for a moment or two, each lost in her own thoughts.

'When I told Marion about the Sussex Sisters,' Lillian went on, 'she didn't seem to be at all interested.'

'That's odd too,' said Stella. 'Wouldn't you think she'd be proud of Pip?'

'She strikes me as a bit cold,' Lillian remarked. 'And here's me thinking that twins were supposed to be close.'

There was a loud squeal in the hallway as Georgie leapt out of the cupboard under the stairs with a growly voice. Stella and Lillian looked up and grinned at each other as they heard the girls clattering away in their high heels.

'Come to think of it,' Lillian went on, 'whenever she has turned up, she's never stayed long.'

'I reckon we'd better keep a weather eye on the situation,' said Stella. 'Whatever that woman is up to, the last thing we want is Pip getting hurt.'

Pip felt as nervous as a kitten. She sat in the front passenger seat of Marion's car trying to look calm, but it wasn't easy. Her suitcase was on the back seat, with

223

presents for her mother and Marion on the top. She had bought her sister a fountain pen and matching pencil set. It was quite expensive and had taken a lot of coupons, but it was worth it. She had dipped into her savings for her mother's present: a brooch from Pressleys, the jeweller's in South Street. It left a sizeable hole in her bank balance and she would have to forgo a few post-war credit certificates, which were issued as recognition of higher taxes paid to the government to help the war effort. Thankfully, the shop rents were stable, and she hadn't had too many repairs of late. She'd been lucky that when the Heinkel crashed into Reydon the previous year, her shopfronts had stayed intact. A few doors down, the pub had had all its windows blown in, as had many houses nearby.

'Where are we going?' Pip asked as they headed towards Chichester.

'A place called Wimborne,' said Marion.

'Wimborne?' Pip gasped. 'But that's miles away.'

'Which is why I told you to bring a suitcase,' her sister retorted in a patronizing voice.

'Is that where Mum lives now?' She couldn't remember where their first house had been, though she knew it was somewhere in London. All she had was memories of the sitting room and sitting on Daddy's lap while he read a bedtime story. Later, when he'd died, they had moved to Devon, and whenever she thought of her mother, she always pictured her there.

Marion had one hand on the steering wheel and the

other in her handbag. She fished out her cigarette case and handed it to Pip. 'Light one up for me, will you?'

Pip took a cigarette out of the case and put it between her lips.

'There's some Swan Vestas in the bag,' said Marion.

Pip found the matches and lit the cigarette before passing it over to Marion.

'Have one yourself,' said Marion.

'I don't smoke,' said Pip, putting everything back in the bag and replacing it in the footwell.

'Oh, bully for you,' Marion snorted sarcastically.

It was not a kind remark. Pip sucked in her lips and gazed out of the window. She might have enjoyed the ride if she'd been with someone else. They trundled along pretty country roads. The war had altered the landscape, but beyond the barricades, army camps and bomb craters, the beauty of the English countryside was still there. War-weary people, dressed mainly in browns and greys, waited at bus stops, rode bicycles or shopped in the high streets. Every now and then, she could see a spot of colour: a bright headscarf, a child wearing red scuffed hand-me-down shoes or the occasional straggly rose hanging over a garden wall. The weather was pleasant for the time of year, chilly but not cold, although everyone was wearing their winter coats, including Pip and Marion.

They sat in silence for such a long time that conversation became awkward.

'Will I be staying with you and Mum?' Pip asked eventually.

'Of course,' said Marion, winding down the window to dispose of her third dog-end. 'We'll stop in a minute for a break.'

They turned into a town called Romsey and looked for the public toilets. They found some in the town centre and spent a penny. When they came out, Marion suggested a cup of tea.

'You haven't told me much about yourself,' said Pip as they sat down and Marion lit yet another cigarette.

'Not much to tell.'

'Do you have anyone special in your life?'

'Good Lord, no,' said Marion.

'Can you tell me more about your job?' asked Pip.

Marion drew her finger across her lips as if zipping her mouth and Pip knew not to ask any more. She sipped her tea. 'Will Mum be home?'

Marion picked a speck of tobacco from the end of her tongue. 'Yes.'

Pip sighed. Yes. Was that all? Why was she making this such hard work? 'Is Mum in good health?'

'I told you before. She's fine,' said Marion impatiently. She looked at her watch and started to gather her things. 'Come on. We'd better get going. We don't want to be late.'

'What for?' Pip called after her as she hurried from the tearoom.

But Marion didn't answer.

CHAPTER 21

They arrived in Wimborne at 2.30 p.m. The remainder of the journey had been as awkward as the first part and Pip was exhausted. All she wanted to do was have a cup of tea and something to eat, and lie on her bed for a while. She couldn't wait to see her mother's house, but to her surprise, her sister suddenly said, 'Before we do anything else, we need to see Granny's solicitor.'

'Why?' Pip's question went unanswered as they crossed a small humpbacked bridge and headed towards the town. They parked outside Peak, Hall & Ellis, Solicitors, which was next to a short pedestrian footpath adjoining Woolworths.

Without a word of explanation, Marion picked up her handbag and led the way. Pip was beginning to feel annoyed. Why all the mystery? What was Marion up to? She'd said Granny had died shortly after she'd left home. She was sixteen back then and had taken a job as a nursery assistant in a children's home because it was the only way Pip could get a roof over her head and a job at the same time. If Granny had died nine years before, why on earth were they going to see her solicitor now?

The offices of Peak, Hall & Ellis were through a door between two shops and up a narrow staircase. There were some chairs lined against the wall on the landing. A woman came out of an office, and when Marion told her who they were, they were asked to sit down. As soon as they were comfortable, the woman walked along the corridor and knocked gently on another door.

Pip turned to her sister. 'What's this all about, Marion?' she said coldly. 'Why have you brought me here?'

Once again she was met with silence.

Pip stood to her feet. 'Well, if you won't tell me, I'm going,' she said crossly.

'Sit down,' Marion scowled.

'No, I won't,' said Pip. 'Not until you tell me what we're doing here.'

'It's to do with Granny's will,' said Marion sullenly. 'There's a clause in it that applies to me and you.'

Pip lowered herself back down onto the chair. 'Go on.'

'She left us some money,' said Marion, 'but we had to wait until we were twenty-five before we could have it.' She glanced up at Pip and added sarcastically, 'Happy birthday, darling.'

The secretary was back. Pip's mind was all over the place. Granny had left her some money? How thoughtful, how kind, but why had Marion kept it secret until now? If anyone else had done that, she would have thought it was a birthday surprise, but with Marion at the helm, it felt altogether different. She followed the two women into the office.

Mr Ellis was a small, twittery man with a balding head and glasses. He was obviously self-conscious of his looks because he had grown some side hair very long and combed it over the top of his head to disguise his baldness. The ruse hadn't worked. As he extended his hand for them to shake, he was unaware that the long hair had fallen down and hung out like a limp and broken wing. They all shook hands and sat down. Unusually for a private consultation, the secretary remained in the room. Mr Ellis opened a large brown envelope and tipped the contents onto his desk. As he smoothed out the pages, Pip stared at the upside-down writing. *The last will and testament of . . .*

'Here is the relevant part,' said Mr Ellis, turning the page. '*As for my dear granddaughters, Marion Eleanor Abbott and Philippa Gillian Abbott, it has always grieved me that they didn't get on. I therefore have decided that if they reach an age of maturity and have become not only loving sisters but best of friends by their twenty-fifth birthday . . .*'

Pip glanced across at her sister. Marion was smiling, her eyes were bright with excitement, and her breathing quickened with every word Mr Ellis spoke. So this was it. Marion had gone to all this trouble and sought her out for money! Pip's cheeks flamed with anger as Mr Ellis droned on and on.

'*To this end, if they come to the offices of Peak, Hall & Ellis on their twenty-fifth birthday or in the year following and, in the presence of a witness, will declare and affirm—*'

'Would you mind reading that bit again?' said Pip.

Mr Ellis stopped speaking. All eyes were on Pip. Marion leaned over and touched her hand. Pip snatched it away.

'Which bit?' Mr Ellis asked.

'There's no need to make Mr Ellis read it again, darling,' Marion interrupted. 'You can read it for yourself when he's finished.'

'The bit from "an age of maturity",' said Pip.

Mr Ellis repeated the words.

'Well, we haven't,' said Pip.

The secretary's mouth dropped open.

'Beg pardon?' said Mr Ellis.

Marion jumped to her feet. 'Mr Ellis,' she blurted out in a smarmy voice, 'we've both had a long journey and my sister is tired.'

'We haven't been reconciled,' Pip said in ringing tones.

Grabbing the arms of Pip's chair, Marion leaned towards her and hissed in her ear, 'If you don't say we're friends, we don't get the money.' She stood back up with a wide smile. 'Just my sister's little joke.'

'I'm afraid we've rather wasted your time, Mr Ellis,' Pip said calmly, rising to her feet. 'Marion and I are not loving sisters, nor are we best friends, and what is more, I have an awful feeling we never shall be.'

Marion pulled on her arm to stop her leaving the room, but Pip snatched it away. She held out her hand to the astonished solicitor. 'I imagine someone else will reap the benefit of all this,' she said in a deliberate tone. 'If that is the case, I would be grateful if you would tell whoever it is that I am glad and I wish them well.' And stepping round the chair, she walked from the room. She allowed herself a small smile as she reached the stairs. It was a long time since she'd felt this good. A very long time.

Marion clattered down the stairs behind her. 'You bitch. You bloody bitch!'

Lillian had taken Flora to the pictures for the afternoon. It was a dull day and already getting dark. As she turned into her gate, Lillian was aware of someone lurking by the hedge. Being November, she knew Dorcas would have lit the fire and it wouldn't be long before the sitting room was warm and cosy. Nudging Flora towards the front door, Lillian glanced back. 'Who's there?'

A man stepped from behind the hedge. 'It's only me,' he said. 'I'm sorry. I didn't mean to frighten you.'

Lillian took in her breath. 'Nigel?'

'Yes,' he said, moving into the light. Her heart skipped a beat. He looked even more handsome in his mackintosh and trilby hat, which he lifted politely as he spoke.

'Just a minute,' said Lillian, and guiding Flora to the front door, she turned the key in the lock and said,

'You go on in and find Granny. I'll be along in a minute.'

'Who is that man, Mummy?' Flora asked. 'Is that my daddy?'

Lillian shook her head. 'No, sweetheart. It's just somebody who wants to talk to me about something at work. Now, off you go. I'll be with you in a sec.'

She closed the door again and turned back. As she came closer, he had pushed his hat back on his head.

He reached out his hands and took hers. 'I know I shouldn't ask this, Lil,' he said nervously, 'you being a married woman and all, but would you like to come out one evening with me for a drink?'

At first, she was surprised. She hadn't been expecting that, but as she opened her mouth, he quickly added, 'No funny business, I promise. Just a drink.'

Lillian relaxed and smiled. 'I think I would like that, Nigel,' she said. 'Yes, I'll come out with you. I'd like that very much.'

It was about 4.15 p.m. and the light was failing as Pip burst onto the street. She was so anxious to get away from Marion she almost knocked someone over.

'Oh, I do beg your pardon,' she began, but as the woman looked up, Pip got a surprise. 'Mum!'

Marion came flying into the street behind her just as Pip, all the hurt and anger momentarily forgotten, opened her arms to give her mother a hug. Over Pip's shoulder, she didn't see her sister's eyes lock with her mother's. Marion curled her lip and shook her head slowly.

'Oh, Mum,' Pip whispered. 'I've missed you so much.' When she leaned back to look at her mother, Maud Abbott wore a stony expression. The lines around her mouth may have been harder, and her hair was greyer and perhaps not as thick as she remembered, but she was still Mum.

'What's wrong, darling?'

Pip smiled until she realized her mother wasn't addressing her but her sister.

Marion was sobbing. She had become a little girl again and was creating such a scene that people turned their heads. With a look of contempt, Maud pushed Pip to one side and put her arm around Marion's shoulder. That look felt like a knife going into Pip's heart. Nothing had changed. She was still on the outside looking in.

'She wouldn't do it, Mum,' Marion gulped. 'The stupid bitch told him we'd never be friends.'

Maud Abbott turned to Pip and rounded on her. 'How could you?'

'Let's go somewhere for a cup of tea, Mum,' said Pip, 'then we can talk about it.'

'The shops will be closing soon,' said Maud.

Pip spotted a place a couple of doors down opposite the minster and persuaded the pair of them to come in. They sat in the window seats. The waitress was probably going to tell them they were about to close, but when she saw the state Marion was in, she gave them an uncomfortable smile. Pip ordered tea and sandwiches.

'You're looking well, Mum,' said Pip, taking off her coat. 'I hoped I might see you.'

'Marion says you have two children,' said her mother.

'Yes,' Pip smiled. 'Georgie is seven, nearly eight, and Hazel is five.' She opened her handbag and pulled out a photograph to show her mother. It was of the two of them playing in the garden. 'They're a bit older now. I had it done to send to my husband, only I haven't been able to get it to him. He's a POW. Did Marion tell you? He was captured by the Japs.'

They were interrupted when the waitress brought the tea.

Pip laid her hand over her mother's, but Maud took it away to pour the tea.

'I brought a present for you, Mum,' said Pip, taking a bite from a Spam-and-chutney sandwich. Gosh, she was hungry. 'It's in the car.'

'What happened in there?' her mother asked.

'I can't wait for you to meet Peter,' Pip went on. 'Unfortunately, he was caught up in the fall of Singapore. Everyone thought it was impregnable, but . . .' She stopped. Her mother wasn't even looking at her; she was waiting for Marion to finish drying her eyes.

'All you had to do was tell him we were friends,' Marion hissed. 'I know we've had our ups and downs, but we were all right in the car, weren't we?'

'You hardly even spoke to me,' Pip retaliated. Then

desperate to lighten the mood, she added, 'This is a nice place. Do you live in Wimborne, Mum?'

'Don't change the subject,' Marion spat. 'You cow. This is the second time you've tried to ruin my life.'

'Oh, don't be so melodramatic,' said Pip. 'I might have cooperated if you'd told me what you were up to.'

Marion harrumphed.

By the looks on their faces, the atmosphere was becoming toxic.

'Listen, I'm sorry,' said Pip. 'I don't want to fight with you, but you really got up my nose in there.'

'Then come back with me,' said Marion.

Pip shook her head. 'I'm not prepared to pretend something that isn't true. I don't tell lies. No amount of money is worth selling myself short like that.' She glanced up at her mother. 'Shall I order cakes?'

Her mother, who hadn't eaten a thing, looked out of the window. Pip wriggled a little in her seat. 'Well, if you'll excuse me for a minute, I need the toilet.'

She rose and walked to the back of the room. There was only one toilet, and as they were closing, she found herself behind a queue of two women. Pip struggled to compose herself. This wasn't at all what she'd been expecting. She knew it wouldn't be easy, and she wasn't naive enough to imagine a warm and tearful welcome from her mother, but she had hoped they could try and talk over their differences.

By the time she reached the toilet, Pip was on the verge of crying with disappointment and hurt. With no one else waiting to come in, she allowed herself a couple of minutes to shed a tear or two, then washed her face. After that, she got out her almost depleted pancake compact and applied a fresh coat to her cheeks. There wasn't much left, but pinching her cheeks to make them pink and putting on a spot of lippy made all the difference. Having satisfied herself that no one would know how upset she'd been, she made her way back to the window seat. Her mother and sister were gone. On her plate, Pip found the bill. Beside the plate, she found her mother's present and the one she had bought for her sister. When she looked down, her suit-case was by the chair.

CHAPTER 22

'Mummy, Mummy.' Hazel's excited squeals as she leaned over the bars of the gate to Stella's house alerted them to Pip's return. They had been expecting her, of course, but seeing her *walking* down Salisbury Road with her suitcase in her hand was a bit of a surprise. When she was about halfway towards them, Stella opened the gate and the children ran to meet her. Pip kneeled down and hugged them so fiercely Georgie wriggled to be set free.

Lillian was coming towards them. 'Where's your sister? We were expecting Marion to be with you.'

Georgie was wrestling Pip's hand. 'Can I carry your case, Mummy? Let me carry your case.'

Lillian was still looking for Marion's car. 'Why did she drop you at the top of the road? She could have at least brought you to the door.'

Georgie took the case and staggered along the road with it, while Hazel grabbed her mother's hand. As Pip stood to her feet, Stella and Lillian could see that she was exhausted.

'You look all in,' Stella said.

'I am pretty tired,' Pip confessed.

'What the hell—' Lillian began, but she was stopped short by the nudge Stella gave her in the ribs.

'Let's get you indoors to freshen up,' she said. 'The others will be here soon.'

'Others?' said Pip faintly.

'You've forgotten,' Stella said apologetically. 'It's your birthday party.'

'We've been blowing up lots and lots of balloons,' said Georgie.

'And Auntie Stella let me make jellies,' said Hazel.

'And me,' Flora chipped in.

Hazel tugged on her mother's arm. 'Come and see, Mummy,' she said, her face shining with excitement. 'Which colour will you have? I like the red one best. Auntie Stella says it tastes like strawberries.'

As they pulled their mother indoors, Lillian and Stella exchanged anxious looks behind her back. What on earth had happened? And where was Marion?

'Perhaps we should cancel?' Lillian whispered.

'Too late now,' said Stella. 'They'll be here in less than an hour.'

'But where's Marion?' Lillian whispered. 'Oh God, this is awful.'

They followed the children into the sitting room, where gaily coloured balloons bobbed all along the picture rail. Bunting trailed from corner to corner, and across the bay window, pieces of paper spelling out the words 'Happy birthday, Pip & Marion' clipped the light coming into the room.

238

The look on Pip's face said it all.

'This is a disaster, isn't it?' Lillian whispered to Stella.

'Look, Mummy,' cried Hazel, pointing to the table groaning with food. 'We've made lots of sandwiches too.'

'And sausage rolls,' said Georgie. 'Can I have one now, Auntie Stella? You said I could have one when Mummy comes.'

'Not yet,' Stella said firmly. 'Now, I want you children to go back outside and tell me when you see the first guest arriving.' As they clattered back outside to wait by the gate, she called after them, 'No squabbling, and don't get dirty,' but they were already arguing about who was going to stand on the bottom rung of the gate first.

Pip hadn't moved. She stood, shoulders hunched, staring at the party food.

'If you'd rather cancel . . .' Stella began.

'No, don't do that,' said Pip. 'It's lovely, and you've all gone to so much trouble.'

'Maybe we should have waited,' said Lillian glumly, 'but it seemed like the ideal moment to celebrate.'

'And it is,' said Pip, her voice small and strained.

'I'm sorry, Pip,' said Stella. 'We rather presumed that Marion would be with you.'

'Yeah,' said Lillian, touching Pip's arm. 'Is Marion all right?'

'Oh yes,' said Pip. Her voice had an edge to it. 'Marion is fine. Couldn't be better.'

Stella and Lillian exchanged an anxious glance. 'Did she bring you home?'

'I came on the train,' said Pip, turning to look directly at them for the first time since she'd arrived. 'Look, if you don't mind, I'd rather not talk about it right now. Like you say, people are coming, and I would like to have a wash and change my frock before they do. I had to stay in a horrible, cheap boarding-house last night and I feel like I've been dragged through a hedge backwards.'

'Yes, yes, of course,' said Stella. 'Come upstairs. We took the liberty of bringing one of your dresses over. It's hanging on the back of the door in the bathroom.'

Alone in the bathroom, Pip sat on a small wooden chair at the end of the bath and stared out of the window. It was already getting dark. The garden looked empty and cheerless. Stella scarcely had time for gardening, so what little borders there were were overgrown with weeds. It did nothing to lighten her mood.

Looking up, Pip could see a spider's web stretching from the window to the drainpipe. For some time she stared at a fly desperately trying to free itself from certain death. It had probably spotted the spider waiting in a hollow between the drainpipe and the wall, and knew what was coming.

She stood to her feet and, grasping the edge of the sink, studied her own reflection in the mirror above. She looked a mess. Her hair was all over the place, her face, devoid of make-up, was blotchy, and her skin was dry. She felt as if she'd aged ten years since she'd last stood in front of this mirror.

Why was this happening? Why did her mother dislike her so much? Marion was her sister and yet the minute Pip had refused to collaborate in a lie, she had no time for her. They say blood is thicker than water, but where was the love in all of this? What had she done to deserve such treatment? It was unfair. It was cruel and heartless. Pip sighed. She felt ill used and miserable.

She glanced down and saw that Stella had loaned her a brand-new, fluffy white face flannel, as soft as down. There wasn't time for a bath, so she ran the hot water into the sink and the pipes clanked in protest. Pip soaped the flannel, then rubbed it over her face. She could feel herself giving way to tears again, but she mustn't do it. For the sake of her children and her friends, she had to put it all to one side for the moment.

She lifted her blouse and the petticoat underneath, and washed her tired body. It was only then that she realized that the soap was scented. A delicate rose-petal perfume filled the room. These days, scented soap was as rare as hen's teeth. How kind of Stella. She must have been saving it for a special occasion, maybe for the time Johnny came home on leave, and yet she had given it to Pip.

When she was washed and dry, she spotted her dress hanging on the back of the door. Someone had ironed it beautifully. As Pip pulled it over her arms, she saw a transformation begin in the mirror. Doing up the buttons and the belt, she began to return to her old self. She pinched her cheeks to make them pink and brushed her hair vigorously.

Almost ready, she noticed a small china dish next to where the flannel had been. When she lifted the lid, Pip gasped. Lillian had placed her brand-new lipstick inside. There was also a powder and puff, and a diamanté hair slide. Pip's eyes smarted. Her mother and sister may be unfeeling and heartless, but here was love. Love in a flannel, the soap, the ironed dress, the lipstick and the powder. She took a deep breath. Why should she feel sorry for herself? There was no need. Her family might not care much about her, but she was rich in love and friendship.

When Stella came back downstairs, Lillian said, 'What are we going to say when people ask where Marion is? If we don't have a good answer, they'll be asking questions all evening, and it's obvious that Pip doesn't want to talk about it.'

'We'll say Marion is indisposed,' said Stella. 'We'll say she's come down with something.' She glanced helplessly at Lillian.

'Chickenpox?' Lillian suggested. 'Mumps? Shingles?'

'Yes, that's it,' said Stella. 'Poor Marion has shingles.'

It was a bit of a squash in the sitting room, but the party went well. There were barely enough chairs to go round, so it was just as well that one of Stella's teaching colleagues hadn't turned up.

'I can't think why she's not here,' Stella told Lillian as they made tea in the kitchen. 'She was perfectly fine yesterday.'

'Perhaps she forgot,' said Lillian, trying to be helpful.

'Got the time wrong more like,' Stella chuckled.

Everyone enjoyed themselves, and if Pip looked a bit sad, they put it down to the disappointment she must be feeling that her sister had been unable to come. They chatted and ate, then ate and chatted. Later, they played silly games, like musical chairs for the children and charades for the adults.

The guest list comprised the people who mattered most to Stella, Lillian and Pip. For Pip, there were a couple of the children she looked after, along with their mums. Phyllis, Stella's mother, was there, of course, and she had invited three teachers from her school, though only two had turned up, while Lillian had not only invited her mother, Dorcas, but also Iris, Betty and Mr Knight in an attempt to be more friendly.

The station cafe had been quiet when, heart in mouth, Lillian had walked in a few days ago. Iris, hostile as ever, gave her a haughty glare. 'What do you want?'

'You remember me talking about my friend Pip,' Lillian began.

'Can't say that I do,' said Iris, polishing the counter.

Lillian bit her tongue. 'She's one of the Sussex

Sisters,' she went on, 'and she's got a birthday coming up.'

'And?'

'She's just found her long-lost sister, so we thought we would throw a special birthday party, and I wondered if you would like to come along.'

She could see by her expression that she'd taken the wind out of Iris's sails. Lillian suppressed a small smile.

'It's at Salisbury Road,' Lillian went on. 'It won't be late, because most of us have got kiddies, but you'd be very welcome to come.'

'Welcome to come to what?' a voice interrupted. It was Betty.

'A party,' Lillian said. 'It would be lovely if you'd come along too.'

'I'll think about it,' said Iris, but surprisingly, they had both turned up on the doorstep. Lillian was delighted. Mr Knight had accepted his invitation too. Perhaps at long last Iris had buried the hatchet and they could all start again. At first, they sat stiffly, only speaking when spoken to, but as Lillian had fussed around them like an old hen, slowly but surely there'd been a noticeable thawing.

As eating the nibbles drew to a close, Stella gave Pip her birthday presents. There was a pile of equal size for Marion, which Stella put on the sideboard with a promise to do her best to get them to her. Everyone enjoyed seeing Pip open her presents, which although not expensive were well received. In fact, Pip thought each one was terrific.

'Anyone got a party piece?' Stella asked eventually.

To everyone's surprise, Mr Knight asked for a pack of cards. Then he amazed them all with some very clever card tricks.

'How on earth did he do that?' cried Pip. He had shuffled the pack and separated it into two piles, and then, at the end of a complex method of deciding which ones to get rid of and which to keep, he had ended up with the very card she had chosen. No wonder they all applauded enthusiastically.

'I had no idea he was a magician,' Lillian whispered confidentially.

'He used to be on stage before the war,' said Betty.

'He's really good,' said Pip as Mr Knight produced the ace of hearts from behind Georgie's ear. 'I can't think why he hides his talent.'

'Probably because of his wife,' said Betty, clearly enjoying being the fount of all knowledge. The others waited with bated breath. Mr Knight was asking one of Pip's mums to write her name on the front of the king of diamonds.

'His act was called the Great Fabio,' Betty told them out of the corner of her mouth. 'His wife was his glamorous assistant, though in my humble opinion, she isn't that good-looking.'

Pip grinned.

'When he came back from Dunkirk with only one eye, she left him for a trumpet player.' Betty sniffed.

'He's very bitter about it. Personally, I don't blame him.'

Mr Knight was asking the lady to open her closed handbag. The king of diamonds was inside. Everybody clapped.

'He seems all right now,' Lillian remarked.

Stella came to join them.

'By the way, you've come undone,' said Lillian. She pointed to Betty's brooch. The pin had come undone and was hanging from her blouse collar in a precarious way.

'Silly thing,' said Betty. 'I keep meaning to get it fixed.'

'It's very pretty,' Stella remarked.

'I got it from the market,' Betty said.

'One of my other customers had one,' said Iris. 'They're quite popular.'

'They're not very well made,' said Betty, refastening the brooch.

'You'll lose the darned thing one day,' Iris remarked sniffily, 'you mark my words.'

They rounded off the occasion with a sing-song round the piano, and by the time the party was finished, Pip looked all in.

Everyone was putting on their coats when the doorbell rang.

'Oh, don't tell me this is Carol here at last,' said Stella as she went to open the door. 'She never gets the time right.'

But it wasn't her teacher friend. It was a telegram

boy. As soon as she saw him, Stella put her hand to her mouth and let out a small whimper.

'What is it?' said Pip.

'Mrs Edmund Bell?' The boy, a spotty-faced fellow aged about fifteen, held out a buff-coloured envelope. 'Any reply?'

'You must have made a mistake, love,' said Pip, taking charge. 'This is Mrs Bell, but her husband is Mr John Bell.'

'Actually,' said Stella, interrupting, 'I am Mrs Edmund Bell. My husband is Edmund John Bell.' She turned to Pip. 'He doesn't like his first name, you see. That's why he uses his second name all the time.'

'Is there an answer, madam?' said the boy, holding out the telegram.

'Everyone calls him Johnny in the regiment,' Stella went on. She knew she was babbling, but she couldn't help it: anything to delay opening the damned thing. 'Everyone except his mother, of course. She calls him John. Funny that, isn't it? Calling your child by one name, then using his second name.' Her laughter was brittle.

'Stella,' Pip said gently, 'the telegram boy is waiting.'

Stella snatched the envelope.

'Shall I wait for an answer, madam?' the boy said again.

Stella looked down at the envelope in her trembling hand.

'Shall I open it?' said Pip.

Stella nodded. By now, the others had gathered

247

round her in the hallway and Phyllis had pushed her way to the front.

Pip tore it open. 'Oh, Stella,' she gasped as she read the contents. 'I'm so sorry.'

Phyllis slipped her arm around Stella's waist and pulled her close. Stella, completely motionless, stared into space. Lillian leaned over Pip's shoulder, but before she closed the door, she said to the waiting boy, 'There's no reply, thank you.'

'Read it,' said Stella.

'I think you might like to read it on your own,' Pip began.

'Read it!'

Pip took in a breath. '*It is with deep regret . . .*'

But the rest of the sentence was completely lost under the sound of Stella's howl of unbridled grief as she sank to her knees and covered her face with her hands.

CHAPTER 23

Lillian was nervous but excited. She and Nigel had arranged to meet in a pub called the Mulberry Arms in Goring-by-Sea. They had been meeting regularly for the past few months, usually in a pub close, but not too close, to home. Gradually they'd got to know each other and become firm friends. Lillian secretly hoped for more, but for now she had settled for 'no funny business'.

In the weeks since Stella had had that telegram, meeting Nigel had been the one thing that kept Lillian going. The Sussex Sisters had come to a grinding halt. Stella had been too ill to carry on. She'd also had to give up her teaching. Some people cruelly remarked that other people suffered just as much and managed to keep going, but Lillian and Pip didn't see it like that. Stella had kept going all the time Johnny was a prisoner. She'd been brave, and she'd been a great encourager of others, but when she heard that he was missing, believed killed, it was as if the legs had been chopped from under her. Phyllis had taken her to Broadwater for a while, and when now she'd finally returned home,

Judith sometimes took her around with her on her WVS assignments. Apart from Pip and Lillian stopping by and one of the mums from the school, a Mrs Dennison, who came calling with cakes every so often, Stella, a shadow of her former self, saw no one.

The Mulberry Arms was quite posh and a fairly new building. The Peacock Hall Hotel had stood on the site until 1937, when it was rebuilt as a roadhouse. The surroundings seemed a world away from the bombed-out areas of the big cities and the pockmarked streets of Worthing, where German pilots machine-gunned the houses before returning home. However, even the better-off had their share of sadness. The terrors of war had reached the sleepy village of Goring-by-Sea, when the landlord and his wife, Len and Rebecca Knight, had lost their son in the sinking of HMS *Hood* in 1941.

When she got off the bus, Nigel was waiting outside the bus shelter.

'I've been on tenterhooks that you wouldn't come,' he said, grasping her hands eagerly.

'I nearly didn't,' she admitted. 'My mother is expecting me home tonight.'

'Do you think she'll worry?'

Lillian shook her head. 'She knows I've been spending time with Stella. With a bit of luck, she'll think I've missed the bus back.'

Nigel nodded. 'How is Stella?'

'Getting there,' said Lillian. 'She's lost a lot of

weight, but perhaps the country life will suit her better.'

By the time Christmas 1943 had come round, everybody was really worried about Stella. She'd lost nearly two and a half stone, something that even her mother felt she could ill afford to do, so with the coming of the new year, they'd packed her off to Mrs Elkins at the farm in Pulborough.

Mrs Elkins was such a motherly type that everyone was convinced that some mollycoddling and a bit of home cooking would do the trick. Stella was improving, but it was obvious that it would be a long, slow haul. She had sunk into a deep depression and no one was quite sure how to help. Pip went for the day every now and then, and Lillian was on her way back from there, having spent a couple of days with their friend.

Lillian shivered.

'Let's get you in the warm,' Nigel said, taking her suitcase and leading her towards the entrance.

The inside of the public house was even more like a hotel. Modern chairs were scattered in semicircles of fours round small, highly polished tables. The Art Deco walls and panelling gave a rather superior feel to the place. At one end of the room, a cheerful fire blazed in the hearth. The bar was lavish rather than seedy, and waiters glided between the customers with their drinks on silver trays. Nigel found them a quiet table hidden discreetly in a corner.

'What would you like to drink?'

Lillian wasn't sure what to ask for. She'd only ever

been in a posh pub once before, and that was on her wedding day, when she and Gordon had stopped at the Swan on the High Street on their way back from church. Compared with the newness of the Mulberry, it had been a little lacking.

'Do you like sherry?' Nigel asked. 'Or port?'

'Sweet sherry will be fine,' said Lillian, remembering the taste from a Christmas past.

She watched him as he called the waiter and ordered their drinks. Good-looking, strong and dependable. When he'd promised 'no funny business', she'd welcomed the opportunity to get to know him. Her courtship with Gordon had been non-existent, but back then he'd been in a terrible hurry and she'd been curious. Their relationship had only ever been about sex. But by the time she and Nigel had made the final arrangements to meet at the Mulberry, they'd both known 'no funny business' would prove to be a promise much too hard to keep.

Her mind drifted back to the first time they'd met. With their drinks in situ, Nigel, shyly to start with, had told her something about himself. Apparently, he'd been a sickly child. He'd missed out on his schooling, but his mother had arranged for him to have piano lessons.

'That was something I could practise on my own whenever I was well enough,' he had explained.

Lillian had been impressed to hear how hard he'd worked. He had reached a high standard and had been a soloist in more than a dozen concerts. When he left school, Nigel had been apprenticed to a sign-writer. He'd enjoyed the work, but when the war came along, he'd tried to enlist but had been refused for all three services because of his weak chest. In the end, he'd applied to the Lancing carriage works.

'I was a bit puzzled when you said you were a sign-writer,' she'd told him. 'All the signs were taken down for the duration.'

'The work is a bit dreary,' he'd admitted, 'but there are plenty of other signs needed on a train. I write the bit above the communication cord. You know – "Penalty for improper use £20." Not to mention putting the carriage numbers on the outside.' He grinned. He was on a roll now. 'Then there's "No spitting" and "Ladies only" on at least one carriage per train. Oh, and "Gentlemen, lift the seat"!'

'OK, OK,' she laughed.

'It's not earth-shattering stuff, but at least I feel like I'm doing my bit. Your turn now. Tell me something about you.'

There wasn't much to tell, but she'd explained how one minute she'd been a schoolgirl and the next minute she'd been swept along by Gordon and got herself into trouble. She'd told him how difficult things had been. 'He hated the idea of getting married as much as I did,' she'd said, 'but we had no choice. The only thing I don't regret is having Flora.'

That was the first time that Nigel had looked her in the eye. 'I'd like to meet her sometime,' he said softly.

Lillian had blushed as his finger, wrapped round his

pint on the table, touched the back of her hand and her heart raced. She'd moved her hand away, but it was as if he'd left an indelible mark on it. That was probably the moment she'd fallen in love with him.

Nigel leaned back in his chair. 'Do you think Stella will ever sing again?' he asked, bringing Lillian back to the here and now.

'I think so,' said Lillian. 'She did mention it a couple of times while I was there.'

'I'm glad,' said Nigel.

'But she's definitely not ready yet,' Lillian cautioned.

He toyed with her fingers across the table. 'Have you ever thought about going solo?' he asked. He had a furtive look about him, as if he was embarrassed to ask.

'Solo?' said Lillian. She was slightly shocked, but at the same time she felt a tingle of excitement.

'I'm not suggesting that you desert the Sussex Sisters,' he said, 'but until Stella is well again, you could easily do it on your own.'

'Solo,' she said again.

He looked down at his beer mat and traced his finger round the edge. 'I'd be happy to play for you if you like.'

Their eyes met.

'Oh, I don't know,' she blurted out. 'I wouldn't want to upset anyone. I've never really thought about it. What would Pip and Stella think? Oh, I don't know.'

'It would be a shame to waste such a talent,' he said. 'Promise me you'll think about it.'

She nodded. 'Funny how . . .' She paused. Her voice was high and squeaky. She cleared her throat. 'Funny how,' she began again in a normal tone of voice, 'we both enjoy music, isn't it?'

'That's because we're soulmates,' he said huskily. He took her hand in his. 'There's still time for you to back out if you're not ready, my darling.'

'I don't want to back out, Nigel.'

She looked up and their eyes locked.

'I have booked us a room,' he said. 'First floor, front.'

She glanced about her nervously.

'Nobody knows,' he said reassuringly. 'We are Mr and Mrs Wentworth, so as soon as you're ready . . .'

Her hand shook as she sipped the last of her sherry, but she gave him a wobbly smile. Yes, she was ready now, as ready as she'd ever be. She was really going to do this. Stella was right. When you love someone, really, really love them, you want it more than anything else in the world.

CHAPTER 24

Betty, Iris and Mr Knight were the first to know that Lillian was thinking about going solo. The atmosphere between them had changed markedly since Lillian had invited them all to Pip's party. Iris always had a cup of tea waiting for her when she got to the end of her shift, and right from the word go, Mr Knight had never failed to find out where the Sussex Sisters were playing. He made sure that he was in the audience. The three of them always enquired after Stella when Lillian had been to see her, and Betty told Lillian she couldn't wait for the Sussex Sisters to get back together again.

'Do you think I'd be being disloyal if I went solo?' Lillian asked. 'I don't want to offend Stella and Pip, but it really doesn't look as if the Sussex Sisters are going anywhere, and I do so enjoy singing.'

'I reckon if you told them, they'd cheer you all the way,' said Mr Knight. 'They seem like a lovely bunch of girls.'

'Mr Knight is right,' said Iris. 'It would be such a shame if you gave up now.'

'And you've got a lovely voice,' said Betty. 'Hasn't she, Ron?'

Mr Knight nodded vigorously.

'Would you come and see me if it was just me on stage?'

'Like a shot,' said Mr Knight.

As Lillian went back to her duties, he smiled after her. 'That girl has restored my faith in human nature,' he said.

Georgie hated being put in the pram, but Pip insisted.

'It's too far for you to walk all the way to Chaucer Road,' she told him.

They were on their way to a birthday party. Georgie hadn't minded going in the pram when he was younger, but now that he was older, the bigger boys teased him mercilessly and he hated it. 'Little Georgie Porgie been for walkies in your pram?' they'd say in a sing-song voice, or else they'd croon, 'Rock-a-bye baby, in the treetop . . .' and fall about laughing. He would go bright red and ball his fists, but there was nothing he could do about it.

Even though the springs groaned under the combined weight of Georgie and Hazel, once Pip had got the momentum going, it seemed far quicker than having to stop every now and then to wait for tired little legs to catch up with her. She often wondered why, when they had such energy in the garden, children would drag their feet and complain when she was in a hurry to be somewhere.

Usually, as soon as his mother lifted him up to put him in the pram, Georgie would begin to make a terrible fuss, but today she didn't seem to notice that he was a willing passenger. Pip had talked about taking out the boards that kept the mattress flat to give them more room for their legs, but to Georgie's great relief, she'd changed her mind.

'No, I'd better leave them where they are,' she'd said. 'I need a flat surface for the plates of food.'

There was a great pile of food between their legs, and Hazel was holding on to six balloons, each tied with a piece of string. The party was for Sarah Hollick, a little girl who had been coming to Pip's house since she was three. Now that she had reached the ripe old age of five, she would be going to school after the Easter holidays.

As they bumped along the pavement, Georgie heard a rolling noise coming from the well of the pram. He held his breath and glanced anxiously at his mother. He knew what it was, and when Hazel put her head on one side as if she was listening, he had to act quickly. Whatever happened, he couldn't let his mother lift the boards and look underneath. Throwing his head back, he struck up a loud rendition of 'Ten Green Bottles', and after a few bars, Hazel joined in.

'You're in fine voice today, Georgie,' said his mother. 'You sound very happy.'

'That's because I like parties,' he said. 'When I grow up, I shall have one every day.'

'Silly boy,' Pip chuckled. 'The reason why parties are such fun is because we don't have them very often.'

When they reached Sarah's house, Pip parked the pram by the wall and hauled Georgie and his sister out. With the brake on, the rolling noise stopped.

'Wait here,' said Pip.

'You'd better not leave Hazel here with those balloons,' said Georgie, doing his best to sound helpful. 'I bet she'll let go of the strings.'

'Will not,' said his sister indignantly.

'Georgie's right,' said Pip. 'You'd better come with me, darling.'

'I can hold on to them, Mummy,' said Hazel. 'Really I can.' But much to her brother's relief, her mother led her away.

Georgie glanced around. He was alone, but he'd have to be quick. Shoving the food to the top of the mattress, he fished about and pulled up one of the three boards that lay over the bottom of the pram. Pushing his hand into the well underneath, he felt around. It wasn't there. Taking out his hand, Georgie leaned heavily on the handle and heard it roll towards him. When he put his hand under the mattress and lifted the board a second time, the jagged edge of something almost broke the skin on his fingers. He grabbed the first piece of shrapnel and stuffed it into his pocket. The second piece was a lot smaller, but he had it in a trice. As his fingers touched something hard and cylindrical, he could hear his mother coming. A second later, Goliath was in his pocket. All he had to do now was put

259

everything straight. As he wiggled the false bottom into place, one of the plates on top of the mattress shifted sideways and a couple of sandwiches slid off.

'Oh, Georgie,' said a cross voice behind him. 'What on earth do you think you are doing?'

'Sorry, Mummy.'

'Why don't you leave things alone?' said Pip, exasperated.

Georgie widened his eyes and with an innocent expression said, 'I was only trying to help, Mummy.'

'Hello, you two.'

Thankfully, they were interrupted by Auntie Lillian's cheery call, and a second later, the two women headed into the house carrying the plates of sandwiches. Georgie patted his pocket. After a whole winter being locked up in his father's shed, he'd finally got Goliath and the shrapnel back.

While Mrs Hollick played pass the parcel with the children in the kitchen, Pip and Lillian were sent to the kitchen to make a pot of tea, and it was here that Lillian asked Pip what she thought about her going solo.

'I think it's a marvellous idea,' cried Pip, secretly relieved. 'And if Nigel is willing to play the piano for you, why not?'

'It's only until Stella is well again,' Lillian cautioned.

'Of course,' said Pip.

'And you're really sure you don't mind?'

'Absolutely not,' said Pip.

The kettle was boiling and they searched for cups. 'Have you seen anything of Stella lately?'

Pip shook her head. 'Not for a couple of weeks,' she said, laying a tray, 'when I took the children over on the bus for the day. Have you?'

'I went a couple of days ago,' said Lillian. 'I told her about going solo and she was all right about it. I must say she looks a lot better.'

'Any sign of her coming back?'

Lillian shook her head. 'Her house has been requisitioned as a billet, so she says she might as well stay with Mrs Elkins for the duration. She says being away from Worthing helps.'

The kettle whistled and Pip poured the water into a teapot.

'I can't say I'm surprised,' said Lillian, getting a bottle of milk from the cold-water bucket in the larder. 'She took Johnny's death very hard, and she gets on well with Mrs Elkins. In fact, I'd be surprised if she ever came back to Worthing. I wish this damned war would end soon.'

'You and me both,' said Pip.

When the party was over, the two women walked home together.

'Tell you what,' Pip suddenly said. 'I've got a couple of evening dresses in my wardrobe. I haven't worn them in years. If you fancy borrowing one of them, you're most welcome.'

Lillian beamed. 'Thanks, Pip.'

Flora and Hazel were tired and glad of a lift, but Pip

261

had let Georgie walk beside them. She stared at his pockets. They were bulging. 'What have you got in your pockets, Georgie?'

'Nothing, Mummy.'

'Yes, you have. They're sticking out. Come here.'

Her son dragged himself reluctantly back to his mother. Pip put her hand in one pocket and pulled out two jagged pieces of shrapnel. 'Georgie!'

'It's all right, Mummy. It can't hurt you.'

'No, but it can make a nasty hole in your trousers,' she scolded. Lillian turned her head and tried not to smile. Pip frowned. 'What's that in the other pocket?'

'Only my hanky,' said Georgie, holding it up.

'Oh, all right, then,' said his mother, 'but I'm keeping this until we get home.'

Stuffing his handkerchief back in his pocket, Georgie walked on ahead. Phew, that was a lucky escape. Good job she hadn't taken the hanky as well. Goliath was wrapped up inside and he was sure she would never let him have it back.

Back at Pip's house, Lillian followed her upstairs and into her bedroom. Neat and tidy, the dressing table was dominated by a picture of Peter. Pip was already looking in the wardrobe, but Lillian hesitated by the door. 'I don't suppose you've heard from your Peter yet?'

Pip's face clouded as she shook her head.

'It must be awful for you,' said Lillian. 'I don't know how you keep going.'

'I have to,' she said, 'for the sake of the children.'

'How long has it been since you heard from him?' Lillian began again.

'Almost two years,' said Pip. 'He was captured in February 1942.' Lillian shuffled her feet awkwardly. 'It's all right,' she went on, her tone flat and expressionless. 'I've got used to it.' They regarded each other for a moment or two; then Pip added, 'What about you? Your Gordon has been a prisoner a lot longer.'

Lillian shrugged. 'He's all right. Apart from losing his freedom, he's having it cushy.'

Pip looked a tad surprised.

'Think about it,' said Lillian. 'No bombing, no queuing; he gets Red Cross parcels from just about everywhere, and from what I can gather, they put on shows and play cricket all the time.'

'It must get a bit boring,' said Pip.

'I wouldn't mind swapping with him,' said Lillian.

Pip giggled. 'I bet you wouldn't. You'd be in your element with all those men.'

Lillian pretended to be shocked. 'Why, Mrs Sinclair, I don't know what you mean.'

There was always something to do on the farm and Stella was beginning to love it. It felt as if she had, or was, emerging from a very long tunnel. She had arrived in Pulborough just after Christmas, but she hardly recalled a single day. All she remembered was the pain in her chest. It was physical and it was deep. At times, it was so bad she could hardly breathe. She was exhausted, and as weak as a kitten. She had experienced grief before, when her father died, but this gnawing emptiness was nowhere near the same.

When she had visited the farm way back in the summer, the days were long, with up to seventeen hours of daylight between sunrise and sunset. With her arrival in the winter, the days were much shorter, with only eight and then nine hours of daylight, and yet there was always something to do. Silted ditches were cleared, fences repaired and some farm machinery given a good overhaul. Once the really bad winter weather set in during January and February, Mr Elkins and the Italian POWs seconded to work on the farm spent their time caring for the animals. With frost and snow on the ground, the cows, horses and pigs had to be housed and fed inside, which meant a lot more work keeping them clean. The advent of spring took the workload up a gear. Lambing was in full swing by February, and at the same time several sows farrowed. Although Stella helped on the farm and in particular helped Mrs Elkins in the house, she had another string to her bow.

It began when she took a walk into Pulborough. Her thoughts were all over the place, albeit mostly on Johnny, but when she passed the place where she, Pip and Lillian had shared afternoon tea with Brenda, she couldn't resist going in.

She'd sat in the same window seat and enjoyed sandwiches and cake. Brenda had been moved over to Horsham, but they still kept in touch, and Stella thought it would be nice to invite her back on her day off. The room was much the same, except that the piano was silent.

'What happened to your pianist?' she'd asked the waiter.

'He got called up.'

Stella gave him a sympathetic nod and carried on eating. As time went on, she began to feel the pull, and before long her fingers were itching to touch the keyboard. She looked around. The waiters had momentarily left the room and all at once she found herself seated on the piano stool and lifting the piano lid. She chose something soothing and restful – part of Beethoven's 'Moonlight Sonata' – and as the notes filled the air, a reverent hush spread over the room. Stella quickly became totally absorbed in the music and found herself drifting on a haze of lovely memories. As she played the last note, she realized her cheeks were wet. Hastily she brushed the tears away with her hand and made to stand up. It was only then that she realized everyone in the room was applauding. She bowed her head in acknowledgement of the sea of smiling faces, and after listening to their pleas, she placed her hands back on the keyboard. Since that day, Stella had played the piano in the hotel every afternoon except Sunday. Her music not only gave pleasure to the hotel guests but it somehow helped her to find healing.

Lillian, Pip and their children travelled over to see her, as did her mother and Desmond and Judith, but Stella couldn't bring herself to return to Worthing. It would be like picking at a scab. The memories were too painful, too raw.

'Are you going to Lillian's show?' Betty asked. She and Iris were in the cafe washing out the teapot and emptying the urn at the end of another day.

'I can't,' said Iris. 'My sister is coming from Winchester tomorrow. I haven't had a minute to myself and I've got to get the place straight.'

'Oh,' said Betty, clearly disappointed.

'Why not talk to Mr Knight?' said Iris. 'He'll take you.'

'Oh, I couldn't,' said Betty, her face colouring. 'I wouldn't have the nerve.'

'Why ever not?' said Iris. 'It's not as if you've got a silly schoolgirl crush on him, is it? You're just supporting a work colleague.'

'Well, if you put it like that,' Betty said.

As it turned out, Betty had a wonderful time. She and Mr Knight had caught the bus to Lancing and walked along the seafront. Lillian had given their names to the guard on the gate, and once they'd produced their identification cards, they were in. The show was in the canteen, and almost as soon as they'd arrived, they'd blended in with the workers.

Mr Knight bought her a cup of tea and they sat fairly near the front. Betty felt very spoiled. It was a long time since she'd felt so happy. She knew they weren't on a date, as everybody called it, but she enjoyed the company of this man. He made her feel comfortable and she knew she could make him happy, she was sure of it. There were a couple of supporting artists and then Lillian was announced. She glided across the stage in a pale blue full-length evening dress with a sequinned neckline. It hugged her body and showed off her trim figure. She looked every inch the star. Mr Knight's eyes shone, and along with everyone else in the canteen, he applauded enthusiastically. Her pianist played an introduction and Lillian began with 'Miss You', a song made famous by Dinah Shore.

At the end of the show, a hooter sounded, and late as it was, it was time for everyone to go back to work. The Lancing carriage works worked a twenty-four-hour day in three shifts. Mr Knight wanted to hang around with the hope of speaking to Lillian, but their 'minder' escorted them back to the gate.

As they waited for the bus to return them to Worthing, Mr Knight hummed to himself. Eventually, he glanced at Betty, his eyes bright with excitement. 'Magic,' he whispered. 'Wasn't she magic?'

By May, Stella had made a whole set of new friends. She had no desire to continue with the Sussex Sisters, and it seemed she wasn't alone. Lillian had embarked on a solo career, with that nice man from the Lancing carriage works playing the piano for her. Stella wondered vaguely if there was anything going on between them. Lillian was certainly looking a lot happier, but Stella didn't like to ask. As for Pip, after that rather unsavoury business with her twin sister, she seemed to have settled back down. Her children were a credit to her, and although it would have been nice for her to get a letter from Peter, she apparently had no problem in keeping the faith that one day he would come back to her.

Stella's walk to the hotel was particularly pleasant today. As the sun grew stronger each day, everything had that fresh, green, bursting-from-the-bud look about it. In the hedgerows, blackthorn was in flower, primroses danced beside the ditches, and she spotted the blue haze of bluebells in a little copse. A blackbird sang in a willow tree, and in the fields, newborn lambs frolicked and played.

The hotel receptionist, Mr Grant, greeted her as she walked into the lobby. 'Ah, there you are, Stella. Mr Wingate wants to see you.'

'Before or after I play?' Stella asked as she took off her hat and gloves. Although spring was well under way, there was still a nip in the air, and it would be a bit chilly by the time she walked home at four-thirty.

'Now,' said Mr Grant. A dapper little man dressed in his usual suit with waistcoat and watch chain, he was usually serious-faced and businesslike with her, but today his face was lit up. He was actually grinning. She couldn't recall ever seeing him like that before. She stood for a moment, simply staring. With a flick of his hand, he waved her on her way, and as she turned into the corridor, she could have sworn she heard him

268

chuckle. What on earth was all that about? And why would the hotel manager want to see her?

As she headed for the office, she became aware that she was the object of some curiosity. Hotel guests huddled together in small groups and turned away as she approached. The odd thing was, their actions didn't seem to be malicious. They were pleased, happy, smiling.

Stella knocked politely and pushed open the office door. Mr Wingate, who was seated at his desk, rose as she walked in. 'Ah, Stella,' he beamed. 'We have had a telephone call from your mother.'

For a second, Stella's heart almost stopped, but then it occurred to her that he was still smiling.

'In fact,' he went on, 'we have had a deluge of telephone calls. Your father-in-law, your friend Mrs Sinclair, Mrs Elkins . . .'

'Mrs Elkins?' Stella said faintly.

'They are all desperate to get hold of you.'

'But why?'

Mr Wingate came round the desk. 'I'm pretty sure why they want to talk to you, but first I want you to come into the staff rest room. There's someone I want you to meet.'

He took her arm and they crossed the corridor together. He pushed the door open and indicated that she should go in ahead of him. The room was unusually tidy, and there were fresh flowers on the table. Someone was standing looking out of the window onto the formal gardens. A man in uniform. Her heart

269

began to thump. Stella heard the door closing softly behind her and the man turned round. She gaped at him open-mouthed.

'Hello, Freckle-Face.' Then he opened his arms and she ran to him with a cry of delight.

'Johnny! Oh, my darling Johnny.'

CHAPTER 25

'I thought you were dead.' Stella's first words of greeting reverberated round and round his head. As soon as he had arrived, Johnny had booked a room, but when Mr Wingate discovered who he was, he had put them in the bridal suite at no extra cost. It was very plush, with a big double bed and a comfortable sofa overlooking the water meadow. At first, he'd headed for home. The officers billeted at Salisbury Road had given him quite a shock when they'd told him they had no idea where Stella was. From there he'd gone to his parents'. As soon as he'd found out where Stella was staying, he'd wanted to leave straight away, but it didn't seem fair to his mother. After a few agonizing hours, he'd set out for Pulborough. He'd told them not to tell her. He wanted to surprise her.

They had been shy at first, like new lovers, but gradually, as they lay in each other's arms, they rediscovered each other. He had a lean, hungry look as they made love. The first time was much too quick. Johnny was apologetic.

'I'm sorry, Freckle-Face. I'm a bit out of practice. It's been too long.'

Putting a finger over his lips to silence him, she snuggled into his arms. 'They sent me a telegram saying you were missing, believed killed.'

'I escaped,' he said.

'Was that when you wrote the letter telling me that you had a plan? I wondered what that was all about.'

'That was the first time I escaped,' he said. 'I didn't last long on the outside. Have you got any cigarettes?'

She shook her head. 'But there should be some complimentary ones in the box on the table.' He got out of bed and went to get one. He was naked, but she watched him, conscious that he was very thin. He lit a cigarette and came back to bed with the ashtray.

'We got sent to Benghazi until Monty came back to finish the job,' he said. 'The first time I had a go at getting away, Nobby Clarke and I found some Italian uniforms and a motorbike. We didn't last long, and when they caught us at a checkpoint, they said we were going to be shot.'

Stella shivered. He leaned over her and smiled. 'But don't worry, Freckle-Face,' he teased. 'As you can see, it was a hollow threat.'

'And the second time?'

'When the Eyeties threw in the towel, the Germans were rounding up all Allied prisoners to take us to camps in Germany,' Johnny said after a long draw on his cigarette. 'Nobby and I legged it then.' He paused. 'We were lucky. An Italian woman found us a safe house until the partisans came. They hid us in the mountains for several months until it was safe enough to get us to Switzerland.' He sighed. 'While we were with them, we joined with the guerrillas for a while. The fighting was fierce and the stakes were high.' He looked away for a second and, chewing his lip, added, 'I'm afraid poor old Nobby didn't make it.'

He stubbed out his cigarette and looked down at her. 'What about you? They tell me you're a pretty good singer.'

'You should know,' she quipped. 'You've heard me in the bath often enough.'

He laughed. 'Where did you sing exactly?'

'Didn't you get my letters?' she asked.

'I did,' said Johnny, 'but they're ages old. What have you been doing recently?'

'Mostly the camps,' she said, 'but we did a couple of performances at Worthing Hospital and at the Canadian hospital by the station in Shaftesbury Road. It was all for charity.'

'Sounds wonderful,' he said. 'Will I get to hear you?'

Stella looked a bit uncomfortable. 'I gave it all up when I got the telegram.'

'Oh, darling,' he said sympathetically.

'I felt like I didn't want to go on without you.'

He kissed her tenderly. 'I couldn't let you know I was alive. It just wasn't possible.'

'I know,' she said. 'Anyway, now Lillian has gone solo, I don't suppose the Sussex Sisters will ever get back together again.'

Downstairs, they heard the dinner gong. Stella pulled back the bedclothes and started to get up. Johnny pushed her back down gently.

'They'll bring us something to eat when I ring,' he said. He traced his finger along the line of her body from her waist to her thigh. It felt deliciously sexy. 'You do know I'm going back.'

She stared at him, horrified.

'I have to, darling,' he said. 'The Allies may have invaded, but it's not over yet. I get the feeling that Jerry will fight on to the last man standing.'

'But you've already done so much,' she protested. Her eyes filled with tears. This was so unfair. She'd thought he was dead for months and months, he'd only just got back, and now he was going again. 'Do you have to go? Don't tell me you volunteered.'

He laid his hand across her hip. 'I haven't volunteered, but I do have some very useful contacts. I must go back, darling. My knowledge could save lives.'

'Oh, Johnny.' Her voice was thick with emotion.

'I know,' he said, kissing her. 'I know.' That lean, hungry look was there again as he rolled over on top of her, but this time it was in her eyes as well.

The audiences absolutely loved her. Lillian was intoxicated by standing ovations, the flowers, the nylons and the bottles of perfume she received after every performance. The money was good too. Her one and only evening dress (on loan from Pip) became two and then three. The money she had saved from her pay rise was put to good use. She posed for photographs and did publicity shots, and was invited to sing at official functions. It had only been a few weeks since she'd decided to go it alone, but she was riding high, and Nigel was the icing on the cake.

Whenever they met, they made plans for their future. She told Nigel she would write to Gordon and ask him for a divorce. She was utterly convinced that he wouldn't mind as his letters were so few and far between now. Because she didn't want Nigel's name dragged through the mud, Lillian said she was willing to pay a professional to act as a co-respondent. 'I'll book a room in a hotel in Brighton,' she told Nigel as they lay in each other's arms. 'People do it all the time.'

But Nigel was horrified. 'But that means you'll be labelled an adulteress.'

Lillian giggled. 'Which is what I am, I suppose.'

'Darling, you don't understand,' he went on. 'If you get a bad name, Gordon can get custody of Flora.'

Lillian sat up. 'Could he?' She frowned thoughtfully. 'I don't think he'd do that. He never wanted her in the first place, and he's been away so long, he doesn't even know her.'

Nigel shook his head. 'All I am saying is, you can never be sure what people will do out of spite.'

The thought of maybe losing Flora hit home. 'Oh, Nigel, what are we going to do?'

He drew her close. 'Let's leave things as they are for

the moment. The war is dragging on forever. It could be years before Gordon gets back.'

'But I want us to be married,' she said petulantly.

'And I do too,' he said, 'but let's talk to Gordon when he gets back. That would be much better than putting it in a letter.'

She lay back with a sigh. Nigel was right. It would be kinder to wait until Gordon got home, but in the meantime . . .

Georgie managed to skip along the back alley without a care in the world, but when he reached the corner, he was surprised to see Billy waiting for him. In an uncharacteristic move, Billy put his arm around Georgie's shoulder.

'Don't look round,' he said quietly right into Georgie's ear, 'but your mum has followed you.'

Georgie stiffened and almost turned his head.

'*Don't* move,' Billy hissed. Then beckoning Norman over to them, he said quietly, 'Here, Norm, give him one of your sweets.'

It was obvious that Norman wasn't too keen to share his booty with Georgie, but nobody argued with the gang leader. He handed him a farthing chew and Georgie stuffed it into his mouth.

A couple of seconds later, Gideon, who had been sitting on the rim of the fence, jumped down. 'It's OK. She's gone now.'

Georgie turned round. 'Why would she—' he began.

'She was just checking that we're not bullying you,'

said Billy, giving him a playful smack on the side of his head.

In May, it was time to get new ration books again. On previous occasions, everyone had to queue at the town hall. The authorities made it as easy as possible by spreading the letters of the alphabet over certain days, but everyone had to watch the newspapers to find out which particular day their name was available. It didn't work. There were always people who forgot or turned up on the wrong day. This time, it was a lot easier because the council deployed travelling vans. As she was registered in the town, Stella was forced to return to Worthing for her new book. She had no home of her own, but it was good to meet up with old friends. Johnny had gone back, but she got regular letters now. There was still the fear that he might be killed before it all ended, but Stella was back to her old self. Moving in with Phyllis in Broadwater helped a lot.

'We heard that Johnny made it home,' Pip said when they met up again. 'I bet it was an absolute joy to see him.'

'It was,' said Stella. She felt a little coy talking about it. 'We had a day and a half together.'

'Is that all?' Pip sympathized as she pushed up her turban, which was falling over her eyes. They were in one of her shops and she was busy wiping out a cupboard to get ready for a new tenant. 'That's rotten luck.'

'What about you?' Stella asked. 'Do you miss being in the Sussex Sisters?'

'Yes and no,' said Pip. 'I miss being with you and Lillian, but it was quite hard to find babysitters and things.'

'We never gave it much thought,' said Stella apologetically. 'Lillian has Dorcas, but of course you were on your own. I'm sorry.'

'What for?'

'Being thoughtless.'

Pip smiled. 'Don't worry about it.' She resumed battle with the cupboard. The previous tenant had obviously dropped something slimy inside. Pip still had no news of Peter. It seemed extraordinary that she had been in the dark for so long. Stella admired her tenacity. Peter had disappeared behind Japanese lines over two years ago. At the cinema, the newsreels were littered with stories of Japanese atrocities. Of course, no one mentioned that to Pip, though she most likely knew all about it.

'Can I do something to help?' asked Stella.

'You've got your nice clothes on.'

'You must have an apron somewhere.' She found one hanging on a nail on the back door. When she put it on, Stella wasn't sure if she'd get more dirt from the apron than the cleaning. 'Have you heard any more from that sister of yours?' she asked as she returned with a scrubbing brush from under the sink.

'Absolutely nothing,' said Pip.

'And are you OK with that?'

Pip shrugged. 'It hurts, I can't deny that, especially when it comes to Mum, but what can I do?'

Stella set about cleaning the countertop. 'What are you going to do with this place when it's ready?'

'I've already got another tenant lined up,' said Pip. 'Mrs Hollick is opening up a wool shop.'

'Proper little businesswoman,' Stella teased.

'Oh, I have one or two irons in the fire,' Pip grinned. 'I quite enjoy a challenge.'

'Mrs Hollick – is she the woman whose little girl had the party?' Stella asked.

'That's right,' said Pip. 'Sarah's at school now, so her mum thought she'd have a go.'

'Has she got a husband?'

Pip shook her head. 'He was a fisherman. He was killed when his boat hit a mine.'

Stella shuddered. 'Damned war,' she muttered.

Lillian and Nigel were getting careless. When they first embarked on their romance, they went to out-of-the-way places and made sure that Lillian had a reason for being late or staying with a friend. She was so comfortable with Nigel it was hard not to let it show. Despite six months passing by, their passion for each other hadn't abated one bit, which was why it was inevitable that they would be found out.

Dorcas was on duty on High Salvington, but when she got there, there had been a mix-up with the duty roster. Emily Cooke was already in the hide doing the observations. There were plenty of planes going over towards France, but the number of German bombers had slowed down recently. Now, the biggest fear came from robot-plane raids. The aerial jet-engine plane was pilotless and shaped like a Spitfire. Called a V1, it was painted in a dark colour and flew at low level on a straight course. An orange flame at the rear of the robot was the only visible part at night, and when they appeared, RAF Typhoon fighters were kept very busy over the Southern counties. When the engine stopped, the plane was little more than a flying bomb, and there were reports of people having only five to fifteen seconds to take cover before it exploded.

'You should be on duty tomorrow,' said Dorcas as she lifted the canvas blackout.

'I asked to change,' said Emily.

'There's nothing on the noticeboard.'

'My gran died,' said Emily. 'I have to go to the funeral tomorrow.' Her eyes filled with tears. 'She lived in Emsworth. I told Mr Sallis I couldn't get back on time.'

Mr Sallis was full of apologies when Dorcas reported to his hut a little further down the hill. Faced with such a heart-rending story, what could she do?

'That girl of yours singing tonight?' he asked.

'Not tonight,' said Dorcas, turning her bicycle round. 'If she was, I'd be babysitting.'

'You must be very proud of her.'

Dorcas smiled. 'I am.'

The drone of an aircraft engine distracted him and he hurried to the observation hide.

Dorcas biked back to Worthing. It might be quite nice to have an evening with her daughter. They didn't get many of them now that Lillian was accepting more engagements.

She didn't call out when she went in. She didn't want to wake Flora. There was a light under the sitting-room door and she pushed it open and got the shock of her life. Lillian lay on the sofa, her legs akimbo. Nigel was across her, his trousers and underpants half-way down his bare bottom.

'Oh!' Dorcas cried.

'Mum!' cried Lillian as she tried to sit up and cover her naked breasts. Her cheeks flamed with embarrassment.

Nigel sprang up, almost losing his trousers altogether.

Dorcas glared at her daughter. 'Make yourself respectable, madam,' she hissed. 'And you,' she said, turning to Nigel, 'get out of my house.'

Lillian and Nigel dressed hurriedly; then she hustled him towards the front door.

'Let me talk to her,' Dorcas heard him say.

'She won't listen,' Lillian whispered. 'Let me handle it.'

Dorcas felt the cold air as Lillian opened the front door.

'Remind her she was young once,' Nigel said, and Dorcas bristled.

'I will, I will,' said Lillian. 'Now go.'

Dorcas heard them kiss.

When she came into the kitchen, Dorcas could hardly look at her daughter. Her heart was pumping hard. She had never felt so angry or betrayed.

'How dare you!' Dorcas spat. 'And in my house too.'

'Mum, I'm sorry.'

'Sorry!' Dorcas exclaimed. 'How long has this been going on?'

'Mum, please don't be angry,' said Lillian. 'You don't understand. We love each other.'

'You're a married woman,' cried Dorcas.

'And whose fault is that?' Lillian retorted. 'If you hadn't made me—'

She was silenced by a stinging blow to the side of her face. Lillian reeled backwards from her mother's hand.

'I should have thought you'd learned your lesson the last time,' Dorcas spluttered. 'This has always been a respectable family, but here you are behaving like a guttersnipe, with your own daughter upstairs.'

'You've got no right to hit me like that,' Lillian shouted. 'What gives you the right to be holier than thou? Are you so perfect?'

Dorcas glared at her daughter. 'Your father was the only man I ever knew in the biblical sense. I met him at seventeen and I never, ever looked at another man. But you – you take your knickers down at the drop of a hat. Well, let me tell you, if you bring any more trouble on yourself, you're on your own, my girl.' She stopped for a minute to draw breath before adding,

'And as soon as you can find a place of your own, you can get out.'

Now Lillian was angry. 'Oh, so you would throw your own granddaughter on the streets, would you?'

'I'm not talking about Flora,' said Dorcas. 'She's got a home here with me for as long as she needs one. I'm talking about you and that fancy man of yours.'

Lillian was beginning to feel uneasy. This was getting out of control. Everybody knew how difficult it was to find a decent place to live these days. She had a nice home here with her mother and a built-in baby-sitter. If she left home, she would take Flora with her, of course, but how would she manage her growing stage commitments with no one to help look after her? Her mother was angry. It was unreasonable but understandable. She'd been embarrassed. 'Mum, please don't do this.'

Her mind was already moving forward. She would have to be more careful. If she did get pregnant with Nigel, what would she do? She couldn't marry him even if she wanted to, not with Gordon still around. And what if it got out that she'd been unfaithful with Nigel? Gordon might take Flora away from her.

'Mum?'

Dorcas was standing by the sink, her hands resting on the draining board and her back to Lillian. 'I don't want that man in my house again.'

'OK,' said Lillian. 'I'll tell him to stay away.' She put out her hand to touch her mother's shoulder, but Dorcas moved aside.

'And I'm telling you now,' said Dorcas stubbornly, 'if you end up in the family way, you're on your own.'

Dorcas heard her daughter leave the kitchen and relaxed her shoulders. She caught sight of herself in the mirror on the wall. Her face was white and she looked old. She wasn't crying. The women of her generation had learned years ago that crying solved nothing, but she could feel a lump in her chest the size of a brick. Lillian, oh, Lillian, why do you have to play with fire? She closed her eyes and put her head back. 'Please God, don't let her get into trouble again.'

CHAPTER 26

Since returning to Broadwater in August, Stella hadn't been feeling too well. At the beginning of the school term, she had started a teaching post in the cookery school on Richmond Road. Her students were school leavers who had a flair for domestic science and were destined for jobs in factory canteens and hospital kitchens. The course itself was comprehensive, taking in the preparation and management of food, health and first aid, personal finance, textiles and the care of clothes, hospitality and family life. The students also learned basic housekeeping skills, such as how to mend a fuse and change the washer on a tap. She taught them how to clean work surfaces, remove hard-water deposits with acid solutions, grease with alkaline solutions and which cleaning agents become toxic if mixed together. They took turns to cook meals, and Stella taught them good kitchen hygiene and how to make the meagre rations into filling and nutritious meals.

The problem was, certain foods made her feel nauseous, and she was constantly tired, so Stella made an appointment to see Dr Kirkwood. He gave her a thorough examination, and while she dressed behind the screen, he washed his hands.

'I would say we are looking towards the end of February,' he said, sitting at his desk.

'February?'

He looked up at her. 'Surely you know?' he said. 'Mrs Bell, you are four and a half months pregnant.'

Stella stared at him blankly. Pregnant? Of course! How could she have been so stupid? She'd never given it a thought. Her periods had always been a bit erratic. When was the last time she had one? Before Johnny came back. Yes, it must have been. The doctor was droning on and on about midwives and not overdoing it, but she wasn't taking anything in. A baby. She was going to have Johnny's baby.

My darling Johnny,

Forgive the small writing and the fact it's so close together. I want to get as much as possible on the page. I never thought we would be apart for so long when I waved you goodbye way back in 1940. I honestly believed it would only be for a few months, until Christmas at the most. I lived for your letters, and when they stopped after you'd escaped, I found it very hard to bear. This time, although our separation is still dreadful for me, I know I shall get through it.

I shall never forget our time in Pulborough. It was all too short, but Johnny, my darling, it has changed our lives forever. After all this time, and all the years before the war of trying, it's happened at last. You told me at the station that you hadn't had the time to go and buy me something special – something for me to remember you by. But, my darling, you have given me something much more precious than anything money can buy. Johnny, I am expecting your baby. He or she will be born at the end of February, so it looks as if 1945 will be a very special year for us. I do hope you will be home and the war will have ended long before then, but even if you aren't home and it hasn't ended, I shall tell our baby all about his or her wonderful daddy, what a lovely man he is and how much I really and truly love him.

The teaching post is most enjoyable. I am living with Mother at the moment. Desmond and Judith are overjoyed about the baby and fuss over me like a couple of old hens. The officers billeted in Salisbury Road move out at Christmas. My plan is to finish work then, which gives me two months to get the house ready for when baby comes.

Dr Kirkwood says I am very fit and healthy, so I should have no problems with the birth. My two dear friends Lillian and Pip are sure to start knitting, so baby will have plenty of warm clothes to wear. Pip is an excellent knitter, but I'm not so sure about Lillian! By Christmas, I shall be the size of a house, so any talk about reviving the Sussex Sisters has gone out of the window. It doesn't much matter. Pip seems to be getting on with her life, and Lillian is in great demand. I think she'll be on the radio in no time.

I'd better close now. I am scribbling this in bed and it's past eleven o'clock. Baby sends a kiss, or is that a kick?

All my best love,
Stella

* * *

Georgie entered a competition. He had to find a slogan for Salute the Soldier Day, which was to be held in Homefield Park on Saturday September 9th. Lillian was singing during the celebration, so everyone had pinned their hopes on his success. The slogan had to be eight words or under. Pip insisted that Georgie should think of the slogan himself, but she was on hand to give advice. The top prize was seven pounds, well worth having for an eight-year-old boy. It was hard work, but eventually he came up with 'They gave everything. Will you give something?' Pip was quite impressed.

The girls had decided to be there when Lillian sang in the fund-raising concert in support of the British soldier. Even though everyone's mind was fixed on what was happening on the other side of the Channel, it was a good day. The weather was more settled and the crowds gathered. There were donkey rides, egg-and-spoon races and knobbly knees contests, which caused a lot of hilarity. While the children were enjoying themselves in the sandpit, Stella told them her news. Lillian and Pip were over the moon.

'Pregnant! Oh, Stella, that's wonderful!' cried Pip. 'When is it due?'

'End of February,' said Stella. Already she was basking in the warm glow of pregnancy. 'I shall stay in the cookery school until Christmas and then I'll give up work.'

'Hopefully Johnny will be back home by then,' said

Lillian. 'The war must end soon, especially now that Paris has been liberated.'

'Everything seems to be winding down, doesn't it,' said Stella. 'Six months ago, we wouldn't have had an occasion like this.'

'There's still a lot of fighting over there,' Pip cautioned, 'and nobody knows when the war will end in the Far East.'

The girls made no comment, but Stella squeezed Pip's arm.

'Are your mum and Flora here?' asked Pip.

Lillian shook her head. 'Mum said she had things to do at home. I left Flora playing in Mrs Armitage's garden.'

'Oh no,' cried Pip. 'If I had known, she could have come with me.'

'Don't worry about it,' said Lillian. She felt slightly guilty, but it hadn't even crossed her mind. Flora would have enjoyed being with the others, but what with getting ready for her performance, she hadn't given it a thought.

Behind them, they heard a shout. Mr Knight, Iris and Betty had turned up.

'What time are you on?' asked Iris, once the introductions were over.

For a second, Lillian seemed mildly irritated. Pip was aware that Mr Knight followed her everywhere, and Lillian had remarked, rather unkindly, Pip thought, that he was beginning to look like a faithful old dog. After she'd said that, Pip had begun to notice that there were times when he stood a little too close to Lillian. He'd never touched her or anything, but it was embarrassing the way he latched on to her.

Lillian looked at her watch. 'Ooh, ten minutes. I'd better head off.'

'We've been looking forward to this,' said Betty, 'and you couldn't have picked a better day for it.'

'Let's hope they make a lot of money,' said Mr Knight, looking around at all the families enjoying themselves.

'I'm sure they will,' Lillian smiled as Nigel hurried over to tell her it was almost time to go on stage. 'Wish me luck,' she said as she went with him.

'Break a leg,' Pip called after her.

Lillian turned for a second to wave and then looked up at Nigel. As she watched them, Stella felt a stab of discomfort. She glanced over at Pip and saw the same concern in her eyes too. Neither of them actually voiced anything, but Stella was sure they had both had the same thought. There was something going on between Nigel and Lillian. She replayed the last few minutes over in her mind. The way she looked at him. The way he spoke to her. He'd only said, 'It's time to get ready, Lillian,' but there was something in his voice. Something unmistakable, a tenderness, a warmth not apparent in other conversations. She didn't want to believe it, but there was no doubt about it: Nigel and Lillian were in love.

After the performance, Iris and Betty sat in the tea tent. Mr Knight had offered to buy them a cup of tea and was getting it right now. The two women looked at each other long and hard. Iris was the first to break the silence.

'You saw it too,' she said. 'The way she looked at that pianist?'

Betty nodded. 'I hope it wasn't what I'm thinking.'

'If it is, it's disgusting,' said Iris. 'She should be ashamed of herself, a married woman and all.' She sniffed and looked away. 'After that party at Mrs Bell's house, I was willing to give her the benefit of the doubt, but not any longer.'

'Oh, I know, dear,' said Betty. 'If anyone believed in her, it was you.'

Iris let out a long sigh. 'It seems I was right all along. I feel a right fool now.'

'You know what they say,' said Betty. 'Them that lives longest sees most.' Iris frowned as if she was trying to work that one out. 'Don't be too hard on yourself, dear,' Betty went on. 'You've got a good and generous heart.'

They turned their heads towards the tea counter. Mr Knight was coming back with a tray of tea and cakes.

'Better not mention anything to him,' Iris counselled.

'My lips are sealed,' said Betty.

Halfway through the afternoon, everyone crowded round the makeshift stage for the announcement of the winner of the Slogan for a Soldier Competition.

Sadly, Georgie's effort didn't win. The slogan chosen was 'Invest all you have to back the soldier.'

'That doesn't have nearly as good a ring to it as Georgie's,' said Stella.

Pip sighed. 'He'll be very disappointed.'

When Georgie snuck off down the alleyway that evening, there was a large 'for sale' board in the grounds of the derelict house. He was going to mention it straight away, but Norman Peabody had turned up with a real German revolver.

'Where did you get that?' Georgie gasped.

'My brother,' said Norman. 'He came home on leave, and when he went back, I found it in his wardrobe.'

'Got any ammo?' Gideon asked.

Norman shrugged. 'Dunno. Might have.'

'Go and have a look,' said Billy.

'I'll have to wait until my mum's out,' said Norman. 'She doesn't like me going up into his room.'

Georgie was gutted. Until then, the tail fin Brian and Christopher had given him when he went to Pulborough had been the gang's best trophy. Gideon, who was the fount of all knowledge, had told them it was the sort of thing they dropped on London. Brian and Christopher had also given Georgie a couple of Nazi badges they'd found in the fields after two airmen had parachuted down and been arrested two miles away at Bury Hill. They'd had pride of place on the mantelpiece – until now. The real revolver knocked everything else into a cocked hat and there it stood, leaning against the wall and facing the door.

Norman gave them a smirk. 'My mum don't like me going into my brother's room on account of these.'

He threw three magazines onto the table.

'What are they?' Billy asked.

'Naked women,' said Norman.

'Ugh,' said Georgie, making a sick noise, but much to his surprise, the other boys pounced on them. 'Let me have a look,' Georgie said, trying to grab one.

'You can't look,' said Gideon. 'You're much too young for that sort of thing.'

Georgie watched as the other boys compared pictures and giggled over the girls. From what he could see, they weren't up to much anyway. And they weren't naked either. They may be lying on a rock with no clothes on, but they had a wispy bit of gauze across their legs. What was so exciting about that?

As soon as everyone, except Georgie, had had a proper look, they got on to the subject of the 'for sale' sign outside. The DD Gang were anxious and upset.

'Did you win the comp?' Billy asked Georgie.

Georgie shook his head.

'Shame,' said Billy.

'It was that Violet Lake,' said Gideon. 'It's not fair. She always wins things.'

'Well, she is the mayor's niece,' Leslie Hoare, sitting at the back, called out.

'If you'd have got that seven pounds,' Billy said

accusingly, 'we could have put it towards buying this place.'

Georgie felt terrible.

'I've got seven and six in my moneybox,' Lionel Brown called out.

'Don't be daft,' said Gideon. 'A place like this costs fousands.'

'But it's falling down,' said Lionel.

'It's the land,' said Georgie sagely. They all turned to look at him. 'That's what my mum says. She says they'll pull down the house so they can use the land.'

'Maybe they'll put up some swings and a slide.'

'Nah,' said Gideon. 'They'll put up another house more like.'

'But that means we'll have nowhere to put our stuff,' cried Billy.

It was late. The house was silent. Everyone was asleep. If it was going to be done, it had to be done now. If it was ready by the morning, it could go in the post on the way to work. How long would it take to reach him? Not long now, the way things were going. Having chased the Nazis out of Brussels earlier in the month, the Allies were already in Holland. It wouldn't be long before the British prisoners of war started returning home and it was imperative that he should know before that. The pen hovered over the page and then began to write,

Dear Gordon,

I'm very sorry to have to do this, but I thought you should know. I hate to see a good man being made to look a fool. You can tell me to mind my own business, but when a wife is out nearly every night, I think her husband has the right to be told.

I'm sure that you've heard that Mrs Harris used to be part of a singing group called the Sussex Sisters. I have enclosed a newspaper report for your perusal. They were very good, but now she's taken up with the pianist and she's gone solo. I've seen her in his car in evening dresses that leave little to the imagination, and the way she looks at him, I know there's something going on. All I can say is that it's a good job her mother is there to look after your little girl. Sorry to be the bearer of bad news, but I thought you should be prepared for when you come home.

A well-wisher

CHAPTER 27

Pip was just getting the children's tea when she heard a knock on the door. She hurried to answer it and was surprised to see Terry Wilcox on the doorstep. For a split second, she felt a rush of anger. When she bought those twenty acres of land way back in 1939, he must have known they were waterlogged and useless. To her way of thought, he and his farming friend had taken advantage of her. She couldn't blame him entirely, of course. She should have done her homework. She should have gone over there to take a look at the field for herself, but instead she had completely trusted Mr Wilcox. It never entered her head that he might be up to no good. Why should it? He was a valued customer at Peter's shop.

'Mr Wilcox!' Her voice betrayed her surprise.

He lifted his hat. 'Mrs Sinclair. I wonder if I might have a word.'

'I was just about to get my children something to eat,' Pip said stiffly. She wasn't in the mood to be talked into another transaction, no matter how tempting it might be. Her savings were still a lot less than they were when she'd paid for the land. In these hard times, it was very difficult to come by any spare cash, and when she did have something left over, she felt obliged to buy war bonds. Besides, she had learned her lesson. Terry Wilcox was a wolf in sheep's clothing.

'It won't take a minute, dear lady,' he said, positioning himself in such a way that she had no option but to step back and let him pass.

She showed him into the kitchen. Georgie and Hazel were playing shops in the sitting room and she didn't want to disturb them when they were playing so nicely. When he sat at the kitchen table, she didn't offer him refreshment but rather pointedly got on with what she had been doing.

'It's about them acres you bought off Tobias Light,' he began.

Pip pretended to be confused. 'Tobias Light? Do I know him? Oh, you mean the man who sold me that land near Durrington Station?'

'That's right,' Terry smiled. She regarded him stonily. Funny but she'd never noticed before just how surreptitious his smile was. He had a shifty look in his eye as well. 'You bought twenty acres for four pounds an acre, I believe.' He got out his wallet. 'Well, I would like to buy them off you.'

Pip watched him count out eighty pounds and lay them next to her teapot. When he'd finished, their eyes met and he put his wallet back into his jacket. Pip was furious, but she was careful not to let it show.

'Actually, Mr Wilcox,' she said, smiling sweetly, 'I think you'll find I paid five pounds an acre.'

'Did you?' he said smoothly. 'I do beg your pardon, dear lady.' And reaching for his wallet again, he counted some more notes onto the pile. 'One hundred pounds.'

Pip didn't bat an eyelid. 'Why would you want the land? You do know it's completely useless?'

'I know, dear lady,' he said. 'At the time you bought it from Tobias, I was strapped for cash. He offered me a few quid if I could find a buyer. I'm not proud of what I did to you, but it was always my intention to reimburse you the money as soon as I could. My conscience has plagued me for years, so here it is.' His dentures dropped slightly as he spoke. 'One hundred pounds.'

Pip hesitated. The money was tempting, but he looked so smug and she didn't trust him as far as she could throw him. What was he up to? 'I'm not sure where the paperwork is,' she said.

'Mrs Sinclair,' he said smarmily, 'we've known each other for a very long time. I trust you. We'll shake on the deal now and I'll pop back in a day or two to collect the deeds.'

Pip widened her eyes in an attempt to make herself look as if she was way out of her depth. 'My husband is very punctilious about business matters,' she said, delighted that he seemed confused as to what the word 'punctilious' meant. 'I know you trust me completely, but I must insist that we do everything the right way.'

'I promise,' he said, rising to his feet and putting out

his hand, 'that I won't breathe a word of this to him. It'll be our little secret.'

'No,' she said doggedly. 'I'm sorry, Mr Wilcox, but you'll have to come back another day.'

'But the money is on the table,' he protested.

'Then please take it with you,' she said.

'All right,' he said, sitting back down. 'You drive a hard bargain, Mrs Sinclair. Six pounds an acre and that's my final offer.'

Pip put her hand to her mouth and made a small sound, but she was only teasing him. 'Mr Wilcox, you are not listening to me. I've asked you to come back another time. Now please go.'

She saw his nostrils flare. He was clearly shocked by her attitude. 'Look here, love,' he said, his whole demeanour changing, 'if I have to come back again, I might not be so generous.' He had become very red in the face.

Pip brushed past him and went into the hall. She waited for him to stuff his money back into his wallet, then walked to the door in front of him. 'Like I say, if you come back in a day or two,' she said politely, 'I'm sure I'll have found the deeds by then.' She opened the door. 'Good afternoon, Mr Wilcox.'

Pip closed the door behind him and stared for a minute or two at the wood. What was the old devil up to? As sure as eggs is eggs, he wasn't settling a troubled conscience. People like Terry Wilcox didn't have one!

For almost a month now, Lillian had sensed a certain coolness towards her when Iris was around. She was polite but not inclined to be drawn into conversation with her any more. She wondered about tackling the woman about it, but she hadn't the stomach for it. It was bad enough at home. She and Dorcas hardly spoke to each other, and sometimes you could cut the atmosphere with a knife. Fortunately, Flora didn't seem to notice. She was too excited about playing the innkeeper's wife in the forthcoming school nativity play. She only had a small line to learn – 'Come and see the infant king' – but she'd practised it to perfection.

Lillian still saw Nigel, of course, but these days their unions were hasty and often down some dimly lit alleyway or out in the country, and the ever-present threat of being caught was beginning to take its toll.

'Run away with me.'

'I can't. You know I can't. I can't leave Flora.'

'Then bring her with us.'

'And who's going to look after her when I'm on stage? Anyway, if Gordon comes home, he'll track us down and take her away from me – you said so yourself.'

'I can't go on like this, Lillian.'

'I know, I know, but what can I do?'

When she dropped the children off at school a couple of days later, Pip headed for Ham Bridge Halt and bought a ticket for Durrington-on-Sea Station. The station itself was easily a mile from the village, but Pip didn't walk down the boulevard; she headed west. Apart from a couple of well-built houses, the rest was farm and nursery land along little lanes. It was a pleasant stroll to get to her twenty acres. The day before, at the town hall, she had discovered that this whole area was earmarked for a huge housing estate. With the war almost over, people were beginning to look to the future. The Lord alone knew how much housing stock had been bombed out of existence or bomb-damaged, and people needed somewhere to live.

She studied her deeds and found the place. It was quite a long way from the main road, so it would take a while for building work to get this far (if it ever did), but it was definitely part of the planned Maybridge estate.

A man walking his dog came towards her. 'How do?' he asked, tipping his hat.

'Good morning,' said Pip. 'I'm just looking to see where all these new houses are going to be.'

'Right down to the Littlehampton Road, so I hear,' he said. 'Sad to see the open spaces going.'

'I agree,' she said, 'but people need homes.'

'Too right,' he said, 'and to tell you the truth, the land wasn't much good for growing anyway. Too wet.'

Pip frowned. 'So how can they build houses on it?' she asked. 'Surely they'll have the same problem.'

'Not any more they won't,' said the man. 'Drained it, haven't they. Piped the springs straight into the Rife over yonder.' He waved his hand towards the village of Ferring. 'You can do anything when you've got the money.'

Pip folded away her map. 'So the land must be worth a bob or two now.'

'I should say so,' said the man. 'There was a time when old Tobias Light was offering to sell it off at three pounds an acre, but nobody wanted to buy it.'

'Three pounds an acre,' Pip squeaked.

'That's right,' said the man. 'I wish I'd taken some. Back then, he couldn't even give it away, but they say it's fetching anything up to eighteen pounds an acre now.'

Lillian was kept busy during the run-up to the Christmas season and she could always count on her two greatest fans to be there: Mr Knight and Betty. Iris didn't come any more. She apologized, saying she had to do fire-watching duties on the Town Hall roof. Lillian expressed her sympathy, but she wasn't too bothered. She didn't want to fall out with Iris again.

Nigel still played the piano for her, but their relationship was definitely cooling off. They were in Sompting Village Hall when everything came to a grinding halt. Nigel had wedged the back of a chair under the dressing-room doorknob as they took advantage of a brief moment together. It was rushed, as usual, and Nigel was having a bit of a problem. Lillian's mind was all over the place, and if she was honest, she wasn't enjoying the sex any more. Right now, she just wanted him to get on with it.

There was a sharp rap at the door and a voice outside called, 'Three minutes, Miss Lillian.'

Nigel jumped and lost his rhythm.

'Come on, darling,' she whispered. 'Hurry up.'

He jerked himself up sulkily and turned his back to dress.

Lillian, who was only in her underwear, reached for her panties. 'Sorry, darling, but I haven't even done my hair yet.' She pulled on her dress and sat in front of the brown-spotted mirror. 'Oh, how I hate these dim and dingy dressing rooms,' she said, powdering her flushed cheeks. 'I'm sure I could top the bill in any decent theatre. I'm seriously thinking of getting an agent.'

Nigel stood motionless by the door, one hand on the doorknob and the other on the chair wedging it shut. 'I can't do this any more, Lillian,' he said quietly.

She frowned and tutted under her breath. 'Look, Nigel, I really can't discuss this at the moment,' she said irritably. 'We'll talk after the show, all right?'

He pulled the chair away and opened the door. As he left the room, she knew they wouldn't be discussing anything after the show. What was the point?

After the worst weather for forty years, with terrific gales and tremendous downpours of rain, the news elsewhere was improving. When the weather allowed, the anti-tank defences on the Sussex Downs were being filled in, and the government announced that every child between the ages of six months and eighteen years would be entitled to an extra half-pound of sweets for Christmas. Both events were greeted with a great deal of pleasure. 'At last we've got somewhere to walk off all the calories,' Pip quipped. There was also the promise of boxes of Iraqi dates in the shops. They would be sold at tuppence a packet and one point in the ration book. Abroad, General MacArthur headed an invasion force in the Philippines with not one ship lost.

The girls decided to meet up for Christmas again this year. They planned to go to Phyllis's place in Broadwater and all chip in together for the meal because rationing and shortages were just as bad as ever.

Johnny was still in Italy. His regiment had been helping to mop up any resistance left behind, rounding up war criminals and helping the hard-pressed Italians to get back to normal life again. Apart from telling her how excited he was about the baby and what a clever girl she was, he had written to say that his demob papers were in the pipeline but that he may be posted to the Far East before then. It seemed grossly unfair to Stella, and she wasn't the only one. In fact, there was a brewing rebellion among the ranks. All the men wanted was to go home. Demob papers didn't mean freedom. Rumour had it that a man might have to stay in the army for anything up to two more years before getting his final discharge papers.

With Christmas over and a few more days of the school holidays left, Georgie and the DD Gang were bored. They hadn't found any good trophies lately, and apart from the doodlebugs, nothing much was happening now. There was even talk of the war coming to an end. Everyone agreed that Norman's gun was the best thing they'd found during the war, but, try as he might, he couldn't find any ammo. The gun was followed as a close second by Goliath, but they couldn't get it to fit in the chamber of Norman's gun. Leslie suggested using a hammer to bang it in, but so far that hadn't been attempted. Apart from the odd bit of shrapnel, there wasn't much else to be had.

Gideon had nicked two cigarettes and some chocolate off his gran. The boys shared the chocolate around.

'It's very small,' said Norman. 'I've never seen chocolate like this before.'

He was right, but there were enough squares to have one each, with one left over. It was dark and rather bitter, but chocolate is chocolate, so they munched it happily.

'I don't like it much,' said Billy. 'I ain't ever seen it in the sweetshop. It don't taste like Cadbury's.'

Georgie turned the wrapping paper over. '*EX-Lax*,' he read aloud. And before anyone could stop him, he scoffed the last bit himself.

It was time to light their cigarettes. At first, Billy told Georgie he was too young to smoke, but after a strident protest from Georgie himself, and cries of 'Aw, go on' from the other boys, Billy relented. Georgie took a long suck from the end of the cigarette and smoke filled his mouth. He swallowed and the next few minutes were pure agony. He coughed and spluttered so hard he thought his lungs would come out of his mouth. It brought tears to his eyes. As his friends rolled around the floor laughing, Georgie made up his mind that this was his first and last ever cigarette.

'See!' Billy cried triumphantly. 'I told you so. You're too young to smoke.'

That rebuke was worse than the pain, and Georgie slunk away into a dark corner to recover. A little while later, the boys came to the end of both cigarettes.

'I've got some fag papers,' said Leslie. 'If we could find a few dog-ends, we could make our own ciggies.'

But nobody had any dog-ends and the boys commiserated with each other.

'I know where there are plenty of dog-ends,' said Georgie. 'Shall I get them?'

'You said your mum never smoked,' Billy accused.

'She doesn't,' said Georgie, 'but I can still get some.'

When he came back a few minutes later, the boys were surprised by how many he had. They counted thirty-five. Some were obviously very old, but nevertheless, thirty-five!

'Where did you get them?' cried Gideon.

'In the alleyway outside my house,' said Georgie.

'Somebody must be keeping an eye on your house,' said Leslie.

'Perhaps it's someone from MI5,' Derek Fox piped up.

'Maybe your mum is a German spy,' Colin's brother Arthur suggested.

'You shut up about my mum,' Georgie cried as he pushed the boy hard. The boy retaliated and before long they were having a proper scrap, with everybody cheering them on. In the end, Billy pulled them apart; then Colin Watts and Derek set about splitting the fag ends and extracting the few strands of tobacco left. They rubbed them together and managed to make another three rather skinny cigarettes. They all smoked one and saved the other two for another time. Because it was winter, it was far too cold to stay very long in the cellar anyway. There was another problem as well. A funny smell. Gideon accused various people of doing a blow-off, but each boy denied it. The smell lingered, so no one protested when Billy decided it was getting near teatime and the boys had to go home.

'All them dog-ends,' Billy said to Georgie as they left. 'I reckon someone really is watching your house.'

Gideon nodded in agreement. 'Yeah. Who is it?'

Georgie shrugged. He'd never really thought about it before. He'd simply noticed the increasingly large number ground down in the dirt. 'Do you think I should tell my mum?'

Billy shook his head. 'Women can't deal with things like this on their own,' he said gravely, as they put the bits and pieces back to hide the doorway. 'They need a man around to handle the tough stuff.'

'You never know – he could be a German spy,' said Gideon.

'We might have to creep up on him and grab him like this,' Billy went on, using Gideon to show how it could be done.

As he watched the two boys scrapping, Georgie felt

a delicious shiver of excitement. Could he really catch a German spy? Gosh, wouldn't his dad be proud of him if he did that?

Pip still had no word at all from Peter, and the war in the Far East was as bitter as ever. Poor Georgie had had a dreadfully upset tummy of late. She thought it was some sort of bug, but fortunately Hazel didn't catch it. He'd had a couple of accidents in his bed, which meant a lot of washing, so when Mrs Armitage offered to have the children over to her place, Pip treated herself to an afternoon at the pictures. In the newsreels, she'd been moved by an iconic image of General MacArthur, flanked by members of the Philippine Government, coming ashore at Leyte. Apparently, no landing craft was available, but he was so determined to keep the promise he'd made two years before that he waded through the waves. His speech gave Pip a real hope that Peter might be freed soon. 'People of the Philippines,' MacArthur had said, 'I have returned. We have come dedicated and committed to the task of destroying every vestige of enemy control . . .'

That night, Pip cried herself to sleep.

In the end, she sold the land in Durrington, not to Terry Wilcox, or Tobias Light for that matter. The man she'd met that day by the field had a few acres at a reasonable price, and the rest went to Worthing Borough Council. They were offering a little below the market price, but by the time she'd enquired about it, that had topped twenty pounds an acre. Pip walked away with almost four hundred pounds. It was time to put her other plan into action.

There was one thing, however, that was slightly more pressing. She'd had a letter from the Wimborne solicitor. The headed paper from Peak, Hall & Ellis had come as a surprise. It was to inform her that because she had been unable to reconcile with her twin, and that a year had passed, the legacy was to be passed on to another beneficiary. There was no indication as to who that was, but Mr Ellis indicated that a certain person wanted to be put in touch with her, a Mr Stanley Abbott.

As she read the words, Pip took in her breath. That wasn't possible. How could it be? All those years ago, her mother had told her and her sister that their father was dead.

CHAPTER 28

'But surely you want to find out what happened to your father?' said Stella.

Pip stared at the floor. Having spent the past three days thinking about it, she had decided to confide in someone. After everything they'd been through, Stella and Lillian were the obvious choice. They were ensconced in Stella's sitting room in front of a roaring fire.

They had spent the day helping Stella clean up her house. The army had handed her home back, but they'd left it in a hell of a state. Stella had big plans, but she'd made them without much thought about her condition. Christmas had come and gone. It was a strange one this year. Everybody carried on as best they could, but with their men still far from home, it felt rather like they were being denied the one thing they wanted most. With Stella in the final stages of her pregnancy, spending the whole day slaving over a Hoover, scrubbing kitchen floors and washing windows was more than a tad beyond her now.

'You can't ignore this, Pip,' said Stella. 'This could be your very last chance to hear his side of the story.'

'Stella's right,' said Lillian. 'You ought to find out what happened to him. If not for yourself, do it for Georgie and Hazel.'

Stella was right. On the face of it, it seemed obvious that Pip would want to know what had happened all those years ago. Hadn't she grieved for him? Hadn't she often said, 'If only Daddy was here'? But now that she'd discovered he wasn't dead, she was angry. Why had he suddenly turned up after all this time? What gave him the right to expect her to come running? It was the stuff of miracles, but the more Pip thought about it, the crosser she felt. She handed Stella the letter from Mr Ellis.

Stella read it carefully before passing it on to Lillian. 'You never did tell us what happened when you went to Wimborne with your sister. Does that have any bearing on this letter?'

'I thought Marion was taking me to Wimborne to meet my mother,' said Pip, 'but there was more to it than that.'

'We always thought you were on your own,' said Lillian. 'It came as a bit of a shock to discover you had a family.'

'I left home at sixteen,' said Pip. She saw them glance at each other. 'I always felt like the odd one out,' she continued, her voice beginning to sound desperate. 'Mum didn't have a lot of time for me. Marion always was her favourite. I know it sounds petulant, but I promise you it's the God's honest truth.'

'We believe you utterly,' said Stella. 'You know that.'

311

She stood up and waddled to the drinks cupboard. 'Anybody fancy a little elderberry wine?'

Pip and Lillian gave her a curt nod. Then Lillian said, 'You left home at sixteen. Was that because of Marion getting burned?'

'I'd already planned to go,' said Pip. 'I had a job lined up and everything, but they wanted me there for the party.'

'So you last saw your dad at the party?' said Stella, coming back with two glasses.

'Oh no,' said Pip. 'Daddy had gone years before. That's what made it so hard. It had always been Daddy and me, then Mum and Marion. I was five when he died and we moved house.'

'Only he didn't die,' said Stella, returning to her chair with her own glass of wine.

'Apparently not,' Pip said bitterly.

'So where has he been all this time?' asked Lillian.

'Exactly,' said Pip. 'And why did he let me go on believing he was dead? Why didn't he contact me?'

'Just a minute,' said Stella. 'Did anyone in the family know where you were?'

Pip felt her face colour.

'A friend of the family could have told him where she was,' Lillian suggested to Stella.

Pip shook her head. 'No, she's right. No one knew where I was. When I last saw my mother and sister, they were living in Devon, in a little place called Hemyock.'

'So your mother moved twice,' said Stella.

'Three times,' said Pip. 'Marion and I were born in

London. We moved to Hemyock when Daddy died, and now, of course, she's in Wimborne. Although come to think about it, I never went to her house, so she could be anywhere.'

'Who told you your dad had died?' said Stella. 'Did you actually see his body?'

Pip shook her head.

'Do you remember his funeral?'

Again Pip shook her head. 'He never had one. I thought it was odd at the time but Mummy got cross when I asked her about it.'

Pip sighed. She was beginning to see things a lot differently now. Daddy hadn't died at all. Her mother had run away and left him. She'd made a whole new life for them in Hemyock and neither of the girls had realized what she'd done.

'Perhaps it wasn't his fault that he didn't get in touch with you,' said Lillian.

'I think you might be right,' said Pip, 'but how did he find me after all this time?' She looked at the letter again, and somewhere in her head, a light dawned. 'It was this legacy,' she went on. 'He must be the other beneficiary. After all, Granny was *his* mother. He must have been told the terms of the will and asked Mr Ellis to put us in touch again.'

'So will you let Mr Ellis give him your address?' Stella asked.

Pip looked uncertain. 'I don't want to be party to a family feud. I know I may be denying Georgie and

Hazel a grandparent, but I don't want them to put up with what I have. I want to spare them that.'

'I think that's perfectly understandable,' said Lillian.

'But perhaps your father has been wronged as well,' said Stella. 'Maybe none of this is his fault.'

Pip swirled her wine round its glass. 'Oh, I don't know what to do,' she wailed.

Stella changed seats and sat next to her. 'Why don't I come with you?' she said.

'Count me in too,' said Lillian. 'Ask Mr Ellis to get your father to meet you on neutral ground somewhere. That way, he won't know where you live. Then if you're still unsure, you can walk away.'

Pip dabbed the end of her nose with her hanky. 'OK.'

'But don't leave it too long before you set up a meeting,' said Stella, stroking her bump. 'In a couple of weeks, I won't be able to risk going very far from home. I don't want to end up going into labour on a bus somewhere.'

When Georgie got in from school, his mother wore that tight-lipped you've-done-something-and-I'm-annoyed-about-it expression. As he dashed upstairs to change out of his school things, Georgie wracked his brains to think what it could be. Had he left his washing on the bedroom floor? No. Had he forgotten to feed the rabbit? No. Had he annoyed his sister? No. Well, no more than usual.

It was far too cold to play outside, though the

evenings were a little lighter. He longed to be able to get out and play in the street. He might even venture a little further if no one was looking. The sea defences were slowly being dismantled, and they hadn't heard Moaning Minnie for yonks. It seemed that bombing raids were becoming a thing of the past. The Allied planes continued going over to the Continent, but the German planes were non-existent. The grown-ups said it was all over bar the shouting, which for Georgie and his mates was very disappointing. The war had been the most exciting time of their lives.

He came downstairs and ambled into the kitchen with his head down. His sister had been sent into the sitting room to play, so things looked bad for Georgie.

'Sit down, Georgie,' said Pip.

He did his best to look as shocked and innocent as possible as his mother laid three dog-ends on the table in front of him. As soon as he saw them, Georgie felt his face flame. Stupid, stupid, stupid. He'd forgotten about them altogether. He'd got to the den last Saturday, but nobody was there. Too cold. He'd picked up the dog-ends on the way back, meaning to put them somewhere safe until the gang reassembled.

'Have you been smoking?' Pip accused.

'No, Mummy.'

'Then how do you account for these? I found them in your trouser pocket.'

Georgie swallowed hard. 'I picked them up.'

'Picked them up? Where?'

'In the back alley.'

315

Pip frowned.

'I was trying to be tidy,' said Georgie.

His mother looked sceptical. 'Are you sure you didn't smoke them yourself?'

'No, Mummy!' He hoped the horror in his voice at such a suggestion would be enough. After all, he was telling the truth. He'd never smoked a dog-end.

'Because if I find—' Pip went on.

'I haven't, Mummy. Really I haven't.'

She threw the dog-end in the waste bin. 'I don't want you picking up things like that,' she said. 'It's dirty. You don't know whose mouth it's been in.'

He was about to tell her about the German spy watching in the alley, but then he remembered what Billy had said. 'Can I have something to eat?'

'We'll be having tea before long,' his mother said, reaching for the potatoes to peel.

'Aw, Mum,' said Georgie. 'Can't I have some toast?'

Pip grinned. 'Oh, all right,' she said, putting on the grill. 'Only one slice, mind, or you'll spoil your tea.'

'Thanks, Mummy.'

'You can do a slice for your sister as well,' said Pip.

When the toast was done, Georgie reached for the dripping. He dug the knife in deep. There was some lovely jelly at the bottom and he didn't need to guess which one of them was going to have that.

As it turned out, the wheels of officialdom move very slowly and so the birth of Timothy Michael Bell came before Pip met her father. He was born on Sunday

February 25th 1945. At seven pounds five ounces, he was a good weight and had a lusty cry. Stella had him at her mother's place in Broadwater. That seemed the best option. Phyllis would be around virtually all the time if she were needed, and if she had to attend to any of her WVS duties, her daily, Mrs Wilshaw, would be on hand.

It wasn't until Easter that the arrangements were finalized for Pip to meet her father for the first time in twenty years. The solicitor had suggested the Grand Hotel in Brighton as the venue, but then it was discovered that it was still under orders from the army. Group Captain Stanley Abbott agreed to meet all three of them for afternoon tea in the Norfolk Ramada Jarvis Hotel, just along the road, not quite as large as the Grand, but apparently every bit as posh. Pip, Stella and Lillian were very excited.

'I've never even been in a place like that,' Lillian gasped. 'I can't wait.'

Pip had been all for catching the bus to Brighton to meet her father, but Stella wouldn't hear of it, especially when she'd learned of the solicitor's suggested meeting place. 'You can't possibly go swanning up to the Grand Hotel with a bus ticket in your hand!' she'd cried. So they'd spruced up the car and filled the tank with petrol.

They'd put on their finest clothes, of course. Lillian looked the best, in a smart grey dress with ivory buttons. She wore a white hat and carried a pair of white cotton crocheted gloves, which matched perfectly, though she could only wear one and carry the other: the person who had made them hadn't got the pattern quite right. There were only three fingers on the left hand.

Pip wore a mid-blue wrap-over dress with dark blue gloves and a rather jaunty hat with a curled brim. She carried a brown clutch bag and wore tan-coloured brogue-fronted shoes with the regulation two-inch heels.

Stella had almost got her figure back, but she decided to wear a fairly loose cherry-red dress with a gathered waist and white Peter Pan collar. Her hat was cream felt.

Lillian drove, with Pip in the front passenger seat. Stella took up the whole of the back seat because she had Timothy Michael in a Moses basket beside her.

Stella was happy to let Lillian drive, and Pip looked every inch the lady sat in the front passenger seat. There wasn't much conversation as they motored to Brighton. Stella was keeping a watchful eye on her son, and Pip was too nervous for lively chat, so Lillian talked about something that was becoming her favourite subject – her new career.

'I shan't be driving the railway van any more after the end of this week,' she told them. 'Monty is confident I shall be working full time before long.'

'Monty?' said Pip absent-mindedly.

'Oh, do stay awake, Pip, dear,' said Lillian, slowing down to take a corner. 'Montague Rankin, my agent.

318

He's already got me a couple of nights at the Hippo-drome in Eastbourne and a week in a variety show over in Croydon. There's even some talk of a slot on *Variety Bandbox* on the radio.'

Pip was delighted for her friend. 'It's all happening now, isn't it?'

'Mother is going to look after Flora for a while,' Lillian went on. 'Just until I'm established, you know. By that time, I should be earning enough to pay for a nanny, and then she can travel with me.'

'What about Gordon?' Stella asked.

'I'll cross that bridge when I come to it,' Lillian said dismissively. 'Did I mention that Cyril Fletcher is on the bill at Croydon?'

They loved the look of the West Pier in Brighton, though there was no chance of taking a stroll. Every pier in the country had been crippled just after the war started. The thinking was that if a larger ship could get its troops near the shore, it would aid an invasion, so the middle decking had been removed. Today, a group of soldiers were removing the Bofors and Lewis guns that overlooked the sea. There was no threat of invasion now. It was really beginning to feel that the war was coming to an end at last.

They collected their things and swanked across the road and into the hotel. The Grand was by far the poshest place Lillian had ever seen, though Canadian and, later on, Polish soldiers had been billeted in its rooms since D-Day. Outside the Norfolk, a concierge in a very smart uniform with brass buttons down the front and gold fringes on his shoulder lappets greeted them at the door. They climbed the steps and he pushed open the monogrammed door panel. They found themselves in a foyer with pillars and a glistening marble floor. They'd planned that they would wander in looking confident and as if being in a place like this was second nature, but instead they gazed open-mouthed at the huge square staircase leading to the hotel rooms. None of them had ever seen anything so ornate.

At the reception desk, Stella explained that they were here to meet Group Captain Abbott and a pageboy was assigned to show them into the lounge area. By this time, Pip was a bag of nerves, so Lillian slipped her arm through hers and gave it an encouraging squeeze.

Despite the war shortages, the Norfolk lived up to its name, with sixty-four rooms on four floors. On the outside of the building, the three mansard roofs still retained their wrought-ironwork decoration, despite the wartime salvage schemes. The main entrance had Corinthian columns, and the cantilevered four-storey staircase took their breath away. They were shown into the dining area. As they came into the room, a tall military man rose to his feet in an alcove near the window and Pip caught her breath. Lillian and Stella held back as she walked towards him. Her step was uncertain, as was his.

'Daddy?'

'Pip, my dear.'

She stood in front of him for several seconds; then he opened his arms and she went to him.

CHAPTER 29

Pip had been in a bit of a dream since meeting her father. She'd kept noticing silly things, like the way he held his teacup to his chest as he drank, the way he tweaked the end of his moustache or the way he stood in the doorway as they said their goodbyes. Before they'd met, she'd made up her mind to be angry with him. She'd rehearsed what she'd say again and again. *How could you just up and leave like that?* she'd tell him. *Why did you let me go on believing you were dead? And why turn up after all this time? What exactly do you want, Daddy?*

All those questions were obsolete now. Lillian's hunch had been right all along. As he talked, she'd realized he had been wronged as much as she had been. It seemed that her mother's bitterness had spilled over and poisoned everything. No wonder she couldn't remember her father's death: it never happened, and that's why they'd moved away with such haste.

Her father spoke of days searching for his family, even hiring a private investigator, but to no avail. His eyes moistened as he recalled the pain and frustration he felt. Pip began to understand the devastating effect it must have had on him.

According to her father, her mother had refused him from the day she and her twin sister had been born. He told her that he had tried to be the loving husband but it seemed that Maud only looked for ways to hurt and humiliate him. She'd refused to go out with him, she'd send back invitations from friends without telling him, and only spoke to their children. Amazingly, he was without malice or bitterness but Pip could see the hurt in his eyes. As he explained, she could hear her mother's voice in her head: 'If only you knew what I suffered bringing you into the world.' It all made sense now. He'd been willing to stick it out for the sake of the children, but one day he'd come home to find they had all gone.

She and her father had been awkward with each other at first, but gradually they'd felt more comfortable together. He had brought a lady he called his wife, a pleasant-looking woman roughly the same age as him, who clearly adored him. They'd ordered tea, but by the time the tray came, Timothy Michael had been becoming fretful.

'Why don't you come up to our room?' Elspeth Abbott suggested. 'It will give you some privacy to change and feed him.'

When Stella agreed, Lillian took the opportunity to make an excuse to go to the powder room, leaving the group captain and Pip alone.

'Are you and Elspeth really married?' she asked.

The group captain sighed. 'I spent years looking for your mother, but in the end I went to court and divorced her in absentia on the grounds of abandonment.'

Pip's heart went out to him. 'It's not been easy for you, has it, Daddy?'

'I'm happy now,' he assured her. 'And I'm really, really happy to have found you again. Tell me about your childhood,' he said, handing her a cup of tea.

'There's not a lot to say,' said Pip. 'I wasn't exactly happy. Marion and I fought a lot, and Mummy always took her part, but it was pretty ordinary until my sixteenth birthday. That's when Marion got burned.'

'Yes, I was sorry to hear about that,' he said. 'The solicitor explained what happened.'

'It wasn't my fault,' said Pip desperately, all the old feelings of guilt flooding back.

'I didn't think for one moment that it was.' Her father smiled. 'Do you want to talk about it?' His voice was gentle.

'Not really,' said Pip, flicking an imaginary piece of fluff from her skirt. 'No one ever believes me anyway.'

'Try me,' he said.

'We were sixteen,' she began with a sigh. 'I'd already decided to leave home. I'd got a job in a residential children's home. It was the only way I could think of to keep a roof over my head.'

Her father nodded. 'Good thinking.'

'Mother bought us new dresses. I liked the blue one better. Blue is my colour.' Pip looked away, a lump forming in her throat. She hadn't spoken about this for years, not in detail. 'But Marion wanted the blue, so I had to have the magenta dress. I didn't like it much and I guess I let it show.' She glanced back at him. Her father was listening impassively. 'We were in our bedroom and we rowed about it. I said some bad things. I remember calling her selfish and mean. She didn't care. She was just twirling herself round in front of the mirror. I was so angry I wanted to clock her, so I came downstairs and waited in the hall. That's when I heard Marion scream. I belted back upstairs and she was just standing there with her dress on fire.' Pip's eyes filled with tears. 'She'd been trying to pat the flames out, but she looked like some grotesque torch. I tried to make her get down. I was screaming at her to roll on the carpet, but she hit me away and tried to run downstairs. Mother came upstairs and between us we got the flames out, but she was horribly burned.'

The group captain leaned forward and took Pip's hand. 'It must have been awful for you as well.'

Pip looked up at him and burst into tears just as Lillian came back from the toilet and Elspeth returned from their room. It was an awkward moment. Lillian was furious, convinced that Pip's father had said something terrible to upset her.

'What have you done to her?' she demanded.

Elspeth seemed slightly embarrassed, but eventually they realized it was all right and they calmed down.

'I'm so sorry, my dear,' said the group captain eventually. 'I had no intention of making you cry.'

'It's all right,' Pip hiccupped, glad that the table was in an alcove. 'It's just that you're the first person who has ever considered how badly I felt about it.'

It was such a relief for Pip that she no longer had to protest her innocence.

'Mother was convinced I had moved the fireguard,' she went on, 'and Marion told her I'd pushed her, but I hadn't. Really I hadn't. I only wanted to get her onto the floor.'

'Why do people put a mirror over a fireplace,' the captain mused. 'She must have leaned a little too close.'

Lillian and Elspeth looked at each other and nodded.

'Mother never liked me,' Pip said. 'I couldn't understand why, but she never did.'

'It always was you and me, and Marion and your mother,' said the group captain, reaching for Pip's hand again. 'We had some good times together, didn't we?'

Pip's eyes were welling up again as she nodded. 'I don't know what I did wrong, Daddy.'

'You didn't do anything wrong, sweetheart,' he said, his voice cracking with emotion. 'Your mother was a difficult woman with everyone, not just you.'

'I think I can guess why she took against you,' said Elspeth. They all looked at her, their expressions those of mild surprise. 'Well,' Elspeth continued, 'you're the spitting image of your father, aren't you?'

'Marion and I are twins,' said Pip.

'But not identical,' Lillian reminded her.

* * *

Georgie had been amazed when she'd told him his grandfather was a group captain in the RAF. 'You mean he flies Spitfires?' he'd said, his eyes bright with excitement. 'Cor, wait until I tell the boys at school!'

'I'm not sure he actually flies them,' Pip cautioned. 'He's more like the man in charge.' But Georgie wasn't really listening. He was running around the garden with his arms outspread as he made engine noises.

Hazel was a little more circumspect, and slightly confused as to where he fitted in the family.

'Granddad is my daddy,' said Pip.

'But where has he come from?'

She decided it was easier to explain that in just the same way that her father was away fighting the war, so too had her grandfather been. She would tell Hazel the full story when she was old enough to understand.

When Pip had finished, Hazel nodded gravely. 'When is my daddy coming home?'

When indeed? Pip pulled her roughly into her arms and hugged her lest she see the tears in her eyes. 'I don't know, darling, but let's hope it's soon.'

Later that evening, when Pip was locking up and making sure everything was in its place before going to bed, she opened the door to the children's room. They were fast asleep. Hazel's favourite dolly lay on the pillow beside her, one eye open and the other shut. There was something wrong with the mechanism. She would look at it when Hazel was at school. Perhaps she could work out how to fix it.

Georgie was growing up so fast. Peter would have

a job recognizing him when he got back. Pip was sure he would come back. They'd heard awful stories of what the Japanese prisoners had gone through, but she remained positive. She always told herself that she would know if something bad had happened to Peter. Some of the mothers who brought their children for her to look after told her she was brave. Pip didn't feel in the least bit brave. She just knew her husband was coming home. She pulled the covers back over Hazel's shoulders and tiptoed out of the room.

Their grandfather was coming to see them next week. He'd be a male role model for Georgie, which would be good. Her son was surrounded by women. She smiled to herself as she tried to imagine how the children would react to seeing her father in the flesh.

As she closed the children's bedroom door, she noticed the curtain at the other end of the landing wasn't quite closed. It didn't matter too much now. After the D-Day landings, the risk of air attack, especially from hit-and-run raiders, had diminished and the blackout regulations had been replaced by dim-out. For the first time since the war, street lights were back on, not as many as before, but at least you didn't have to walk about in the pitch darkness any more. And if the newspaper reports were to be believed, even the dim-out would soon be a thing of the past.

Pip went to draw the curtain, but as she did so, she noticed a small red glow by the hedge at the bottom of her garden. She pulled herself back and watched as the red glow grew brighter, then dimmed. Someone was in the alleyway, someone who was smoking. Even though the street light in Lyndhurst Road was on, she couldn't see who it was, but it was definitely a man. What was he doing there? Why was he watching Lillian's house?

She hadn't seen Lillian for a couple of weeks, maybe three. Their paths didn't cross so often now. Lillian was making quite a name for herself, and with the war almost at an end, even the doodlebugs had stopped coming over, so Dorcas was no longer needed on her radar post. There was talk of the observation buildings on High Salvington being abandoned.

It was then that Pip remembered the dog-ends Georgie had put into his pocket. She never had properly investigated that, had she? She'd meant to look in the alleyway, but she hadn't got round to it. The cigarette grew bright again and she saw him begin to move. She watched him turn away and disappear from view. How odd, she thought as she pulled the curtain and went to her room.

CHAPTER 30

Gordon was the first to be on the move. He and his fellow prisoners were sent on a forced march through Germany because rumour had it that the Russians were coming. After four months of what seemed like aimless marching, Gordon had had enough. Sleeping out in the open and only having scraps of food was no life, so while everyone was still sleeping, he grabbed the opportunity to slip away. He didn't get far. While walking across a field, he was suddenly faced by a German officer coming towards him. His heart went into his mouth and for a split second he was tempted to make a run for it, but where could he hide in the middle of an open space? The game was definitely up. What a damned fool he'd been, and how ironic to survive all this time and then get himself shot in the middle of nowhere.

The officer lifted his gun and Gordon closed his eyes, but instead of shooting him as he expected, the officer handed him his weapon. It was only then that Gordon saw the British Army tank coming up the road behind him. There had been no finer sight since he'd been on foreign soil.

Once liberated, he and his companions were taken to a small village nearby. They were billeted in German houses, while the villagers were made to sleep in a makeshift camp in the surrounding fields. The tables were turned at last. After a week, they were taken to an airfield and flown to Belgium. Two days later, Gordon was in England, where he was given a clean uniform and sixty days' leave. While he was waiting for the paperwork to be done, he wrote to tell Lillian he was on his way home, and his excitement mounted with each passing day.

There were other troops on board the train. The men passed the journey by showing each other photographs of their wives and families or their girlfriends. He could hear them swapping stories of times past and their hopes for the future, but he didn't join in. He felt too emotional for conversation, so he stared through the dirty carriage window at the once-familiar countryside. The war had changed the landscape. Every now and then, the train would pass a scattering of bombed-out houses, a blackened tree or a field with a large crater in the middle of it. The women waiting by the barrier gates as the train sped on looked tired and shabby. Even the kids looked scruffy in their threadbare jackets and cut-down trousers, and a sobering thought crossed his mind. We may have won the war, but the country is broken.

A tight knot of excited people were waiting on the

platform at Worthing. He watched as his travelling companions fell into the arms of those they loved. Fathers lifted their children into the air and kissed their wives. There was laughter and gaiety everywhere. He scanned the crowds, but he couldn't see Lil or the kid. He hung around for a while, but eventually bowed to the inevitable. She wasn't coming. He didn't know whether he felt disappointed or angry.

'You all right, soldier?' The man's voice jolted him from his melancholy. He turned to see a porter with an eyepatch and what looked like a war injury. It was only then that it occurred to him that Lillian could still be working. What time did her shift end? He hadn't a clue, so it was perfectly possible that she could be somewhere on the station concourse.

'I was looking for my missus,' he said. 'She works here. Lillian Harris.'

The man's face broke into a wide smile. 'Are you Gordon?'

'Yes,' said Gordon, a little unsure.

'My name is Ron Knight,' said the man, giving him a clap on the shoulder. 'We all love your missus. Come in the cafe and have a drink.'

'Is she around?' Gordon asked as he was being gently propelled towards the bright lights of the cafe.

'Lillian doesn't work here any more,' said Ron. 'She left some time ago.'

'Left?' Gordon was stunned, but by this time, he was inside the cafe and having his hand pumped by just about everybody in sight. A cup of tea, laced with some of the stationmaster's medicinal brandy, and an iced bun were placed before him as he sat in a chair. Some people wanted to hear his story, while others were telling him what an amazing woman Lillian was.

'I've been to see nearly all her shows,' Ron told him. 'She's wonderful up on that stage.'

'But she left the railway,' he said, feeling a bit of a fool for not knowing. Did that mean she wasn't in Worthing any more? And if not, where was his kid?

'She's got a proper manager now,' said Betty. 'He's made a big difference to her career. We went to see her at the Connaught last month.'

'The Connaught?' said Gordon, munching his bun. 'What, the Connaught Theatre here in Worthing?'

'That's it, lad,' said Mr Knight. 'You should be right proud of her.'

An hour later, he left the warm welcome in the cafe, but only after he had promised several customers that he would be sure to come into the Buckingham, the Thieves' Kitchen or the Jack Horner and have a pint with them. They finally let him go as they slapped him on the back and pumped his hand once more, congratulating him on his safe return.

Gordon's boots rang out in the empty streets as he marched along Railway Approach towards North Street, past the Rivoli Cinema and on to Lyndhurst Road. Everywhere looked much the same until he reached St George's School, where the jagged gap in the row of houses opposite was a stark reminder of the hostilities now past. Mr Stevens's newsagent and sweetshop was gone, blown to kingdom come by some Jerry aiming for the gas works across the road no doubt. All that remained was a pile of rubble. He remembered the four chews for a penny and the gobstoppers he'd bought in that shop as a kid. He thought about Mr Stevens, tall, gaunt and a little bit scary in his rimless glasses. He used to peer over the counter at any young boy in his shop, making sure they weren't tempted to nick something. Whatever happened to him? he wondered.

The brandy and the tea had warmed him, but he still felt ill at ease. The folks at the station had been friendly enough. He'd been aware that Lillian was on stage, but he'd had no idea that she was so well known. It would be hard for her to give it all up now that the war was over, but he wanted them to settle down and get a place of their own. He'd been forced to marry and he'd resented it at the time. Five years as a POW had changed his outlook on life. Now he was keen to take up his responsibilities towards his kid and make a go of his marriage.

Gordon was shocked to see more war damage on Reydon, the house on the corner of Lyndhurst and Homefield Road. Half of it was just a pile of rubble. Lillian had mentioned it in one of her letters, but he'd been more interested in the news that little Flora had been burned. For the first time in his life, it created a surge of paternal affection. He'd been angry and upset that his little girl, his baby, had been hurt. He'd wanted to punch somebody, anybody, but preferably a bloody Nazi. How was Flora now, poor little lamb?

When he knocked on the door, his mother-in-law opened it. They stared at each other in disbelief, until Dorcas finally regained her senses and said, 'Come in, come in.'

Dumping his kitbag in the hallway, Gordon walked into the sitting room. It was so normal, so comfortable-looking that it almost reduced him to tears there and then. A little girl with a red ribbon in her blonde hair sat at the table drawing. She only glanced up at him for a second before carrying on with her work.

He turned to Dorcas. 'Is that . . . ?'

She nodded and went over to the child. 'Flora,' she said gently, 'this man is your daddy.'

Flora looked up, but she didn't move. She looked so grown-up. She'd only been a babe in arms when he'd last seen her.

'Hello, love,' he said, coming towards her.

Flora slid from the table and hid behind her grand-mother's skirt.

Gordon turned to Dorcas. 'Where's Lil?'

'She's away,' said Dorcas. 'She's got a week in Croydon in a variety show.'

'Fine homecoming this is,' he said.

'We hadn't a clue that you were coming,' said Dorcas helplessly. 'Nobody said.'

He glanced at the mantelpiece and saw his letter leaning against the clock.

335

'Is that from you?' she cried. 'Oh, Gordon, I had no idea. It came the day she left.'

Gordon looked down. Flora was watching him, but as soon as their eyes met, she hid again. Gordon pulled a small dolly from inside his jacket and held it out to her. 'Aren't you going to give your daddy a kiss?' he said, bending down to her. But she'd already started to cry.

He was close to tears himself and bitterly disappointed. All these months he'd been dreaming of his homecoming and what it would be like. It sure as hell wasn't supposed to be like this. He hadn't expected bunting and a big party, but he had thought at the very least that his wife would be here to meet him. He hadn't seen Lillian for nearly five years. He knew she was a popular singer, but he hadn't expected her to be away from home. Bloody Croydon? She wouldn't be home tonight, that was for sure. Tossing the dolly onto the table, Gordon turned on his heel.

'Where are you going?' Dorcas called after him.

'To get drunk,' he said as he slammed the front door behind him.

Pip's father had sent her a letter. She'd read it at least six times, and every time it made her cry.

> *My darling Pip,*
>   *I am so thrilled to have found you, and I can't wait to spend the rest of my life getting to know you and my beautiful grandchildren. I couldn't be more proud*

of all of you. Pip, you have done an amazing job in bringing them up on your own, and I'm sure that when Peter gets home, he will be delighted. They are both lovely children.

I know what I am about to do will, I am sure, raise a protest from you, but I will not hear 'no' for an answer. We finally met up through Peak, Hall & Ellis, and I understand that under the terms of her will, my mother wanted you and Marion to have an inheritance. She knew how difficult things had been for you throughout your childhood and she was desperate for you and Marion to be friends, but I know that this has proved to be impossible. However, in these difficult times, I don't want you to lose out. For this reason, the enclosed cheque is from Granny. I shall send an equal amount to Marion, without condition. I have no idea where she is, of course, but Mr Ellis promised to post it on. As for your share, do with it what you will. You are under no obligation to anyone.

All my love,
Dad

Pip turned the cheque over in her hands once more. What an amazing gift. What an opportunity.

The DD Gang were all together for the first time in ages. The old derelict house had lost some of its appeal, mainly because of the smell. Now that the weather was warming up, it was worse than ever. They had noticed some funny-looking mushrooms growing on the walls, and the cellar was very damp. Norman had a weak chest and it made him cough a lot. Everywhere smelled musty and old.

'I don't like coming here any more,' said Norman. 'It stinks.'

'We'll be able to play on the beach soon,' said Billy. 'They're clearing all the barbed wire and the mines.'

'There ain't no mines,' Gideon scoffed. 'They only put the notice up to scare off the Germans.'

'So shall we make this the last time?' said Colin.

'We'd better get our stuff,' said Georgie. 'I don't want to leave my tail fin and Goliath here for somebody else.'

'I know,' said Norman. 'Let's have a party to say goodbye to the old place.'

'Good idea,' said Gideon. 'We could pile everything in the middle of the floor and blow it all up.'

'Don't be daft,' said Billy. 'We'd blow ourselves up and all.'

Several boys pounced on Gideon and pulled him to the ground. The scrap was a good one, with everybody egging them on.

'I know what I'd like to do before we go,' said Georgie.

Billy slipped his arm around Georgie's shoulders. 'Oh, and what's that?'

Georgie grinned. 'Find a way to fire Goliath.'

Lillian came back on Tuesday afternoon. Gordon had been dozing in the armchair in the sitting room. He'd been to the pub until closing time and had brought a couple of bottles home. The kid was at school, and his mother-in-law had gone to the shops.

A car door slammed and he heard voices outside in the street. He rose to peep round the curtain. Lillian was standing on the pavement beside a black Humber. She was dressed in an expensive-looking suit. A flash-looking geezer got out of the car and opened the boot. He pulled out a suitcase. 'I'll bring it for you.'

Lillian took a compact out of her handbag and powdered her nose. 'Thank you, darling.'

Gordon bristled with anger.

They walked up the path and she put the key in the door. Gordon hovered by the sitting-room door.

Lillian came in and turned to her companion. 'Pop it down there, Monty, there's a dear.'

Monty put the case in the hallway. Then Lillian put her arms around his neck and they kissed on the lips. It was only when he saw Gordon that he pulled back. Lillian's face paled as she turned round. 'Gordon,' she gasped. 'You're home.'

There was a pregnant silence and then she said, 'Monty, this is my husband, back from the war.' She walked towards him and brushed his cheek with her face, kissing the air beside it. She smelled the beer on his breath and wrinkled her nose. 'Gordon, you haven't met Monty. He's my agent, Montague Rankin. He's doing wonders for my career.'

'Is that what you call it?' Gordon said acidly.

Lillian turned to Monty. 'I'd better let you go, Monty. This is a special occasion. I'm sure you'll understand

– my husband coming back. See you soon.' She closed the door. 'Really, Gordon, you could have been a little more civil,' she said peevishly. 'When did you get back?'

'Saturday,' he said, lighting a Player's Navy Cut. 'I thought you might be there to meet me.'

'I was working,' she said. 'Monty has been very busy.'

'I bet he has,' said Gordon.

'It's not like that,' said Lillian, tossing her head.

'Are you sleeping with him?'

'Don't be ridiculous,' she cried indignantly. 'He's my agent.' She took off her coat and hung it on the hall-stand. 'Look here, Gordon, I'm pleased to see that you got home safe and sound and all that, but you've been away for a long time. Things have changed. We're not the same people any more. I've got a life of my own now. I'm becoming famous. Monty says it won't be long before I'm a radio star.'

Gordon took a long drag on his cigarette. She certainly looked the part. That suit didn't come from the jumble sale, and she even smelled expensive.

'How long have you got before you have to go back?' she said, looking at herself in the hallstand mirror and patting her hair. 'Or have they given you your discharge papers?'

Gordon pushed himself against the doorpost to stand up straight. 'I've got two months' leave,' he said, moving towards her. 'You're looking good, Lil.'

She stepped away. 'I'd better go upstairs and change,' she said. 'Where's Mum?'

'Shopping.' He caught her wrist. 'She'd only just gone,' he said suggestively. 'We could go upstairs together.'

Lillian tugged at her arm, but he held on. 'Gordon, I'm tired,' she said firmly. 'Monty and I have been on the road for hours. Besides, Flora will be home from school soon.'

'I'm your husband,' he said crossly.

Lillian snatched her arm away from him. 'Oh, grow up, Gordon. You're drunk.'

CHAPTER 31

Maud Abbott had been staring at the envelope for most of the morning. The solicitor's name on the left-hand corner intrigued her – Peak, Hall & Ellis. Why were they writing to Marion again? Well over a year had passed since that first letter came with her mother-in-law's strange bequest. The solicitor had given Marion no clue as to how much she might get from the estate had Philippa agreed to pretend they were reconciled, but Maud had a shrewd idea it wouldn't be a large amount. Darcy Abbott wasn't rich, but she wasn't a pauper either. The twins had been given a year to resolve their differences or their inheritance would go to another. That time was long gone, so why write a second letter?

Marion was at work. She'd done quite well for herself. She was only a secretary, but working for Sir Keith Samson was certainly a feather in her cap. He respected her, probably realizing that her appearance would curtail any office flirting. There had been one man who had shown more than a casual interest in her daughter. Richard Lynch didn't seem to mind how she looked. There had been invitations to the theatre, concerts and even a candlelit dinner, but when Marion brought him home to meet her, Maud had soon put a stop to it. She didn't have to say much. A veiled hint that although Marion was a perfect daughter, she would never be a mother and poor Maud would miss having grandchildren was enough. It wasn't true, of course, but it certainly helped Richard to turn his attentions elsewhere. Afterwards, she'd felt a little guilty about it, but they were happy as they were, and if she was brutally honest, who would look after her in her old age?

Maud took the envelope down from the mantelpiece and steamed it open. She lowered herself into a chair as she read it. Mr Ellis, the solicitor, had written to say the benefactor of her mother-in-law's will had enclosed the following cheque as a gift. There was no indication as to who the unknown person was, but Maud was in no doubt as to his identity: Stanley Abbott, her husband. She unfolded the cheque and gasped. Five hundred pounds! Her hand trembled. Now she was faced with a dilemma. Her instinct had been to tear it up, but five hundred pounds would make such a difference to their lives. Should she give it to Marion and pretend she had opened the letter by mistake? She couldn't do that either. As far as Marion was concerned, her father was dead. How could she confess after all this time that she'd faked his demise to stop the twins from asking questions? She'd been apprehensive enough when they'd met Philippa in case she knew Stanley was still alive.

She laid the cheque on the kitchen table and looked at it carefully. It was made out to 'Miss M. E. Abbott'. With some careful pen-work, she could change the name. If she added a small loop over the 'i' in 'Miss' and joined it into the first 's', she could make it look like a capital 'R' – MRS. Her first initial and Marion's were the same. What luck that Stanley hadn't written her name in full. That 'E' could easily be changed into her second initial, 'B' for Beatrice. Maud felt a tingle of excitement. It wouldn't be like stealing, would it? After all, if her mother-in-law had simply given her granddaughters the money when she died, without all this 'let's make up and be friends' rigmarole, she would have looked after the money anyway. She would have had to. The twins had been seventeen and still minors in the eyes of the law, so where was the difference if she looked after Marion's share of the money now? Maud placed the cheque back in the envelope and put it into her handbag. All she needed was some ink in the same colour and a little practice. She was only taking what she deserved, and Marion would get it when she passed on, so where was the harm?

Pip and Stella were surprised that Lillian hadn't bothered to mention that Gordon was home before.

'How marvellous!' Stella cried. 'How is he?'

Lillian shrugged. 'All right, I suppose.'

They had arranged a get-together at Pip's place for

a cup of tea and a catch-up. Pip and Lillian had both brought a present for the baby. Pip had made a beautifully smocked romper suit in blue, while Lillian had brought Stella all Flora's old baby nappies.

'They've been in the loft since she was about eighteen months,' she said, 'but Mum's washed them and they've come up lovely. There's still a lot of use in them.'

'Thank you,' cried Stella. 'You can never have enough nappies.' She gave her friend a nudge. 'And if you ever need them back—'

'I won't,' Lillian quickly interrupted. Embarrassed, Stella and Pip avoided her eye.

'Could Gordon be the person I saw in the alley-way?' said Pip. Her two friends gave her a puzzled look. 'It was a couple of nights ago,' she went on. 'I saw someone out there smoking. It was late: ten or ten-thirty. I couldn't see who it was, but I'm pretty sure it was a man, and he headed off towards your back gate.'

'That wouldn't surprise me,' said Lillian dispassionately. 'Gordon smokes like a chimney.'

'Has he got his discharge papers, then?' Pip wanted to know.

Lillian shook her head. 'Not yet. He's got two months' leave and then he has to report to Bovington.'

'What does Flora think,' said Stella, with a smile, 'about having her daddy back again? She would only have been tiny when she last saw him.'

'She's finding it hard to adjust,' said Lillian. 'She's

345

used to coming into my bed halfway through the night, but of course all that's stopped now. She's very upset about it.'

'Oh dear,' said Stella with a chuckle.

'You don't seem very happy either,' Pip observed.

Lillian chewed her bottom lip. 'To be perfectly honest,' she began, 'I'm not. Oh, don't get me wrong. I'm glad he's home safe and sound. I wouldn't wish the man any harm, but I've got my own life now. I've told him I've no intention of going back to being just a housewife again.'

'That's what he would expect,' said Stella.

'I don't care,' Lillian said. 'I'm not having it, I tell you. I'm not having it.'

Her defiant glare told her friends the discussion was over. Outside the back door, Timothy Michael began to stir. Stella got up, reached into the pram and picked up her son.

'Oh my,' said Pip, glad to change the subject, 'he's put on weight.'

'Nearly ten pounds now,' said Stella proudly. 'I posted a photograph to Johnny last week.' She sat back down and opened her blouse. 'Always hungry, aren't you, darling?'

'What about your father, Pip?' Lillian asked.

Pip went to the dresser and pulled a large envelope from one of the drawers. 'Elspeth sent me this,' she said, emptying the contents onto the table. The envelope was full of cards. Pip sifted through them, placing them into two distinct piles. 'My father didn't know where we were, but every year he bought Marion and me a birthday card and a Christmas card. Look, there's the one he gave me for my tenth birthday, and this one for my seventh birthday. That one was for the Christmas the year I was twenty-one.'

'You say Elspeth sent them?' said Stella.

'Daddy kept them in a drawer,' said Pip. 'Apparently now that we've met, he wanted to get rid of them, but she sent them to me instead.'

'I guess she wanted you to know that he'd never forgotten you,' said Stella. 'What a lovely woman.'

Pip nodded. 'It's not hard to see why he fell in love with her.'

'They're organizing a street party for when Victory Europe Day is announced,' said Lillian, changing the subject. 'It can't go on much longer, can it?'

'Not for us,' said Stella, 'but Pip might have to wait a bit longer. Any news of your Peter?' she said, finally voicing the one question neither of them liked to ask.

Pip shook her head. 'But I shall join in with you all, don't you worry. There's a lot to be thankful for. I've still got my kids, and now I have my father as well.' There was a semi-awkward silence. Then she said, 'Tell you what, though. When Peter does come home, we'll have the party to end all parties.'

'Mrs Sinclair,' said Mr Fisher, holding the door open to allow her through.

Pip, dressed in her best clothes, squeezed past his huge girth and entered his small office. She lowered

347

herself onto a wooden chair in front of his desk and waited for him to waddle round to the other side. There was a buff-coloured folder on the desk. He opened it and leaned back in his chair.

'As you instructed me,' he began, 'I am pleased to tell you that both parties have agreed to accept your offer at the suggested price.'

Sitting primly on the chair, Pip showed no reaction, except perhaps to grip the handbag perched on her lap a little tighter.

'I have drawn up the papers,' said Mr Fisher. 'All that's needed is your signature.'

Pip nodded.

Mr Fisher leaned forward in what he hoped was a fatherly way and put his elbows on the desk. Pressing his fingertips together, he gave her a concerned look. 'However, I would be failing in my duty if I did not advise caution.'

Pip didn't move. She knew exactly what he was going to say. Her plan was a good one, commendable under the circumstances, but she would not make nearly as much money as she would if she thought about investing in housing. People need somewhere to live, he would say. With the war drawing to a close, she was turning down the opportunity to make a wise investment. If she had come to him sooner, he would have advised hanging on to that twenty acres on the Maybridge estate. In five or maybe ten years' time, she could have made a killing. It wasn't entirely her fault, he would say. Women need a man's input and sound advice. He didn't want to sound presumptuous, but as her husband wasn't around, she should have come to him.

'While I value your opinion,' she interrupted, 'my mind is made up. I have worked for years to this end, and with the capital I now have, I cannot wait a moment longer.'

'It is a huge undertaking, Mrs Sinclair.'

'I know,' she said. 'Now, where do I sign?'

The cashier looked up as she came to the window. 'Good morning, Mrs Abbott, and how are we today?'

Normally his banal greeting irritated her, but today she was too nervous to be cross. She had dressed with care because she wanted to create the right impression. She wore the jersey suit she'd had made up in the style she'd seen Barbara Stanwyck wearing in a film. It was a trifle too hot in this weather, but she knew she looked every inch the lady when she had it on. Her matching hat and the three strings of pearls round her neck added that je ne sais quoi. With a bit of luck, the cashier would be more interested in her than the cheque.

'Fine, thank you,' she said, passing the paying-in book and the cheque over the counter.

He opened the book and glanced at the cheque.

'Are you doing something special this Whitsun?' Maud hoped she could distract him.

The cashier smiled. 'The wife and I are taking the kids to Weymouth.'

Maud had not the slightest interest in him or his wife and kids, but she cried, 'How lovely! Let's hope you have the weather for it.'

He pressed his banker's stamp onto the pad and rocked it in the ink. 'I hope so too,' he said as his stamp hovered over the paying-in book. 'Last year, it poured the whole time.' He thumped the slip and then the stub.

'I shall certainly keep my fingers crossed for you,' said Maud.

'And what about you, Mrs Abbott? Have you got any plans?'

'Oh no,' said Maud. 'My daughter and I like a quiet life.'

The banker's stamp crashed over the cheque and he pushed the paying-in book back towards her. 'There you are, all done. Good afternoon, Mrs Abbott.'

'Thank you,' she said humbly. 'You've been a great help.'

Outside in the street, she had a job not to laugh out loud. Indeed, he had been a great help. He'd brought the stamp down right over her alterations.

The sound of Gordon crashing up the stairs was enough to wake the dead, but Lillian turned her face to the wall and pretended to be asleep. As he burst into the bedroom, the door banged against the chest of drawers. He clicked the light switch, but nothing happened. How could it? She'd taken the lightbulb out of its fitting.

He sat on the edge of the bed and pulled the chamber pot from underneath. A moment later, the sickly smell of warm urine filled the air. Ugh. Lillian curled her lip. Why couldn't he go to the privy before he came up to bed? He pulled back the bedclothes and she heard him throwing his clothes over the end of the bedstead. As he clambered between the sheets, there was a loud report and a foul odour hovered between them. 'Whoops,' he muttered, and giggled. Lillian despised him more with each passing day. The people in the theatre treated her like royalty, yet every night she came home to this. It took every ounce of strength not to sit up and scream obscenities at him.

She tensed her body as she felt him pawing her back. He was trying to get close to her. He cursed. 'Damn it. What have you done with the bed, girl?'

She stayed silent. He wouldn't have his way this time. It was becoming more and more difficult to fend him off, even though he was drunk every night when he came to bed. She had rigged the bedding so that he was between the sheets, while she lay on top of them. He sat up and tugged at them. 'What have you done, Lil?' His voice was getting louder.

'Shh,' she said, 'you'll wake Flora.'

'I don't care if I wake the 'ole of blurry Worthing,' he said, his voice even louder. 'And what 'appened to the lights?'

He struck a match and tugged at the bedclothes. The blanket came off at the same time as the match went out. She heard him lumber towards the window, where he pulled back the curtains. The darkness in the bedroom became less inky because of the street light. He stumbled back to the bed. She had grabbed the blanket again and was trying to hold on to it, but he was astride her now, his boozy breath making her head spin.

'No, Gordon. Stop it, will you? I don't want to.'

'Aw, come on, Lil,' he pleaded. 'I've been home a blurry month and you've never let me come near you.'

'Get off me,' she said, desperately trying to push him away. She couldn't let him win. She couldn't even bear the thought of it, and if she got pregnant now, he would ruin everything. She might be willing to take a risk with someone she really liked, but not with Gordon. She couldn't understand what she ever saw in him. He was a loser. They were both wrestling with her nightie now, her trying to keep it on, him trying to pull it off.

She hit the side of his head. 'No, Gordon. Stop it.'

He stared at her in shocked silence, then hit her back. The nightdress ripped and Lillian cried out in pain.

They heard Dorcas knocking on the wall, and in the distance, Flora was crying.

'Now look what you've done,' she said, gaining mastery at last. She got up, and snatching her dressing gown from the nail on the back of the bedroom door, she left the room to comfort her child.

It was tempting to spend the rest of the night with Flora, but she knew she had to go back and sort this out once and for all. When she returned, he was sitting on the edge of the bed with his head in his hands. Lillian got another nightdress out of the drawer.

'I'm sorry, Lil,' he said brokenly. 'I shouldn't have hit you, Lil. I'm really sorry. I only want what's mine by rights.'

'I don't want you, Gordon,' she said coldly. 'I want a divorce.'

'A divorce?' he said incredulously. 'People like us don't get a divorce.'

'We never should have got married in the first place,' she said stubbornly.

'You loved me back then.'

'I was young and foolish,' she said. 'I don't even think I understood what love was. I've told you before. We're not the same people.'

'All I want is a home, a wife and a family,' he said. 'I'll treat you well, Lil. You'll be my princess. That's enough for me.'

'It might be enough for you, Gordon, but it certainly isn't for me,' she said, climbing back into bed. 'I've had a taste of real life. Do you realize that I can get as much as twelve pounds a week in variety shows? And you want me to give all that up and go back to the kitchen sink? Oh no, Gordon. It's not going to happen.'

'When did you become so hard-hearted, Lil?'

'And when did you become a drunk?'

'I wouldn't be if—' he began.

'Oh, don't start that again,' she snapped. 'If I'm hard, it's because I've had to be. While you were sitting on your bum in Germany, moaning about Red Cross parcels, I was keeping a roof over Flora's head and trying to give her some semblance of normality.' She threw herself back against the pillow. 'Now let's get some sleep, shall we?'

Dejected and beaten, Gordon lay in the dark feeling like a whipped dog. It wasn't his fault he'd been made a POW. She shouldn't speak to him like that. Divorce? She'd got to be joking. If he went home and told his dad she wanted a divorce, he'd knock him into the middle of next week. Oh no, he wouldn't give her a divorce. He'd sooner kill her.

Outside in the alleyway, a shadowy figure took a long drag on their cigarette and threw it down. Raised voices again; he couldn't hear what was being said but it was becoming a habit. What on earth was going on in there? What a disappointment. How hurtful. What on earth was wrong with the man? It was enough to make anyone sick to their stomach. Grinding the cigarette into the soft earth, the smoker took one last look at the bedroom window before hurrying away into the night.

CHAPTER 32

Georgie and Hazel were very excited to meet their grandfather, and Pip had taken a lot of trouble with their appearance. Hazel looked as pretty as a picture in a yellow-and-white patchwork dress that Pip had made from oddments. Her hair was tied with a yellow ribbon – a rarity she had bought at the haberdashery at the corner of Montague Street. As for her son, although he still wore short trousers, Georgie looked every inch the English schoolboy in his first ever two-piece suit. Pip had made it from the material in a suit of Peter's. She hadn't opened his side of the wardrobe for ages, and when she had, she'd been horrified to discover the sleeve had been damaged by moths. It meant a total clear-out, a thorough washing of the inside of the wardrobe itself and mothballs in every pocket when she hung his clothes back up again. While she'd been doing that, she'd spent a moment or two holding his things close to her cheek just to get the smell of him. It had been so long, too long.

Pip had pulled herself up sharply. She mustn't give way. The suit was ruined as far as Peter was concerned, but the rest of the material had been far too good to waste. Pip had never tried making anything tailored before, and although the jacket collar was a little off centre, the suit looked quite good. Georgie, who had no idea that his mother had made it, was very proud of it.

The visit of the group captain and his wife coincided with a gift to the nation of twenty-two million eggs from Canada. With the promise of six to ten eggs per ration book, Pip was able to make a Victoria sponge cake in the traditional way. She'd virtually spring-cleaned the house and waited nervously for his arrival.

They arrived on time, and after a few shy and awkward moments, it was as if they'd only parted yesterday. In no time at all, her father had delighted Georgie with first-hand stories of the Battle of Britain and its heroic pilots.

'We had a Heinkel come down here,' said Georgie.

'Did you really?' said his grandfather, even though Pip had already told him the tale.

Pip, Elspeth and Hazel left them swapping experiences to attend to things in the kitchen.

'It looks as if things are finally coming to an end,' said Pip, settling Hazel down at a table in the hallway first. Her grandparents had brought her a doll's house. It wasn't new, but it had absolutely everything. Elspeth explained that it had been in her family for years.

'Are you sure you want Hazel to have it?' Pip had asked.

'Absolutely,' said Elspeth. 'I have no children of my own and it's time to pass it on.'

Although it was the end of April, it was far too cold to sit in the garden. The radio said that there had been as much as six inches of snow on the Kent coast. Worthing, protected by the South Downs, had only had a sprinkling, but coupled with some sharp frosts, it had been enough to damage the new season's potatoes, runner beans and soft fruits. Stella's parents-in-law had been devastated to see their plum tree, which was in blossom, totally decimated and the strawberry beds completely ruined.

Once they were alone in the kitchen, there was a chance to speak more freely. Elspeth helped to load the tea trolley with the sandwiches and cakes Pip had made.

'There's a rumour going round that Hitler is already dead,' said Elspeth. 'They haven't said as much on the news, but Stanley is convinced that it's true.'

'I don't usually wish anybody dead,' Pip said with a sigh, 'but let's hope so.'

'Where are the children from your little nursery?' asked Elspeth.

'I gave myself a holiday,' said Pip. 'This is a special occasion. It's not every day you get to entertain the father you've only seen once in twenty years.'

Elspeth gave her a grin. 'Will you carry on with the nursery if the war ends?'

'Oh yes,' said Pip, 'and I have plans to expand.'

Elspeth looked around. Pip didn't have a lot of space as it was. Where would she expand?

'I'm hoping to create a purpose-built nursery,' Pip went on. 'I've just sold some land, and now I'm in the process of buying a property to convert.'

'My word,' said Elspeth, clearly impressed.

'You see, I think times have changed,' Pip said as she poured boiling water into the teapot. 'The war has given women a taste of freedom. They've had their own money and so I think that even when the men come back, they'll want to carry on working, or maybe they'll *have* to go out to work. In any case, they'll want somewhere to put their preschool children. Hence yours truly.'

Elspeth smiled admiringly. 'You're an amazing girl,' she said. 'Most men think women are too stupid to run a business.'

'Ha!' Pip cried. 'Since Peter has been gone, I've been renting out two shops, running a small nursery from my own home, and I've got my finger in a couple of other pies as well.'

Elspeth chuckled. 'You're definitely your father's daughter.'

Just as they were about to push the laden trolley towards the sitting room, Georgie came running into the kitchen. 'Look, Mummy. Look.' He was holding up a picture of an airman.

Pip glanced at the photograph. 'Ooh, that's Ginger Lacey, isn't it?'

In the photograph, the flying ace who was credited

with bringing down the Heinkel responsible for bombing Buckingham Palace was receiving a parachute and scarf especially made for him by the women of Australia. Pip turned her attention back to the trolley.

'You're not looking properly, Mummy,' Georgie complained.

Pip looked again at the man with the beaming smile in the foreground; then her eye strayed to the back of the picture and the knot of people behind. There, in the background, were her father and Elspeth.

'My goodness,' cried Pip, glancing up at Elspeth. 'You were there!' She took in a breath. 'That means you met the King! How wonderful.'

'And that's not all, Mummy,' Georgie cried as he held up a life jacket with Mae West's picture on the front. 'Grandfather says I can have this!'

The pub door swung open and Gordon walked inside. He had forgotten the weird licensing laws and had been standing outside for ages. Public houses in England and Wales were open from noon until two-thirty. They closed until six-thirty and then opened again until nine-thirty. He glanced up at the clock. It was thirty-one minutes past six.

'Ah, here he is,' said a voice at the bar. 'Better late than never, lad.'

Ron Knight had a pint waiting for him on the counter.

'How did you get in?' said Gordon.

Ron thumbed his nose and pushed the glass towards

Gordon. He drank it greedily. All he wanted was oblivion.

Gordon wasn't the only ex-POW in Worthing, but he was the only one who had Lillian for a wife. Whenever people found out who he was, he was regaled with stories about how wonderful she was. People recalled the early days when she was one of the Sussex Sisters and how she'd put down some sleazy git in some factory who wouldn't leave the girls alone. They told him how she'd raised hundreds of pounds for the Red Cross and Worthing Hospital. He heard that she'd held the hand of some dying old man and comforted his wife after the old boy had gone. They reminded him of how brave she'd been when their little girl had been burned by the fire when Reydon was hit in 1942. As he listened, Gordon squirmed inside. Little did they know that this same woman was somebody else behind closed doors. While he was being pushed away from the marital bed and humiliated in his own home, his own child still ran from the room when he came in. Dorcas said it was only because she was a bit jealous that she was no longer allowed in her mother's bedroom. His mother-in-law told him that given time, she'd come round, but they had no idea how much it hurt him, and being a man, he couldn't tell anyone, of course. They'd think him a wimp and a cissy. They'd tell him to give her a slap and take what was rightfully his, but Gordon wasn't the sort of man to take anything by force, especially not a woman. Only the drink helped. It dulled his senses. It made him everybody's pal. All they had to do was keep the beer coming.

'She was a little gem all through the war, that wife of yours,' said Ron. 'I kept a weather eye on her while you were away. I never once saw her misbehaving.'

He wondered if he should tell Ron about the poison-pen letters he'd received while still in camp. He'd spent days brooding over them. He'd been angry and bad-tempered, but he'd finally come to terms with them. It was sour grapes on somebody's part. Whoever wrote them was probably jealous, so one night he'd burned the lot, but they kept on coming. They always started the same way, *Dear Gordon, I'm very sorry to have to do this, but I thought you should know* . . . and ended, *Signed, A well-wisher.* Letters full of accusations and innuendo. He should know that she wasn't faithful. He deserved better. They poisoned his mind and filled his nights with thoughts of revenge. Perhaps they were right. She hadn't let him touch her since he'd got back. That was no way for a dutiful wife to behave, now, was it?

Ron had once confided in Gordon that his wife had been unfaithful. She had run off with some actor or some such when he'd got back from France. Apparently, she'd left him a note saying she didn't want to live with a one-eyed whelk. Gordon had sympathized with him, but he hadn't told him how things were with Lillian. Ron seemed to think Lillian could do no wrong. He desperately wanted to tell someone how things really

361

were, but he wasn't sure his newly found friends would believe him.

Another pint appeared in front of him. The barman indicated that it had come from a woman in the ladies' bar. Gordon leaned forward to peer behind the wooden partition and saw Betty waving her hand. He nodded his appreciation and lifted the glass. Betty Shrimpton followed Ron everywhere like a devoted sheepdog. He glanced over at him. He was smiling, a cigarette hanging from the corner of his mouth. Gordon frowned. If by his own admission, Ron had been to all Lillian's concerts, could she have been unfaithful with him? It was a possibility. Ron never stopped talking about her. There were times when Gordon had wanted to shout, 'Shut up. You don't know anything about her. She's *my* wife.' He reached in his pocket for his cigarette packet, but Ron got there first. He was holding out his cigarette case. Gordon took one.

While Ron searched for his lighter, Gordon decided that he was letting his imagination run away with him, but then the thought of Lillian staring up at Ron all doe-eyed filled his mind. He could just imagine her parting her lips, and Ron's mouth covering hers. His breath became faster as he could almost physically feel his body becoming aroused at the thought of Ron's hand creeping from her waist to her bottom. Gordon's eyes narrowed. Yes, that was it. Ron was the sod who was having an affair with Lillian. All this pally-pally stuff was just a smokescreen, and for all he knew it was still going on.

'I wanted to have a word with you,' said Ron. He held the lighter towards him, and at the same time a swarthy-looking man bumped into them and Ron spilled his drink onto the bar and all over his sleeve.

'Watch it,' said Ron irritably as he came back to the bar to sup his beer.

'Sorry, mate,' said the man. 'Here, let me get you another one.'

Gordon lit his cigarette and Ron put the lighter away. 'It's about you and your missus,' he went on. 'I don't think you're treating her right.'

Gordon stared at him, his nostrils flaring slightly as he balled his fists.

The barman had poured another pint and the man paid up. Pushing it towards Ron, he said, 'Who are we talking about?'

'Lillian Harris,' said Ron. 'Not that it's any of your business.'

'Plucky little cat's meow that one. Lovely knockers too,' said the man, just before Gordon's fist hit him in the mouth.

Lillian and Dorcas glanced nervously at each other. It might only be teatime, but the person banging on the door was doing it loud enough to wake the dead. Dorcas grabbed a saucepan and stood a little to the left as Lillian opened the door. She gasped. It was Pip.

She burst into the kitchen, her face wreathed in smiles. 'I've heard from him,' she cried. 'Peter has made contact.'

A second later, they were all dancing around the kitchen, laughing and smiling. 'Of course, it's not a proper letter,' said Pip, 'but at least I know he's alive.'

She produced a grubby-looking card. It wasn't much, and the message had obviously been written by someone who had a poor knowledge of English, but Peter's signature was at the bottom.

> *Our precent quarters and work is good. They rains have finished, it is now beautiful weather. I am working healthily. We receive newspapers printed in English which reveel world events.*
>
> *We had joyfully received a payment of some milk, tea, margarine, sugar and cigarettes from kind Japanese authorities.*
>
> *We are very anxious to here from home, but some prisoners have received letters or cables.*
>
> *Everyone is hopful for speedy end to the war and with faith at the future we look forward to happy soon reunion.*
>
> *With best wishes from*
> *Peter Sinclair xx*

Although overjoyed, Pip was under no illusions, but after more than three years of silence, it was something to celebrate.

The boys in the DD Gang were awestruck. Georgie's Mae West life jacket had to be the most amazing war trophy ever. Georgie was bursting with pride.

'And you say this was actually worn by Ginger Lacey himself?' Billy said as he stroked it reverently.

'Yes,' said Georgie. He could feel his face heating slightly. He didn't know that this particular jacket had been worn by Ginger Lacey, but his grandfather had shown him the photograph and then given him the life jacket. He hadn't thought to ask if the two went together, but it was perfectly possible, wasn't it?

The day before, the boys had been told that the Germans had surrendered. The war was over. Today and tomorrow were holidays. When the news came, the whole town had gone mad. People were dancing in the street until late last night. Respectable men and women were kissing each other all over the place. Today, just about everybody else's mum or dad had a hangover, so the boys were left pretty much to themselves. Georgie's mum was busy making stuff for the impromptu street party tomorrow, and Auntie Lillian's husband was in the police cells for starting a brawl in the Thieves' Kitchen. Georgie didn't much like Uncle Gordon. He smelled of beer and he never seemed to be able to walk straight. He and Auntie Lillian shouted a lot, and Flora told him and his sister that he frightened her. Still, he was locked up now, and Hazel and Flora were playing together in the garden, so he'd snuck off to the house for one more time.

The smell in the old house was worse than ever, and they were all aware of the creaking timbers. It wasn't nearly as much fun as it had been, so nobody wanted to stay long.

'You know we always said we would give Goliath a

bang when the war was over,' said Gideon. 'Well, I think I've worked out a way to do it.'

The boys listened bug-eyed as he told them his plan and they all agreed that it was an absolutely brilliant idea and that they would do it. After that, they cleared everything else from the den and took it home.

'The party starts at three,' said Gideon, 'so everybody needs to be here in their place at two-thirty.'

The boys parted, their eyes bright with excitement.

CHAPTER 33

Betty Shrimpton glanced up at the clock and tutted to herself. She had told him six o'clock and here it was a quarter to seven already. It really was too bad. If he was much longer, the pie in her oven would be spoiled beyond redemption. As it was, it was difficult keeping everything warm without overcooking. She'd done everything possible to make this meal special. She'd even managed to get a bit of beef. It had cost her an arm and a leg, and of course it was black market, but she was so looking forward to it. It was ages since she'd eaten beef. She'd cooked it slowly with onions and gravy; then just before six, she'd put a pie crust on the top. The plan was that she would offer him a drink in the sitting room (she had a lovely fire in the grate) before the meal. That way, he'd experience all the home comforts, but that part of the plan wouldn't happen now. They'd have to eat straight away. She looked at the clock once again. Five to seven. For goodness' sake, where was he?

Today was Ron Knight's birthday, which made it the ideal occasion to ask him over for a meal without looking too forward. She'd even bought him a lovely wallet, but she couldn't make up her mind whether to give him the present as soon as he came in or after they'd eaten. She'd got it in the market. The trader had told her it was genuine imitation leather, so she'd paid a fair sum for it, but she didn't want him getting the wrong idea. She was a respectable woman and she'd trailed after him for long enough. She might be too long in the tooth for chasing rainbows, but she wanted to settle down to married companionship.

She put some more coal on the fire and went back into the kitchen to check the pie. It was getting a bit too brown, so she turned the oven down and put a sheet of greaseproof paper over the top. The sound of the door-bell came as a great relief. She almost missed it. It was one of those wind-up bells, and after a few uses, the cap became loose. The sound should be high-pitched and loud, but now it was more like a low clunk. Her little dog, Dilly, shut away in the bedroom, barked like mad.

Ron Knight stood on the doorstep dripping wet. She hadn't realized it was raining.

'Sorry I'm late, Betty,' he began. A stream of water ran from the edge of his hat. 'And I hope you don't mind but I've brought someone else along.'

Mind? Of course she minded. She minded terribly, but what could she say? It was then that she noticed that Ron was sporting a black eye and his bottom lip was swollen. 'What happened to you?' Betty gasped.

Ron didn't answer, but as he moved to one side, she saw Gordon Harris standing on the step behind him. It took all her willpower to stick a smile on her face and say, 'Oh, Gordon. Do come in. You're most welcome.'

'He was in the pub when I popped in for these,' said Ron, thrusting two bottles of milk stout into her hands. 'He's had a bit of a rough time and I thought he could do with some company.'

And I bet you stayed for a couple of pints, she thought acidly. She could smell the beer on his breath. Betty wrinkled her nose slightly. She'd soon put a stop to that when they were wed.

'Come in,' she said cheerfully. She led the way to the kitchen. 'Gordon, maybe you could bring that hall chair with you and I'll lay another place.'

'Summat smells good,' said Ron as he came up behind her. Betty felt a warm glow of pleasure. Ron moved a little closer. 'The poor lad got himself locked up last night,' he went on. 'Some mouthy bastard insulted his wife, so he punched him.'

'What about you?' Betty asked.

'Remind me not to stand in between next time,' he said with a grin.

Betty pursed her lips disapprovingly.

There wasn't a lot of room in her small kitchen, but they pulled the table away from the wall and made a bit more space. Betty bustled around them, taking the pie out of the oven (just in time, it would seem), draining the potatoes (which had begun to break up, so she'd have to mash them using some of her precious butter ration) and dishing up the cabbage. She heaped the men's plates and put a much smaller portion on

369

her own. She had planned to have enough left over for Ron to take a bit of pie home, but having Gordon here put the kibosh on that. The men tucked in.

'Umm, this is champion, Betty,' Ron said appreciatively.

Betty lowered her eyes modestly. 'There's apple pie for afters,' she said.

Inevitably, the conversation came round to Lillian. Betty didn't say a lot. What could she say? She was Gordon's wife, and Ron was besotted with her.

'What will you do when your demob comes?' Ron asked. He leaned back in his chair, his plate empty.

'Move away,' said Gordon.

Ron sat back up again. 'Move away?' he repeated. 'Where?'

Gordon shrugged. 'As far away as possible,' he said.

Betty let out a secret sigh of relief.

'What does Lillian think about that?' cried Ron. 'What about her career?'

'She won't care,' said Gordon bitterly. 'Why should she? She's having the time of her life.'

'I don't understand,' said Ron. 'Surely she'd want to keep up the contacts in this area. This is where she's well known. And what about the Sussex Sisters?'

'I don't know and I don't care,' said Gordon. 'She wants a divorce, and I want a new start.'

The colour drained from Ron's face. 'You're getting a divorce?' he thundered. 'What's the matter with you, man? After all she's done for morale, you want to get rid of her?'

'Perhaps Gordon would rather not talk about this,' Betty interjected. 'After all, what happens between a man and his wife is a private matter.'

Gordon was keeping his head down as he fiddled with the edge of the tablecloth.

'That little lassie is a good wife and a good mother,' said Ron. 'You don't know what side your bread is buttered on.'

'Who wants apple pie?' Betty said desperately.

Gordon rose to his feet. 'I hope you'll excuse me, Mrs Shrimpton,' he said stiffly, 'but I have to go. Thank you for a lovely meal.'

He hurried from the kitchen without a backward glance. Dilly, still shut in the bedroom, started barking again. Betty hurried after Gordon and helped him into his wet coat. 'I'm sorry about that,' she said. 'Are you sure you want to go? Perhaps if we change the subject . . .'

'Thank you, Mrs Shrimpton,' he said stiffly, 'but I'm sick of people giving me their opinions when they don't know the half of it.'

She closed the door behind him and patted the back of her hair. 'Be quiet, Dilly,' she said sharply. 'Go to your bed.'

'Well,' she said, returning to the kitchen, 'that was a turn-up for the books.'

'The man's mad,' said Ron. 'A lovely wife like that . . .'

'Oh, Ron, surely you must have seen what's been going on?'

He stared at her with a blank expression and she

supposed she'd have to spell it out for him. Why were men so stupid?

'The pianist,' she went on. 'Surely you could see the way she looked at him? I reckon they've been having it off for ages.' Ron continued to stare, so she reminded him of a couple of other occasions.

'Lillian was always faithful to her husband,' he said stubbornly. 'It's him that doesn't appreciate her.'

'I knew what sort of woman she was from the minute I saw her,' said Betty, dishing up his apple pie. 'Soon after she came to work on the railway, I saw her kissing a Canadian in the Ilex Way.' She curled her lips disapprovingly. 'French-kissing they were, and with her little daughter standing right next to her.'

Ron jumped to his feet, scraping the chair on the kitchen floor. His face was puce with rage. 'You women,' he spat. 'You're all the bloody same.'

'I beg your pardon,' Betty said indignantly.

Ron was already in the hallway putting on his coat. Behind the bedroom door, the dog was hysterical.

'What did I say?' Betty cried as she ran after him. 'I only told you what everybody knows. You ask Iris.'

'Thanks for the meal,' he said formally.

'But you haven't had your present yet,' Betty wailed.

Ron yanked the door open and stepped out into the night.

It was about nine when Lillian heard a muffled knock on the door. She was alone in the house with Flora. As far as she knew, Gordon was still in the police cells, and her mother had gone over to Lancing. Gordon had got into a fight in a pub, and having decked a couple of the regulars, he'd been carted off by the police. Dorcas wanted to celebrate this evening with her sister, so they'd arranged for her to stay overnight and come back on the bus tomorrow in time to help with the party. The Sussex Sisters were going to sing for one last time in the evening and Lillian was looking forward to it. She wondered what peacetime would bring. She hoped it would usher in a new chapter in her life, one without Gordon and one with something much more palatable – fame and fortune. Although her mother wasn't too keen on the idea of her and Gordon getting divorced, Dorcas had agreed to look after Flora if she had to travel, and Monty had set up some amazing contacts. It really looked as if she could be in a variety show next month, and if she was lucky, she might even get the chance to go abroad to entertain the troops in their peacekeeping role.

She'd been in the sitting room tidying music sheets in preparation of tomorrow evening. It was fun going over all the old songs once more, though there was a slight worry that the weather might scupper their plans. It was raining cats and dogs out there right now. Pip and Stella had come round in the afternoon and they'd picked out the old songs they had sung in the group – 'You Always Hurt the One You Love', 'Don't Sit Under the Apple Tree', 'I'll Be With You in Apple Blossom Time', 'The Trolley Song', 'Let Him Go, Let Him Tarry' – the list was endless, but Lillian had

373

insisted on singing a couple of her new solos as well. 'People like to hear me singing my new songs, and there's no time to rehearse them together,' she'd said. 'You do understand, don't you?'

She'd laid herself a place at the table in the kitchen and dished up some macaroni cheese, which was cooling on the rack. Lillian was in her dressing gown and she pulled it around her as she reached the back door. She was just about to open it when the clothes pulley slipped a bit. Lillian ducked, but luckily it stayed where it was. She heard the sound of shuffling feet. Was it Gordon? Had they let him out of jail? She really didn't want him here tonight, especially now that her mother wasn't around.

Lillian leaned towards the wooden door and called, 'Who is it?'

A voice on the other side said, 'It's me.'

Puzzled, Lillian opened the door and the light flooded out. 'Oh,' she said, surprised. 'It's you. You'd better come in.'

CHAPTER 34

Flora woke up early. Now that she was six, she washed herself and got dressed before going downstairs. She couldn't wait to put on the lovely dress Mummy had bought her for the street party. It had pretty baskets of flowers all over it and a swirly skirt.

In the kitchen, the big pulley was down, but Flora was able to walk underneath. Granny said they'd get it fixed someday, but nobody ever got round to it. It was very heavy, and the wooden rungs were held together at either end in an iron frame.

Mummy wasn't up yet, so Flora decided to get her own breakfast. There was a plate of food on the table, but it was cold and congealed, and Flora didn't fancy eating it. The loaf in the bread bin was whole, and she knew she wasn't allowed to use the big bread knife, but fortunately, there was half a slice next to it. It felt a bit hard, but with some jam (a little more than Mummy usually let her have), it went down a treat. There was no tea in the pot and very little milk, so she made do with a glass of water. She glanced at the clock on the wall. The big hand was on the twelve, and the little hand was on the nine. Mummy still wasn't up yet, and last night she'd said they had to be at Auntie Pip's by eight-thirty.

Flora crept back upstairs and knocked softly on Mummy's bedroom door. There was no answer. She called out. Still no answer, but as Flora pushed the door, it opened slowly. She knew she wasn't allowed in Mummy's bedroom any more, but seeing that Mummy was alone in the big bed, she was very tempted to run in and jump on top of her. She chewed her lip for a while before deciding not to do it. This was a very special day and she didn't want to make Mummy cross.

'Mummy,' she said softly. 'Can I come in?'

Her mother had her back to her and she didn't move.

'Mummy,' Flora said a little louder, 'we have to go to Auntie Pip's. We're going to be late.' She hung around, but her mother remained still. 'Shall I go first?'

Puzzled and hurt, Flora went downstairs. When the little hand was between the nine and the ten, and the big hand was on the three, she put on her coat and ran to the back door. It only took a minute to get to Auntie Pip's.

As Georgie opened the door, Flora heard Auntie Pip call from the kitchen, 'Who is it?'

'It's only Flora,' said Georgie, stepping back to let her in.

Auntie Pip came out of the kitchen. There was flour on her apron and some on her cheek as well. 'Now, you kids are going to have to make yourselves scarce if we're going to get this party under way. Auntie Stella, your mum and I have a lot to do.'

'Did I hear my name being taken in vain?' said a voice behind Flora. Auntie Stella was coming up the path with the big Silver Cross pram. Inside, Timothy Michael was fast asleep.

Hazel came bounding downstairs. 'Can we take Timothy Michael for a walk?'

Auntie Stella hesitated, but when Flora joined in with, 'Oh, please, Auntie Stella, please . . .' she relented.

'All right, but not too far, and if he wakes up and starts to cry, bring him straight back.'

'Hazel, ask Maisie at number four to go with you,' said Pip. 'She's a sensible girl.'

'Oh, Mummy,' Hazel protested.

'Run along now,' said Pip, 'and be back by lunch-time.' She turned to her son. 'Georgie, make sure you're home by then as well. We start at two o'clock.'

The children set off.

'Flora,' Pip called as they reached the garden gate, 'where's your mother?'

'In bed,' said Flora.

Pip and Stella were making good headway with the sandwiches. A couple of other neighbours had joined them in the kitchen, and with pooled resources the mountain was growing. Pip had knocked up some fairy cakes, and Mrs Armitage from the corner house had dug out half a packet of icing sugar. It was almost solid, but after some patient sieving using the back of a spoon, it was eventually usable.

Outside in the street, the men were putting up the trestle tables. They'd set them in a 'V' shape, and other neighbours were putting white sheets over the top. Men were up ladders hanging bunting and Union Jacks, while the women began laying the tables. Everywhere there was the sound of whistling, and the jokes and banter came a-plenty.

'Is somebody going to say grace before we eat?' one of the women called out.

'If my wife's been baking them cakes, it'll be better to pray *after* we've eaten,' said a male voice.

'Oh, you naughty boy, Jack Armitage,' another woman cried. 'I thought you were happily married.'

'My wife and I had twenty very happy years,' said Jack. 'And then we met.' His wife cuffed him on the arm as everyone enjoyed the joke.

At ten to eleven, there was still no sign of Lillian. Pip had moved from being cross and thinking she was getting out of all the work to genuine concern.

'She must have a hangover,' Stella joked. 'From what I hear, that was quite a party in the pub last night.'

Pip, who was busy making tea for all the helpers, suddenly looked up with an anxious expression. 'Lillian was on her own last night,' she said. 'She would never have gone out and left Flora alone in the house.'

'So why isn't she here?' said Stella, wide-eyed.

Leaving Mrs Armitage to pour the teas, the two friends hurried to Lillian's place. Stella knocked but to her surprise, the front door was open. She glanced at Pip.

'That's odd,' said Pip. 'Flora isn't tall enough to reach the catch, so who left the door open?'

They went inside calling as they went. The house was silent. They searched the sitting room and the kitchen before going upstairs. The floor in the kitchen was littered with cakes of earth, mud that had dried out overnight. The overhead pulley was down. Pip looked around. That's funny. Where were the clothes to hang on the drier? Stella went to the bottom of the stairs and called up. There was no reply. Glancing at Pip, she began to climb.

On the third stair, Pip spotted a brooch. It looked vaguely familiar. The pin on the back was too short to do it up. Tossing it into a dish on the hallstand, she followed her friend up the stairs.

'Flora said she was in bed,' said Pip.

At the top of the stair, Stella pushed open the first door she came to.

'That's Dorcas's room,' said Pip, coming up behind her. 'The one at the end of the corridor is her room.'

The door was ajar. They could see Lillian lying on her right side facing the wall.

'Lillian,' said Pip. 'Lillian, are you all right?'

The figure remained motionless. They glanced at each other, a terrible feeling of foreboding clutching at the pair of them. They walked to the bedside together and Stella reached over to touch Lillian's shoulder. Her hand reeled back almost immediately as she gasped. 'She's cold.'

Pip tugged gently at Lillian's sleeve until she had enough leverage for her to roll back. Then they both cried out. There was dried blood on the pillow. Lillian's face was purple and congested, and she had vomit round her mouth and on her cheek. She also had an ugly bruise just above her eye. The blood had come from her ear.

'Dear God in heaven, Stella,' Pip cried. 'She's dead.'

CHAPTER 35

At the bottom of the stairs, the two girls turned to comfort one another. They hugged and wept on each other's shoulders until they heard the sound of children's voices and laughter outside. They stepped back to wipe their eyes.

'One of us will have to go to the phone box and ring the police,' said Pip.

'I'll do that,' said Stella. 'Oh, Pip, I can't believe it. I can't believe this has happened.'

'One thing is crystal clear,' said Pip darkly. 'She didn't die of natural causes.'

'But who could have done such a thing?'

Pip gave her a penetrating stare.

Stella gasped. 'You don't mean . . . You can't possibly think it was Gordon?'

'Who else?' said Pip. 'They've been rowing a lot lately, and the neighbours tell me they can't even remember the last time they saw him sober.'

'She's not very nice to him, I grant you,' said Stella, 'and she did say she wanted a divorce.'

Pip nodded. 'Dorcas said Gordon wasn't too happy about that.'

'Yes, but murder,' said Stella. 'No, no. He's a bit of a twerp, but I can't believe he would stoop to murder. Oh, poor Flora.'

Pip hesitated.

'What?' said Stella, looking around nervously. 'What is it?'

'We don't have to tell Flora just yet, do we?' said Pip. 'I mean, we could make sure she has a really happy afternoon first.'

'But people will know there's something wrong,' said Stella. 'They'll see we've been crying.'

'They might put that down to the fact that we're disappointed that the Sussex Sisters won't be singing.'

'Someone is bound to ask why not,' said Stella.

'Because Lillian is in bed,' said Pip. 'She can't sing.'

Stella frowned uncomfortably.

'Well, it's the truth, isn't it?' Pip challenged.

'I suppose so,' said Stella uncertainly. 'Oh, Pip, I'm not sure I can carry it off.'

'Yes, you can,' said Pip. 'We're doing it for the sake of the kids, remember?'

Stella nodded.

Pip squeezed her shoulder. 'We've managed to keep our peckers up all through this damned war. Let's do it for just one more day, eh?'

'Do you really think it was Gordon?'

'I don't know,' Pip said helplessly. 'I suppose it could be, couldn't it? Perhaps he just snapped.'

'Poor little Flora,' Stella said again. 'If they hang him, she'll be without a mother and a father.'

The front door began to move. They turned together, both holding their breath. As it swung right back, Dorcas was on the doorstep.

'Oh, it's you two,' she said brightly. 'When I saw the door open and heard your voices, I thought we might have burglars.' She threw her overnight bag into the hallway.

Pip and Stella glanced anxiously at each other.

Dorcas frowned. 'What's up? You look a bit upset.' Her voice became fearful. 'Is everything all right? Where's Flora?'

'Stella,' said Pip, 'you'd better go and make that call. Dorcas, come into the sitting room for a minute, will you?'

'Tell me,' said Dorcas as Pip steered her towards the sitting room. 'Just tell me.'

Stella hurried out of the house. By the time she reached the front gate, she heard the sound of Dorcas's anguished cry.

The Desperate Dan Gang had gathered at the old house for one last time. They were all dressed in their Sunday best because of the VE party later in the afternoon. Somebody said a photographer from the *Gazette* was coming to take a picture, so every mother wanted her child to look their best. They had to be careful not to get dirty. Everyone got safely through except Norman, who snagged his sleeve on a nail.

'Aw, no!' he cried as he lifted the unravelled wool. 'My mum will kill me.'

'Push your sleeve right up your arm,' said Gideon, 'and your mum will be none the wiser.'

The smell inside the building was awful. It had always been bad, but today it was worse than ever. They hurried down to the basement. To set up the experiment, Gideon had brought some sturdy-looking plyers from his granddad's shed. Georgie volunteered to hold Goliath between the plyers while Billy held a nail against the end of the machine-gun bullet and then Gideon would hit it with a hammer. The main bone of contention was where to point the bullet.

'Try over there,' said Derek.

'That's too near the doorway,' said Billy, brushing a spider's web from his trouser leg. 'What if we hit the doorpost? We might not be able to get out.'

'And if somebody else comes down,' said Colin, 'we might kill them.'

'Don't be daft,' said Norman. 'Who else is coming down?'

'I dunno,' said Colin.

'I think Billy is right,' said Georgie.

'Who cares what you think?' said Colin. 'You're just a kid.'

'It's my bullet,' Georgie reminded him sniffily.

'Well, if we point it that way,' said Norman, 'it's too close to the window.'

'I reckon we should aim it at the shelves,' said Gideon.

Every boy smiled as he turned towards the shelves, where row upon row of Kilner jars full of unidentifiable fruits stood side by side. They were imagining the satisfying crash as Goliath smashed into the wall, dislodging shelves and sending the Kilner jars crashing to the floor. What could be a more fitting end to the war? And it would be something they'd remember for the rest of their lives.

'Yeah,' said Georgie breathily. 'Let's do it.'

They had to move the table onto its side; then everybody stood behind it. Colin made sure he was in the doorway so that he could make a run for it should anything go wrong. The atmosphere in the cellar was charged with excitement. Georgie crouched down with his head bowed while he held Goliath in the air between the plyers.

'It's not going to work,' said Billy. 'He can't hold it steady enough for me to bash it.'

'It needs to be firm,' said Gideon. 'What we could do with is a vice.'

'That's something rude, isn't it?' said Derek.

'Nah,' said Gideon. 'My dad's got one in his shed. You use it to hold wood and stuff when you're sawing it.'

But there was nothing remotely like a vice in the cellar.

'I know,' said Georgie. 'Why don't we make that hole in the top of the table a bit bigger?'

'We can't shoot Goliath into the floor,' cried Derek.

'Of course not,' said Georgie, 'but now that the

table is on its side, we could ram Goliath into that hole. That way, it'll be easy to bash the other end.'

'Good thinking,' said Gideon.

They chipped away at the wood until Goliath fitted snugly. 'We've made it into a flipping great wooden gun,' Norman chuckled.

Billy held a six-inch nail against the end of the machine-gun bullet.

'Ready?' said Gideon.

'Ready,' said Billy.

The gang held their breath. Georgie stared at the wall, waiting to see what got hit first. Some of the others had their fingers in their ears. Norman held a smelly old cushion in front of his face, while Colin got ready to run. Gideon swung the hammer and missed. Everybody groaned.

'Here, let me,' said Derek.

'Get orf,' Gideon protested as they jostled each other. In the tussle that followed, the hammer was dropped.

Georgie picked it up and took aim. He wasn't bothered about the nail. He intended to bash the end of the bullet. 'Ready,' he shouted, then brought the hammer down.

They heard someone shout, 'No!' and then there was an almighty explosion of light, followed a split second later by a loud bang. The boys standing nearest went deaf. Billy was screaming his head off because when the flash came, something had hit him on the arm and the gases made him cough. Even though Georgie had done it without using the nail, when the hammer struck, it had hurt his fingers. There was a hole in the wall and the shelves began to topple, slowly at first, but then they gathered momentum.

'Get out,' a voice boomed. 'Get out, all of you!'

Dust was falling from the ceiling, and as the jars began to slide onto the floor, the sound of splintering glass filled the air. The noise was terrific as the jars exploded and dark red fruit, probably plums, splattered everywhere. They'd been there so long, they stank. The boys nearest the door, who were unaware that Billy had been injured, thought it terrific fun, until they heard a different and more sinister sound. It was a low whining noise followed by the sound of falling timber, and then the whole room filled with dust as the roof of the cellar caved in.

Everyone was bitterly disappointed when Stella broke the news that the Sussex Sisters wouldn't be performing. After listening to a cascade of complaints and grumbles, she had a job controlling herself. She longed to say, 'Believe me, Lillian couldn't help letting you down: she's dead,' but she couldn't breathe a word. Not if she was to remain true to her promise. Flora and Hazel were playing musical chairs. Flora was winning. Stella watched her happy face as she raced to the next chair and squealed in delight as she got there before the other remaining participants.

Nobody noticed the police car that stopped at the other end of the street. Stella supposed everyone thought they were in attendance because of the celebrations. The chance to hear the Sussex Sisters once more had certainly brought in the crowds, but with the announcement that the concert was off, people began to turn away, saddened and upset.

'Is Lillian all right?' Mr Knight asked. He had Betty with him.

'We'll know more in the morning,' Stella said diplomatically. She was slightly puzzled by the state of Mr Knight's face. He was sporting a rather large black eye, and his lip was scabbed over.

'Shame,' said Mr Knight. 'I wanted to have a private word.'

Stella smiled grimly. 'It can't be helped.' Lillian had become wary of the man, and Stella didn't blame her. He was becoming far too familiar.

'What's wrong with her?' asked Betty.

'I can't really say,' said Stella casually. Betty looked over his shoulder and stared down the road towards Lillian's house, so Stella added quickly, 'But her mother is with her, so there's no need to worry.'

'Let's go over to the Alexandra,' said Betty to Mr Knight. 'My treat, seeing as how it's VE Day.' She slipped her arm through his, and much to Stella's relief, they wandered off.

A sudden sharp noise made everybody stop in their tracks. 'What was that?' Stella asked Mrs Armitage, who was standing right next to her.

'It sounded like a gun going off,' said Mrs Armitage. They exchanged an anxious look.

The sound was followed by a low rumble. 'My God,' someone cried. 'Something's happened.'

Now everyone was on alert. 'Where did it come from?'

'Dunno. Down the road somewhere.'

Behind the trees, a pall of dust rose into the air.

'It looks like it's near the old derelict house,' Stella shouted.

'Keep an eye on the kids for me,' cried Pip as she began to run.

A policeman had come out of Lillian's house and he started running too. As soon as they saw him, everyone else ran. As they headed towards the corner, a voice cried out, 'The old house – it's collapsed. It's gone.'

Sure enough, behind the high fence, they could see the pile of rubble where the derelict house used to be. Everyone stared in horror, but there was worse to come. Staggering over the pile of bricks and covered in dust was a small boy.

The men found a hole in the fence big enough to let a full-grown adult through, so several people, including the policeman, tumbled through.

'Colin!' cried his mother. 'What on earth are you doing in there?' She reached out for him and he collapsed into her arms. His face was covered in dust, and his best clothes looked as if they'd been rolled in flour. Colin was spluttering and coughing.

'Anyone else in there with you, sonny?' said the policeman.

Pip pushed her way through the hole in the fence.

When he managed to stop coughing, Colin nodded. 'The gang,' he said, his voice hoarse and dry.

'Gang?' said the policeman. 'What gang?'

'The Desperate Dan Gang,' said Hazel, coming up behind them.

'What are you doing here, young lady?' said Pip crossly. 'Go back to Auntie Stella right now.'

Hazel pouted and turned back.

'Hang on a minute,' Pip said, changing her mind. 'How do you know about them?'

'Oh, Mummy, we all know. The boys think they've got some big secret, but everybody knows about it. They meet in the cellar and drink beer and smoke cigarettes and stuff.'

'What!'

Someone had got Colin a drink of water. 'We never drink beer,' he spluttered.

'I saw you,' said Hazel.

'Did not,' cried Colin, 'and anyway, girls aren't allowed.'

'OK, OK, son,' said the policeman. 'So how many boys are in the cellar? Can you tell us who they are?'

'My brother, Georgie,' said Hazel counting on her fingers, 'Norman Peabody and Derek and Gideon.'

As Pip took in her breath, she heard several other mothers do the same.

'Plus Billy Stanford, Leslie, Lionel and my brother Arthur,' said Colin. 'Nine of us altogether.'

'What happened down there?' Pip asked.

'We fired Goliath,' said Colin with a grin.

'Fired what?'

'Goliath, our machine-gun bullet,' said Colin, his eyes bright with excitement. He didn't seem to notice the collective gasp of horror from the crowd. 'It was as big as your hat, Mum.'

'And you fired this bullet in the cellar?' said the policeman incredulously.

'Yeah,' said Colin. 'It was great. It went off with one hell of a bang.'

'Language, Colin,' said his mother.

'Sorry, Mum,' said Colin, 'but you should have heard it.' He waved his arms and shouted, 'Boom!'

Stella had joined them. 'I'll take Hazel back home.'

Pip waved her hand dismissively. Her attention was totally focused on Colin and the policeman.

'Where are the others, son?' said the policeman.

Colin looked at the pile of rubble. 'Still down there. In the cellar.'

His words brought an instant reaction. Men and women began clawing at the rubble, throwing bricks every which way. Pip began doing the same. Georgie was down there? Buried alive . . .

Billy's mother fainted clean away and her neighbours carried her off the site.

'Hang on a minute,' said the policeman. 'We don't even know where the cellar is. You may be digging in the wrong place. I'll have to get hold of the owner first.'

'My son is under there,' said Norman's father. 'How long is that going to take?'

'Not long,' said Pip, snapping into action. 'I'm the owner of the building and I've got the plans indoors.' And outrunning both her friend and her daughter, she dashed back home.

CHAPTER 36

By the time Pip came back with the plans to the house, the men were trying to work out how the collapse had happened. Friends and neighbours had already formed a human chain and were moving debris to the far corner of the site. Every now and then, the air was punctuated with the sound of women crying, but on the whole, everyone worked in silence, not wanting to voice their deepest fears.

The policeman had been joined by several colleagues and a couple of off-duty soldiers. They studied the plans.

'What good will all this do?' Pip said irritably. She hated the thought that they'd stopped working. Georgie was down there somewhere. What sort of state was he in? How much air did he have to breathe? Had he broken a limb? His leg or his arm? He could be in pain. Someone should get to him fast.

'With a bit of luck,' said the policeman, 'we can work out which way the walls have fallen. They could be in a cavity and be protected from the worst of it.'

Wringing her hands, Pip looked away. Oh, please God, please . . .

A cry went up. Someone had spotted a child's hand. Quickly but carefully the team moved the bricks and roof tiles out of the way. They came to a different sort of rubble. A framed picture of Constable's *Haywain*, an old photograph, more bricks, a mountain of dust and bits of timber, then a boy's head. He was on his side and motionless. Everyone moved forward, making the area around him more unstable.

'Get back, please,' someone said. His voice was authoritative. 'If you all stand here, the whole lot is liable to give again and he'll be crushed to death.'

'Who is that man?' Pip whispered.

'Mr Dennison,' said Mrs Powell, Gideon's mother. 'He works for the council.'

Reluctantly, people, particularly the anxious mothers, stepped back. The child had been protected by a beam, which although fallen, had wedged itself just above him. When they finally got him out, he had an injured leg and was out cold. He came round as the soldiers laid him on the ground and Marjory Davies, the doctor who lost her house and surgery when the Heinkel came down in 1942, pronounced that he was not seriously injured but needed to go to hospital to be checked out. Someone handed her a wet flannel, and when she wiped away the dust and muck from his face, the boy called for his mum.

Mrs Peabody, who was at the back of the crowd, had pushed her way forward. The relief on her face was palpable. Norman was safe. As he was stretchered off to hospital, the man who had taken charge called for silence. It took a minute or two, but the area became quiet. Mr Dennison kneeled down by the place where Norman had been found and shouted, 'Is anyone there?'

They caught their breath as far below ground, they heard the unmistakable sound of a boy's voice. 'Get me out. Help, help. Get me out. I want my mum.'

Mrs Fox, Derek's mother, her eyes wide with fear, came forward, her white face tear-stained. Just as she was about to throw herself at the hole, Mr Dennison tugged at her arm.

'Listen, love,' he said, 'I want you to stay calm. Don't let him know how worried you are. That'll make him panic. Just talk slowly and tell him we're on our way.'

With a sniff into her hanky, Mrs Fox nodded and kneeled down by the hole. Everyone held their breath.

Pip felt someone slip their hand in hers. She turned. It was Stella.

'Don't worry about Hazel,' she said. 'I've taken her back to yours.'

A wave of black guilt rushed through Pip's veins. Since she'd been standing here hoping and praying that Georgie would be all right, she hadn't given her daughter a thought. The last time she'd seen her, she'd been standing right next to her, but she wasn't there now. Then she remembered: Stella had offered to take her home, but Pip hadn't even bothered to say good-bye. Her eyes filled. What sort of mother was she?

'Are you all right?'

Pip nodded dully.

A cup of tea was pushed into her hands. 'Here, drink this, darling,' Stella said.

Behind her, Pip could hear Mrs Fox's wobbly voice saying, 'Stay still, Derek. The men will soon get you out. You'll be fine. Mummy's here.'

'Is Hazel all right?' Pip asked Stella.

'She's fine,' said Stella. 'She's happy helping me to look after Timothy Michael, so I thought I'd pop over and tell you everything's OK. My mother-in-law is keeping a weather eye on them both until I get back.'

'What about Flora?'

'She's back with Dorcas,' said Stella.

'So she knows about her mum?'

Stella nodded. 'They've taken Lillian's body away now,' she said, lowering her voice to a whisper. The pair gave each other a quick hand squeeze; then Stella added, 'I'd better go now. I don't want to leave the kids too long. Keep your pecker up. We're all praying for you.'

It was difficult work. The men had to make sure that every brick, every piece of timber and every artefact was safe to be moved. If they pulled an unsupported beam out of the rubble, there was every chance it would cause another fall. They ended up tunnelling their way to Derek, who apart from a gash on his arm, was in remarkably good shape. Gideon Powell was close by, but he didn't look so good.

'I tore the sleeve on my best jumper,' Derek said as they dragged him out. 'I'm sorry, Mum.'

Mrs Fox took in a sharp breath. 'Let's not worry about that now, son,' she said through tears of relief.

As soon as Gideon was released, he was packed off to hospital, and the men had a change around. Those who had begun the rescue were told to stand down and a fresh team took up the task. There was a bit of an argument from those who had been working since five to three, but eventually they could see the sense of it. It was now five-thirty and they were tired. Sandwiches from the street party were brought on site and everybody ate as they worked. No one wanted to stop. For Pip and the other waiting mothers, it was agony.

As they worked their way down, the smell got worse. 'What is that smell?' said one of the team standing close to Pip.

'Dry rot,' said a man. 'This was bound to happen sooner or later. The whole place was as rotten as a pear.'

Pip sucked in her lips and wiped a renegade tear from her eye. This promised to be the longest day of her life.

As dusk came, there was a call for lights. People dug out every torch, tilley lamp and even oil lamps until the sappers managed to rig up an electricity supply. The work carried on regardless. At nine-thirty, there was another call for silence. They had come at regular intervals since Derek and Gideon had been found but with no response. This time, they heard two voices, faint but audible. The teams swapped again and everyone worked with renewed vigour. Mrs Hollick had joined Pip in her vigil, and someone had put a blanket around her shoulders. She was shivering, though she didn't know it. Mrs Hollick tried to coax Pip indoors, but like the other mothers, she didn't want to move. Billy and Leslie were brought up an hour and forty minutes later. Only three boys remained missing: Lionel Brown, Arthur Watts and Georgie.

No one could persuade Pip to leave but when her father and Elspeth arrived, her father put his arm around Pip's shoulder and she gave way for the first time.

'Come along, my dear,' said the group captain, as she wept on his shoulder. 'Let's get you home.'

'I can't,' cried Pip. 'I can't leave him. He'll think I've given up hope.'

'You need to give yourself a moment or two,' her father said firmly. 'You'll be no use to him when he comes out if you collapse with the strain of it all. Let's get you home and give you something to eat.'

Although she wasn't used to being told what to do, Pip allowed herself to be led away, but only after she'd extracted a solemn promise from the men that they would come and fetch her the moment Georgie was found.

As she walked through the door of her kitchen, Pip

was greeted by a delicious smell. Judith had made some vegetable soup, which was simmering away on the gas cooker. Stella had laid the table. Elspeth stood at the drop-down dresser making more sandwiches for the rescuers.

On her way to the bathroom, Pip stopped by Hazel's bedroom. Her little girl lay in her usual position across the bed. Her face was flushed, but she slept soundly, with her toys scattered around her. Pip tidied a few teddies and gently stroked her daughter's hair. Her heart was aching and she had but one thought in her mind.

Georgie. Oh, Georgie . . .

In the bathroom, she stepped out of her dirty clothes. They were covered in brick dust and stank of dry rot. Almost as soon as she'd washed her face and underarms, Pip felt refreshed. Back downstairs, she sat at the table as she was bidden, but after a couple of mouthfuls of the soup, her throat closed.

'How did my father find out?' she asked.

'I told him,' said Stella, pushing a cup of tea in front of her. 'You need your family around at a time like this.'

Pip frowned. Family? It seemed odd using the word after all this time. Georgie and Hazel had been the only family she'd had for such a long time, but she was glad her father and Elspeth were here now.

'Where's Daddy gone?'

'He's taking a look at the site,' said Elspeth, putting

the sandwiches into a tin. 'Your father has some experience of incidents like this.'

'I don't understand what the boys were doing in there,' said Pip, shaking her head in disbelief. 'They should have kept away. That's why I arranged for the fences to be put up, and there were notices all around the building. What more could I do?'

'You mustn't blame yourself,' said Judith.

'Boys will be boys,' Elspeth said with a shrug.

'You arranged?' said Stella, puzzled.

'I bought the damned place,' said Pip angrily. 'It was an eyesore and nobody was doing anything about it. I planned to turn it into a proper nursery. I never thought for one minute that those dreadful boys would be firing guns down there . . .' Her voice trailed off.

Stella, Judith and Elspeth exchanged a glance.

'What?' Pip demanded. 'Why are you looking at each other like that? Tell me.'

'Rumour has it that it was Georgie who had the machine-gun bullet,' said Stella.

'What?!'

'Apparently, he found it after the plane came down on the corner,' Stella went on. 'They fired it by way of a celebration that the war had ended.'

Pip stared at her in horror, then closed her eyes. 'Oh God,' she whispered. 'What a terrible day.'

When she opened her eyes again, Pip rubbed her forehead with a shaky hand. 'What about Lillian?' she said quietly.

'Don't concern yourself with that now,' said Stella.

'You concentrate on Georgie. That's enough to worry about.'

'Did he kill her?' asked Pip. 'Was it Gordon?'

Stella shrugged helplessly. 'I guess somebody did. The police have been there ever since.'

'Excuse me,' said Elspeth. 'Am I missing something?'

'I'll fill you in later,' Stella said dismissively.

'What about Dorcas and Flora?' Pip wanted to know.

'They've gone over to Dorcas's sister's place in Lancing.'

Timothy Michael drew everybody's attention as he stretched in his pram and made a contented baby noise.

'I can't stay here,' Pip said, suddenly getting to her feet. 'I have to go back.'

'You need some rest,' said Stella. 'Sleep.'

'I can't,' said Pip, grabbing her coat. 'He's my son.'

When she got back to the site, she discovered that Lionel and Arthur Watts had been brought to safety. Only Georgie remained unaccounted for. Mr Simpson, the local postman, grabbed her arm. 'We've heard a child's voice,' he said urgently. Pip's heart rate soared and she staggered, almost fainting. 'He's a long way down,' Mr Simpson added, 'but he sounds OK.'

He went on to explain that they'd heard Georgie calling out about ten minutes before. Apparently, he couldn't move, apart from his hand. 'We asked him if it was his left hand or his right, but he didn't seem to know,' said Mr Simpson. 'He seemed a bit confused.'

'He never does know his right from his left,' said Pip solemnly.

'After being underground for so long, I'm amazed that he sounds so compos mentis,' said Dr Davies, coming up behind her. 'He's been down there, what – ten hours?'

The men called her over and Pip was taken to a reasonably stable pile of rubble. She kneeled down and called Georgie by name. 'Are you all right? We're coming for you, darling. Don't give up. It won't be long now.'

'I can't move, Mummy.' His voice, which was like music to her ears, was faint, but it sounded strong. 'The man is still on top of me.'

Pip froze. She turned to the others, who seemed equally shocked. Pip took a deep breath and said as calmly as she could, 'What man, Georgie?'

'Uncle Gordon.'

They had to saw through several beams as they went down, but eventually they made a burrow about four feet deep. Dr Davies put her hand down and made contact with Georgie's wrist. His pulse was about ninety beats a minute.

With Pip calling encouragement, Georgie kept talking to his mother until his head was completely uncovered. The rescuers pushed a rubber tube down beside his face and told him they were going to send some water down.

'Rinse your mouth, Georgie,' Pip called. 'It'll make you feel better. Spit it out and then we'll send down a drink.'

They heard him splutter and then the sound of spitting. When he was ready, they sent down some warm, sugared tea. Pip's relief was palpable.

'He's not out of the woods yet, lady,' one of the rescuers cautioned.

The men worked doggedly until someone cried, 'The kid's right. There is another chap down here.'

Pip took in her breath. She recalled the smoker she'd seen in the alleyway. Could that have been Gordon Harris? Had Lillian chucked him out? She could have done, Pip supposed. She was determined to have a new life, wasn't she? Maybe that was why Gordon was camping out in a cellar with a crowd of small boys.

CHAPTER 37

Dr Davies wriggled down the hole until she was beside Georgie's exposed hand and head.

'Where does it hurt, Georgie?'

'I want my mummy.'

'All in good time, young man. Are you in any pain?'

'My legs,' he said. 'I can't feel them at all.'

The doctor explained that she was going to give him an injection. 'You may feel a sharp prick,' she said, 'but it will help you.'

Once the rescue squad had managed to get a soldier's kitbag out of the way, they gained access through the rubble to the side of Georgie's body. It turned out that he was in a crouched position, his face pushed down to the floor. They knew once they moved him and the blood flowed freely again, he would be in some discomfort, but the eighth of a grain of morphine Dr Davies had just given him would help. It appeared that Gordon lay across Georgie's lower back. He wasn't moving, but he had a faint pulse. At first, they thought Georgie's feet were under him, but as they extricated the child, it turned out that Georgie's knees were under his chest. All that remained was to get Gordon out as well.

As Georgie was hauled to the surface, Pip wanted to snatch him away and hold him tight, but the doctor had to examine him first. She had no hesitation in declaring him in reasonable condition, but she wanted him to go to hospital for a proper check-up. By the time Pip got close enough to hold Georgie's hand, his rescuers were tousling his hair and calling him a brave young fellow. The medics put him on a stretcher and walked across the road to the hospital.

He was woozy from the morphine, and he complained that his legs were all pins and needles, but apart from that, he seemed relatively well.

'Mummy, why didn't you come sooner?'

'You were a long way down, darling,' said Pip.

'I was scared.'

'I know,' Pip said gently. 'So was I. Somebody said you fired a gun.'

'I didn't have a gun, Mummy. I only hit the bullet with a hammer.'

Pip was alarmed. 'Oh, Georgie, fancy doing a silly thing like that.'

'Aw, Mummy,' he said. 'You should have heard the bang. It was fantastic.'

As her mother-in-law brought Timothy Michael into the bedroom, Stella woke from a deep sleep to the sound of his lusty cries. Bright sunlight snaked its way between the curtains, which weren't properly closed. Had she overslept? What time was it?

'All changed and ready for his breakfast,' said Judith.

Stella pulled herself sleepily up the bed and took her son into her arms. A second or two later, although she was still half asleep, he was drinking greedily. She glanced at the clock. A quarter past six.

Judith was still in her nightdress with a matching lightweight dressing gown. Her hair was in a long plait, which reached halfway down her back. As she left the room, it occurred to Stella that she had never seen her mother-in-law looking so casual. She was always in her uniform, or smartly dressed for some occasion, or in an evening gown. She was even smartly dressed when she was in the garden.

A little later, Judith reappeared with a cup of tea. 'How are you feeling?' she asked as she put the cup on the bedside table. 'Did you sleep well?'

'Like a log,' said Stella. 'I feel dreadful that I didn't even hear him.'

'We moved the pram into my room and I put him next to our bed,' said Judith. 'After yesterday, I thought you could do with an uninterrupted night's sleep.'

It was Stanley, Pip's father, who had arranged for Stella and Timothy Michael to spend the night with her in-laws. It was only when Pip got home from the hospital and told them that they were keeping Georgie in overnight that it occurred to everyone that there weren't enough beds in the house. Stella was all for pushing the pram back to Salisbury Road, but the group captain felt that under the circumstances, it wasn't a good idea for her to be alone. Staying with Desmond and Judith was the obvious solution, even though at first Stella wasn't so keen. She liked them well enough, but Judith, with her exacting ways, always made her feel slightly inadequate, and besides, she'd never actually stayed at their house before. However, her apprehensions were brushed aside, and a little while later, she was standing outside the door of the Knowle with Timothy Michael in his pram. Desmond welcomed her with open arms. Judith was kind and efficient. She quickly made up the bed in Johnny's old room for Stella, and after Desmond had taken the pram apart and carried it upstairs, Timothy Michael was left on the landing outside the door simply because there was no room in the bedroom.

Stella had been exhausted, so they'd had little conversation. Her parents-in-law had been very sad to hear what had happened to Lillian. They had walked down to the street in the evening to hear Stella sing with the Sussex Sisters in what was to be their last appearance. When they heard what had happened at the derelict house, it was Judith who had rallied the WVS canteen to make tea for the rescuers. Apart from the time she had taken a drink to the site for Pip, Stella had stayed in the house looking after Hazel.

She sat Timothy Michael up to wind him and noticed Judith's winsome smile. All at once Stella felt guilty. Judith was his grandmother, but she hadn't made a lot of effort to foster that relationship. She had never stopped Judith and Desmond from 'dropping in', but that wasn't Judith's way. How many times had she taken Timothy Michael to the Knowle? The answer was not many.

Their eyes met and Judith made to go.

'Please stay,' said Stella, indicating the small chair beside the bed. Judith hesitated but sat. 'Did you breastfeed Johnny?' It was a very personal question, but somehow it seemed appropriate.

They chatted amiably for some time about Johnny and his babyhood, and Judith seemed to soften as they talked.

'I miss him,' said Stella.

'I do too,' said Judith, and they exchanged a smile.

Timothy Michael finished feeding and Stella sat him up to wind him.

'I'm sorry about Lillian,' said Judith cautiously. 'That was a terrible thing to happen.'

'Yes,' said Stella. 'Awful.'

'It must have been a ghastly shock for you both finding her like that,' Judith went on. 'Have the police said anything more?'

Stella shook her head. 'It keeps going round and round my head. She could be difficult at times, but she was funny and she was feisty. Her fame was changing her, but I can't imagine why on earth anyone would want to kill her.'

Timothy Michael burped and gave his grandmother a lopsided smile. Stella held him out to her. 'Well, Timothy

Michael, now that you're all tanked up, how about giving your granny a cuddle?'

Pip woke with a jolt. Her bedroom door was creaking open as Hazel came cautiously into the room. Her hair was tousled, and she was still in her nightie. Looking every inch the frightened little girl, she held her knitted golly by one leg and twiddled her hair with the other hand. Pip lifted the bedclothes and her daughter ran to the bed and climbed in.

'Are you all right?' Pip asked, cuddling her close.

Hazel nodded. 'When is Georgie coming home?'

'Later on today,' said Pip. 'The doctor wanted to keep an eye on him, but he's fine.'

'Pat Tumber said it was Georgie's fault that the house fell on top of him, but I said it wasn't true.'

'Pat may be right, darling,' said Pip. 'Georgie has been a very silly boy, but thankfully he wasn't badly hurt. Isn't that good?'

'Will our house fall down?' said Hazel, looking around anxiously.

'No,' said Pip. 'Our house is very strong.'

'I missed you, Mummy.'

'I know you did, and I'm sorry I had to leave you, but you had Auntie Stella as well as Granddad and Auntie Elspeth to look after you. Mummy had to stay near the old house in case Georgie needed me.'

'But he didn't?'

'He did for a little while,' said Pip, 'but when they got him out, we took him to the hospital and then I came straight back to you.' Hazel looked up at her with wide eyes. 'In fact,' Pip went on, 'I came into your room and kissed you on the nose.' She tapped Hazel's nose as she said it. 'But you were fast asleep.'

'Auntie Elspeth read me a story,' said Hazel.

They settled back on the pillow to doze, but Pip couldn't get Lillian out of her mind. How on earth was she going to tell Georgie and Hazel that Auntie Lillian was dead? One thing was for certain: she'd have to do it soon. When she'd come home last night, the whole street had been buzzing with the news.

At eleven, Pip went back to the hospital as per their instructions to bring Georgie home, but before she went to the children's ward, she headed to the men's ward to make enquiries about Gordon Harris, who had most likely saved his life. It was still a complete mystery to her as to why he was in the house.

'He's doing well,' the ward sister told her. 'He has a bit of a bump on the head, which knocked him out for a while, but apart from that, all he's got are some cuts and abrasions and two broken fingers. All things considered, he got off lightly.'

'Can I bring my son in to thank him?'

The sister arched an eyebrow. 'Visiting hours are from three to five.'

'My son is supposed to rest when I get him home,' Pip said. 'It would be so much easier if we could pop in now. I think it's important for Georgie to appreciate just how lucky he is.'

'Well, if you put it like that,' said the sister. 'But don't stay too long. It interferes with the ward cleaners.'

Georgie's clothes were covered in dust and torn to shreds, so Pip had brought a bag of clean clothes with her. The sister of the children's ward called Pip into her office first.

'Doctor is very pleased with your son's progress,' she began. 'He seems virtually none the worse for wear, but keep an eye on him. Make sure he gets plenty of rest and give him time to talk. He's had quite an ordeal.'

'Thank you,' said Pip. 'I will.' She stood to leave.

'There is one other thing,' said the ward sister. Seeing her serious expression, Pip lowered herself back down onto the chair. 'Your son's friend Gideon Powell. I'm afraid he didn't make it. Gideon died at four this morning. I thought it would be better if you told Georgie.'

Pip swallowed hard. Oh no! After all they'd been through. They'd survived the war virtually unscathed, but on the very day peace came, both she and her son had lost a dear friend. Poor Mr and Mrs Powell. They'd been faced with every parent's nightmare. Pip could think of nothing worse than losing your own child. The sister stood up. Pip stood as well. 'Thank you,' she said hoarsely.

To Pip's immense relief, Georgie was sitting up in bed playing with a woodpecker on a stick. It was a toy designed for a much younger child, but Georgie was fascinated as he put the woodpecker to the top of the stick and watched it slide to the bottom. The bird was attached to a round disc with a spring on the side. Perfectly balanced, it gave the appearance that the woodpecker was pecking its way down.

Her son was delighted to see her, and as Pip helped him to dress, she explained that Uncle Gordon was in the ward next door. 'I think you should take the opportunity to go and thank him, don't you?' she said.

Georgie nodded but seemed a bit nervous. 'Is he badly hurt?'

'Not at all,' she said, realizing that Georgie was worried that he might see something scary. How was he going to react when he discovered his friend was dead? 'We won't stay long,' she promised. 'Just long enough for you to say thank you.'

The patient was at the far end of the ward. They walked past patients who were sleeping, some reading the newspaper and others just lying quietly on their bed. Gordon Harris was sitting up, but he had his eyes closed. Pip took in her breath. She had never been formally introduced, but a neighbour had pointed him out one day, and she recognized him from the photograph at one end of Dorcas's mantelpiece. And now she probably owed her son's life to this man!

He had a bandage on his head and another on his right hand, with what looked like splints sticking out from it. Pip's heartbeat quickened. Should she say who she was? Should she mention Lillian? Did he even know about his wife's death? He was dressed in a hospital gown, but his clothes were in the locker. The door was open and she could see them hanging out. His army boots were thick with dust.

Georgie tugged at her hand. Pip cleared her throat and Gordon opened his eyes.

'Apparently,' she began uncertainly, 'you saved my son's life. We've come to say thank you.' Oh Lord, she hadn't meant that to sound so formal and unfeeling.

'Thank you,' Georgie said dutifully.

Gordon looked at him and smiled. 'That's all right, son,' he said. 'You take care now.'

'If there is anything I can do for you . . .' Pip went on. 'Wash your clothes, clean your boots . . .'

'I'll be fine,' he said.

As it was impossible to shake his hand, Pip nodded. She and Georgie turned to go, and two men in mackintoshes came into the room. They headed straight for Gordon's bed and stood on either side of it. Pip, ushering Georgie towards the door, didn't turn round, but she heard one man say, 'I am a police officer. Gordon Chester Harris, you are under arrest for the murder of Lillian Anne Harris—'

'What?' Gordon shouted. 'What are you saying? Are you telling me my wife is dead?'

The ward sister sailed past Pip with an angry expression on her face and an argument followed. Pip was doing her best to push an open-mouthed Georgie into the corridor before the policemen had finished. She managed it, but not before they had both seen Gordon being handcuffed to the bed.

CHAPTER 38

By the time she got home, Pip realized that she had no alternative but to tell Georgie and Hazel what had happened. Her father and Elspeth had to leave the house to see an old friend who lived in East Preston, so she and the children soon found themselves alone. It seemed the right moment. Hazel burst into tears. Pip held her close and stroked her hair.

'That policeman arrested Mr Harris, didn't he, Mummy?' said Georgie.

'Yes, he did,' said Pip.

'It wasn't Mr Harris,' said Georgie. 'I bet it was the German spy.'

Pip frowned. 'What German spy?'

'The one who used to smoke in the alleyway,' said Georgie.

Oh my goodness, thought Pip. He must mean the man she'd seen lurking by the hedge. She'd forgotten all about him.

'You should have told me about him,' said Pip.

'I couldn't, Mummy. Billy said girls can't deal with the big stuff like spies and things.'

414

Pip gave him a watery smile. Hazel sat up and she wiped her daughter's tear-stained face.

'Why did Auntie Lillian die?' Hazel whimpered. 'I didn't want her to be dead.'

'Nobody does, darling,' said Pip, struggling to push away her own feelings of grief and loss, 'but it can't be undone.'

'We saw the police arresting Uncle Gordon,' said Georgie, his statement a mixture of shock and excitement. 'They put some handcuffs on his wrist.'

'Georgie,' Pip cautioned.

Hazel's eyes grew wide. 'Did he really do it, Mummy?'

'I don't think so,' said Pip. She had no reason to believe what she was telling her children, but would a cold-blooded killer rush to save several small boys trapped in a derelict building? It hardly made sense.

'Do you think we should tell the police about the German spy?' Georgie asked.

'I think perhaps we should,' said Pip, 'but not today. The sister on the ward said you have to rest, remember?' She pulled the blanket up and gave him a book.

Hazel wanted to go round to Lillian's to play with Flora, but Mrs Armitage had already told Pip that Dorcas had taken her granddaughter to Lancing for a while.

'Not today, darling,' she said, and anxious to bring some sense of normality back into the house, she added, 'How about you and I go into the kitchen and make something nice for tea?'

Stella and Pip didn't meet up for a couple of days. Leaving Elspeth and her father as willing babysitters, Pip set off to walk to Salisbury Road. The day was typical of the onset of summer: blustery, cold and wet. On the way, she called into Thurloe House, the local police station, a rather forbidding Victorian building on the High Street. Known locally as 'the Gallows', it had gained its nickname after a Victorian policeman had spotted two men loitering outside a shop across the road. After the men were arrested, it transpired that they were wanted for the murder of a man in Portslade. They were tried, convicted and hung.

Pip wanted to talk to Gordon, but she was told he had already been transferred to Lewis Prison to await his trial.

'I suppose there can be no doubt?' she asked the detective constable.

'None whatsoever,' he said firmly.

'It's just that he saved my boy's life,' said Pip. 'It seems a little odd that a murderer would hang around after doing such a thing. Wouldn't it be more likely that he would make a run for it?'

The detective constable smiled. 'If you don't mind me saying so, madam,' he said, 'I think you've been watching too many American films.'

'But he seemed awfully surprised when you arrested him,' Pip protested.

'Don't be fooled by a bit of acting,' said the detective constable. 'This is a cut-and-dried case. He's been a POW for the duration of the war. He comes home to find his wife all dolled up and on the stage. He doesn't like it, and what's more, she's been playing around. He finds out. He doesn't like that either. She wants a divorce. They argue. He loses his temper and bashes her over the head. It's a story that's as old as the hills.'

Pip frowned. There were so many things that didn't add up. 'Yes, except—' she began, but the detective constable was having none of it.

'Now, don't you worry your pretty little head about it, Mrs Sinclair,' he said, coming round the desk, putting his hand between her shoulder blades and giving her an encouraging push towards the door. 'We've got our man, and you mark my words, he'll hang for it.'

Outside in the road, Pip bristled with anger. Pompous ass. How dare he be so patronizing? She was still annoyed when she got to Stella's place.

They sat in her newly decorated sitting room and tried to console each other. First, there were tears and memories. The night they'd all slept in this very room in 1942 when the Heinkel came down, Lillian learning to drive, the times when they'd practised their routine, the midnight-blue material followed by the siren suits and headscarves . . . The list was endless.

'Do you think everyone realizes what's happened?' said Stella.

'I should think so,' said Pip. 'Bad news travels fast.'

'I was thinking about Mr Knight and Betty,' said Stella. 'They followed Lillian wherever she went.'

'He was beginning to annoy her,' said Pip with a sigh.

'I know,' said Stella, 'but when all is said and done, he was a loyal admirer.'

Pip frowned.

'What are you really thinking?' Stella went on. 'You think the police have made a mistake about Gordon, don't you?'

So she reminded Stella about the single place laid on the kitchen table and the untouched meal. Lillian hadn't been expecting Gordon. She was eating alone. Then there was the mud on the kitchen floor. Lillian would never have gone to bed and left such a mess.

As she went on, Pip could see by her face that Stella had begun to share her concerns, so she mentioned the open front door. 'We all know it has a funny catch. Anyone who had been to the house before would know how to close it. If it had been Gordon, he would have closed the door behind him. No matter what he'd done, he would never have left Flora alone upstairs with an open front door.'

Stella listened with a grave face as Pip went on to talk about the pulley that had been down for the washing, though as far as she could remember, there was no sign of any washing in the kitchen.

'You're right,' said Stella. 'All the surfaces were bare.'

'Gordon's shoes were sticking out of his locker in

the hospital,' Pip went on. 'They were dusty but not muddy. In fact, the more I think about it, I reckon Gordon was sleeping in that derelict house. That's why they found his kitbag in the rubble.'

'So if Gordon didn't do it,' said Stella, 'who did?'

'I don't want to jump to conclusions,' said Pip cautiously, 'but I'm beginning to wonder about Mr Knight.'

'Mr Knight!' cried Stella.

'At first, I thought the man I saw hanging around in the alleyway at night was Gordon Harris,' said Pip, 'but the more I think about it, it could have been Mr Knight.'

'Are you sure?' said Stella.

'Why not?' said Pip. 'I think we both agree that he had an unhealthy fixation on her, and when I found all those dog-ends in Georgie's pocket, it was ages ago, long before Gordon came back home.'

'That's creepy,' said Stella. 'He's much older. Oh, Pip, Lillian was so full of life.' Stella blew her nose for the umpteenth time. 'I can't believe she's gone.'

'Of one thing I am certain,' said Pip. 'I don't believe for one minute that Gordon killed her.'

Stella looked at her steadily. 'Neither do I now.'

CHAPTER 39

Iris had just begun to clear up in the cafe. She used to give herself a good fifteen minutes to pack up, but just lately she'd needed a little more time. She was getting slower and there was so much to do. She had to wipe all the tables and sometimes the chairs as well. People left crumbs everywhere. The children were the worst. They thought nothing of putting their jammy hands all over the backs of the chairs or hiding bits of pie behind the menu. After she'd cleaned them all, she had to wipe down the shelves and remove any stale buns. The sinks had to be scoured and the teapot emptied. After a busy day, it was hard going, and she couldn't even put her feet up when she got home because there was Mother to see to.

The cafe was open from seven-thirty to five, and it irritated her when someone came in five minutes before closing time, but somebody always did. The doorbell jangled at ten to five.

'We're closed,' she said sharply. She was bending down to put the empty milk bottles in the crate ready for the milkman in the morning.

'We know,' said a gentle voice. 'That's why we've come to see you.'

She rose to her feet to see Pip and Stella in the doorway.

'Could we have a word?' said Pip.

'Of course,' said Iris, flustered and surprised.

'Mind if I wheel the baby in?' asked Stella.

'Not at all,' said Iris. 'Be my guest.'

'We've something important to tell you and Mr Knight and Betty,' Pip went on.

'They'll be here in a minute,' said Iris. 'They always help me finish up.'

Pip held the door and Stella wheeled Timothy Michael inside. 'I remember Lillian telling me that once,' she said.

The expression on Iris's face didn't alter. As she took the empty milk bottles outside, Pip whispered to Stella, 'She doesn't know.'

'We heard about that old house collapsing and your boy being inside,' said Iris. 'Is he all right?'

Pip nodded. 'Yes, thank you. He's back home now and will recover fully given time.'

They could hear Betty rolling down the shutter on the ticket office, and a moment or two later, she joined Iris behind her counter. At virtually the same moment, Mr Knight came into the shop and turned the sign on the door before locking it behind him. He jumped when he saw Timothy Michael's pram tucked away in the corner.

'Mrs Sinclair and Mrs Bell have something to say to

us,' said Iris. She had made a fresh pot of tea and was pouring everyone a cup. Pip reached for her handbag and purse, but Iris shook her head. 'On the house,' she said brusquely. 'So what's this all about?'

Pip glanced at Stella, but she avoided eye contact.

'We've come about Lillian,' Pip began.

'What's the little minx been up to now?' Mr Knight said acidly.

His remark took both of them by surprise. 'Why do you say that?' Stella asked. 'I thought you were an admirer of hers.'

'I'm very disappointed in that girl,' said Mr Knight. 'I had her down as a good wife and mother, but I've changed my mind.' He was busy doing up the buttons on his coat. 'I'm afraid I shan't be stopping for my tea tonight, Mrs Keegan,' he added stiffly.

'Mr Knight,' Pip called as he returned to the door, 'please don't go. This is very important.'

'Anything you have to say about Mrs Harris is of no concern to me,' he said huffily. 'I wash my hands of her.' He turned to unlock the door.

'Mr Knight, Lillian is dead.'

Everyone in the room froze.

'Oh no, no!' cried Betty.

Iris took in her breath noisily. 'Dead? What do you mean, dead? What happened?'

Mr Knight turned slowly. His face was white.

'We found her,' said Pip, her eyes beginning to fill.

'She was dead in her bed,' said Stella, slipping her arm through Pip's and giving her an encouraging

422

squeeze. 'And her husband, Gordon, has been arrested for her murder.'

There was a collective gasp. Mr Knight came back to the counter.

'Sweet Jesus,' said Iris, crossing herself. 'I can't believe it.'

'We came because we weren't sure if you knew,' said Pip. 'You've always been such faithful followers of hers.'

Mr Knight lowered himself into a chair. 'Gordon arrested, you say?'

Pip laid a gentle hand on Mr Knight's shoulder. He seemed genuinely shocked and surprised. She could feel his body trembling under his coat. 'When did you last see her?'

'At the Connaught,' he mumbled. 'She was magnificent.'

'I stopped going when I saw her kissing that Monty bloke,' said Betty.

'They all do that,' said Ron dismissively. 'It's show business.'

'Well I was very upset about it,' said Betty. 'First the pianist and then that Monty. It isn't right, I tell you. I mean, she's a married woman.'

'With a child,' Iris interjected.

'But you both came to the street party to hear the Sussex Sisters for the last time,' said Stella.

Mr Knight looked slightly awkward.

'Ron and I only went there because he was going to give her a piece of his mind,' Betty interjected.

'Hush, woman,' Mr Knight snapped. He glanced over at Pip. 'Betty always told me she was a wrong-un but I didn't want to believe it, see?'

'What made you change your mind?' asked Stella.

'Gordon told me she wanted a divorce,' he said bitterly, his lip curling. 'You women, you're all the same. That man gave the best years of his life to serve king and country and when he comes home, she tosses him aside like an old rag.'

'I'm sorry she's gone,' said Iris tossing her head, 'but I for one won't be shedding a tear.'

'I admit I was annoyed with her,' said Ron, recovering slightly, 'but I don't want to speak ill of the dead.'

Pip's eyes went to the lapel on Betty's coat. The material on the left side was slightly faded, and then she remembered the brooch. Obviously Betty had dropped it again. Pip knew she had seen it quite recently, but where?

'I can't take it in,' said Mr Knight, shaking his head. 'Mrs Harris, Lillian gone?' His eyes were watery. 'In the beginning, I tried to look out for her. There are some weird people about these days, and being in the public eye, a woman as good-looking as that can attract all sorts. I never told her, but I often used to stand in the alley behind her house until she'd gone to bed. Just keeping her safe, that's all.'

'Like a father to her, he was,' said Betty.

'I did it a couple of times after he got back,' Mr Knight went on.

'Gordon?' said Pip.

Mr Knight nodded glumly. 'I heard the rows they had. Terrible, they were. It wasn't right.' He paused. 'How did he do it?'

'Her head was battered,' said Stella. 'She'd obviously been sick in the night and choked on her own vomit. When we found her in the morning, she was quite cold.'

Pip watched as Betty's eyes grew wide and she pressed her handkerchief to her mouth. All at once, the pieces of the puzzle fell into place. 'You were there too, weren't you, Mrs Shrimpton?' she said. 'At Lillian's place.'

'I don't know what you mean,' said Betty haughtily.

'Don't deny that you were in the house,' said Pip. 'I know you were. You left a calling card.'

Betty's hand trembled as she looked around helplessly. 'She was alive when I left her,' she protested loudly. 'She was a bit dazed, but she was talking to me.'

The room had gone very quiet.

Betty began twisting her handkerchief in her hand. She turned to Pip and Stella. 'He thought the world of that girl and there she was, playing around with other men, acting like a tramp and behaving like some sort of prima donna on the stage. Well, I wasn't having it. Somebody had to tell her what's what. It was disgraceful.' She looked helplessly at Mr Knight. 'I only did it for you.'

'Exactly what *did* you do?' asked Pip.

'I went in the back way so that I didn't draw too much attention,' said Betty. 'She invited me in, but then she saw the mud on my shoes, so we only stayed in the kitchen and I told her off.'

'Then you hit her,' said Stella.

'No, I didn't,' cried Betty. 'That pulley thing fell down. It gave us both a shock. It was all skew-whiff, so when it fell, it hit her on the side of the head and she slipped on the floor. She went down with such a whack, and she hit her head on the handle of the oven door.' Betty looked from one to the other. 'I helped her up and she said she'd be all right.'

Timothy Michael began to stir. Stella went to rock the pram.

'You should have got a doctor,' said Iris.

'I was going to,' Betty protested, 'but she said, "Just help me to bed and I'll be fine." So that's what I did.'

'And you dropped your brooch on the stair,' said Pip.

Betty's hand automatically went to her lapel and her face reddened. 'She was fine when I left her,' Betty insisted.

'Tell us what happened next,' said Stella from the back of the room. 'When you left the house.'

'I couldn't bear to go back out through the kitchen,' said Betty, 'so I opened the front door. Trouble is, it's got a funny catch and it wouldn't close properly.' She plonked herself down on a chair and burst into tears. 'I never laid a finger on her, I swear.'

Nobody moved.

'All she had was a bump on the head,' Betty protested. 'She said she'd have a bit of a sleep and then get undressed, so I pulled the eiderdown over her shoulders and left her to it.' Her gaze went back to Mr Knight. 'I never meant her no harm. I admit I was angry, but I never touched her. I just wanted her to know how much she'd upset you.'

'Mrs Shrimpton,' said Stella, 'you have to tell the police.'

'Oh no, I couldn't,' said Betty. 'I just couldn't.'

'But you must,' said Pip. 'Gordon Harris has been accused of her murder. They'll hang him for sure if they find him guilty, and in that case, poor little Flora will have lost both her mother and her father.'

'But I didn't do anything,' Betty wailed.

'For God's sake,' Mr Knight snapped. 'All you have to do is tell the truth, you silly woman.'

'I only did it for you,' she complained.

'I don't need looking after,' he said stubbornly as he stood to go.

'Gordon Harris is a good man,' said Pip. 'He doesn't deserve this. Don't you think he's suffered enough?'

Once again the room went quiet.

'I'll go with you, if you like,' said Stella.

Betty wiped her eyes with her sodden handkerchief.

Nobody spoke, but a couple minutes later, Iris was alone in the cafe. She locked the door one more time and turned back to the counter. No one had drunk so much as a mouthful of the tea she'd poured, so she tipped it all away and washed up the five cups. She emptied the washing-up bowl and hung the dishcloth on the hook to dry. Then taking a deep breath, she turned to face the wall and allowed her tears to fall.

CHAPTER 40

Worthing, 1995

'We can't find it, Granny Pip.'

Pip tilted her head back and called to the ceiling, 'It's in the big chest of drawers, bottom drawer.' She listened as her great-grandchildren ran to the other side of the bedroom; then she heard the heavy drawer opening. 'Under the old siren suit.'

The door to the sitting room opened and the children's mother came into the room with some coffee cups. 'I think I'd better go and give them a hand,' Susan said, putting the tray onto the low table, 'before they wreck your bedroom.'

Pip grinned. She still enjoyed it when everyone came to her house for Sunday roast, but because cooking the whole meal by herself was a bit much these days, the whole family now chipped in with the preparations. Pip put the joint in the oven, while her daughter-in-law, Margo, brought the roast potatoes and the vegetables. Susan always brought pudding, usually from Iceland. It was a system that worked well and reminded Pip of the days when she and the Sussex Sisters pooled their meagre resources to make a feast.

Georgie handed her a coffee cup and Pip smiled up at her son. It was odd to think that her little boy was now a grandfather and she a great-grandmother. When did she become so old? Georgie had married Margo in the late 1950s and they'd had two sons, William and Bob. Bob had emigrated to Australia, while William had married Susan and they'd had Josh and Angela.

Settling back in her chair, Pip felt cosy and relaxed. These occasions might be a little tiring, but Pip loved to hear the sound of children's voices in her house again. The children's footsteps thundered down the stairs, and a few seconds later, Josh and Angela flung themselves into the room. She'd never seen them quite so animated before. This school project had certainly fired up their imagination.

This year, 1995, marked the fiftieth anniversary of the end of the Second World War and the school had given each pupil a project. Josh's class had to write an accurate account of an incident in Worthing during the war. He had been researching in the library and happened to mention what he was doing while the whole family were sitting by their beach hut.

'I remember when the Heinkel 111 came down on a house at the end of my old street.' Pip's remark had been casual, but it had begun a chain of events that seemed unstoppable. Granddad George remembered

430

the same incident from a child's point of view, and the children listened with open mouths as he and Pip told them the way each of them had seen the same event. He recalled finding Goliath, and later on, taking it to the secret den. She talked about the wartime friendship between Lillian, Stella and herself that had begun that very night.

Angela's class had been asked to find out how people amused themselves during the war years and what was being done to boost morale. The story of the Sussex Sisters was the perfect answer. Pip shared memories of things she hadn't thought about for years. The family was so interested that Susan, the children's mother, decided to research the family tree, and Georgie's son William, the children's father, planned to write a play that could be performed in the community.

'We need to make a proper record of things before it all gets lost,' William told her, so Pip was given free rein to recall anything and everything she could. That had been weeks ago and the whole project had culminated in today's family gathering at her home. Pip had never been one to hark back to 'the good old days'. She cherished her memories, but life was for living in the present. Even so, this had been an enjoyable experience.

They were all gone now – all except her. Her father, for all his generosity, had never heard from Marion again, although she'd cashed his cheque. Pip could only hope that the five hundred pounds had made a real difference to her life. It had certainly changed her own in more ways than one. Did Marion and her mother take a holiday, perhaps? She would never know, but she had long since forgiven them for the way they had treated her. Pip refused to allow bitterness to blight her life the way it had her mother's, but she did sometimes wonder what had happened to them. Their paths had never crossed again, but then real life, she told herself, doesn't always have a story-book ending.

Pip had not long had her seventy-seventh birthday, a vast age and one she couldn't quite believe, but she was fit and healthy. She still walked her little dog, Chalky, twice a day, though he didn't get long hikes on Highdown Hill any more. She told herself that it was because Chalky was too old for such excursions.

Georgie (even though everyone called him George, she could never think of him as anything but Georgie) could remember the collapse of the old building and the tragic loss of his friend Gideon, but he was a little short on detail, especially when it came to Gordon Harris.

'As soon as Betty told the truth of what had happened that day,' Pip told him, 'he was released from prison.'

'I never knew that,' said Georgie. 'What happened to him?'

'He came back to live with Dorcas for a while, but a few years later, he and Flora became one of the first of the ten-pound Poms.'

The expression was lost on Josh and Angela.

432

'The Australian Government were desperate for people,' their father interjected, 'so they offered anyone and everyone a passage to Australia for ten pounds.'

'It was a wonderful way of having a new start after the war,' Pip went on. 'Gordon married a girl he met on the boat going over and they all settled in Sidney. We exchanged Christmas cards for a few years, but,' she added with a shrug, 'you know how it is.'

Susan was keenly interested to hear Pip's personal experiences as a wife during the long years of separation, but it wasn't until she'd talked about how she'd felt that Pip realized how hard it had been. Somehow, with everyone else going through the same privations, it didn't really register at the time. Susan had been shocked to hear about the constant queuing for food, the lack of a proper toilet in the house ('What? You had to go outside? Even in winter?'), hand-washing sheets and bedding, sooty fireplaces, scrimping and saving and sometimes going to bed hungry, but for Pip, it was normal life, so you just got on with it.

She explained that although Peter had made it home, he was never the same man. The horrors of Japanese internment were just as bad as she'd imagined, if not worse. He'd been released in September 1945 but had been too ill to come home with the first of the POWs. He had to be sent to Australia and nursed back to a measure of health and strength before beginning the long passage home. Although their reunion was delayed, Pip considered him one of the lucky ones. Some of his companions who were sent home immediately hadn't survived very long. When a person's stomach had been reduced to the size of a plum for years through malnutrition, they had to be gently weaned back on to nourishing food. There were stories of men tucking into a much-desired steak and dying.

She still had one letter Peter had sent her. She never did get round to asking him exactly when he wrote it, but it must have been before they moved him to Australia. He was at a point of despair.

My darling wife,

After three years of living hell, now release is in sight, I am feeling pretty rotten. I feel I only have a small chance of making it home. I have left several letters to you with different people in the hope that you will at least have something to remember me by. I don't expect to survive much longer.

These past three years have been an absolute nightmare, my darling. With the exception of you, everything I once held dear has been taken from me. My whole world, our whole life is gone. If I ever reach home, it will be a miracle, and how will I pick up where I left off after all the terrible things I've seen?

Our life together seems like a million years ago, but, Pip, I love you, my darling, just as much as I loved you on the day we got married. When the Yanks landed in the Philippines, I received the precious letters you sent me. I am only sorry that I was not permitted to write to you until now. They only let me send typed cards. How thoughtful of you to send photographs. How the children have grown. Georgie looks a sturdy fellow, and everyone thinks Hazel is a sweetie. I am so proud of

434

you, sweetheart. You have brought them up so well. I
wish you had sent a photograph of yourself.

I did my best to do my duty and help to relieve the
suffering of some of my fellow prisoners. I have not
been paid since May 1942, so everything I have or own,
all money and allowances owing to me, I want you to
have in order that you can take care of our children.

I will say goodbye now, my darling. I pray every
night that I will see you again, but in case it is not to
be, thank you for being such a wonderful wife to me.
The happiest days of my life were those I spent with
you. I'll always love you, my darling. God bless you
and keep you.

All my love,
Peter xx

When he finally made it back to Worthing in time
for Christmas 1945, Peter was still terribly thin. He
had returned by ship, a six-week voyage, but the medics
on board had made sure that he'd had a carefully con-
trolled diet. After a period of convalescence, Peter was
deemed too frail for manual work, but by then Pip was
already making a good living. She'd shelved the idea
of running a nursery to care for her husband, so as
soon as he'd come home, she'd sold the pile of rubble
and the land on which it stood for three hundred
pounds more than she'd paid for it. This led to a series
of property deals, which brought in a steady income
of rents and sales, an absolute boon while Peter was
ill.

After a year or two, he'd got a desk job, but he
didn't make old bones. His body had been seriously

weakened by his terrible ordeal and every winter he became susceptible to chest infections. He died in 1969, aged fifty-three, a man old before his time.

When she'd told the family about the Sussex Sisters, they could hardly believe their ears. Georgie was aware of them, but he hadn't appreciated the contribution they'd made to the war effort or how famous they'd been. It was then that Pip remembered the old tin in the bottom drawer and sent the children upstairs to look for it.

When Josh laid it on her lap, Pip ran her hand over the lid. She hadn't looked inside for years. As soon as the lid came off, she was transported back to the war years. The programmes, the flyers and the newspaper cuttings were all there. She pulled a photograph from underneath and there they were smiling up at her. Stella at the piano had been a staunch friend for nearly forty-five years until cancer took her. She and Johnny had moved into the Knowle after his parents died. They'd brought up four children. Timothy Michael became a doctor, Sally a musician, Penny kept a smallholding in East Preston, and Andrew worked at Shoreham Airport. Johnny still rattled around in the Knowle resisting all attempts to persuade him to sell up and move into a smaller place.

'Is that you, Granny Pip?' Angela was pointing to the middle person of the trio. Pip nodded.

'Wow,' Josh breathed. 'You were a real babe.'

Pip chuckled. 'I'll take that as a compliment, shall I?'

'You wore funny clothes,' Angela remarked.

'Siren suits,' said Pip, and followed up with a brief résumé of the whys and wherefores.

'Was that your siren suit on the top of the tin?' Susan asked, and Pip nodded.

'Oooh, can you put it on, Granny Pip?' asked Angela.

Pip laughed. 'I'd never get into it, darling. Not now.'

'Mummy would,' Josh blurted out.

'I expect it's too precious to Granny Pip,' said Susan. 'After all these years, she wouldn't want it to get torn or something.'

'Do you know what?' said Pip. 'I think it would be a really good idea if Mummy put it on.' She turned to Susan. 'I was about your size back then. If you put it on, William can take a photograph.' She turned back to the children. 'I'm sure you'd be the only ones in your class to have something like that in your project book.'

'Are you sure?' Susan cautioned.

'Absolutely,' said Pip, 'but have your coffee first.'

Pip turned her attention to the photograph in her hand. The girl on the end was Lillian. She ran her arthritic thumb lovingly over her face. How pretty she was, and how young they all were. Of course, poor Lillian would stay that way forever. Should she tell them what happened on the day of the street party? At the time, she had softened the blow for her own children, but children of the 1990s were so much more resilient.

437

'There's something else you should know about the Sussex Sisters,' she began.

Lillian's story was exciting, fascinating and different. Everyone listened in rapt attention. There was one other picture in the tin. It was from a newspaper cutting about their concert at the Lancing carriage works. The Sussex Sisters were flanked by their greatest followers, Mr Knight on the left and Betty on the right.

'Is that her?' Georgie asked. 'The one who did it?'

Pip nodded. 'Her confession to the police was enough to make them re-examine the evidence. After Lillian had died, Dorcas had had the pulley taken down. It was tossed into the garden ready for the bin men. When the police arrived, they found traces of blood on the iron rests. They also found minute specks of blood on the oven door handle, and strangely enough, there was a skid-mark on the linoleum floor where she'd fallen. Dorcas told the police that no amount of scrubbing would get rid of it. We all thought it was a bit creepy, as if Lillian herself wanted the truth to be told.'

Pip fished through the papers in the tin. 'And this was the brooch I found on the stair.' She held it up for them all to see, a lurid parrot on a tree branch. It was only a cheap old thing, mass-produced and not very well made. 'Half the women in Worthing bought one from that stall in the market,' Pip went on. 'I can't recall anyone who didn't have trouble with the pin.'

When they all looked closely, they could see that the

pin was too short, which was why it had fallen from Betty's lapel.

'The police didn't need it, so after Betty's confession, I took it from the dish on the hallstand one time when Dorcas wasn't looking,' said Pip. 'It's the only thing I've ever stolen in my life, but I did it to spare her feelings.'

Susan went back upstairs to get the siren suit, while the children and their father collected together the photographs and Peter's letter. While Margo cleared away the coffee cups, Georgie found a stout envelope and put everything into it.

Pip was looking at the brooch once more. It crossed her mind that so often the big things in life swing in a different direction because of flimsy little things. What a blessing that Betty was always losing that brooch. She was exonerated of any wrongdoing, of course, but Pip had no idea what happened to Betty, or Iris and Mr Knight. She supposed they carried on working at the station until they retired, but she would hazard a guess that Mr Knight wasn't nearly as friendly as he once had been.

As she smoothed out the newspaper cutting to lay it flat, a little air escaped from her lips. The brooch in her hand was a parrot on a branch. The brooch on Betty's lapel was a woodpecker. Good Lord! The brooch Pip had found on the stair wasn't Betty's after all. Dorcas must have bought one too. When she and Stella confronted Betty in the station cafe all that time ago, Pip had assumed that she had Betty's brooch. Betty must have assumed the same thing. If Betty had realized her brooch had been lost somewhere else, she might never have blurted out what really happened to Lillian, and poor old Gordon might have been found guilty of a murder he hadn't committed and been hanged.

The door opened and Susan, dressed in Pip's old siren suit, walked into the room. She looked amazing and Pip was transported back in time. She remembered the nights she'd sat hunched over her sewing machine as she opened trouser legs to give a little flare, and how she'd taken the big, blousy pockets off to make everyone look slimmer. The colourful turban neatly tied on Susan's head looked really attractive. The children squealed with excitement as their father clicked away with the camera. They had to have one with Granny Pip, of course, so with Susan sitting on the arm of her chair, Pip smiled for the camera.

All at once, Angela cupped Pip's face and looked into her eyes. 'Can we sing one of your songs, Granny Pip?'

Pip hesitated. 'Well, I . . .'

'Oh, please,' Josh pleaded. 'Please say yes.'

Everyone was looking at her. 'Well, if Nana Margo plays the piano . . .' she began.

Everyone rushed to collect the music, choose a song and position themselves. Margo sat at the piano, and Susan put her arm around Pip's shoulder. With the children sitting cross-legged at her feet, Pip listened as the music swelled. 'We'll Meet Again' had always been Vera Lynn's song, but she didn't say anything. She was beginning to understand a great truth: in good times and bad, it's the song that keeps people together. *Keep smiling through* . . . Long after she'd gone, this would be a memory for her children, grandchildren and great-grandchildren to treasure. A song people would still be singing a hundred years from now.

The song ended and Margo picked out another tune, 'I'll Be With You in Apple Blossom Time'. Now, *that* was a Sussex Sisters song. Pip's voice wasn't what it once had been, but as she sang, just for a moment, the years melted away and she could see the delighted faces of the audience as they clapped and cheered for more. In her mind's eye, she could see Stella, not Margo, seated at the piano, and there was Lillian, dear Lillian, always making everybody laugh with her jokes and limericks.

Now Margo was searching through the music sheets for another song.

Georgie turned round. 'All right, Mum?'

Pip nodded.

Susan squeezed her shoulder, and Josh looked up at her with a soppy grin. Pip wouldn't forget this day easily. Her heart was filled to bursting with love for everyone around her. This was why they had sung all through the dark days of the war. It was for precious moments like these.

ACKNOWLEDGEMENTS

I would like to thank Jan Spooner Swabey for her invaluable help with this book. Over the years, I have watched her encouraging people of all ages and abilities, including my own daughter, and changing them from timid and unsure into award-winning singers, so who better to ask when creating The Sussex Sisters!

My thanks also goes to Caroline Hogg my editor and Juliet Burton my agent. Where would I be without you both!

Blue Moon

by *P*AM *W*EAVER

Worthing, 1933: Ruby Bateman works at the prestigious Warnes Hotel on Worthing seafront. She enjoys her job and the camaraderie with the girls at the hotel, but she also loves a day off . . .

On an outing to the Sussex Downs, Ruby meets handsome photographer Jim Searle and instantly falls for him. The only cloud to overshadow her otherwise perfect trip is the dark mood of her father when she returns home. It's the first of many clouds to loom threateningly over the hardworking Bateman family.

When a tragic accident shakes each family member to the very core, Ruby's older brother Percy turns to the Blackshirts – a group who have recently started making trouble in the town – for support. But when unrest escalates to violence, will he see right from wrong?

Ruby dreams of a life outside of the seaside town with Jim, but it falls to her to hold the Batemans together. However, a long-buried family secret may just undo all her hard work.

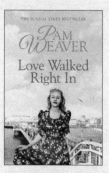

Love Walked Right In

by PAM WEAVER

Worthing, 1937: Ruby and Jim Searle run a guest house, but the newly-weds have had a rocky start to their marriage. Their troubles are only set to get worse when Jim starts to unravel a dark secret from his past.

The guest house is in high demand, and Ruby is asked to take in two German schoolboys on a cultural exchange. She agrees, but when they arrive they seem more like grown men and their activities are far from innocent. The Germans' arrival is followed by that of two Jewish refugees, and Ruby does as much as she can to help these young girls whilst they're in her care.

As the country gears up for war, Ruby throws herself into war work as a distraction from her troubles at home. But revelations from Jim's childhood continue to surface, with devastating consequences. And when war is declared, Ruby's life is changed forever . . .

Always In My Heart

by 𝒫AM 𝒲EAVER

1939. When war is declared, twins Shirley and Tom are evacuated to the coastal town of Worthing. Almost fourteen, they are very close to their mother, but leaving London is the only way to keep them safe. The twins are taken in by a local farmer, but their new home quickly proves to be far from a rural dream. Tom is forced to do back-breaking work and sleep under the stairs each night. The farmer's wife is heavily pregnant, and seems to live in fear of him. Their new teacher at the local school notices that something is not right with the children, but the farmer keeps the twins from seeing anyone, even their own mother. As the cold weather sets in and Tom falls ill, will Shirley be able to find a way out for them both?

The People's Friend

**If you enjoy quality fiction, you'll love
"The People's Friend" magazine. Every weekly
issue contains seven original short stories and
two exclusively written serial instalments.**

**On sale every Wednesday, the "Friend" also
includes travel, puzzles, health advice, knitting
and craft projects and recipes.**

It's the magazine for women who love reading!

For great subscription offers, call 0800 318846.

**twitter.com/@TheFriendMag
www.facebook.com/PeoplesFriendMagazine
www.thepeoplesfriend.co.uk**

extracts reading groups
competitions books new
discounts extracts
competitions
books
new
events books
extracts
new reading groups
interviews
events extracts
discounts
new books events
events new
discounts extracts discounts
www.panmacmillan.com
extracts events reading groups
competitions books extracts new